The
Gilded
PROSPECT

Philip Thurman

 Creation House Press

THE GILDED PROSPECT by Philip P. Thurman
Published by Creation House Press (CHP)
Charisma Media/Charisma House Book Group
600 Rinehart Road
Lake Mary, Florida 32746
www.creationhousepress.com

This is a work of fiction. The characters portrayed in this book are fictitious unless they are historical figures explicitly named. Otherwise, any resemblance to actual people, whether living or dead, is coincidental.

Select CHP products are available at special quantity discounts for bulk purchase and for sales promotions, premiums, fund-raising, and educational needs. For details, email chp@charismamedia.com, or telephone (407) 333–0600.

Scripture quotations are from the King James Version of the Bible.

Cover design by Nathan Morgan

Library of Congress Control Number: 2011940586

International Standard Book Number (Paperback): 978–1–61638–684–9

International Standard Book Number (Hardback): 978–1–61638–849-2

E-book International Standard Book Number: 978–1–61638–685–6

First Edition

11 12 13 14 15 — 987654321
Printed in the United States of America

For Donna, Matt, Elizabeth, and Paul

My compass and harbors

Acknowledgements

Publishing a first novel is the most unique experience an author will ever know. Once the pages are printed, the leap of faith has passed. A lifetime of relationships and events contribute to the storytelling process. They develop, simmer, and mellow until prepared for release. To all of you, my eternal gratitude.

I offer thanks to Atalie Anderson, manager of Creation House Press, for this manuscript's initial assessment through the eyes of a true reader. Also, my unending appreciation extends to Virginia Maxwell for her original copyediting and writing style preservation. She recognized perspective without sacrificing the creative voice. Nathan Morgan devoted his heartfelt dedication finalizing the cover art with insightful imagination and a keen eye.

Mom has and always will provide gentle counsel no matter the challenge. Dad, you never told Jeff or me how to be men—you demonstrated it every single day of your life. My most sincere acknowledgement is devoted to the love of my life and to whom this novel is dedicated, my wife, Donna. Words are hollow expressions compared to the devotion and love we share every day.

And finally, I distinguish the first kind reader who enjoys this novel—thank you. I have no more significant satisfaction than your discovered insight and abandonment in the story. With your help, many more will follow.

But where shall wisdom be found? and where is the place of understanding?

Man knoweth not the price thereof; neither is it found in the land of the living.

The depth saith, It is not me: and the sea saith, It is not with me.

It cannot be gotten for gold, neither shall silver be weighed for the price thereof.

It cannot be valued with the gold of Ophir, with the precious onyx, or the sapphire.

The gold and the crystal cannot equal it: and the exchange of it shall not be for jewels of fine gold.

No mention shall be made of coral, or of pearls: for the price of wisdom is above rubies.

The topaz of Ethiopia shall not equal it, neither shall it be valued with pure gold.

—Job 28:12–19

Prince of Morocco, Act II, Scene VII

O hell! what have we here?
A carrion Death, within whose empty eye
There is a written scroll! I'll read the writing.
All that glitters is not gold;
Often have you heard that told:
Many a man his life hath sold
But my outside to behold:
Gilded tombs do worms enfold.
Had you been as wise as bold,
Young in limbs, in judgment old,
Your answer had not been inscroll'd:
Fare you well; your suit is cold.

—William Shakespeare, *The Merchant of Venice*

Skagway, Alaska
May, 1898

Abe recognized the knife-blade depth in Dobson's cream, stubbled throat from a single candle's wavering flicker. Pulsing gushes decreased to a spreading magenta stain across the folds of calendric creases. Still-opened eyes stared at a thumping canvas drum above his head as if searching for stars. Abe leapt toward hoof slaps and pushed back the rear tent flap. A simultaneous wind gust extinguished the candlelight, and he watched two galloping blurs fade away beneath the downpour. He shook the vision and grasped a red trunk's brass handle on one end, attempting to swing it across his shoulder. The box scraped across raw timber before mud squirmed through his boot-sole holes. Each successive step was a hydraulic squish as he leaned forward and allowed his momentum to propel him on a straight path toward his mount. With a grunting heave, Abe tossed the trunk onto Sack's hindquarters, and the horse whinnied in protest.

Melting rain sheets continued flooding and obscuring hillside rows of off-white tents and campfires struggling to remain lit beneath the deluge. Sack's hooves clomped and slid through the narrow ruts while he steadied the balanced weight with each step. Ragged makeshift shacks lined one edge of the cobbled-fabric neighborhood menagerie where a piano plinked, glasses clinked, and women's laughter cackled through the rain. Wind roared while Abe bent his head forward to diminish pelting ice pinpoints against his face. Eyes lifted just long enough to register wrought-iron chimes against a steel anvil cutting above the rushing splatters.

"Boy!" Greeley's voice thundered loud enough to spur random neighs and whinnies down the stall row and a hammer's hesitation in falling to rest. Abe tied off his rib-stretched animal to a post and clomped boot mud across the planks. "Thought you musta drowned out there," the towering man bellowed, wide and solid beneath a coal dust-blackened leather apron. His bottom lip and glistening bald head reflected the glowing forge inferno. It sizzled with sweat and escaped ceiling drips. Abe bent forward and dragged the trunk across the floor with both hands. He rose and shook the saturation from his coat, shivering and clapping his hands together before blowing on his fingers. "Ah, you got it," Greeley's face loosened and he retrieved a shoe with long-handled pliers. He submerged shaped iron into a bucket, steam squealing and rolling across his slick puffing features.

"Yessir."

"Let's see if old Dob's brother came back with all o' them nuggets he was braggin' about." He grunted down onto one knee, but his fumbling fingers pushed on an unrelenting latch. He rubbed his knuckles. "Come on, boy, give us a hand, we still got a pair o' Arabs needin' two new front sets for the mornin'." Abe tossed his coat aside and rotated the red chest so fired coal illuminated the face. He too pushed and struggled without result.

"Step back," the other man commanded. Greeley picked up his pliers and swung a smashing blow against the iron plate. The catch clicked. Greeley bent forward and threw open the lid. Abe watched his eyebrows' gradual descent and a sudden spasm twitching his jaw. His initially prodding hands now flew, tossing paper, linen scraps, and brick shards across the sawdust-covered timber floor while sweat poured and beaded into his eyes.

"There a problem, sir?"

"It's not here. Shod that team up over a week ago and I still ain't seen a cent." Greeley jumped to his feet and threw the pliers, chipping away a section of furnace-blackened red brick. He unfastened his apron cord. "I'll come take it outta his hide," he threatened and started stomping for the door after bundling himself under his coat and hat.

"Sir, don't believe you're gonna have any luck," Abe offered while cringing behind the stock rack.

"Young man?"

"He's dead." Greeley stopped and tilted his head.

"What makes ya say something like that?"

"Saw the knife sticking outta him and two fellas beatin' it for the hills." Greeley crumpled his hat and threw it against the rack of tools, metallic clanking overtaking the slowing rain. He turned and landed a solid boot kick across the trunk. It twisted and turned, skidding across the planks and colliding against the coal bin.

"Might as well burn the thing to keep this fire lit the way things are goin'."

"If you wouldn't mind, sir, I might find a use for it."

"Good use, eh? Fine, consider it your week's wages. Now stoke up this furnace—we got a long night ahead."

CHAPTER

1

Snohomish County, Washington
Today

Charlie no longer sensed his feet. He passed the same broken fence slats he had been promising Karen he would fix for almost a year. Foofoo's unchanged, darkened dog house remained slanted in One-Eyed Chamber's yard across Milford Street, vacant from the cocker spaniel's death last spring after too many tennis ball chases into evening traffic.

The constant, almost barren maple still retained its tapered fingers stretching into a late-night sky. His feet shifted toward another route, down to the pavement's end, and right toward the river. At this late evening's hour, most porch lights were dark. Only one or two windows glowed with a single lamp's illumination or a television's blue glow beyond closed-eye snoring. A cat darted from a low-cut hedgerow with a quick-crunch, dry-leaf flash, and Charlie didn't offer the slightest reaction.

Karen's distorted expressions of concern, blueprint patterns in his subconscious, churned his concentration. He realized that no phone calls would raise suspicion. There was no word choice or delivery method, just intimate tonal knowledge transmitting the event. Synapses cracked and sizzled with cascading images and how to compact so much into a single word, sentence, or expression.

Autumn air suspended silence without a single fluttering sway past quiet cottages and ancient plots; a star array across the vast night sky spun him in disorientation. In the valley below, a single, blinking neon light flashed with intermittent bursts among fast-food incandescent signs and streetlamps. From his considerable distance, Charlie recognized the pinpoint lights set at regular intervals around the yard's chain-link fence. Fourteen years passed during the half minute he stared down, recognizing the forklifts and stacks still moving around the kilns. Every moment, both inane and what seemed critical in the passage of his years, was clothed in the same blue uniform jumpsuit of Deen and Sons Lumber. Even now, the day's pine resin still clung to his nasal passages.

A blaring horn shocked Charlie, and he leapt to the roadside ditch, unaware of his drift toward the median. An upward glance contrasted almost naked sycamores against the stars. Their thin black bodies rose with upward-slashing illusion while Charlie waited for a single, thin tendril of shadow to curl down and reach across his throat. Darker leaves scattered across the front lawns were browner, the night sky more vast, and his little angel's red cheeks that much farther away.

He descended a hill toward the Malcolm C. Jay Memorial Bridge. The ancient iron span was early 1920s construction for Western National Passage hauling timber into downtown yards. Even after years of abandonment for faster, sleeker, newer, more efficient modes of transportation, it was the longest county commission demolition tabling due to insufficient funds. Its newer cousin, a poured-concrete, bland track platform, paralleled only a short distance to watch its older cousin decay into the grave. Gradual rushing water broke above hushed night sounds, a consistent crescendo rising above all else.

Charlie zipped his coat and yanked up the collar, stifling cool gusts that brushed back his neck hair. Prior total stillness transformed to a consistent breeze when he took an initial hesitant step on the first creosote-saturated wooden trestle. Wobbling, rust-penetrated iron spikes shifted beneath his weight and released protested groans. His gloved hand reached out and grabbed a low side railing. Even with the moon hanging as no more than a cream-colored, bleached, stark crescent, enough light remained for Charlie to navigate narrow beams beneath his feet. Through the splintered path, whitewater rushed through boulders and jagged slate more than forty yards below.

Railing sections were missing or shifted in random leanings with the DANGER—KEEP OFF sign hung upside down by a single rivet at the end of the span. Charlie sat on the platform's edge, dangling his feet over the side after reaching the center of the river. He leaned forward and allowed metallic coolness to chill his forehead. White, whooshing water lulled his frenetic shifting thoughts of how he would tell Karen. For that matter, what he would tell Karen. Charlie gripped an orange rusted cable no more than a foot beyond the railing with both hands. Squeezing his palms tight against the woven wire and slipping off the platform edge, he heard far-off rivets screech while suspending himself. He swayed, dangling in air with the whitewater churn beneath him.

Charlie's grip release began with his right hand; it was not complete muscle relaxation but a personal experiment, seeing just how much strength remained if each finger, one after the other, was loosened. Awareness blurred from reality—scattered bills across the kitchen table like a whiteout, first finger, Karen's frightened eyes attempting a brave reflection, second finger, a life of undetermined choices, third and fourth fingers. Charlie's entire weight now dangled by a single clutched hand with lungs sucking deep, night-air swallows. Looking down at the low murmur of boiling ripples, he heard a mechanical thrumming sound, repetitive and fast, vibrating through the metalwork. He turned at a whistle shriek cutting through the night.

Diesel engines churned.

Pistons slammed.

Sleek aluminum lines reflected the moon while thundering past Charlie's outline. He watched illuminated yellow window squares flicker past like frames from an ancient black-and-white movie. Some heads paid no attention while others leaned forward and strained to see, if for the briefest of moments, a man dangling above the water outside the comfort of their seats. Each window blinked a year from the previous thirty-two: mostly blank, some curious heads, some ignorant of the world outside, but each one having no control how fast or where their train took them.

Even with his continuing hand-lock on the cable, sweat slicked his skin within the glove. Near the end of the car succession, a child's small form leapt from her seat. Charlie watched her crimson bereted head pass down the rows until shoving her face and deforming her nose against the rear plate glass.

She raised an open hand against the night, and Charlie was certain he caught the briefest glimpse of a grin. The girl's features metamorphosed into his daughter, Charlotte. The smirk disintegrated into a frown. Reddened lips pushed an exaggerated pout while her head shook back and forth in admonition.

Charlie could not identify the moment his body swung back to the platform's edge. He beat dust from his coat bottom and slapped both hands on the railing. Energy returned to his arms, but strength now staggered in his legs as he bent forward to watch the engine light eye cut through a distant black pine scruff. Car after car continued clanging across steel echoing tracks, sending neighborhood dogs into frenetic protecting howls. Charlie slapped himself across both cheeks and straightened his stature. Sudden closed-fist punches against unyielding metal crawled pins and needles dancing across his forearm skin. Bones shuddered beneath, each a thrust at Charlotte's antiseptic sheets.

No lights were on when Charlie first spotted their front porch, turning the corner for a final pass. Paper bag-rustling maple branches obscuring lamp-coned light tricked his eyes, flashing intermittent reflections towering above the front windows. He hoped the lamp beside the living room chair wasn't still casting shadows. He measured each step up the worn wooden front porch steps, years of repetition like a pianist's fingers knowing just where to exert pressure and avoid horrible loose-plank screeches. But the screen door offered no forgiveness. Its echoing shriek cut through the silence.

Pausing after opening the door just wide enough to slip through, he fumbled his keys and unlocked the handle, senses tuned for any indication of Karen realizing his arrival. Charlie knew the eventual face to face but prayed it wouldn't occur prior to sunrise. After self-assurance that the only sound was his own ear-throbbing heartbeat, the door clicked behind him, and Charlie explored a path to the kitchen, flipping on the stove light.

Charlie's adjusting vision scanned a note taped to the refrigerator door:

> Leftovers ♥ in green bowl.
> Figure you and George
> had to go somewhere
> Kiss Kiss Hug Hug

He swiped the paper scrap, holding it up to the light, and examined her lettering, still in the same manner she once wrote him in high school, complete with scribbled hearts where everyone else dots the *i*'s. Charlie collapsed at the table, pulling off his coat, boots, and each meditated glove finger. He pushed back stacks of unpaid bills, just an image in earlier thoughts. Hunger was the last sensation of his effort. Taping the note back to the door, he pulled one of Charlotte's particle-paper crayon-and-marker masterpieces and his neck relaxed. His eyes drank the brilliant grass green surrounding their house and sun ray angles engulfing a vast blue sky in childish, innocent exaggeration.

Desperate dryness coated his throat, and he poured sputtering tap water. Charlie rose and scuffed into the living room, holding his coat in one hand and Charlotte's drawing in the other. He twisted the small chair-side lamp, his throat gulping the water while his eyes drank Charlotte's winding colors and shapes.

When Charlie awoke, the glass hovered on the table's edge, coat in his lap, and his Sweetpea's picture still clutched in one hand. Opened lids revealed Karen's brown eyes staring down at him. "Hey there, mister. Keeping some late hours, aren't we?" she smiled and grasped his free hand. Charlie turned his head, unable to return her gaze, staring through parted curtains where a new day's sun lightened the horizon and peeled away stars. "That's some sort of greeting for such a loving, devoted wife," she continued in feigned disdain. Still, Charlie could not isolate nor form any response. "Charlie?" she asked, playfulness washing from her expression. "Charlie?" she again searched and dropped to one knee, now taking his hand full into her own.

"How long has it been since I've told you how much I love you?" Words drifted without effort.

"I love you, too, but—but—that dark purple under your eyes," Karen's voice crumbled as she brushed a thumb across one of his puffed lids.

"Take a look," he instructed, raising his coat and shielding his face at the same time. Her thin fingers rummaged through a pocket, removing a wadded pink scrap crumpled into a loose ball. Random corners unfolded while she examined it beneath the lamplight. Her jaw loosened and with a final brow furrow, Karen smoothed the paper, folded it with precision into a perfect square, and reinserted it into his pocket. She rose, her head dropping forward to an angle where Charlie saw the pale whiteness of her scalp between parted hair as her chin rested against his thumping chest. Charlie's neck tightened, prepared for whatever words next spilled from her lips.

Karen stood in silence, pushing aside the curtains to reveal the morning's horizon breaking into pink-purple and spreading across branching-spire curvatures. Final star twinkling receded from the impending sunrise. He had no resistance, eyes remaining open to admire light glancing across her cheek contour. She turned and dropped into his lap, wrapping both arms around his shoulders and leaning her head against him. Charlie inhaled deep breaths of lavender in her hair.

"Listen to me, Charlie. It's going to be all right."

"You don't know how good it is to hear you say that. Whether those words are true or not, as long as you believe it," he offered a weak smile while her forearms tightened around his neck.

"Haven't we been through a lot already? Haven't we been through more than most people could possibly handle? And look at us—we're still here safe, alive, and knowing a brand new day is about to start. I believe we've gotten used to challenges."

"At least we've already gotten her birthday presents. Whether or not we get tossed out of here in a few months is another matter," he strained each successive word. His concluding sigh rolled backwards with his head, staring up at the splitting-plaster spider webbing across the ceiling.

"You've already been through so much—Grampy passing away, of course Charlotte, Benjamin finally reappearing in your life after what, seventeen years? And now this—you know, it's almost too much for one man to handle all by himself, no matter what a loving and supportive wife he may have," Karen turned up to pinch his chin and tried pushing a grin across his stubbled jaw with no result.

"Ah yes, the renowned Benjamin J. Sutcliffe," he mumbled with closed eyes.

"You really should—"

"No, Karen, don't say it, please, just don't say it. I know what you're about to say, and I just can't hear it right now. I know he's only two miles away, but Benny shows up after all these years, and everything is supposed to be normal again. With the money that man must have from his travels, he can't toss a few scraps our way?" Charlie's eyes closed once more, and he rubbed them with clenched fists. "I am a thousand years old."

"Maybe George might have some ideas. Seems like he knows everyone."

"It's not just the paycheck. Walking around earlier, I started asking a lot of questions I've never really asked. In my entire life, I can't recall a single deliberate decision I've ever made—not one. It's almost as if I've only existed day to day, year to year, just letting events tell me what to do rather than choosing direction. Even when Mom died all those years ago, and he took off, I never took a stand." Karen stroked the small hairs across the back of his neck.

"Want some coffee?"

"No, thanks. Just need sleep," Charlie exhaled and rose from the chair with resistance, one hand pushing against the

8

armrest while the other remained around his wife's hip. He didn't bother pulling back sheets and collapsed across the mattress. Far away, he heard a train-whistle shriek cutting through the early morning hour.

CHAPTER

2

The late afternoon glare hypnotized Charlie's gaze across a shallow oval pond's rippling surface scattering kaleidoscope colors. If he stared long enough, Charlie almost convinced himself that the green bronze oxidation covering the statuettes rising from the pond's center grew darker from countless hours already dedicated to his bench. Water splashed upwards from the open mouths of surrounding scaled bronze koi. Metal returned his stare and bragged in silent ability to withstand extremes of sun, cold, day, or night. Alloys stared past him without necessity of food, water, or air.

Leaves fluttered with a few breaking free and dwindling to the water's surface. They took casual random flips until reaching contact and radiated shy ripples, vanishing in the gentle action. Their soft curves contrasted with the towering black window-and-concrete hospital geometry of the surrounding four walls rising high above his field of view—massive rectangle dark eyes staring across at one another. Pink and purple pansies dotted in well manicured islands lining a fieldstone pathway. It encircled the pond while white lilies bloomed their greenish pads spanning a shallow covering across the far edge. Other empty benches were scattered around the circumference with IN MEMORIUM tarnished bronze plaques bolted to their frames. By now, Charlie could close his eyes and recite both the names and dates of each monument.

"How is she?" Karen's voice rose from behind, and Charlie's shoulders snapped forward. During the same moment she asked her question, both arms slipped over his shoulders, and she allowed her head to fall on his own scalp with the pressure of sunlight. He turned to absorb slow inhalations of long brunette hair and allowed the fine strands to wash across his forehead and face. The stone rolling between his fingers for the previous half hour skipped across the pond and ended with a vacant hollow crack after colliding against a seraph's left foot. It offered no response, perched among the other bronze sculptured angels, sheep, goats, and deer.

"'Bout the same I guess. Strong as ever. You want to hear something funny?" he asked and turned.

"What?" she asked with softened widening eyes and moved around the bench to sit and press herself against her husband.

"How old am I now? Our baby girl is almost eight years old. How is it that in eight short years she has more strength to deal with this than I have in over three decades?" Charlie concluded his question never intending for an answer and smirked without control.

"She is something pretty amazing," Karen mimicked his laugh and forced a finger curl around his hand. A cooing mallard squawked a few feet away, spreading its dripping wings in pursuit of two brown females dancing and darting around the third angel. "You get a chance to talk to Dr. Benedict?"

"Nope," his response emerged as no more than a whisper.

"Must have just missed him. I only caught him on the way out to the parking lot." Her grip tightened around his hands.

"And?"

"The latest round of results are back. I could tell what he was going to say before he said it, you know, the way he pulls that ear? The last treatment round hasn't shown any significant improvement." Charlie listened to her last statement as if the words came from the doctor's own mouth even with her sigh grasping every effort to maintain steadiness in her voice.

"Benedict, five months...Karen, five months!" Charlie bolted to his feet as if kicked from the bench, tearing away her grip. He turned with both hands on his hips, and lungs forced air in and out with no control. Charlie spun and kicked the bench's iron framework, forcing it to lunge to one side with audible straining bolts shrieking above chasing ducks. Karen grabbed an armrest and wooden strap, preventing it from crashing across worn stones. He again collapsed, head in his hands. Karen returned an arm across his back and rubbed his shoulder. "Saw some orderlies earlier hauling boxes down the hall marked CHRISTMAS. That's months away. Last Christmas, I'd never even heard the words *intrahepatic cholestasis* in my entire life." He hesitated to stare at everything and nothing.

All resumed silence below the duck chanting and streaming water droplets splashing against the angels. Lights popped on beneath the surface, illuminating live orange and yellow koi slithering and shifting like blurred phantoms. Charlie sensed warmth edging to the corners of his eyes. No matter how intense the desire for release, wetness would not come.

"You've got to believe, Charles." He turned to glance at her cheeks in late soft light and the slight upward curves of her mouth's corners.

"You haven't called me Charles in longer than I can remember." Her head rested on his shoulder.

"Benedict said the treatment in Salt Lake is looking like our best option." Charlie knew Karen chose careful words, reclining against the back rest and releasing breaths in shallow bursts.

"Karen, we both know that we simply don't have the money, and if we did, the transplant waiting list could be almost a year. We can barely keep the house lights on now," he said and threw another pebble, this time the angel's leg clanging with the impact and koi scattering in every direction. "We're already in debt past our eyeballs just staying here, insurance ran out over a month ago, and who knows when I'll get a call back, if ever. I spent fifteen minutes this morning rummaging through the couch cushions for change." She turned to look into his eyes. "No, absolutely not."

"How do you know what I'm going to say?"

"My wife will never, ever work in a greasy dump like that place again." Karen offered no protest.

"I understand. But you have to believe," she responded, accentuating each word's syllable with drawn-out assertion. "Getting sort of late and we've got service in the morning," Karen reminded him and patted one knee, rising and drawing her jacket around her shoulders. Her profile angled down, and she waited for a delayed response.

"Think you better go without me this time," Charlie murmured, unmoving in both face and body, continuing an unwavering stare across the faces of angels.

"What? You haven't missed a Sunday in years."

Charlie now rose, a hesitant breaking tightness in his jaw pulling back his lips. "Just don't see the point anymore. Can a God exist who would allow something like this to happen?" Charlie wasn't certain if he wanted her answer or not. He turned, the final allowance of a single struggled wet stream wandering down one cheek.

"Charles, that's the very reason why you must go."

"You should know by now how much I love you and our daughter up there," he turned and pointed to one of the downward staring black windows. "But, I don't know if I believe anymore." Karen released her own sniffle and leaned into Charlie's chest after standing face to face. He couldn't resist allowing her hair's aroma to slow his heartbeat.

"Do what you think is best. I've never told you what to believe and I never will. You coming home?"

"Go on ahead, I won't be too late. Think I'll go on in and see her to sleep," Charlie's words rose upwards as he removed the sedan keys from his front pocket and tossed them through the air where Karen snatched them with a gloved hand. "Anyway, Gup said he was coming by sometime this evening, and I'll get a ride back with him." She strolled back, reaching up to embrace his shoulders and plant a quick kiss across his forehead. Charlie watched her drifting across the close-cut grass. "Karen?" he called the moment her hand reached the door handle. She stopped short and turned. "I love you. Thanks."

"Love you too. Don't be too late. Dinner will be waiting for you," she finished and blew a kiss, vanishing back into the hospital's main annex.

Charlie resumed his seat on the bench. His mind reeled with recollections from the first days of vomiting and fever, uncontrolled spasms, and nights of sweating sleeplessness. His stare never wavered from the darkened window until the hue changed with an interior light glow. Charlie rose and used his scarf to wipe chilled remnants of wetness from his cheek, entering the main hallway's automatic swooshing double-parting doors. Nurses, orderlies, doctors, and interns all filed past and around him like stockyard cattle, their distinct scrub colors identifying differences of discipline. The Sutcliffe Stroll no longer required conscious thought: follow the red stripe to the end of X-Ray, take the second service elevator to the third floor, turn right at Medical Records, proceed past the lounge, acknowledge the recognizing nods, take the stairs up one more floor, exit right after Neonatal, and enter Pediatrics on the opposite side. Charlie tried keeping his head down and his hands in his pockets.

"Mr. Sutcliffe, good to see you again," came a woman's voice behind the nurse's station with a thick island accent.

"You, too, Rosie," he replied and forced a smile.

"Thought you'd be going home with the missus. Sure must be proud of that little trooper. She ate all of her dinner and talked about you so much between mouthfuls that I didn't know if that plate was ever gonna come clean. Hold on, I'll buzz you inside," she said, her dark head rising above the partition as she smiled with broad white teeth. He heard a familiar buzz followed by magnetic locks releasing within the walls. The door-swoosh opening poured more antiseptic aroma into his nostrils. Hallway lights dimmed, turned down for evening hours.

Different random cartoon voices emanated from passing televisions. Some beds remained empty, some with tiny forms encased in plastic shining shells, some with little men and women, tubes emerging from various orifices and needles jabbed into delicate pink skin. Stainless steel and plastic supported still developing bones while wanting eyes groped for the passing tall figure, hopeful anticipation that someone would turn looking for them.

Charlie stopped short at the last door on the right. It remained cracked open, and he leaned forward, recognizing the voices and shapes of Charlotte's favorite cartoons bouncing off the portion of visible wall. After a clearing cough, he swabbed his eyes and cheeks with a final wipe, and rehearsed several wide, tooth-filled smiles. He pushed open the door. "Who's my favorite pumpkin in the whole-wide world?" Charlie shouted and jumped through the doorway. The girl in the elevated bed leaned forward and released a high-pitch squeal.

"I am!" she shouted in triumph.

"You bet you are! Come here and hug the stuffings out of me," he returned, collapsing on the edge of her bed and leaning forward. His arms reached through and around various tubes and wires escaping from beneath her sheets. Charlotte's warm, shallow breath reached across his neck.

"Daddy!" she exclaimed and her hands caressed his stubble.

"Whoops, sorry there, didn't mean to crush Mr. Snuggles," Charlie leaned back and smoothed her purple stuffed rabbit's fur. He pulled it from a reluctant embrace, holding the animal up to the light and examining a torn button that had been one of its eyes, a ripped leg seam, and chunks of filling stuffed back into its chest. "Mr. Snuggles here looks like he's had a lot of loving, Princess. Want me to take him home to Mommy so she can get him all fixed up?" Charlie's question was met with an immediate stern, forehead-wrinkled response as she plucked Mr. Snuggles and squeezed him against her chest, foam stuffing now bulging further between the seams. "Okay, okay. There's something happening next month, but I just can't remember what." He turned with his head cocked up in the air and one hand rubbing his chin's stubble.

"Daddy," she cooed and pried away his hand.

"Ohhh, that's right, it's the birthday of the most beautiful, smart, and loving little girl in the entire world," he smiled in laughter and a tickle under her chin. Charlie allowed his glance to drift for less than a second at the beeping monitor, but it was long enough for his façade to collapse. However brief, it was enough. Charlotte allowed the purple rabbit to flop to one side, raising her free hand to Charlie's cheek.

"Don't worry, Daddy. I'm gonna get better. Mommy and God told me so."

"They did?" he turned at his daughter's deliberation.

"You have to believe that everything is going to be all right," her voice squeaked and she brushed her fingertips across his cracked lips.

"You are the second person to tell me that today."

"I am worried about someone."

"Oh?"

"Yeah, Mommy. She cries but I can tell. She told me she was just putting on her make-up without the light on, but she had raccoon eyes when she came by." Charlie laughed at the image. Charlotte mimicked his giggle until amusement blossomed to the point where they both held their hands over their stomachs in uncontrollable laughter.

"Miss Rosie is right, you are a most special angel," he said after rising and clearing his throat. Charlie brushed a gentle kiss across her eyebrow.

"Am I interrupting something here?" a voice called through the still-opened door.

"Uncle Guppie!" Charlotte's voice again lit up the antiseptic starkness. George crept low with both hands raised and shifting in front of him, taking long and slow deliberate steps. His head shifted to each side with a pouncing cat's spring, and both hands shot forward to tickle her ribs. Charlotte burst into laughter until she doubled forward and released a series of sporadic coughs from her rattling lungs. A monitor rose and emitted a high-frequency beep. George retreated with all expression vanished from his features. Charlie leaned over to give

Charlotte a glancing slap across her back, and the monitor returned to its consistent drone.

"Sorry about that," he muttered and folded his hat in his hands. "Gotcha something." George pulled a coloring book from his back pocket and a box of crayons from his coat. Charlotte's eyes illuminated in recognition.

"Ponies!" she cried and grabbed both gifts.

"Thought you might like these and you know what? When you get better and outta this place, guess what we're gonna do?" Charlotte pushed herself forward, staring up with straight, fresh teeth glowing in the television light. "We are going on a pony ride," he exclaimed and began dancing around what little open area of the cramped room remained, galloping and holding imaginary reins while Charlie now also stood and clapped his thighs.

"Can we, Daddy? Can we?" she pleaded.

"We'll see. Now I believe it is getting close to your bedtime, isn't it?" he asked to a frowning response. Charlotte offered no defiance and scooted back beneath her covers. Charlie adjusted her bed back down to a horizontal position with humming electronic-controlled gears. She leaned forward to kiss his cheek.

"You too, Uncle Guppie," she directed and George bent low.

"All right, beautiful, you have sweet dreams of butterflies, rainbows, and candy canes," Charlie hushed. George had already entered the hallway and was studying wall charts.

"Daddy?"

"What?"

"Aren't you forgetting something?" Charlie stood looming, his shoulders framed above her bed and protecting the curving light across her nose. He said nothing in an uncertain stare. "Bedtime prayers?"

"Oh yeah, yes, of course," he snapped back and sank down until both knees met hard white linoleum.

"If you don't mind, I'd like to say this one tonight between Him and me," she whispered. "That okay?"

"Of course, Little Angel." Charlie rose and turned, listening and straining, but he struggled to identify her soft mumbled words. The incessant monitor beeping drowned any sense of the phrases emanating from her lips until he recognized a definitive "Amen." Charlie turned and leaned forward, pulling the blanket higher over her chest and Mr. Snuggles, tucking in both sides.

"Goodnight, Daddy."

"Goodnight, Little Princess," Charlie finished, kissing her cheek for a final time and slipping from the room in silence.

CHAPTER

3

Roads melted beyond vision. "Shouldn't be much farther, should it?" Karen's just-waking voice jolted Charlie from his trance as they descended the mountain grade down a series of sharp switchbacks. A late morning peaked through naked-branch shadow fingers crawling across split pavement. He cracked the window, allowing a face-washing chill.

"Another mile or so."

"I can't remember it taking this long." The tears from Karen's previous sobbing now dried across her cheeks. Her words were among the few since they left. The image of Christmas three years before remained clear in Charlie's mind as if he had woken up that morning. Even the Parkers and McDills came up from the holler. The first stroke was the series' worst. Karen called late in the evening after he returned from work, knowing he would drive through the hills in a mad dash. The closest medical care was sixteen miles away, and with recent floods, half of the roads remained washed away enough to prevent any vehicle from maintaining control. His grandfather's stay at Memorial had lasted six weeks; and he returned home with an entire array of heart monitors, breathing assistance, and a motorized bed. The equipment accompanied regular scheduled home-health workers dropping in on him twice a week.

Karen's voice entered his ears as random whispers from a crowded restaurant's far table. She offered faint observations but remained motionless, clutching her seatbelt and gripping the door handle at the same time. "You haven't said it, but I can see the memory of your mom in your eyes." Her words were a staccato-syllable stumble.

"I guess I should have known, but I was young at the time, just before high school. She was always so tired. Then more and more trips into town. You know the biggest giveaway?"

"What?"

"She used to make dinner every single night. Six o'clock and we had better be at the table. Then, it was later and later. Then, only every other night. By the time I figured out something was seriously wrong, Benny was picking up fast food every night of the week," he stated and poked at radio dials. Charlie's slight chuckle was met with Karen's sharp head-turn. He noticed from the corner of his eyes but continued waiting for her reaction. "Only a few years later, they probably would have been able to successfully treat that lymphoma. Not that Benny would have been around to help."

"Then why save the postcards?" She noticed his wince at the phantoms.

"Charlotte, of course."

"Even the one a few months ago from the Extendastay? Isn't she going to wonder why her grandfather sent her a postcard with no stamp?" Charlie punched the radio dials with increased determination, the morning still fresh in his memory, when he opened the front door and noticed a white rectangular card. Benjamin Sutcliffe's signature curved with boasting recognition.

As they progressed forward, surrounding past acquaintances increased—half-decayed barns absorbing back into the earth, a mailbox series lined one after the other with a rusted rooster perched on the last, and an abandoned church with rock holes punched through stained glass. "Kavnesh said the fourth stroke was the most merciful. At least that's what he said when he called. The one taking him happened in his sleep, and he didn't even know it."

"Did you see George?"

"No."

"That's okay, it's understandable. Probably too much. It wasn't that long ago."

"What about Benny? My own father? Where was he?" Karen could not nor would not answer.

"Didn't realize the church could hold so many," Karen said, her voice betraying his effort and taking the exchange into a new direction.

"Quite a few I guess. Maybe if we eventually touch enough lives, we never really die anyway," he said with a reflex reaction to the image of the coffin lowering into the ground. "You look tired, Muffin," Charlie spoke from the side of his mouth without glancing away from the windshield. The twisting road ceded to a barren field, descending toward their advance. "Getting close," he said. A semi chugged past them, downshifting gears to compensate for the sharp decline. Charlie tilted a brief glance with a frame-shifting whoosh of air as it passed.

His grandfather's farm opened to their right. The 1932 Deere was still stationed halfway out of a leaning, warped shed with its once brilliant green contrasting brown surrounding weeds. "There she is," Charlie's head turned, "Gretchen."

"Who is Gretchen?"

"Why that old lady taught me to drive," he nodded at the tractor. Poplars were no more than barren spindle sticks lining the split-log fence path. Charlie slowed and turned across a gravel-covered driveway arch, agate and quartz stones crunching like ice beneath their tires. "How far out does it go again? Almost seems like a lifetime," Karen asked, absorbing the same unfolding view.

"Grampy said it was ninety-six and a half acres. Might as well have been the rest of the entire world. This land has been in the family for generations. Almost a hundred and fifty years ago, Grampy said the government gave special land grants to the region's settlers if they helped survey for timber, roads, and such. Grampy said our past generations knew every old trail better than anyone around, so it couldn't have been a better fit."

"What's that over there, again?" Karen raised a hand and pointed across Charlie's nose.

"That stretch hasn't seen a seed in longer than we've been alive. Grampy said that even when they were planting, the yield left for a scarce return." Charlie's eyes drifted further to the forest surrounding the holler's edge, brown bland entanglements fading into gray-and-black illusions. "There it is."

"Are you sure?" Charlie didn't reply but swung his head toward her, the gesture's articulation conveying his response. "I don't know, just seems more compact, simple," she observed after the car scrunched to a halt and she unfastened her seatbelt. He stopped and leaned backwards on the hood, hands shoved into his trench coat pockets. Charlie noticed her ears and nose turning pink behind billows of crystal-turning breath. "I believe it's colder down here than when we were at the top of the hill," her words emerged, trying to scrape frost. He nodded in silence and followed her trudge up the front porch, both sets of eyes concentrating on each measured step.

The two-story framed house shuddered with warped horizontal siding playing at every angle. Window and door frames bubbled peeling paint and sloughed off leprous sheets. Soffits sagged and faded with mildew. "Remember carrying Charlotte up those steps?" Karen heard a crisp tone in his voice.

"How long ago was that?"

"She couldn't have been more than a couple of days old." His statement halted prematurely with the first porch footfalls. Charlie scanned for a pair of split ash rocking chairs, ferns suspended from framing, the ice cream churn, and a hammock where he used to lie during dusk to watch fireflies overtake the evening or listen to the apple tree lullaby whisking branches against the upstairs bedroom window. Karen watched her husband's transition from memory to a structure now no more than wood and stone, concrete and glass. "You still have the key?"

"Somewhere in—here it is," she turned. "I must look a mess," she forced a smile and pushed one of her mascara-streaked gloves across her sniffling nose.

"Wait a sec, the attorney said the power had to be turned back on." Charlie scaled down the steps and located the main electrical box beside the storm cellar doors. The rust-caked box screeched open, and he flipped the central breaker. A distant hum rose. By the time he returned to the front, the door was open and Karen shivered in the hallway.

"Doesn't seem real, does it?" she asked and answered her own question in the same sentence. Switching on the parlor light, they saw the living room and stairs leading upwards into darkness, and just beyond the kitchen's far edge, it glowed in an alien cream light.

Photographs of yellowed and faded pastel-colored age were suspended from the walls, hollow furniture draped in musty, stagnant sheets still watched guard over his estate, and the rose-patterned wallpaper his grandmother had forced his grandfather to hang now peeled from corners and joints. "What is that?" Karen pointed through the shadows.

"The workshop. Well, it was a workshop. Come on," Charlie grabbed Karen's hand, floorboard squealing and timber jostling echoing in the silence. They both poked their heads around the corner and witnessed a vacant room absent of a single chair, table, or any other sign of furniture. "This is where he moved on." They both entered and stood in the hollow space's center, one arm draped across each other's hip. "Grandma would have a fit if she saw the dust and grime on those windows."

"What do you think it must have been like for Grampy with only himself to look after?"

"Musta been tough," was all Charlie could squeeze from the sensory overload. He couldn't imagine his grandfather hobbling past these walls by himself after marriage to the same woman for fifty-eight years. "The attorney was pretty clear regarding the estate."

"Yeah, but doesn't it all still seem a little strange? We know they weren't wealthy by any means, but why did they leave everything to the church?" Charlie didn't answer. She found courage to speak the thoughts that had already passed through his mind.

"Denkins was very precise in reading Grampy's last wishes. Everything except the basement contents is to be liquidated and donated to First Calvary. Wanna take a look?" The same key that unlocked the front door opened the basement as Karen inserted it. Metal works rotated with a spring-snapping click. Charlie shouldered the door open and moved forward, taking his initial descending step. Visions passed through his thoughts without control. Long forgotten pirate caves and castle dungeons commanded any sense of current reality—one of passed forgotten dreams you realize can never be dreamed again. Karen followed with one hand on his neck until he located a suspended string brushing across his nose, jumping back from the sudden contact.

The air remained frozen, breath still clouding around their faces. A quick string tug illuminated the whole room in a single, unshaded bulb's low wash, cobwebs and dust swirling in struggling rays. Only two narrow paths formed between eighty-five years of living stacks. Charlie removed one glove, raising his touch to brush the rough-hewn beams above their heads, worm holes and axe chipping still fresh as if felled the previous day. Almost silent moisture seeps dripped through barren slate walls.

Browned trunks and distorted boxes lay covered beneath molded canvas tarps. Ancient road signs, fishing gear, hunting equipment, snowshoes, paint cans, metal and wood objects he couldn't begin to catalog remained tossed into random piles. Karen stopped, glancing at Charlie's expression. "Grampy was a collector. The funny thing is that I didn't know if he had some sort of neurosis or if it was just to keep Grammy a bit on edge. I can still hear her now: 'Old Man, just what do ya think you're gonna do with all that junk?'" Charlie's hands unclenched in his pockets, and he surveyed unending half-finished projects.

"Did you just hear something?" Karen interrupted. Charlie made no indication through the stature of concentration further than what was contained within their four walls. "Sort of like airbrakes—must be the van." She turned and scaled the creaking wooden stairs while she spoke. Her high knees and delicate footfalls tapped against loose risers, never allowing her hand to grasp the railing. She emerged into what scarce light crept through drawn shades.

Charlie nudged boxes and oxidizing relics with his shoe until the front door swung open. Unintelligible murmurs resonated through floorboards and he rejoined Karen. A squat man with an unlit cigar gripped a clipboard. He wore a baseball cap so grime layered that Charlie couldn't identify the team. Charlie blinked against open front door brightness.

"Sir, ready when you are." Charlie remained abandoned in his silence. Karen blinked at her husband and resumed instructions while he turned and drifted through the kitchen. He would not allow his eyes to recognize the refrigerator—the Frigidaire where his grandfather pulled freezing watermelon on boiling August nights to savor between them. Afterwards, he floated with a bloated belly to the back porch, curled across the wicker lounge, and drifted off to a cricket- and frog-croaking chorus. Charlie unlatched the back-porch screen. In the initial afternoon's barren skeleton woods and sunlight struggling through gray overhead haze, he recognized the tree house's path twisting start at the clearing edge.

By the time Charlie and Karen returned to the living room, bay windows revealed nothing but black exhaust and the truck's rear-door Moving On logo fading down the drive. They both turned at various degrees around the now vacant, foreign shell. Removed furniture specters appeared as solid shapes dotting faded backgrounds, where sunlight weathered bright wallpaper colors, yet paintings and chairs protected original coloring. Still shining varnished floor spaces contrasted a million footfall paths of their family map cut between them.

"What's that?" Charlie uttered with a break from their mutual trance and bent down, brushing his hands across book spines lying solitary in the room's center. His words emerged with a tourist's echo.

"When they were hauling everything away, this was in the basement corner under some old sheets. I know how you've always loved old books, so I thought you might want to glance through them sometime." Charlie turned up and softened. He rose, embracing his wife, both pausing in unspoken reliance and staring down at the abandoned driveway through the open window. Charlie again savored the smell of her hair, the aroma returning his mind to the abandonment of those hot summer nights and cool autumn afternoons. "We better get going, looks like another storm is heading this way," she reached and turned the front door handle. Charlie hoisted the box under one arm and opened her door.

At that night's late hour, the only sound was Charlie's bare feet scuffling across the kitchen linoleum and breaking the refrigerator compression cough. He cracked the refrigerator door and explored drawers, finding nothing more than raw, rubbery vegetables, yogurt, ketchup, and crumpled tinfoil-covered, crust-rimmed bowls. He sniffed and closed it. On most nights, Charlie blocked his mind through years of practice. It was a developed art of concentration. No matter what facts possessed waking moments of open-eyed reality, he could obliterate any images of Charlotte in that bed and her elimination of fear and isolation behind the brave face she tried portraying. This was not one of those nights.

Charlie yanked the breakfast nook's dangling fluorescent light string. It illuminated just enough light to identify the glass of milk he poured but not enough to disturb Karen through their cracked bedroom door. The creaking, worn, white chair settled beneath his weight—an all-too-familiar sound. From between a three-year-old phone book and one of Karen's mystery-stained cooking magazines, he pulled a beaten-cover collection of comic strips and flipped through the ragged pages.

Some pages were almost torn in half or creased, still bearing finger smudges of his own uncalloused adolescent fingertips. Simple, yellowed black-line drawings on newsprint paper released tension in his neck. He scanned block-lettered captions over each drawing's expression and associated these earliest friends when the most important decision to make was between peanut butter and jelly or bologna.

Rising to refill his glass, Charlie tripped over the corner of a box shoved beneath the table. After walking the same path so many countless times, he had no recollection of the obstruction, and his loose grasp sent the glass falling from his hand, but he caught it by the rim. Whatever sleep began creeping back into his nostalgic fog disappeared, and he leaned forward to focus on the box. Cardboard walls were split and eaten through with silverfish. The corrugated interior peeled away in layers. Dim filtered light still allowed him to read the spines—mostly classics of Defoe, London, and Verne.

The titles returned Charlie to his grandfather's animated recitals. His grandfather didn't just read to him, he acted out each character on the back porch or while perched high in their tree house. So many nights after his grandfather drifted off to sleep in his chair, one of these books had remained open across his chest. While his grandfather slept with glasses pushed high on his forehead and resonating snores from his throat, Charlie lifted the pages to continue their adventures on his own.

Of the two dozen hardback volumes, the last five rose higher than the others. He withdrew each and associated a specific image until noticing a flat cover at the bottom. This book was bound in darker leather, scratched, faded, stained, and smelling of forgotten wood. The miniature page collection spread with comfort in his open hands, and brief page separations revealed inked script.

Unlike the others, Charlie saw no title, no stamping or machine print of any kind on the cover or inside page. When he opened the front page in full and read initial words written in strained blocked lines, Charlie realized the hammer pounding the back of his eyes:

YVKON
1898
A.F.S.

Charlie's fingers shook.

His grandfather entertained with unending tales of sea captains, underwater submarine adventures, and rafting down great rivers, but this was a tale heard and repeated so many times it overshadowed any other story he ever told. This was his own blood, his own history. Events and words recorded by his great-great-grandfather were now witnessed with his own eyes.

There was never even the slightest doubt in the innocent truth of Santa Claus or the Tooth Fairy. But their reality faded with the shadow-creeping monster of age cloaking the tales more and more improbable beneath the cynicism of maturity. Always wanting to believe—and that belief stronger so many years before—Charlie, without deliberate decision, convinced himself that those stories would disappear the way of other childish dreams. He didn't bother reading each page but skimmed through the fragile leaves, taking delicate turns. Careful handwritten script, drawings, and maps detailed geology, rivers, vast forest stretches, and blurred landmarks. He dropped forward, turning to adjust a better view in the light.

The moment Charlie's eyes refocused, his elbow nudged the half-full glass, and it plunged from the table, sending glass fragments shattering and milk splattering in every direction. He found the broom was close enough, not requiring a single step. He twisted and swept shards away from potential injury. The bedroom light turned on down the hallway. "What on earth is going on in here?" Karen stumbled and stood in the open door, yawning and stretching. Her eyes remained half-open between puffed lids as she adjusted to the dimness until flicking on the main switch.

"Careful, there might be some more pieces," Charlie cautioned. He reached out with one arm blocking her path and crouched down to scan for any remaining fragments.

"Can't sleep again?" she asked, her words not a question so much as an autonomic statement with the last crash remnants spilling into the trash. "Hon, this has been going on for too long. We both know this isn't healthy." Karen cinched her robe to ward off the chill and placed both hands on her husband's shoulders. "Maybe the next time you see Benedict he might refer you to someone who can help." His rapid eyelash fluttering ceased at the name's mention.

"Maybe I'll just do that. Come on, take a look at this," he turned back to the table with words emerging in a bouncing gasp and his head cocked to one side.

"What am I looking at?" she managed asking. A cavernous yawn escaped. "Isn't that the box of books from Grampy's basement?"

"Yeah, look at this. This is it. This is what I've been telling you about all these years. It's the journal—Absalom's journal," Charlie bubbled with each word rising in his brain's registration as he spoke them. Karen now pulled out an adjacent chair and leaned forward.

"Isn't he the one that was supposed to have headed north after the Yukon strike?" She rose and turned for the cabinet, retrieving a glass and pouring her own milk. "If you weren't telling those stories, it was your grandfather." Her mouth offered a slight curve.

"Nobody could tell it like Grampy." Charlie's eyes wouldn't budge from flipping pages.

"I must have heard those folk tales so many times I almost started believing them myself. I think Charlotte believes them more than Santa Claus," she said and resumed a hand brushing Charlie's hair. "Come on, it's late and you have to get to bed. Even if you can't sleep, the dark and quiet might slow your mind." She rose, pushing her chair back, and forced the book closed in his hands. "It'll still be here in the morning."

"Right as always," Charlie rose and kissed Karen's forehead.

CHAPTER

4

Charlie's hesitant steps followed one another after he parked near the curb, city sounds rising around him. Avenues and boulevards awoke with resonance of movement—cars and buses, taxis and pedestrians, filing to their offices, stands, and stores. But this abandoned back stretch hadn't realized the new day beyond trash-strewn papers blowing across cracked gray asphalt. Charlie lowered his jacket zipper, welcoming morning sunshine and warmth crawling over tenement shadows.

The apartment's front step leaned to one side with graffiti tags curved in squiggled spray lines of yellow, red, and black. Previous covering attempts in slap cream coatings fell short with splattered bleeding colors. Pausing at the top of the stoop railing, he heard faint crunching below. Rats gnawed at the naked ribbed carcass of a rotten, once orange-furred cat. Flies buzzed and swirled while the pack chomped, oblivious to his recognition.

Scanning a vertical nameplate row next to the door buzzers, half of them missing and the remainder faded from exposure, Charlie still knew the correct plastic splintered button. A sick, faraway pang of electrons collided in a fluid grind sounding more like electric-chair straining than a buzzer. No reply. Charlie depressed the button longer, the buzz cracking on and off under the strain. A vague chortle came through the loudspeaker with the clarity of a fast-food drive-thru. "Hello?" came an almost human voice.

"Gup, come on, it's me." Charlie pressed his nose against a grunge-filmed side window, too clouded to identify any interior movement with corner air-drifting cobwebs. He pushed and held the button once again. "Come on, wake up, it's almost ten o'clock."

"C.S.! Hold on, I'll buzz you up." There was a final nauseous vibration of the worn speaker diaphragm, and Charlie heard a distinct grate of metal against metal. A mechanized deadbolt retreated into the doorframe. Stepping inside, the immediate mixture of a thousand unidentifiable odors swirled up into his nostrils from the patch-worn, stained carpet, compressing like a sponge beneath his rubber-soled tennis shoes while his forward steps provided an audible squish. Untold soaking snowmelt winters, dripping garbage bags, mold species yet to be named, and stale beer swirled together in a sensory stew that forced Charlie's eyes to blink. Shining gloss lime-green paint was coated over patched drywall, and straining yellow fluorescence pulsated down vacant corridors.

Charlie refrained from gripping the chipped wood handrails to support his ascent up the stairs. He rose the usual six flights, winded by the top-floor arrival. He took measured steps and keyed his ears for the slightest doorknob twist to avoid encountering George's neighbors. He knocked at the door where a six, a four, and another number once hung but were now no more than newer paint outlines against old. Scanning to each side, he heard stumbling and knocking sounds arise from the door's other side while he gripped the spine of Absalom's journal beneath his jacket.

A series of bolts clicked, and the hollow wooden door cracked open less than an inch. The arc slammed on multiple chain restraints, one at the top, middle, and a final brass short link length near his knees, stopping any further progress. "Oops, sorry about that." Through the opening, Charlie heard the subliminal notes of quiet jazz—a horn playing low. "What's happening?" George's words exploded, still dressed in nothing more than a t-shirt and a pair of shorts. "Come on in," he requested with an unchaining grasp.

"Same as ever," Charlie said as he reached forward.

"Hey man, sorry I didn't get to the service. I mean I really wanted to go—I really meant to go. Even had my suit on, I was tying my tie and—" George stopped short in the realization that his words continued a commitment he did not want to follow.

"Yeah, yeah, don't worry about it. You know he'd understand." Charlie collapsed on the couch between day-old taco wrappers, scattered, stale popcorn, and empty beer cans. Pointed springs jabbed into the small of his back, but he expressed no indication of discomfort. George vanished into the kitchen while he scanned the walls.

Shelves were strewn in ragged naval manuals, ship histories, photographs at various ports of call during his service years, certificates, degrees, and a lifetime's memorabilia. Charlie rose after spotting the final eight-by-ten at the end of a high shelf. Even with the thick dust coat blanketing each surrounding object, this frame remained clean and polished. He traced a finger across the glass. George's big-toothed, wide-mouth grin stared back while he held his wife Debbie in his arms. She beamed back an identical abandoned release.

"You took that one," his friend's voice startled Charlie from behind him. "Remember? Just before I shipped off to Manila? Want one?" George motioned a beer bottle against his elbow. Charlie shook his head.

"Drinking this early? Come on," he admonished.

"Beats what comes outta that tap," George nodded toward the kitchen and tipped back a bottle after releasing a stifled belch. He pulled a blue-and-white striped robe close around his waist and collapsed in the recliner, clicking the remote to turn down a game show elevating above the mellow tenor saxophone. George snatched the frame. His head sank forward, and his fingertips glided across the glass, eyes closing as if his fingers absorbed the image beneath them, tracing uncountable worn-glass caresses.

"What's it been now, almost three years?"

"Three years, sixty-two days." Widening corneas dropped back to the image. "Nobody has to tell me she's gone. It was a morning a lot like this one. I've played that scene over in my mind more days that either of us has been alive."

"Come on, Gup, we've been through this over and over. It wasn't your fault. There was no way you or anyone else could have known. You read the report so many times you should be able to recite it from memory. That van's brakes were worn, he was driving too many hours, and the road was slicker than glass," Charlie rose and stared with a direct focus on George's unnoticing stare.

"But I should have known. We were singing."

"Singing?"

"Yeah. Even to this day, when I hear *that song* on the radio driving or even the melody plays in a crowded restaurant, my hands start shaking and everything goes blurry," he said with fingers still brushing across the glass.

"You sound older than I feel." The comment was offered between two friends knowing one another after so many years— an observation only time's bond would allow.

"My friend, why do I get the sensation that you didn't come here to talk about me? You taking the day off or something?"

"You might say that. I might be taking off a whole lotta days. There's no telling when or if I or the rest of the crew will ever make it back with the Deens this time." Charlie leaned forward and rubbed his reddened eyes. Sleeplessness tinged his stinging lids.

"I knew something was a bit off when we drove back from Memorial the other day. How's Karen taking it?" George asked, no longer drifting through his own memories. He sat his bottle on the litter-strewn coffee table and leaned forward.

"Supportive as always, I guess. She's the last one I'd ever have to worry about," Charlie's words diminished.

"Speaking of which, how is my beautiful little goddaughter enjoying her new pony book?"

Charlie's face contorted into an instant smile with Charlotte's image clutching her stuffed, worn, purple rabbit against her chest. "Little Angel won't put it down."

"Enough of this, come on, let's get some fresh air," George finished and threw his bottle in the trash, clinking it against a pile of more empties. He retrieved a set of keys from the counter and clicked off the television. Charlie followed him back out into the hallway before he turned a deadbolt behind them. Muted voices of other televisions, banging pots, and a distant electrical hum resonated through thin walls. They reached a doorway at the opposite end and ascended a short flight of stairs, emerging into morning sunshine swallowing the rooftop. "Welcome to the garden," George beamed and spread his arms across several buckets of plants in lined rows. The black containers were spaced in measured precision across white-painted tar and air conditioner handlers.

"What's this?"

"Gotta do something with my free time. Look here, I use the handler drain-off for watering. Zucchini and squash, peas down on the end. Getting time for winter crops. Always knew I had green thumbs, my man."

"This is something, Gup. Now all you need are some chickens, cows, and pigs," Charlie laughed. He settled down in an abandoned couch once dragged up the service elevator.

"Sure must be rough, man. Grampy passing on, losing your job, and of course—" George stopped himself short, both men recognizing the unneeded conclusion. They both sat in silence with sunlight warmth across their faces and listened to random stirrings along the sidewalk beneath them.

"Can you believe Benny didn't show?" Charlie remarked between a half question and statement. George studied his toes for a moment, kicking back loose gravel. "Would you get upset if I told you I did?"

"No, guess there's no reason getting bothered over something so obvious."

"There's still more, isn't there? I've got this crazy idea that something else is on your mind," he said as he glanced up with one eye squinting against the sunlight. Charlie said nothing but continued his gaze at early-morning fluttering leaves. His hand reached into his inner jacket pocket and traced the journal's spine. After a concentrated breath, he retrieved the book and dropped it into George's lap. "I need to go see Uncle Tyler."

"What's this?" he asked, opening the front cover and focusing his eyesight across faded ink scribbles. "Someone sure had some horrible penmanship. Old?"

"More than a hundred years." George now sat up and cradled the pages in both hands after Charlie's clarification.

"A.F.S.?"

"Yeah, Great-Great-Grampy. When we were kids, remember the stories Grampy used to tell us? You know, the ones about Absalom?" Charlie turned with a direct stare into George's profile. A grin curved across George's lips while he raised a hand to slap the armrest.

"Do I remember? I can recite every one of those tales as if we were there ourselves, the three of us sitting up in that old tree house. That man had a gift, you know, a real gift for storytelling as if you were right there in the middle of it." George thumbed through the pages with the same eager attention Charlie recognized in himself during his late evening discovery.

"What if I told you they weren't just stories?" Charlie turned.

"Aw, come on, we both loved them, but racing sled dogs for a stake, barroom brawls, killing a bear with nothing more than a pickaxe? And my favorite was the buried Klondike fortune he had to hide from the Indians. Stories told to wide-eyed gullible kids." Charlie offered no reaction, leaning forward instead over a wrinkled-page concern. "So what about them? The stories, I mean."

"They were true, Gup, they were true." George returned the book to Charlie's eager grasp. He peeled a fresh beer bottle label, and his eyes deciphered Charlie's facial features like a topographical map. His own brow twitched between contraction and release. "Don't mistake me, Absalom took some fundamental artistic liberties with most of the stories, but the most important, the main reason—"

"Ahhh, here it comes."

"The main reason for my brief little journey will be locating the gold he stashed. And no, he wasn't killed in an Indian ambush. He died from yellow fever in Skagway. Knew he wasn't going to make it back home, so he hid it before he died."

"And just how do you know all of this is true?" George replied with skepticism tracing his question.

"There's a phrase I keep hearing in unconnected places. 'Sometimes you just have to believe.' These pages are the most real words I've ever read in my life. Karen and I found it in the basement when we were clearing out Grampy's stuff after the service," he said and clutched the journal against his chest. "There are dates, locations, amounts, and quite a few details I would have preferred never knowing. The drawings are a little crude, but I can make out most of the landmarks. The rest shouldn't be too tough for someone like Uncle Tyler. Absalom started out as a blacksmith's apprentice at one of the mining camps. I haven't read everything, but from what I've skimmed, shoeing everyone's horses is how he got all of the hot tips on where to look. Can't say for certain if he was a claim raider or just paid close attention, but it doesn't really matter now."

"You're planning on going all the way to Skagway?" George's voice rose and he shifted forward, waiting to hang on each of Charlie's words.

"He hid it in an abandoned mine northeast from there. I calculated it's about a two-week hike from a little place called Blackhole in Canadian territory."

"Does he say how many ounces he found?" George chose his words with care in both content and timing.

"Ounces? He talks about pounds." George collapsed back in the couch cushions. From Charlie's opposite pocket, he pulled a map copied from the library. Yellow highlighter markings traced over Charlie's crude handwriting. "This is what I've been able to make of it so far." He tapped a finger on the unfolded paper, tracing slowly along the route and trading glances between the paper and George's expression. "I need to get to Juneau, then Skagway, and finally toward Blackhole."

"You have much stuff for that kind of trip?"

"I'll figure it out," Charlie replied without removing his eyes from the paper and thumbing back through the journal's pages with his other hand.

"So exactly what are we going to do when we get to Tyler's place?" George asked.

"When *we* get to Tyler's?"

"Buddy, you don't think I can let you go on this thing alone, do ya? Besides, you think you're gonna be able to carry all of that by yourself?" Through all of the calculated, detailed planning Charlie believed he accomplished, the goal's burden never crossed his determinations.

"Yeah, guess I was so worried about supplies and equipment I never thought about that. Two conditions: one, we don't discuss with anyone why we're going there, and two, we're only about a month from the first real snowfall, so an exact, tight schedule must be maintained. You and I have been through enough winters to know this would be a suicide mission if we got stuck in the bush when the snow sticks. Just how are you going to get away for a month on the spur of the moment?" Charlie asked as the logic conflict interrupted his heart-accelerating journey description.

"Not much to get away from here. If I pay the bills a little late, I'm not here to freeze when the power goes off anyway," he laughed to himself.

"Don't worry, if these pages are any indication of what we'll bring back, you may never have to worry about an electricity bill again." Charlie refolded the hand-drawn map and stuffed it between the journal pages, returning the book to his inner jacket pocket. He leaned back, closed his eyes, and enjoyed sunshine across his cheeks.

CHAPTER

5

Charlie jumped at the sound of Karen's voice interrupting the refrigerator condenser motor clunk cutting on and off during the late hour. "You have that dream again?"

"Oh, sorry, hon, didn't mean to wake you up," Charlie said. "But yeah—a little different this time but basically the same. I'm flying around a night sky, and I see the merry-go-round's spiral red-and-white canvas roof below me. The same creepy calliope music drowns out every other noise."

"Are you at some kind of carnival?" she asked.

"No, nothing like that. Everything is misty. Anyway, the next thing I know I'm on the ground behind this chain-link fence looking through at Charlotte on one of the horses. She's the only one riding. Benedict is wearing a red-and-white pinstripe outfit with one of those old goofy flat-top, round straw hats, and he's laughing so hard he forgets to monitor the speed as it goes faster and faster." Karen pulled a glass from the cupboard, her eyelids no more than tentative slits, stumbling and feeling substituting actual determined motion.

"Then what?"

"She starts spinning her head in every direction and her mouth opens when she sees me through the fence. The horses' eyes go red, and mouths start chomping on their bits, heads twisting and turning. Charlotte's horse starts bucking even as it goes up and down the pole. All of a sudden, Benny jumps over the fence on the other side and starts taking pictures. Pretty soon, he and Benedict are roaring in laughter. I try climbing the fence, and every time I get a few feet off the ground, it grows that much higher until I fall back and wake up." Karen took a sip, rested a hand on his forearm, and kissed his temple. "This must be the third time I've had the same dream and it's so real. Even now, I can smell popcorn and cotton candy, see Benny's flashbulb blinding my eyes, and hear those calliope notes."

"You have to remember, it's nothing more than a dream, and nothing in it is going to hurt our baby," she attempted reassurance. "You're still looking through that book? You've had your nose in that smelly old thing for days. Every time I turn around."

Charlie remained bent forward, one finger tracing across open journal pages and his other hand tapping the map. "Come take a look at this," he stated more than requested. Karen scuffled to the chair beside him and wiped sleep from her eyelids with a balled fist.

"Find something?" Charlie broke from the pages, turning his head to gaze into eyes unrecognizing the stare. Snapping back to the open page, the scribbled ink collection trembled beneath his knuckles.

"He was right."

"Who was right? Want some?" Karen croaked and nudged her mug against Charlie's elbow.

"No, I'm fine. Grampy was right. Absalom did gather a load during the Rush." Karen leaned back in her chair, one hand stroking across unkempt hair flying in every direction from the top of his scalp. "He hid it around six months. Look over here," his fingers spoke while flipping forward. "He knew a fever was setting in, and his partner, his name was Thomas, was about to kill him anyway. So he hid it. Right up somewhere around here," Charlie's pointing finger glided across the yellowed pages while Karen still leaned forward over one shoulder and tried focusing with glassed-over eyes.

"What are you doing with that calculator?" Charlie didn't flinch, the fingers of one hand punching keys while his other hand flipped water-stained pages.

"It's there, Karen. Absalom's find is there. Spent a while down at the library. Everything here tells me it's near some old mine north of Blackhole."

"Where in the world is Blackhole?"

"Over here," he motioned without disturbing his hunched-over gaze. Karen's eyes were now wide and focused, milk splashing down her dry throat. "The man was almost as illiterate as I am, but I've checked these figures over at least ten times. It's in pounds, not ounces, see," he said and pushed a scribbled paper in her direction. His pencil scratched so dull that the final numbers were more wood scrapes than graphite. "This bag is two, this one four, this one two more, this one—"

"Charlie, it was more than a century ago."

"I don't care if it was eight hundred years ago or last year, these are specific recorded events." Charlie hadn't yet recognized the other eyes of their discussion. Deep within the walls, a series of scratching clicks broke the hypnosis, freezing them both after turning to look near the corner. Following a quick hum and drywall shake, the entire house was consumed into darkness. The only surviving illuminations were streetlights and neighboring forgotten porches casting single reflective beams through open kitchen windows.

"Guess I'll get the candles again," Karen released a sigh. Charlie leaned back in his chair, screeching legs punctuating her comment, and he slapped the cover closed. Karen rummaged through the overhead stove cabinet.

"They were just here the other day. You move them somewhere? Charlie?" her words faded, recognizing that she now remained alone. She closed the cabinet, no longer searching for the candles, and required no need to feel her way through the dimness, negotiating the narrow hallway. The front screen door opened with a mild rub of aluminum. Stretched springs and oxidized hinges announced a parting scrape through the early morning chill. Charlie remained at the far end of the porch, cinching his robe with a blanket pulled high over his legs. He stared into a still, sleeping neighborhood. Karen glided to his side, pulled back the blanket, and snuggled into his chest, wrapping the blanket back around both of them.

"Charles?"

"Yes."

"You're thinking of going, aren't you?" Her question came out with lungs barely inhaling a breath. They both stared across the barren patched lawn.

"How did you know?"

"When a man and woman live together this long, she often knows what's on his mind when he doesn't." Charlie smiled. Karen understood his expression without the requirement of seeing his face. Dry leaves crackled in the limbs just beyond the porch roof, scraping and drifting down while he pulled her closer. "I take it you've given this a lot of thought? I know you and your dad went camping years ago up around those parts, well, at least Alaska. But that was so long ago and you were just a kid."

"It may be a lot of years ago, but it can't be that tough."

"Winter's coming soon."

"That's why we can't wait any longer. A few supplies and a way to get up there is all I need." Charlie scrambled for more spoken assurance, as much for himself as Karen. "Anyway, it might be nice to see Uncle Tyler again even if he doesn't recognize me right away or for that matter still live around those parts. I'll find him. If anyone knows how to get me through, it's him."

"How do you know he's still up there?"

"Last I heard." Charlie no longer spoke. Thoughts continued their rumble through his mind, contemplating their effect instead of speaking and then a result. He hung in suspension, waiting for even the first further word from his wife. Their body warmth pressed close together, shunning the night chill while mutual breaths rose and fell. "George has a couple of friends up in Seattle. We sort of kicked around the idea the other day, and he's got an old Navy buddy named Ned doing some commercial fishing. This friend might even be able to get us as far as Juneau."

"George is going, too?"

"I don't think I could stop him."

"We can't even keep the lights on with these medical bills," Karen said in exasperation and pulled away with the avoided coolness rushing across both of their chests. "How in the world are you and George getting up to the Yukon?"

"According to these entries, we won't have to make it all the way up to Dawson. George said he'll work it out, and we can pay passage for work on the boat."

"Even so, what about—" Her mouth fell to silence with a single raised finger from Charlie's free hand.

"My love, there are a thousand questions. I can't promise you that I know a real answer to any of them. But I know this is right. I know this might be our last and only chance." A far-off stray mongrel yelped against the darkness. Karen returned to the warmth of Charlie's chest, her hand sensing his rapid beat beneath the flannel. She took deep breaths of her husband's scent through his t-shirt. "You said it yourself."

"What?"

"Sometimes you just have to believe." The continuing wind hiss sizzled through remaining leaves, their darkened colors fluttering red-and-yellow shadows beneath moonlight. Both Charlie and Karen drifted into the doze of their mutual embrace.

CHAPTER

6

The washer traveled almost a foot by the time the thumping across faded, curling linoleum jolted Karen from her doze. It collided into the wall, contributing additional drywall dents testifying of an extended history of uneven loads and worn bearings.

Hair fell into her eyes, and her shoulder collided against the water heater. She tore open the lid, and scratched white enamel shuddered into stillness. Sunlight poured through open shades while she rearranged the wet clothing, and she collapsed back into her creaking-jointed kitchen-table chair. She stared at the bottom of an almost empty teacup.

Random, different colored lines and painted shapes pulled her eyes toward paper sheets affixed to the refrigerator door with magnetic plastic apples, bananas, and oranges. They formed an interpretation of the house with stick figures of

Charlie, herself, Charlotte, and Mr. Snuggles trailing one purple arm. Surrounding lopsided butterflies, daffodils, and a rainbow stretching across a green sun and flowered field carried her away from the washer. Karen pulled the bottom masterpiece painting and lost herself in the hypnosis of sunlight filtering through the thin paper. She pulled it against her lips as if inhaling her own daughter's breath.

What was supposed to be a front-door Westminster chime resembled more of an electric-shorted frog croak. It struggled twice and vanished with a following knock. Karen pulled her robe up around her shoulders. "Hold on a minute, be right there." The chain remained hooked. Cracking the door, her cup slipped, swinging by a thumb while the other hand remained anchored to the door handle.

"Would you be Karen?" a voice came through the narrow opening. The man on the opposite side leaned a knee on cracked concrete steps, nodding forward and resting his thumbs in suspender straps. Dust-frosted spectacles dangled at the end of his nose above a broad-smiling grin. "Hope you've been well?"

"Charlie's not here," she managed summoning, and she pulled her pink fluff robe even tighter, knowing it would close no further.

"I'm not necessarily here to see him. Might we have a word?" he asked.

Karen hesitated and glanced back at the wall clock, calculating how much time remained until Charlie drove back up the driveway. Seconds passed in silence while the man rocked back and forth on the balls of his feet and his smile faded from cracked lips. "Oh, all right, hold on," she resolved and shut the door. The chain slid backwards, the door reopened, and she shuffled towards the kitchen with her back to him.

"It's a pleasure finally meeting you," he marveled. His head rotated in observation of everything around him. "Oh, is this one of my granddaughter's Michelangelo's?" he asked, turning a page and returning it to the Formica tabletop. "May I?" he inquired. Karen shirked her shoulders and opened a palm toward the opposite open chair. "In all my years of photography, the million or so I've taken couldn't begin capturing this perfect clarity."

"Thirsty?"

"Oh no, I wouldn't want to impose."

"Let's get to it, Mr. Sutcliffe. What do you want?" her question spurted.

"Just because I drop by for a social visit, why is it that you automatically assume I want something?"

"You vanished from Charlie's life all these years, not bothering to come see us even once, not even to meet your own granddaughter," she erupted and still refused a direct look into his bloodshot eyes.

"With something as tragic as my father's passing, can't I simply stop by for the comfort of family?" his eyes dropped to the floor in front of his feet and hands grasped together at his waist. Karen massaged tightness from her eyebrows. Benjamin lifted Charlotte's finger painting once more, eyes rolling across the page and a finger tracing crude shaped outlines. "How is she?" Benjamin's tone dropped to a mutual level abandoning all adult distractions.

"The same. There hasn't been any real change for the worse or better in five months now. Her doctor has a tentative university contact, but they can't do anything without the results from the previous study. She still laughs and smiles all the time like there isn't a care in the world," Karen's words ended, each diminishing in volume when realizing the poor reflection of her daughter's own optimism. "You know she still asks about you."

"Oh?"

"Is that all you can say? Oh?" Karen yelled, asked, and jumped to her feet in unison. Benjamin reeled backwards in his chair, almost crumpling the painting between his hands.

"Karen—I," he stammered.

"Do you know how many times she asks about her Pop Pop? You know what? I quit. Charlie quit long ago. I quit disappointing that little girl. The only thing I can tell those hopeful glowing eyes is that you're still on a trip traveling far away. And you know what? I pray to God you stay traveling!" she screamed with tears bursting hot reflections from the corners of her eyes.

The jogging washer broke Karen's frenzied explosion with another continuous, hollow-echoed thumping. She released a throat exhalation not formable into any intelligible word and stomped back into the laundry room. She slapped dripping clothes into the dryer while attempting to control her heaving chest. The slamming front door interrupted her cathartic release.

Karen jumped and turned with the haunting image of Charlie's arrival and standing face to face with his father. A quick blind parting revealed nothing more than taillights of a black-and-yellow taxi rolling back down the driveway. Her head sank forward, resting on the living room chair's headrest cushions to suppress rolling whimpers heaving through her throat.

Karen returned Charlotte's art to its proper refrigerator door gallery, and she pushed the journal back beneath a clay ladybug her daughter sculpted in the first grade. Neither the television nor the radio blather eradicated the morning after drifting back into the kitchen.

A car engine cut off in the driveway.

The cessation of rumbling was a distant fog. "Anybody home?" Charlie's call from the front yard was preceded with a high whistling tune. The slamming front screen door jerked her back to instant recognition. Karen jumped to her feet. She sprinted around the corner, and her slippers almost lost footing while throwing her arms around Charlie's shoulders. "Whoa, what's this?" his voice rose and concentrated. His open hands folded around her waist, and he leaned back, lifting her into the air.

"So glad you're back," she whispered in his ear and didn't suggest even the slightest embrace release.

"I must be the luckiest man in the world." His permanent smile underscored his voice's rolling lilt. "I get to spend this life with the two prettiest women in the world." Charlie's statement emerged more as a continuation of whistling notes rather than a declaration. Although his grin remained, his eyes shifted focus as he noticed the final remnants of wetness in her clumped eyelashes. Karen's flashed glance betrayed lingering irritation. "All right, what happened?" Charlie asked as he threw his jacket over the back of the living room chair on his way to the bedroom.

"I met your father," she stuttered, studying her memory's disbelief. Charlie stopped in both motion and sound. Karen stood gripping the back of a chair, waiting tortured seconds until again hearing his voice.

"Mr. Pulitzer? What did he say?" Charlie allowed escaping words beneath his breath. His palms tightened around the armchair rest until his knuckles turned white.

"He didn't say anything. The washing machine was acting up again, and I had to dislodge the jam to keep it from hopping right out the back door," she said as her words gathered strength. She dropped onto one of the armrests and outstretched a hand, brushing the nape of his neck with her fingernails. Charlie's eyes grew narrow. She watched a spasmodic muscle twitching above his right eyebrow. He rose and turned through the kitchen doorway toward the back laundry room.

"You didn't leave him alone did you?"

"What? No, wait, yeah, but only for a few seconds after I had to go fix the wash. When I got back, his taxi was already pulling away," her words waivered as she raised both hands to her lips.

"Would it kill him, Karen? Would it kill him just to drop by and see her once, one time to see his granddaughter? The man is one of the most reknowned photographers in the world. If there is anything—" Charlie stopped himself short. His armrest gripping eased, and he rubbed tired blood back into his cheeks and forehead.

"You knew your father better than I ever could. I wouldn't understand him anymore than you," she said, now shifting her weight and sinking into his lap, allowing her head to mold into his neck's curve. She listened to his breathing rise and fall, the thumping of his heart, and breathed in his scent. Slender fingers rose to sift through his hair, heaves growing more shallow with each stroke.

"You should have seen her this morning, honey. We had a tea party with Betsy, Scary Beary, and Mr. Snuggles," he mumbled as if Charlotte were no more than a hug away.

"I don't believe I've met Betsy," she turned and stared, their eyes mere inches of separation.

"Of course you do, you know, about a foot tall, long whiskers and a black tail?" he joked.

"Oh, that Betsy," she sighed in mutual assurance. "Well, tomorrow, I am going to see our Little Princess."

"I braided her hair," Charlie stopped himself short, the depth of breath increasing and a tingle flashing across his skin. His throat swelling couldn't be swallowed away. If even a single following word was spoken, no more than garbling would follow. His eyes closed and his mind emptied, enjoying Karen's cool ear lobe curve against his chest.

The alarm clock's radiating red segments blared eleven thirty-five when Karen registered the first howling yell disturbing a fitful sleep. The violation jolted her upright from the comforter. Panicked images raced through her still-dreaming thoughts as she leapt from the bed and focused on the light beneath the door.

"What in the world are you doing?" she asked to her knees with Charlie on all fours, crawling beneath the kitchen table. Floor-wax bottles, paper towels, and month-old newspapers flew in every direction. His head half-turned to recognize her arrival with a face no more than clenched teeth and sweat beads trembling across his brow.

"Gone! Gone! They're gone!" he howled with Karen dodging papers in a mock blizzard.

"What's gone? What are you talking about?" her voice rose to an equal tone with his. He shoved Charlotte's table-strewn painting pile and slapped open the cover of Absalom's journal. He flipped toward the rear of the book, and Karen's eyes didn't require lingering until recognizing the source of his madness. Jagged tears of fine cotton fibers just past the spine jutted out where there had previously been black-smudged mustard sheets. "I guess it wasn't like that when you found it?" She tried slipping an arm around him, but Charlie's uncontrollable tremors allowed no grasp. He was already sprinting toward the bedroom, tripping over every obstruction with the journal tucked beneath one arm.

Lifting the mattress, he shoved Absalom's journal into the center of the box spring. Not bothering to strip his pajamas, Charlie hopped and pulled on his jeans while groping for the sedan keys across the dresser. "Where do you think you're going?" she asked, still maintaining what she considered a safe distance.

"There's only one question, and we both know the answer," he grunted, reaching for his jacket and shoving his feet into unlaced tennis shoes.

"You don't think Benjamin actually—" she stopped short.

"There's only one way to find out." Charlie stomped toward the front door. "What was the place where he's staying?"

"The Extendastay," she pried into the determination.

"That's it, see you in a while. Love you," he faded, shouting and sprinting down the front steps.

"Love you, too," Karen whispered to a face-slamming door.

The sedan's transmission shuddered, almost snapping from the frame. Charlie made it through three stoplights, one of them green, and entered the highway. Few other vehicles flashed past on the route while he shifted between third and fourth, the gears groaning from abuse. His thoughts were random and scattered; he saw isolated images of Charlotte with a stuffed animal collection perched around a tea party table. They transposed with long buried visions of his mother's farewell. Charlie had no idea what physical manifestation would emerge once confronting his mission's target. He skidded down the main highway's exit, balding tires screeching around every turn, and arrived at the Extendastay's blinking neon sign where the STAY was a pulsing strobe.

After locking to a stop across the gravel-scattered dirt parking lot, Charlie slammed the door, shut loud enough to echo off the L-shaped motel, and sprinted toward the main office. A single green, shaded fluorescent light twitched but remained lit through the venetian blinds, and he threw his shoulder against a rattling door handle. The locked door didn't budge. He cupped a hand to one side of his face and pressed his nose against the glass. The front desk was vacant, and the back room dark with the exception of a glowing reflected television screen light dancing against an obscured wall. Charlie's open palm banging against the plate glass door made it shudder beneath the force. His second and third series of bangs made him believe the glass might shatter from the aluminum frame.

Lights clicked on from a scattering of second- and third-story windows with muffled obscenities spoken loud enough to penetrate balcony walls. With a single final slam of both fists, the television light was blocked out by a man's darkened silhouette stumbling forward from the office back shadows. Black hair covered clenched fingers rubbing his eyes. A half-smoked cigar splashed ash down the front of his pink-stained t-shirt. He bumped into the front desk corner and shook his head, clearing the stumble. Once his vision focused enough to recognize a single raving form beyond the window, sluggish relaxation transformed into a sour, tightened tension across a now-dancing cigar.

Charlie's eyes pleaded with the squat figure, body hair springing from miscellaneous discolored fabric, and a pair of matted-grease hair tufts on each side of a shining scalp not quite reaching his ears. His rough throat-hair stubble blended with indistinct transition into the same slick hair curls spilling from his chest. His lips didn't move as he raised a hand and pointed with exaggeration at the CLOSED—NO OCCUPANCY sign dangling from a chain on the door.

Charlie pounded again.

This time, the man leaned over to retrieve a worn wooden baseball bat, no more than the VILLE still discernable with most of the shellac missing, and waved it in Charlie's direction. "Please, I need your help."

"Can't read? Sign says we're closed," he barked and shook the bat again.

"All I need is a few seconds of your time," Charlie begged and fumbled in his wallet, retrieving a five-dollar bill and shaking it through the partial drawn blinds. Still maintaining a firm grip on his bat, the man waddled closer to the glass.

"So what's all fired-up important at this time of night?" he demanded. His jittering eyebrows furled and flew in every direction, settling into a scowl.

"I have to find someone who is staying here. Benjamin Sutcliffe." Charlie continued waving the bill. The man's forearms eased, and the bat lowered to his side. He rubbed his whiskers in contemplation. Charlie recognized the illuminating instant of recognition popping in the man's eyes only to have the previous irritation revive once more into his glare.

"You know that no-good, rotten trash?" the man's voice rose to a yell.

"Yes, I need to see him. Where's his room?"

"Hold on, hold on," he said, turning and disappearing once again to the back room. He emerged moments later in boxer shorts and an unbuttoned, blue-striped pajama shirt. The door latch clicked. Massive looped keys jingled in his clutch. A squeezed, resonating cough shook his entire frame as he turned and relocked the door behind him. Charlie took a step back from the engulfing odor of cheap scotch and a cheaper cigar. "Come on, but remember, if you get anything out of that worthless piece of garbage, I get my share. Two months behind and he's lucky I ain't had the cops here already."

"Can't tell you how much I appreciate this," Charlie stammered and shadowed his mysterious fumes while climbing the steps behind him.

"Yeah, yeah, remember, he owes me first," he grumbled and wheezed with each step followed by labored-breath gasps. They paused at a door with a dim orange bulb flickering from flying insects swarming and buzzing through the glow. Keys rattled in his shaking fingers, lifting one to make several insertions at opening the lock. After a click, the door swung open with a yawning hinge grate. Charlie pushed him aside and stumbled across frayed carpet, prepared to tackle anyone or anything in immediate sight. Behind him, the manager clicked a switch. Both men froze. Charlie scanned the cramped room in a single glance—dresser drawers were missing and strewn across an unmade bed. Three empty hangar shadows swung in the dimness, and not a soul offered breath.

No sound rose from the man's throat, but in the dim light, Charlie deciphered his lips' formed obscenity. The manager's soundless declaration escaped above open-back-window interstate traffic.

CHAPTER

7

Electronic beeping provided Charlie the needed excuse to escape his tossing fits. Four AM segments hazed and formed a gradual sharpening with no other light except the thin slash peeking beneath a still-closed bedroom door. Awake for hours, he wasn't certain if he had ever slept.

The usual rise and fall of Karen's breath was missing from her side of the bed, but he still flopped over an arm confirming her absence. Water splashed across his face. Pulling down his lids, he glared back at the thin red webs spanning the whiteness. Charlie stumbled into the kitchen.

No more than "Hi" emerged. It was the only word she grasped from the unending mental vocabulary whirl refusing specific sequence. She turned in quarter profile, not far enough to betray puffed lid wetness coating cheeks and eyelashes.

"I bet Charlotte is asleep like she doesn't have a care in the world right now." Charlie broke the silence above an echoing barnyard clock electrical tick suspended on the wall. It was the single common image joining them both into an implicit moment's mutual understanding.

Karen turned with a second coffee cup and leaned over to kiss his forehead after Charlie collapsed in his chair. Her frayed robe skimmed across the top of his feet. He winced from the sear across his mouth roof lining and released a chest-heaving sigh. Turning to stare into Karen's eyes with a half smile, his question rose no higher than a murmur, "Do you really think this is the right thing to do? Am I crazy?"

"If this is what your heart believes, then you are doing the right thing," her words reassured while taking his hand in hers and doubling over the top with her other fingers.

"This does seem pretty far out if you think about it. I mean come on, a grown man, father, husband, traveling a thousand miles to look for buried treasure. If it was anyone else—"

"You know as well as I do that you can't go back now," she said as she sat down and scooted next to him.

"All night I couldn't help but to keep tossing around and questioning my real motivation. Am I really doing this for Charlotte's sake, or is it just a momentary escape from some inevitable future I'm too afraid to face?" Charlie asked and dropped his gaze to his toes.

"Look at me, Charles," she commanded and lifted his chin with a forefinger. "In all the years we've known one another, I cannot recall a single instance of any word spoken or action you've taken in self-interest or greed. Granted, this trip might seem a little odd to the casual observer, but if it's what you believe in, what you believe is best for the well-being of our family, then you have no other choice but to go. If you don't go now, you will regret it for the rest of your life. It's not crazy. It's something I've always loved you for and always will—when you see hope, when you see possibility, you pursue it with every ounce." Charlie's tightened lips loosened, and his distant stare diminished with each successive word.

"I need to go see her one more time."

"I know," Karen replied, now sitting in his lap with both arms encircling his neck.

"Mr. Sutcliffe? Didn't expect you for another couple of hours," Rosie said, her black horn-rimmed glasses peaking over the monitor. "You're looking good on this beautiful afternoon."

"Is she up?"

"Yeah, as a matter a fact, it's just about time her nap was over, and I was going to bring her afternoon snack," she nodded at a cart in the corner. "But I think you would make a better waiter than I would a waitress," she smiled and nodded. Charlie grasped both chrome handles and shoved the cart down the corridor. Charlotte's door was closed. He knocked. A muffled squeak responded.

"Who wants some juice?" he called through the dim light.

"Daddy! Daddy! Daddy!" her squeals shot out in rapid succession. Charlotte's face transformed from a trance-like sleep to a spanning grin, pupils jittering across her eyes. He leaned forward and pulled her close to his chest. "Daddy, you're doing it again."

"What?" Charlotte wrestled free from his embrace long enough to point at the smothered purple rabbit's head poking from beneath her blanket. "Oh, sorry again, Mr. Snuggles. You think Mr. Snuggles would also like some juice?" She cupped one hand to the side of her mouth and bent down, whispering in the rabbit's ear. She nodded her head with enthusiasm. Charlie poured two cups of milk from a small carton, opened a pack of crackers, and peeled a banana. "Do rabbits eat bananas?"

"Mr. Snuggles eats everything. But if he's not too hungry, I can help him out," she garbled, squeezing a reply between cheek-distorting bites. Charlie raised the shade and returned to meet a wrinkled chin.

"What's the matter, Pumpkin?" he asked and rested a hand on her leg.

"You and Mommy, you are both the same. What is it?"

"What's what?"

"With Mommy it's raccoon eyes, with you it's eyebrows."

"What about my eyebrows?"

"Anytime you have something to tell me, your eyebrows wiggle." At her statement's recognition, Charlie's hand rose to stroke his forehead from spontaneous reflex. She giggled and he returned a smile.

"Always said you are the smartest little girl in the world." Charlie tapped his jacket zipper. "How sad would you be if I had to go away for a little while?" Charlie forced the words without thought, not certain courage would remain if he thought about them for too long.

"How long is a little while?"

"Just a few weeks. Don't worry yourself none, I'll be back for your birthday, but there's something I need to go do to help someone out." Charlie studied every soft curve and muscle contraction in her face, hoping they might convey her reaction when words would not.

"This someone sounds kind of special."

"Oh, she is, she is, but I'm going to need your help," he replied, first wiping milk from the corners of her mouth and then Mr. Snuggles. "I need you to say an extra special prayer for me and this special someone every night until I get back."

"I don't even know her name." Charlotte reached a hand up to Charlie's face and brushed back hair falling into his eyes.

"You know what? You're my little Sweetpea from now until the end of time. When I get back, I'll tell you who she is. Then it's okay?"

"On one condition. I get all of the hugs and kisses I missed while you were gone!" Charlotte finished, pushed her tray to one side, and wrapped both arms around Charlie's neck.

Charlie returned to find his boots, duffel bag, socks, and clothes draped across the couch. Neither he nor Karen spoke while he slipped into the bedroom to change. She entered and sat at the bed's edge, springs creaking beneath her weight. A short beeping succession cut through their silence. "That must be him," Charlie observed and bent forward to kiss her cheek. He laced and stomped his boots until his toes reached full insertion. Charlie reached forward and embraced his wife. Another horn blast separated their hold with mutual comfort-forced smiles pushed across their faces, eyes refusing to break the lock.

"Call if you can and remember to give Tyler a big hug for me when you see him." She spoke as if Charlie was only running down to the corner store. "I love you, Charles," she trailed words.

"I love you, too," he returned and slung the bag over his shoulder. He turned while descending the steps to watch her waving from the porch.

"Charlie!" George cried out while he tossed his bag into the truck bed.

"Gup." He collapsed in the passenger seat while George shifted into reverse, and Charlie watched his wife's form grow smaller, turning just once to the abandoned road ahead until she was no longer visible.

"My friend, might as well sit back and get comfortable. It'll probably be a few hours to the docks, and we should make it just after sundown," George exclaimed, trying to shake Charlie from his fog. "Want some?" he motioned to a Styrofoam cup in Charlie's direction. His head shook, continuing a window stare at passing fields and abandoned warehouses once they cleared the city outskirts and darted down the highway.

"You sure this friend of yours is on the level?"

"Oh yeah, Ned and me go way back."

"I miss her already."

"Karen? Charlotte?"

"Both." The truck kept constant speed through farms and villages, rising and falling over thin foothills. George passed other vehicles on occasion, most going in their same direction toward Seattle.

"Think your uncle is even going to recognize you?" George played with the radio dial.

"It's been an awful long time. Sure have missed him. There's a lot of important questions right now. He and Grampy were more like a real—you know, than Benny ever tried to be. You still got anymore of that?" Charlie motioned toward the coffee cup.

"Here, take the rest, getting too wired." The coffee was cool but still strong and black, lubricating the dryness in his throat.

"We've known one another a long time, haven't we?"

"Mrs. McClintic's third grade. Finally broke you of that paste-eating habit." Charlie chuckled and stared across some long-distant vision.

"Shouldn't be much farther," were Charlie's last remembered words as he slipped into a fitful doze of dogsleds, Indians, and crazed lantern-flashing miners.

CHAPTER

8

Charlie's voice interrupted their stride, trailing several paces behind George. "You think our stuff is really safe back there?"

"Don't worry, port security is all over that place day and night. Charlie paused to glance across the glowing Seattle skyline, admiring blinking skyscraper flickers and ribbons of light intersecting and dotting along the highways, rising, curving, and snaking between concrete seas. "I don't know about you, but we better get there soon. Seems like we've been walking half the night. What did she call that place again? Bobby's? Billy's?"

"Billy's Elbow Room," Charlie replied in a hoarse tone, his breath struggling with the rising and falling of the narrow pavement damp with evening mist. Yellow orange glows defined a runway down the narrow deserted tarmac strips with housing a direct reflection of decreased income. They paralleled the waterline with seagull strains screeching above a passing car's brief rattle. Peripheral haze threw dull reflections across darkened windows. A few revealing occasional blue light flickers pulsated from living rooms' occupants falling asleep during late-night broadcasts.

Crickets hyperventilated in low-cut shrubs below while dried leaves hissed steady in the late draft. Charlie unzipped his coat, ventilating sweat and heat formed from the hike.

"Sure hope that crazy woman was right. Did you catch that smell? We shoulda drove." Charlie didn't answer his observations.

"When she said it was just down the street and around the corner, we had no way of knowing it was several blocks down the street and around half a dozen corners," Charlie replied and continued their descent after a hill crest. Streaming music rose in their ears but wavered in discordance and straining identification. As the pair turned a bend, an organ chorus intermixed with what Charlie swore was early Swing. Light and music expanded with each step's progress. Farther down the slope, red and blue neon beer signs blinked in the dark windows of a warped hut, pylons suspending it above water.

While still on the road's domestic side, an Episcopalian church stood with two front double doors swung wide to the evening. Continuous measured notes poured from a phantom organ, accentuated by the framing of various strings and horns. George turned and examined the church as they passed. Light-tapered white altar candles glowed at the central row's far end. Most were more than half consumed. "Come on, I don't want to hang around these parts any longer than we have to," he cautioned and pushed George.

A used car lot of rusted trucks, Jeeps, and a doorless El Dorado spotted the hut's front row parking lot. Farther down, weak light across a creaking wooden pier shadowed several black silhouettes stumbling past one another in cracked unkempt coats.

Neon window flashing blinked while electric humming bugs swirled around a lone domed light suspended above the entrance.

A single distorted wooden door appeared to sag beneath uncounted paint coatings. Boot prints smudged stains across the chipped surface. George followed Charlie.

Not enough light allowed them to distinguish the facial features of the dozen or so figures reeking of sweat, salt spray, and gutted fish. A group of three huddled around a low corner table beneath another ceiling-suspended, tin-shaded bulb.

Rolled-up cuffs revealed forearms of white-curled hairs poking through black-and-blue tattoos stretched with time's passage. More specters hunched on stools. Their hollow gazes draped around the bar with the last vacant-shell face down on stained wood with his spent mug still clutched in one hand. Only one shadow with his back against the wall allowed his cards to fall low enough to notice their entrance. No other eyes lifted acknowledging their entry.

Black nets hung suspended from the ceiling with sea-worn chipped cork floats. A corner jukebox flashed intermittent explosions of color, interrupted from a buried wiring short, and screeched Sinatra in scratching worn shrills. "This is Elbow Billy's?" George shot a wavering murmur from the corner of his mouth and sideways glance in Charlie's direction. His frozen eyes refused to unlock from the menagerie of hollow men.

"She said it was the only place with nets hanging from the ceiling, and I didn't see any lights on or doors open anywhere else along this street. Did you?" George turned and scanned the hundreds of photographs spanning each wall with every size and form of fish that could be taken from the sea. Most were black and white beneath hazed glass covers, but a scattering contrasted brilliant color. Both men advanced toward the extended island bar stretching the shack's length.

Brief coughs and unidentified whispers passed, but there was no common defined indication of their presence. A brass bell hung suspended from one rafter. George reached overhead and grasped the frayed clangor rope. Charlie's hand grabbed his wrist. "Gup, hold on, you hear that?" Charlie asked and tilted his head to strain between the last few booming jukebox chords. George leaned over the bar railing.

Stretched out on the hidden concrete bar floor's opposite side, a canvas Army cot lay along the interior with resounding snores curdling from a shapeless lump beneath trembling newspaper sections. Charlie gripped a mug and slammed it down with an echoing knock, shaking the worn patched shellac. The scraped surface was worn down to the original unfinished teak, edges and corners still retaining the original glass slick surface. The lump jumped in reaction, newsprint scattering in every direction. "Hmpppphhhhh!" came a high-pitched whining protest and random chuckles scattering around the room. George turned at the sound of clomping boots through an open far wall door. The man yanked down his coat bottom, pulled out a fourth chair, and resumed the game.

"Excuse me, think you might be able to help us find someone?" George looked down at the animated skeleton, now perched on the cot's edge and wiping his reddened eyes with age-spotted bony fists. Even after rising, his back remained in a permanent stoop. The gaunt framed relic couldn't raise his head high enough to meet their own but turned to the side for a passing glance.

"Depends."

"John, John Hanover," Charlie forced out and didn't bother extending a handshake as he concentrated on not twitching his eyebrows. The man raised a single eye.

"And him?"

"Oh, he's my brother, Jim." George sensed a welcoming curve start across his lips but repressed the response.

"We're trying to find my brother's friend, goes by the name of Ned Logan. Another friend of ours told—" Every muscle in the man's face squeezed at the same time. From behind, Charlie heard rustling chairs scooting across slick concrete. A trunk-thick hand the size of Charlie's head vice-clamped his shoulder from behind.

"Whaddya got to do with Ned?" growled a faceless voice. Before he could answer, Charlie was spun around, and both shoulders were anchored, the voice pulling him from within an inch of a crooked nose professing numerous breaks received over a lifetime. Whiskey and stale cigar smoke washed across his face with each breath stench blanketing his cheeks. Charlie's eyes filled with tears and decreased to thin slits, masking the burn. He rose to no more than the man's chest and stared up into ragged stained teeth retaining scraps of his previous meal.

"I—I—we need to ask him something," Charlie stammered.

"You got my money?" A fine red blood vessel network bulged around his gray pupils and neck cords strained pale through stubble with every forced exhalation. Whitish pink multiple scars crisscrossed just above his collar. With his peripheral vision, Charlie caught an exposed nickel-plated revolver's glint from the man's waistband.

"Money? Just trying to find our friend, nothing more."

"Oh, I gotcha," he muttered after a noticed relaxation of tension across his features. He rubbed his chin with a single, vast, grime-covered hand, black bands crusted beneath each fingernail. "That no good trash into you too?"

"Yeah, and we ain't waiting no more," George contributed.

"Good luck with that, already shook him." The tower nodded in the rear opened door's direction. He swiveled on a heel, trying to maintain balance with one hand on the bar and refilling his mug from the tap with the other. After several teetering, sloshing lurches and grasping at any surface to maintain an upright path, he rejoined the card table and released a rib-trembling belch after his chair wrenched beneath the weight. Charlie and George exchanged blank stares.

Another back-table ghost nodded over his shoulder to the rear door, only distinguishable from bobbing pier-moored boat lights. As they exited, cigar and pipe smoke swirled and parted like fog. A fine mist drizzle darkened cracked asphalt. Charlie scanned the vacant dock. At the moment he called to George, a pathetic, weighted gasp for air rose from the side alley.

"You? That you, again? No, no more," a cracking voice followed the initial struggled breathing. One hand shot out through a light shaft and clawed at the air.

"Over there," George pointed. Charlie took measured steps wading through and pushing aside haphazard broken crate stacks stained with every form of rotten ooze and crust, stale beer-soaked cardboard boxes, tinkling empty bottles, and a torn plastic garbage bag mountain spilling rubbish.

Two legs stuck out from a body, facedown on the rancid concrete behind a dumpster. The figure's normal paste-white legs were covered in scrapes, purple-green bruises, and surrounding filth.

"Come on, give me a hand," Charlie instructed. Charlie circled around to the body's opposite side, kicking away empty beer cans while George pulled on the man's clay feet. An agonizing groan released the moment he lifted him from the ground. "Careful, careful, we're not going to hurt you," Charlie reassured.

After more kicks and protests, they dragged him into the light and propped him upright against a crate. One eye was swollen shut in a protruding goose egg, and the other was no more than a crimson fissure. His bottom split lip oozed red and swelled in distortion. A normal white t-shirt was blood-soaked black. Skin was slick to the touch while a full head of white hair was now matted, blood-caked, and netted with small scraps of gray lettuce and fruit.

George pulled a wallet from one of his clutching hands, but the man had no energy remaining to resist his force. "This him? The guy's hardly alive," Charlie remarked after retreating for a better view, slipping his shirt neck over his nose and stifling some degree of stench.

"No more. Said I ain't got it yet," the man croaked in a swollen lip lisp and unmistakable Scottish accent, wincing through disfigured bloated features. A slight cough and he doubled over, grabbing the right side of his chest. He sucked air gulps and concluded each in a long drawn-out whimper. His fingers poked with hesitation along his torso. "Nothing seems broken yet," he gasped.

"Take it easy, we aren't here to hurt you." George knelt down on a knee and turned the man's face aside. "Ned, it's me, George Gupford." One lid now somewhat cringed apart. It widened enough for George to identify his pupil darting back and forth after wiping grit from his face.

"Georgie boy!" Ned's voice rose. He winced and dropped the arm back to his side. "Uh, can't do that yet, hurts to even smile." Charlie and George each grabbed an arm, hoisting Ned until he was almost standing. More grunts and moans followed each jarring shift.

"Where we going? In for another drink? Rounds on me, Georgie! Who's this?" Ned slurred and half-giggled to himself.

"Relax, don't worry about that now. We need to get you cleaned up a little, old friend," George reassured.

"Better not take him back through there," Charlie pointed toward the door, and George shrugged in agreement, nodding back down the alley toward the front parking lot. They continued shifting his weight and regaining holds on his thin slipping biceps while returning to the front lot.

"All right boys, I'm driving," Ned rasped, wrestling a clenched arm free and fumbling with keys pulled from his front pocket. He yanked the opposite arm from George's grasp and stumbled forward until dropping across the hood of the El Dorado without doors. "Ain't she a beaut? Got her couple a weeks ago with a pair of threeeeeeeees. Believe it? Believe it?" his question repeated, face straining tight followed with a trembling body.

After the last cough, Ned collapsed limp. He fell forward, arms stretched out to each side and his torso slumped across the hood.

"Now what?" George shook his head.

"Can't stay here all night—grab an arm." George grasped Ned around the shoulders, turned his head to one side, and took the shallowest breaths, avoiding as little reeking inhalation as possible. Charlie opened the wrenching tailgate. George jumped into the bed and pulled Ned in by the shoulders. Both men turned to regain their breath.

Ned's chortling snore rose and lowered from behind them. "Let's get back to the docks," George said and tossed the keys at Charlie. "We'll drop him off at the ship. I don't think I can drive."

CHAPTER

9

George swayed up the gangplank while Charlie stayed near their duffel bags, chain-link handrails tinkling with each step. Two nervous heads twitched and ceased their rope coiling to stare at his approach. Among lining runner deck lights, Charlie's distance disguised specific speech recognition. One figure shoved a cigarette back between cracked red lips, gesticulated with both arms, and with a final turn, pointed toward the bow.

Wind rose and random spray sprinkled across his face. High gulls struggled against the gales, hanging suspended in midair by invisible tethering lines, their beaks pointed up in a rapid snatching rise and fall. Charlie turned and gazed across distant skyscraper profiles. Thoughts of Charlotte's dreams whispered far beyond them. His drift was interrupted by a backward glance and George's frantic overhead hand waving from beyond the railing.

"Hey! Come on up," he indicated in a controlled yell. The plank thudded beneath Charlie's soles. He almost lost his footing as it drifted between sides during the ascent, his duffel throwing him off stride.

The Triton Majestic was a hundred-and-thirty-six-foot steel Eastern Rig Scalloper converted to a long line hauler. Through rust, corrosion, and expanding and contracting plates, multiple roles had been played since her original Boston shipyard launch. When Charlie reached the deck, the two earlier figures vanished, leaving them alone. Shadows revealed vague shapes of wenches, pulleys, stacked equipment, and cargo. "Come on, let's find Ned," George motioned and headed aft with his bag bouncing on one shoulder. George dropped his duffel and ducked through the opening. Charlie followed and pulled both of their gear in behind them.

Narrow hallways and low ceilings collapsed and molded around Charlie's body, suffocating what breath was forced through his tightened throat. His eyes widened as the walls tightened close against his shoulder blades with random turning hydraulic lines and electric conduits. Snapping his vision to the sand-gritted wooden floor allowed distraction from blood pumping through his heart and a cold sweat breaking across his brow.

They passed doors, some shut, others wide open with random sounds drifting from accidental shadows—a crackling television, guttural cartoonish snores, dark silence, and a gibbering sermon in a foreign language he couldn't begin identifying. The air was a sludge of men's sweat and old grease. Charlie remained on George's heels. He noticed George's obvious absorption while scaling steep iron stairs winding to a higher deck.

"Man, this is like coming home," he shot out between labored breath. Charlie noticed fewer hatches on this higher level, the footing beneath them more uniform, off-white, and almost antiseptic; walls higher and brighter. "There he is, last door on the right," George said and cleared his throat while striking a steel door with the back of his knuckles. "Anyone home?" Although not intentional, his knock dislodged the door, and it swung inwards with a whispered metallic grind. After swinging to full view, the opposite side of the quarters was defined by a single dangling lantern and a thin man's back to them, scribbling across rolled-out maps. Mustard smoke clouds swirled around his bandaged head. "Ned?"

"Hold on," he barked, one hand tapping a cigar into an open trashcan and the other rotating a compass across open curling paper. "Now what can I do ya fer?" he turned in a swivel chair and rested his palms on the armrests, squinting through his own smoke. "Georgie!" a clear Scottish accent sliced through the haze, exclaimed during his rise, and a liver-spotted hand, arrayed in mysterious discolorations, extended toward them.

"Great to see you again, Ned," George returned. "You look a bit better than that mess we pulled out of the alley a little while ago."

"Nah, it's all this salt air, you know, good for the skin. And I do believe we've met?" he turned.

"Ned, this is Charles Sutcliffe who I told you about. We go way back." Charlie dropped his duffel.

"Ned Logan, boatswain, engineer, killer of fish, favorite of the ladies, and all-around seaman extraordinaire," he smiled in a half-toothed grin and lifted an imagined hat from the gauze. Features remained swollen with his split lip still crusted in dried blood. "Guess I didn't offer the most auspicious first impression."

"Nice seeing you again, Ned." Charlie took a half step backwards while Ned grew close to his chin, staring up and examining his features. His clawing grasp forced fingertips into

Charlie's biceps, and he slapped him across the lower back. "Hey," Charlie exclaimed in surprise more than discomfort.

"Don't get jittery, just sizing ya up, son. You ever been on a long liner?" Ned's tone shifted.

"Nothing of this size, but I've done my share of hauling." Ned studied the cadence of his response, the rate of his breath, and the blink of his eyes.

"Uh, huh." George said nothing. "Well, just listen to whatever you're told, and you might end up making it to Juneau in one piece. Don't worry, you'll be on the cutting tables most of the time anyways. Just try and not lose too many fingers over the next couple of weeks. May I interest either of you gentlemen in a smoke?" his partial grin widened and revealed a few remaining teeth distributed between his upper and lower jaws. "Go on, these Cohibas aren't more than a month old, practically still in diapers."

"No thanks," Charlie nodded with a sudden lightheaded rush from the lack of air flow and odors coating his exposed skin.

"Charles, Georgie here told me about you and him are goin' up to see your ailin' uncle. Such a shame, seen a lot a good men go like that." His face drew wistful. He sucked a long drag from his almost spent cigar and returned to his chair. Charlie stole a glance at George with raised eyebrows. George returned a shoulder shrug. "Yeah, that's right, no telling how much longer he'll be," Charlie played along with intuition.

"Georgie, as well as I might want to stay catching up on the latest, it's gonna be early morning real quick, and we'll have plenty of time for that sort of thing. Let's get settled and I'll let Mr. Cronsky know you made it. We're making the run with a full complement," Ned continued while exiting into the main hallway. "Nine of us, including the captain, are lifers on this tug, the other seven are half-day trippers and short haulers, including you tourists. Just listen to me and Paco, stay out of Fatso's way, and ignore whatever Chicken Neck tells you. As far as the others, the team will come together with time."

Charlie followed behind, watching Ned's broken gait shifting sides with each lurch down the clanging hallway. Ned offered brief mumbling comments through side-berth doors. "Here we go," he stopped and pushed open a hatch, squealing with pain. Both George and Charlie ducked to enter the berth. Ned remained in the passageway as George switched on a bulb overlooking a short table and opened the porthole latch. Charlie and George bumped elbows.

"There's only one bunk," George observed.

"That's because this only sleeps one. Like I said, we got a full complement. You're rooming someplace else," Ned replied with a palm through the oval opening in a sweeping gesture request. Charlie's face offered a blank stare back to George as the sounds of Ned's footfalls diminished down the corridor.

"Don't worry, I'll come find you later," George reassured him, but words fell deaf while Charlie struggled with his duffel through the narrow opening. Ned whistled with the same swaying swagger to his stride, gripping both handrails and sliding back to the bottom deck they first entered and past the initial sound and odor array. A gray steel bolted door defined the hallway's end. Ned planted both feet firm on the grit-covered floor and strained aged triceps beneath rolled-up sleeves. "Charlie is it? How 'bout giving me a hand?" Charlie reached both arms above the man and exerted outward pressure on the forming crack. The massive door swung open, and Ned dodged the backswing, avoiding a door and bulkhead pinning. Ned flicked a rotary switch on the wall, and the room lit up in a maze of piping, knobs, buckets, mops, and every shape and size of cleaning chemistry. "This is where you'll be bunking down," he said with both hands on his hips.

"This?" Charlie exclaimed, hesitant to let his bag fall and come in contact with the floor. The space beneath his feet shone with a myriad of random filth piles. In the single clear corner, a shallow mattress stretched across the floor with red blotch stains creeping up the sides.

"Sorry as I can be. This is the only space left on the ship unless you want to find a hole topdeck. Can't have you sleeping in the chutes, or you might get a boot in the middle of the night. Better get some rest, first shift's gonna be a long one," he said. Charlie didn't speak another word. Locating a carton of trash bags, he laid out a barrier across the slick squish beneath his boots and dropped his bag. He collapsed into the mattress and ignored random springs poking his back and shifts of living movement within the padding.

Engine humming rattled through steel and penetrated his fingertips brushing across the blank wall above his head. Karen was in bed by now but not asleep. Charlie tugged and pulled at his shirt and jeans, wadding them into a ball as a pillow, and pulled a blanket up to his chin. The journal's sharp-edged cover pressed into his ribcage. He leaned over to one side and opened the pages. The bulb's meager light still allowed recognition of Absalom's handwriting.

Black scratches interspersed with pencil scribbles began straight but drifted into downward arcing jumbles as they approached the page's edge. The hypnotic engine hum continued pushing down on Charlie's eyelids. The journal returned to its nest inside his coat, and he couldn't remember the last thoughts chopping his mind.

"Rise and shine, Newbie," a voice rose from the real world and snapped Charlie from the furthest reach of his senses. A swift kick across his ankles brought the words to immediate recognition. The blow sent a jolt through his shin, shot up his calf, and disappeared somewhere in his lower back. A penetrating flashlight beam danced across his just-opened eyes. Once the bouncing light dropped to one side, Charlie raised his open hand to block the glare.

"What do you think you're doing? Do you have any idea how early it is?" Charlie protested, crouching up from his slumber.

"What am I doing? The question you should be asking yourself is what you're not doing. Guess what the answer is?" Charlie shook his head. "Not enough!" the faceless voice snarled. Charlie rubbed his eyes and swung his feet across the plastic bag rug.

The lone light switch clicked, revealing a gaunt framed man towering across the shadows. He wore a full-length yellow rain slicker too short to reach past his knees. Dirty blonde chin stubble matched the color of his teeth. "'Nough of this—your skinny butt better be at the slaughter slabs in the next five minutes, or I will cut you up myself and string you up on your own personal gangie, Mr. Earlytime," the man sputtered with spittle scattering from cracked skin-chapped lips. He turned back, ducking low out of the doorway.

The man's full round head was supported by no more than a narrow rod of flesh, and his epiglottis protruded like a goose egg, bouncing with every utterance. Charlie lurched to his feet without any further encouragement or need to ask directions to the "Slaughter Slabs."

The earlier ship hum grew more vibrant with faded men's yells and random metallic thumps. As Charlie groped down the hallway, previous grumbled chattering disappeared from open berths, their doors closed and abandoned while his footing pitched and rolled. He didn't mistake a full throttle on open sea. He scaled the stairway at the end of the hall and heard a familiar voice after clearing the walkway. "Hey there, C.S. Sleep okay?" George chirped to a blank returned glare.

"Yeah, hope your accommodations are better than mine. Didn't know I'd be sleeping with an extended rat family between the mops and lye." A broad, uncontrolled yawn consumed his face.

"Can't tell you what it's like getting back out on the open water again. Don't worry yourself too much—talked to Ned some more this morning. Captain's just shy of another ten thousand pounds in the freezer, and there's only one more run until Juneau." Charlie licked his lips at the coffee mug George gripped, steam washing across his features. "Want some?" he asked and motioned the white ceramic toward Charlie. He snatched the handle and took several distended gulps before wincing at the swelling burn across his mouth lining.

"What and where are the Slaughter Slabs?" he asked. A recent voice again broke over rushing water.

"Mr. Earlytime, we ain't waitin' much longer," the crackling voice echoed through an open port.

"Sounds like your number. Ned got me on the hook baiting line. Get moving and we'll meet up later," George said and disappeared toward the aft. Charlie couldn't sputter another word. He turned and sprinted toward the voice's general direction. After his head cleared the deck, a wind gust blasted across his face, and salt spray dripped from his lips.

The horizon was no more than a rose lavender but grew visible enough to discern the boat's violent lunging and pitching. Crashing waves jostled straining metal. The captain struggled to maintain trough position and pointed the bow perpendicular to the rolling water walls.

"Mr. Earlytime," Chicken Neck called. A few others milled around shifting gear, coiling ropes, counting blue tubs, and securing beach ball-sized orange floats, black spray painted with the Majestic's designation code. "This is Paco," he motioned toward a man who appeared no larger than a child. If not for the full beard and mustache masking adult acne, Charlie believed he could get into any movie for half admission. He curled what remained of his fingers in front of his lips and blew across the tips extending from the ends of cut rubber gloves. "You listen and watch everything Paco does, and you might even leave here with more fingers than him. Any questions?" Chicken Neck turned and vanished back toward the wheelhouse, not waiting for a response to his barking roll of directions.

"Mi amigo," Paco turned and craned his neck up to look at Charlie. "Come on, vaminos, let's get going, man," his brief verbal burst shot out in the same delivery as Chicken Neck but with a distinct Mexican accent. Charlie grabbed pipes, chains, random bars, and any other anchor to maintain balance while Paco glided without effort across the open deck. None of the other orange-coated figures appeared to even glance in their direction.

The sea was a heaving, churning mass of black water and white foam. He followed Paco into a narrow opening at the wheelhouse base toward the aft. Only one other man sat squatting on a short wooden bench struggling to pull on his final rubber boot.

Over his shoulder, the wall was lined with hooks, but only three jackets remained. Each hook possessed name plaques scrawled in handwritten marker like accompanying gravestones without dates. "This looks about the right size. Here, try it on." Paco threw the orange coat at Charlie with an identical pair of blue rubber gloves sticking out of the side pockets. He grunted as he pulled the massive coat over his shoulders. "Them ain't gonna do," Paco shook his head with a tsking sound. A low whistle followed, and he waved a hand at Charlie's blue jeans. From an overhead locker, Paco retrieved a matching pair of orange weather covers and dense thermal boots. "See the door at the end over there?" Charlie nodded. "Once you get suited, I'll be outside."

Charlie buckled and strapped, tied and zipped, eventually struggling to his feet and waddling side to side. He thought previous maneuvers were difficult, but now he both leaned forward and swiveled his hips in a gravity-defying dance. Reemerging at the very back of the ship, sunlight crested the waterline and outlined all edges with a golden tinge below a clean, clear sky. He stopped at two tables on each side of the porthole's exit, and next to them, a pair of sluices with constant running water entered from a dark space above their heads, vanishing through the deck floor to an unidentified destination below their feet. The long-ago, white plastic-covered tables bore the slash cuts of a million strokes. "What now?" Charlie yelled over a struggling electric motor's deafening roar in desperate need of bearing replacements.

"Take one of these," Paco demonstrated with a knife. To Charlie, it appeared just short of a saber. Its curved carbon steel blade glinted flint blue in the morning sun while Paco reached down to retrieve a full cod by the gills. Only the thumb, fore, and index fingers grabbed the hilt while the other two absent digits remained inarticulate stumps.

The fish thumped on the table, and his blade moved with such speed and precision that Charlie caught no more than brief metal glimpses. The extended blade entered and disappeared followed by a flash of gutting, splitting, and pieces flopping into a waiting tub. The opposite hand pushed entrails into the running water stream. Charlie pulled another identical knife from a rack behind Paco's shoulder and pulled his own fish to the table. Even though this wasn't Charlie's first dressing, Paco evaluated each available finger extension and wrist turn while measuring the precise blade entry point and pull. "Oh, mi amigo," Paco released another extended low whistle.

"Not fast enough?"

"We could sail this wreck all the way back to San Francisco before you put enough in the hole. We only get another day and the lines go down," he rubbed his whiskers, measuring Charlie and the knife in his hand. "If the bait ain't on the line by the time Cronsky gets to the rift, Fatso'll toss us over."

"What? There's only two buckets here," Charlie pointed at the pair of fifty-five-gallon plastic drums with open tops. Paco's eyes rolled. He stepped to a curtain and swung back the blood-splattered vinyl. Yellow arc lamps reflected off a barrel stack three high, ten wide, and too deep to calculate. Charlie dropped the knife and caught himself on the table's edge. "Just watch and do your best," was the final direction.

Charlie reached up and dropped an empty barrel across the aisle to his own table. His awkward balance soon moved in rhythm to the deck's pitch. After the first two dozen, he developed a routine—drop, slit, gut, dice, push, drop, slit, gut, dice, push. Innards squeezed and slipped into the constant running clear water stream.

"Where does all of that go?" Charlie called out after what he perceived as an hour's passage. Paco flew beyond their universe. Arms and hands distorted with the blade became an extension of his own arm. He hummed a continuous tune Charlie strained to hear over the bad motor's incessant sputtering. "Paco!" Charlie yelled and repeated his question. Paco's vision never shifted from his task, but a slight mouth corner upturn signaled acknowledgement.

"What do you think we all eat for dinner?" With Charlie's already diminished senses, he hesitated, registering Paco's reply, and didn't bother with any further questions. After Paco's fourth full barrel, Charlie hadn't filled a third of his second. Paco stopped to spray blood and slime from his fingers and snatched a radio transmitter from the wall. He mumbled a few unintelligible words.

Within seconds, a man taller and inverse in proportion to Chicken Neck swung around the curtain's end. His massive swallowing shadow blotted out the morning sun. He wore no orange coat or gloves but an open neck and sleeveless t-shirt with enough curled body hair for Charlie to believe he wore a black fur coat. Faded black-blue tattoos of every shape and distortion peeked from beneath his blubbered biceps. A shining bald head reflected above pouting red lips and sunken eyes. He planted both feet and grabbed the edges of Paco's first barrel, rolling it behind the drawn curtain. Charlie kept his head down and continued cutting.

"You," the deep rasping accent called. Charlie recognized it as either Russian or Yugoslavian from his years with the Deens. His towering eyes glowered down into Charlie's barrel and released a chortle. "Oh, heard about you. Keep an eye on this one, Taco." The hulk commanded and stomped from sight.

"Paco, man, Paco!" he yelled. Time was abandoned. All energy found concentration in avoidance of vomiting from the putrid stench of intestines, livers, and hearts.

"Hey!" Charlie felt a surreal nudge against his boot toe, still caked in dried cod gore.

"All right, I'm going, I'm going," Charlie retorted without opening his eyes. His legs refused reacting with intent as he struggled forward and released an uncontrolled yawn.

"Easy there, don't hurt anything," George motioned with a hand, palm outwards.

"Gup, don't break yourself into a sweat, my man." Charlie focused enough to identify the clean button shirt, jeans, and refreshed sparkle in his eyes.

"Looks like you been through the ringer. After a little baiting, Ned got me moved to an easy one."

"What? You're the captain's personal steward or something?" Charlie said drolly with drifting vision.

"Even better, I'm the kitchen help."

"You don't know the first thing about cooking."

"And what do you know about long line fishing? Hope you're working up an appetite. It's spaghetti night. Just thought I'd check in on ya. Anything you need?"

"New feet, new arms, new hands, you name it," Charlie said, pulling himself to a stand by vacant hooks and maintaining one hand against the rolling wall.

"Dinner's at twenty-four hundred hours. Save you a seat. Ned told me we'll be reaching the grounds about this time tomorrow." Charlie scratched his head, and when his eyes opened, George had vanished. He trudged back through the open doorway toward his table.

"Hey, mi amigo, thought you fell asleep back there. Don't let Chicken Neck or Fatso catch you. You don't want to know what they'll do."

CHAPTER

10

The ever-present journal's sharp corners against Charlie's ribs subsided from his consciousness as the muscular cycle of discomfort eased from burn to an elapsed constant numbness. Reeking cod gore stimulated vigilance to prevent inserting the blade through an open palm. Swarms of flies and crawling maggots swirled through his mind at the thought of not having stiff winds and forty-degree temperatures.

After three lather-and-rinse showers where Charlie leaned against the wall to almost raise his hands above his shoulders, the stench still clung to breathing passage linings. It remained buried within the foundation of his pores even through multiple layers of protective weather barriers. He hesitated putting on a fresh set of clothing, uncertain if they too would absorb the odor.

Charlie collapsed backwards on the mattress without arm strength to break the fall. Over the usual engine humming vibrations, he listened to muffled orders and men's replies through the steel walls, their faint responses a floating drift. Hunger pangs remained the sole motivation preventing him from passing out. Charlie shook and staggered to his feet, stumbling through the hallway with both hands gripping the handrails on each side of his waist and applying bone joint stiffness; the support not from lack of sea leg development but the recent comprehensive assault.

The common room occupied the immediate area below the rear wheelhouse, and the hatch was an open explosion of sound and light. Charlie placed a single foot through the opening. At the rear of the largest room he'd seen on the ship, George's head danced over a stretching range of burners and stainless steel through a long rectangular opening in the wall. He glanced up to notice Charlie's arrival. Charlie kept his head to the floor and slipped into one of the eight massive table booths lining each side of the room.

The encompassing saturation of garlic, oregano, and stewed tomatoes peeled away previous odors. An enormous television hung suspended from the center wall, but the screen was blank. Men hunched in random slouches at their tables. The only sounds were flatware clinking against porcelain and an occasional snort, burp, or glass slurp. Charlie rose and stuck his head through the opening, catching another glimpse of George.

"What's a man got to do to get some food around here?" he called out to George who jumped from boiling pot to boiling pot, the edges of his hair damp with steam and sweat.

"Have yourself a seat and you'll find out." George reached behind and untied his apron strings, tossing his hat on the counter. He appeared moments later with two spilling plates of spaghetti and dropped them across the Formica with a pair of water bottles. "Wow, you've seen better days." Charlie curled a lip towards his friend. "Enjoy this time while you can."

"What? Torture?"

"Sitting down for more than five minutes is a welcome gift. The actual fishing portion of the trip is only a fraction of the gear checks, baiting, coiling, tying, barreling, soak, and retrieval. Just be glad we don't have to do the standard maintenance, cleaning, and other thousands of details keeping this bucket's hull afloat."

"Yet."

"Dig in," he instructed through noodle slurping.

"Gup, I haven't been like this in a long time, if ever," Charlie drawled, his eyes remaining closed and his head falling to one side, resting against faux wood paneling. "Muscles, bones, you name it—so spent. I think even my hair is sore," he said, releasing a strained sigh.

"Nothing like getting your energy back with a full belly," George laughed between bites and a garlic bread slice bouncing in the corner of his mouth. "So you made any more sense of that scribbling?" Charlie snapped his head forward, eyes glaring wide as if receiving a hateful curse.

"Not so loud." Charlie kicked his ankles beneath the table and gave a side-to-side glance, bending his head forward to funnel further direct words into George's ears.

"Come on, there ain't nobody around here who could even begin to imagine." Charlie swung a subsequent head survey and returned eye contact in agreement. He lowered his jacket zipper, and the journal slid up to the table surface.

"Take a look here," Charlie whispered and ran an index finger to the creased worn envelope used as a marker. One of his hands remained in careful position on the right side, hiding any possible detection of the missing pages. He dragged a finger across several lines of faded, water-blurred characters, diagrams, and almost legible script. "If we follow this river, continue through that pass, and over these ranges, we only have to finish this long valley stretch until getting here," he concluded with a pointing jab.

"You figured out the coordinates?"

"Still working on them. Just can't make this word out, something like Stilson or Santona," Charlie stopped, surprised at the energy returning to his voice.

"So what do you really think?"

"Think about what?"

"How much gold do you think the old man really stashed away?" Charlie again cringed without control from George's comment, and his friend shrank back, realizing a broken established rule.

There was no vocal recognition, no head turned or eyebrow raised. Neither man sensed the perked ears less than a few feet from their exchange.

"Can't say for sure. There's a bunch of numbers and figures scratched everywhere, even in the margins. Can't connect most of them, but I still stand by my assertion on your apartment roof. The only real decipherable meaning I can gather from Absalom's uneducated spelling is the rough route we need to take." Charlie now chose his words with care, not wanting to disclose the truth that he had no idea of their final destination.

"Ned told me we'll be putting down a twenty-four hour soak, harvesting, and heading into Juneau by Thursday."

"I don't even know what day of the week it is anymore."

"That plate is awful empty. I can get you more—all you want," George indicated with a satisfying belch. Charlie raised a hand over his own distended stomach and gestured deference.

"Can't lift another fork to my mouth, and I'll be lucky to reach my broom closet. See you in the morning." He slipped the journal back into his jacket lining while hearing George gather their empty plates and whistle back toward the kitchen. Charlie hadn't exited the galley for more than two minutes when a figure in the adjacent booth jumped to his feet and followed through the same exit.

When Charlie returned to consciousness from the smash of a tin bucket crashing to the floor, there were no aches or tendon strains.

And then he moved.

In a haze of frenzied cramping, his hands clawed at pipes jutting from the wall until he found rest on a low table beside the mattress. The constant, never-ceasing engine hum of his steel cage continued its grinding vibration. Without windows or any indication of the outside world, time absorbed into relative mutations. He staggered to the door and clutched any presenting support to remain upright. Again, he found the hallway without activity and pushed open the rear hatch.

A sudden increase and roll of the ship sent Charlie's grip grasping for the open portal frame. Instead of morning sunlight blanketing across his face as he entered the open deck, a saltwater airborne spray torrent splashed across his vision. Dense rolling clouds obliterated any distinguishing color of the sky, and even the usual accompanying gulls vanished from perception.

A pair of orange wrapped men wheeled blue tubs in calculated side-rolling arcs when Charlie heard a voice call over the roar from above.

"Mi amigo, decided to join our party? You better get your proofers on before Chicken Neck finishes his coffee," Paco's mouth parted wide from the top deck railing with his single front gold tooth reflecting the runner floods shining through misted glass. The deck lunged forward, and another drenching wall of spray flew across Charlie's face. A second warning wasn't required, and he disappeared into the locker room. Charlotte's face energized the boot push over his socks. After suiting up and sprinting back to the previous evening's tables, Charlie faced a blank drawn curtain flapping in the wind. Even the knives no longer jangled from their rack. "Figured you might be back here, come on, Chicken Neck and Fatso are getting jumpy. New job today. Come on," Paco motioned and waved a finger stump at Charlie.

Both men jogged to the center of the ship, colliding into a controlled choreograph of men abandoned from individual thought. The large round floats scattered across the deck vanished. Every man's hood drew so tight that no more than eyes and noses were visible through the round laced opening of their faces.

Four men with eight-foot gaffs straddled each side of the boat, caribiners latched to their waist harnesses. Enormous wench drums towered between them while a third in each team steadied support against the railing—rope-tied hooks dangling at their ankles. Over the loudspeaker, a command barked, "Throw!" On cue, the hook took an almost straight line as if ejected from a cannon. Charlie leaned closer and watched one of the orange balls clear the railing and clang toward them. As the top rope hooked around a spinning wheel, the line hissed and began coiling.

Enormous mackerel, larger than Charlotte, began flinging over the deck from the curved gaffer hook steel. Glistening eyes blinked in rapid succession at their strange new world. They flopped across the saltwater-soaked black wood, and their gills flared crimson pink in gasps of air-sucking desperation. Three more orange bodies joined Paco and Charlie when another announcement of "Throw" boomed from the wheelhouse and the team on the opposite side of the deck repeated the previous pattern of events. Charlie arranged himself in a fireman's throw line along with the others.

The first man retrieved a massive fish from the gaffers' arms, passed it down the line, and finally shot toward the last man braced at the freezer door several feet down a staircase.

After dropping his first three fish, Charlie once again forced his mind devoid of all physical discomfort thoughts pulsing through his body. Almost frozen water spray was a bonus, speeding the numbness while negotiating the forty-pound mackerel without thought across the pitching deck.

By the thirtieth line, he quit counting. Charlie's inner clock convinced him that the day reached past noon, and the loudspeaker added a new word to his vocabulary—*break*. Charlie turned with both arms extended only to find nothing thrown in his direction. Paco jumped up and down, waving both arms at his sides and encouraging blood flow through his body.

"You know, mi amigo, had my doubts, but you all right," Paco flashed his golden tooth and slapped Charlie's arm.

"Is that it? We're done?" Charlie's words sputtered from numb lips.

"Done? That was just the first round and a little one. Man, we got a whole 'nother string." Charlie's face lost all expression, joining the single file line of orange coats and cigarette smoke heading toward the locker hatch. They filed into the galley where George sprinted from table to table with stacked plates. He held a cooler under one arm where the others snatched water bottles as he passed. Charlie and Paco established their own booth while everyone else collapsed into the first open seats.

"Gup, this is Paco. He's been breaking me in," Charlie motioned toward George.

"Oh yeah, you're the other Greenie Ned was telling me about," Paco raised an eyebrow and gave a subtle nod. "Ned's a good man, and any friends of his has to be okay," Paco snorted with ham dangling from his teeth while chewing. "Better chow, ten more minutes."

"You've got to be kidding, we just sat down," Charlie protested, wiping sweat and salt from his eyes with a napkin while not allowing his eyebrows to betray the intense cramps of his lower back.

"No more words, eat," Paco commanded and tapped his plate with a fork.

The earlier morning's drift and pitch of the deck was a calm pond compared with the rolling whitecaps and water rushing across the deck with each punch of the ocean. Frozen rain blew in sideways, and he squinted from the sting across his cheeks. Minute sparks pelted all exposed skin, and he winced with each microscopic impact. Heat would have risen to his cheeks if not for the numbness now penetrating layers beneath his skin.

Mackerel after mackerel soared through the air with the electrical whir of the wenches' nonstop recoil. Fatso hovered, keeping the lead gaffer and others in order if he noticed even the slightest slowing pace of their rhythm. He barked orders in Russian even though nobody else understood the stiff tongue. Charlie's mesmerized repetition was interrupted by Paco's broken English. "Almost there, amigo."

Charlie reeled back on his heels. An unexpected weight arced into his outstretched arms; the objecting spasm yanked his forearms, and its wide-fanned tail snapped across the bridge of Charlie's nose. The impact jolted his head backwards more from surprise than mechanical reaction, not noticing until red splattering drops combined with water streaming down the blue of his gloves appeared. He soon realized the blanketing dizziness was more than exhaustion.

Both ankles and feet disappeared from beneath him. Through screaming wind and the ice pellet barrage, he heard Fatso's distant commands and lines squelched to a halt. His bulk blotted out the wheelhouse floods, orange popping lights from a sky diminished to dusk. Fatso's exaggerated spittle-flying tirade was interrupted with a drowning louder echo.

Three different heads bobbed in front of Charlie's vision, but he shook away the haze. Enough focus formed to identify the towering Russian rotating his head toward the loudspeaker. A haunting siren blare echoed across the deck. Each bright orange figure ceased immediate motion, snapping their heads in the loudspeaker's direction. The redundant warning froze all movement, tools clanging to the wood in scattered response to the "WAH, WAH, WAH!"

"Come on, man, we gotta get you up and stop that blood," Charlie heard but could not distinguish any shapes other than a gold glint. He draped one arm around Paco's shoulder after the man struggled to help Charlie to his feet. He half-dragged and half-carried Charlie back toward the lockers.

The room spun in altering directions as Paco dropped him across one of the extended wooden benches. Now that truth began a gradual return, so did the awareness of facial swelling until his nose blew up large enough to notice between his eyes. Paco shoved a stained towel beneath his nose and gave it a slight push on one nostril. Charlie winced. "Oh, mi amigo, you so lucky—don't look broke, but you took a good one across la nariz. You sit here, be right back," Paco instructed and the room continued its swirling carnival ride effect.

The blaring horn continued echoing even within the plated metal walls, away from salt and wind spray. Charlie heard a metal grind screech and opened his eyes to better focus on Paco floating beside him.

"That horn, what is it?" Charlie asked, trying to be certain if he also understood the words he just spoke.

"That's the Klaxon. Riffie missed a throw. Line got caught 'round a shaft, and we only got one engine, man. Here, lay back," Paco instructed and pulled Charlie's head back by his hair. "Only a few more lines in the water, and we can take care of it. Come on, let's get you back to your place," he pulled the unyielding orange layers from Charlie's soaked body. He leaned on Paco after regaining his feet. "Don't worry 'bout any shower now until you get that blood stopped. Paco took a restrained stride while Charlie hobbled, gripping tight to handrails and ignoring the magenta blurred spots down the chest of his t-shirt.

Paco swung open the utility hatch and pulled the bulb string. "Mi Amigo, know it ain't much in here, but you ain't very tidy, are you?" he swung his head and scanned the disarray. Charlie lifted his chin and surveyed his cramped space.

Brooms, buckets, and industrial containers he had stacked with precision the previous night were now a scattered pile across both the mattress and entire floor. His duffel bag lay empty in the center, clothes and every other item scattered. Charlie pulled away from Paco's support and allowed his forearm to grasp his jacket poking out from beneath the mattress. His head didn't turn after sensing the journal's hard cover in the inner pocket.

"This isn't how I left it this morning," he said. "Who hasn't been up top today?"

"Coulda been anybody. Here, back again," Paco leaned over and shoved a pile from the bedding. Charlie followed his instruction. "Chicken Neck says we gotta head into the coast, get the load dropped, and clear the shaft. Just in case, you better get into town and see a doctor." Charlie rose to his elbows and motioned toward the sink. "No, no, you don't wanna look in any mirrors anytime soon. Let me know if you need anything. I'm in 10C," he said and vanished back into the hallway, clanging the hatch shut behind him. All noise ceased except for the redundant engine hum.

Charlie couldn't determine the passage of time when his eyes reopened. The throbbing between his eyes pulsated with every breath and rush of blood through his heart. After visual refocus, George sat on an overturned mop bucket with his arms folded across his chest and an ice bag in one hand. "Wow, you really did take a good one, didn't you?" Charlie sat up with his eyes rolling in their sockets. Exploring fingers rose and tapped the swelling, contracting further winces. "Sorry about that but I think we've got something bigger." He shoved the ice bag against Charlie's swollen nose.

"You too?"

"Yeah, looks like someone's also paid you a visit." George scanned the room.

"After that mackerel took me out, Paco gave me a hand back here, and everything was all over the place."

"Like someone was looking for—" Charlie interrupted him when both men uttered the word *something*. No further exchange was necessary, their mutual glance expressing more than any words. "Overheard Ned and the captain. Moving at half a clip right now on one engine, but we should still make it to Juneau by the wee morning hours."

"Let's not make too much noise," Charlie suggested. Blood now ceased flowing, and he rose to the sink, splashing away black caking streaks from his cheeks and chin.

"Agreed. I gotta get back and clean the grill. Want me to bring you anything?"

"Just quiet."

CHAPTER

11

George stirred from a shoulder nudge and rolled to one side. It wasn't a rapid shove following the first returning him to consciousness but the deforming press of his nose against the frozen, fish oil slick-coated hull. Screeching strained rivets ceased their popping struggle to maintain hull plate positions. "Gup, come on man, rise and shine," Charlie whispered an abrupt command. Sensation snapped back like a gushing flood down a dry creek bed, dream images shaking from his subconscious. Charlie held a flashlight beneath his chin. The beam exaggerated his still swollen and bruised features, reminding George of when they tried scaring one another as children beneath a blanket stretched between two chairs. "It's getting late. We need to get out of here before the sun comes up in a few hours."

"What time is it?" he slurred and coughed.

"Time to go. Better make some distance, and this is our best window. We don't wanna be here when the rest of the gang gets back, and we can't take any more chances."

"Where are we going?" George wiped his eyes.

"We're in dock, made it to the coast. They've been out for at least a few hours, probably getting under the stools in town," Charlie whispered and snapped off the light. The only visible identification outlining their forms was a thin light shaft through the portal pulsating between darkness and faint outlines with the ship's rise and fall.

"Sure it's safe?" he asked in identical muted whispers while shoving a blanket back into his duffel. Charlie turned, glancing over his shoulder from instinct, and probed his jacket for the journal's hard-covered reassurance.

"Yeah, Fatso's snoring on one of the galley tables, and Chicken Neck is too interested in gazing at his own navel lint to notice a bomb exploding beneath him. Come on." George braced both feet and lifted the hatch's latch in slow motion, minimizing the tortured screech of metal against metal. It still offered a dull dissonance above the lapping water and distant night dock sounds. George kept one hand on Charlie's shoulder while twisting through the maze, and both took exchanged bumps against blackened steel walls. Light filtered with a degree of shape recognition at the end of the hall, a shaft escaping down the open hatch.

Charlie drew on his memory of the passageway layout. Senses not returned in full, his head lifted too soon and thumped against a low doorway. He crumpled to his knees and hands, not releasing the slightest vocal response to the collision. Any remaining sleepiness wiped clear and was replaced with brief white light flashes. Female giggling in Chicken Neck's berth paused but returned with alcohol-infused murmurs. Charlie suppressed his primal intention of releasing a cathartic yell, but

George still grabbed him by the upper arm and shoved him up the iron ladder rungs. "Good thing we're getting outta here. You're gonna kill yourself without anyone else's help."

With George still waiting at the bottom, Charlie crested his swirling head through the opening and scanned a full circle, not perceiving a single unnatural movement. Bay winds flapped signal flags, and a scattering of gulls picked over the earlier day butcher table scraps. "Well?" he heard the anxious voice beneath his feet. Charlie's vocal cords wouldn't work as he hoisted himself upwards and slid his duffel across the deck. He crept forward, scuffing on his knees. George's head cleared the deck surface, and he also hunched low at the hips. He shuffled toward Charlie's form creeping behind the wheelhouse.

Through smoked windows, they distinguished a figure's black outline but without movement. Further down the dock, a pair of men smoking pipes faced one another coiling rope beneath thick full-length coats. Both pipe bowls traded lava orange flashes. Deep inhalations of iced air mingled with their trailing smoke and blew off across open water. Neither man turned to notice Charlie and George, too wrapped in their own chore and conversation.

"Gup, see that set of pylons over there with the white rings around the tops and that fat gull?" he asked and pointed over George's shoulder.

"Yeah."

"That's our spot." No sooner had he concluded when Charlie jumped from his knees, flashed onto the deck, and sprinted down the gangplank incline, the narrow walkway swaying with each footfall. Metal and wood strained above the water regardless of care taken to mask any sound. Charlie's bag slipped from his shoulder after reaching the boardwalk. At the same time, a light popped on in the wheelhouse. A beam followed behind him no more than a meager moment. Charlie managed grabbing the duffel and snatching it to his side behind the mooring posts.

The gull squawked from its post perch and half-opened one eye, scanning the activity below her. Charlie squinted between a post opening and watched an extended hand from the wheelhouse silhouette scanning across the ship and dock. Charlie's breath shallowed, intensifying his nose swelling.

George waited and watched. Once the flashlight made its final sweep, the shadow returned to a slumped inert blob. Through the intermittent lighting, George recognized two overhead arm sweeps in the air. All distractions blanked from his mind while focusing on the gangplank, chains swinging at this side while clutching his bag to his chest. He descended toward the boardwalk.

The expected flashlight scan return never reappeared. Charlie snatched him around the wide pylons once he cleared the wood. Both men jumped at the gull's objection. She fluttered at the rouse from her sleep, released a splitting caw, and took off in a broad swoop, catching a draft and disappearing into a moonless sky. "Now what?" George asked, words agitated with a punctuating yawn.

"Take a look at those lights," Charlie motioned toward the horizon where fog lifted and illuminated a spanning reflection glow. "That direction." Once clear of the dock and loading bays, both men resumed an upright posture and slung their bags over their shoulders. Slinking past sleeping warehouses and clearing stations, they remained cloaked in available shadows.

The entire arcing bay was a ribbon of bobbing lights reflecting calm water. Charlie blew on his exposed fingers now numbing from stiff Arctic gales. George paused to review the "Welcome to Juneau" sign and turned into an abandoned alley.

"Hey, wait up a second," George gasped from behind him after the thumping drop of his bag. Charlie stopped with cover behind brick walls and released his own gaping yawn.

"Yeah, I don't think we're making too much more distance tonight. We gotta find somewhere to bed down—at least until the sun comes back up."

Charlie struggled keeping his collar as high up on his neck as it reached. His shoulders caved from the duffel's weight, puffing with the yank of each successive step. George's eyes remained locked on the pavement at his feet, breath swirling up in clouds around his head, raising eyes only long enough to notice Charlie also wincing and tearing from funneling wind through another narrow alley. "Think it's safe to get out of the shadows now?" George's muffled voice penetrated through his scarf.

"Yeah, you're probably right. We're gonna freeze to death out here. You think Ned is going to take any heat for us jumping ship?"

"Don't worry about it. Ned's talked himself out of worse situations." They both stopped to stomp some degree of feeling back into their toes. Charlie was on the move again. George watched him turn the corner. One or two trucks lumbered through the late night, their tires splashing gray slush and lingering blue exhaust, the second set of bald tires no more than a rough jumbled echo.

Neon glows were well behind them, and several more turns landed them along an abandoned stretch of commercial warehousing. Struggling arc lamps illuminated their vision. From the bleak darkness, crossed incandescent bulbs flickered. A few of them blinked in random intermittent connection, contrasting against oncoming sleet.

In the doorway of a red-brick, three-story skeleton, a slumped-over shape hugged his knees. George snuck his head around the corner and scanned every direction. Tugging on

Charlie's sleeve, they crept across cracked pavement. The shuddering man in a ragged calico coat mumbled in simple chanting whispers above the wind. Both Charlie and George took broad steps over the garbage bags wrapped around his ankles and knees drawn up tight to his chin. Charlie knocked first with a closed fist. Both men exchanged glances in the quivering wait.

"Hello?" a voice called through the cracked door. Wind gusts pushed it wider and a man appeared. A broad smiling freckle-spanned face greeted them. His copper colored straight hair reached well past his shoulders and was restrained in a rubber-banded pony tail. His random angled teeth reflected the jittering cross bulbs. Behind him, walls danced in reflective wavering glows high up water-stained cracked plaster. "Do you gentlemen need anything this evening? More coats, gloves, warm blankets?" he continued in an alien cheer. Charlie reached a glove toward him, and he returned the greeting with an unhesitant firm grasp.

"No thanks, we're okay. Just looking for some directions."

"We're all gonna catch a permanent chill if we stay out here much longer. Come on in." George stepped forward with such determination he almost knocked Charlie backwards into the anonymous figure at their knees. "How about it, Jake? Lots more room," the man motioned toward the curled-up individual, still crouching and mumbling to himself. "Have it your way, but you know the door is always open." After entrance, Charlie unwrapped his scarf, and warmth embraced his cheeks. He had to catch his balance, almost tripping over more extended legs across the hallway. "That Jake, he's been hanging around for the last three years I've been here and still won't even come in to eat. I have to bring his soup out on the doorstep," he continued. The extended legs didn't budge nor was there any movement from the attached torso.

As they turned a corner, it opened to a vast room with a low iron Franklin stove at the far end. The floor was scattered with various forms beneath blanket layers and stained coats. Some slept in silence while others released cartoonish snores.

The young man weaved through the random sprawls with high steps, contorting his hips and center of gravity as if navigating through a minefield until opening a door on the opposite end of the room. Charlie and George slinked along his same path. They joined him in the adjacent clearing. He lifted an oil lamp from a counter, snapped a match beneath the table, and it flared to life with an immediate knob twist. "Please, have a seat," he gestured toward a table against the wall. "You gentlemen don't look like my usual guests."

"What is this rat hole?" George chattered his question between thawing lips.

"You are comforted in the St. Angelo Mission—a lone refuge in the Alaskan wilderness you might say. My apologies for the late introduction—Father Sullivan Dempsey," he grinned and extended slim white fingers. Both men grasped the extended palm in turn, but George glanced away during the exchange when the man unzipped his sweater and revealed the white square collar beneath his chin.

"Sorry, Father."

"No, please, Sully. Think nothing of it, I hear much worse."

"I'm Charlie and this is my good friend George." Charlie couldn't keep his eyes from wandering past Sully's grin and toward the stove while an unidentifiable stew simmered and grasped his senses.

Sully rose, pushing the chair behind him, and dipped a wooden spoon into the pot. Lips tightened and he turned. "You wouldn't be hungry, would you?" He asked the question while rummaging for bowls and then filling them with broth splatters over the sides.

The spaghetti and garlic bread of their previous meal was no more than distant memory, and all courtesy was abandoned. Charlie shoveled in his third spoonful, shuddering and listening to Sully while soaking heat shed the chill. "As I said, you two don't look like my usual crowd. New in town?"

"Just arrived. Trying to figure some transportation up to Skagway," George managed garbling while Charlie's spoon continued a bowl-to-mouth double step.

"Plan on staying awhile? Might be able to set you both up with some regular work if you're interested," Sully said and tilted his head back to one side, leaning against an open palm. His eye sockets rested low in the dim light with a premature sunken strain.

"Thanks anyway. Just need to get to Skagway. I've got an uncle who lives up around those parts. Haven't seen him in years, and we thought we'd surprise him." Sully continued his steadfast smile, reassuring them with unspoken recognition as if already understanding their determination.

"A place you might consider—Point of No Return."

"Where's she docked?" Charlie asked.

"Not a ship. Sort of an eatery, saloon, and meeting place. It's a local workers club off Bering," he said. Charlie and George swapped looks and broke their spoon to bowl to mouth clanking. "Tell you what, I'll give you, give you—" he paused with a rolling yawn. "Sorry about that, long day. I'll give you directions in the morning since you have no business going anywhere on a night like this. I can save you a few bucks, and you're more than welcome to stay here out of the freeze. The accommodations aren't probably what you're accustomed to but at least it's warm." Sully rose and stretched.

"I believe we'll take you up on that offer," Charlie accepted and stifled a belch. Tense ribs relaxed with the stew's warmth spreading through the length of his chest and tingling returning to the tips of his fingers and toes.

"Fine, no worries, you can bed down here. As you've already seen, the place is crammed to capacity on a night like this, and don't let Nan give you a scare in the morning. She's usually here around five getting breakfast started, but she never minds anyone in her kitchen. "Gentlemen," he finished and fumbled back toward the open doorway with the bouncing lantern. Neither Charlie nor George summoned enough energy for further observations, exchanging quiet required communication. Charlie pushed chairs to one side and unrolled his blanket, using the duffel as a pillow.

Even down the extended hallway, other men's snores filled the air and offered random interruptions to the steady gas hiss of the pilot light beneath a hot water heater. George occupied the opposite end of the narrow kitchen. Charlie didn't have a chance to confer regarding daylight's next step, George adding his voice to the snoring night chorus.

Charlie rubbed his temples but eased the pressure once reaching the bridge of his nose. Lumps remained gray and purple. He inhaled cooked vegetables, meat, and floor wax. Even with closed eyes, his core retained the roll of waves rocking beneath his body.

Images of Charlotte and Mr. Snuggles' barren-patched, purple fur wouldn't shake from his thoughts. He hovered over her bed, holding her hand, and offered every reassurance in both word and gesture while stroking back fine brunette hairs from her forehead.

Charlie awoke with a leg tug. At first, he was uncertain if he kicked the wall by accident or an actual force tapped the bottom of his sock. Dim haze wrapped his eyes with fireplace flickers reflecting a glow down the hallway. "Charlie, come on, Charlie, wake up," he heard George's strained pleading. Contrasting the remaining light against the wall, the silhouettes of two men folded and contrasted their outlines against cracked paint.

"What do you want?" George's eyes grew wide. He shoved a hand across Charlie's mouth, muffling his last word. Further away, voices exchanged low tones while both he and Charlie strained to hear.

"…both early thirties hauling a couple of bags…"

"Let me think," Sully's drawl allowed each word to drip one after the other. Charlie, clearing the haze from his thoughts, focused on the first silhouette in combination of understanding a few identifiable Russian phrases.

"Fatso?" George whispered. He nodded, eyes now also white and wide. The accent deepened and a finger rose to point and shake, almost touching Sully's face who took a half step backwards into the hallway.

"Some of these piles of trash have to be them," Fatso's voice growled in a drunken slur, and his shadow disappeared from the wall. Sully turned to face Charlie and George, recognizing the whites of their eyes. Safe in the knowledge of Fatso kicking his way through slumbering blanketed men snorting and rustling from the disturbance, the distraction allowed Sully to jerk an arm up from his side and point toward the back kitchen window.

"Gentlemen, this is a house of the Lord, and your presence is not welcome. You either leave now, or I will be forced to call the authorities." Charlie heard the crash of an empty bottle against the wall and turned to see Sully's shadow duck to his right.

They scrambled, not bothering to roll up their blankets, tie laces, or any other waste of precious seconds. Charlie pushed

George aside and heaved, shoving open the window with paint flecks sprinkling his hair. First, both bags shot through the small square opening where wind rushed in from the darkness. George pulled a chair beneath the opening without a scrape, heaving Charlie up through the hole.

The back alley was deserted. Charlie scanned from right to left, no more than his head extended beyond the opening. A sudden push from behind shot him forward, and he fell almost six feet onto wet crumbled pavement, tendrils of fire shooting through his impacting shoulder.

"You okay?" all three of George's heads whispered above his sight.

"Fine, just fine. Let's get out of here," Charlie rose and beat the gravel from his coat, checking the journal's security against his chest. George's head popped through the opening and then his shoulders.

Then he stopped.

"Gup, come on, what do you think you're doing?" Charlie pleaded, eyes still scanning to each side of them.

"Go on, go on, I think I'm stuck." George twitched and struggled with his nylon coat scraping across the paint-chipped frame.

"Oh man, we don't have time for this. Breathe in as deep as you can and push," Charlie's voice now rose to an elevated begging pitch while clutching George's shoulders from below. He planted one foot against the wall and collapsed backwards with his entire weight. Seconds elapsed. "Listen, listen, take the coat off and toss it through." George squirmed his way back inside, and his layered black coat shot through the window, followed with an immediate appearance of George's lumbering frame falling headfirst into Charlie.

After a tumble to pavement, George grabbed his coat, hat, and bag, sprinting after Charlie who shot ahead of him down the alley. Both he and Charlie retained singular concentrated focus on the path ahead trying not to trip over each other's untied laces. In the distance, they heard distinctive Russian shouts. Red and blue lights pulsated reflections off slick brick walls. Charlie heard Fatso's final command before a siren drowned his yell.

Their duffels bobbed and danced across the lengths of their shoulders. The alley ended and opened to a vacant lightless parting of square staring rectangles. "Come on, over there." George sprinted the final fifty yards until reaching a stretch of scrub pines and fireweed. "Think we're safe here for the time being," he huffed through gasping breath. Charlie bent over holding both knees and drew in morning air inhalations. The sky remained navy blue with a barest pink bleeding across the waterline.

"Still can't stay out here for what remains of this night. Look," George pointed to a chain-link fence well disguised through the brush. Their boots relaced, breathing resumed a normal rhythm. They rose and stopped short between shrubs, Charlie in the lead. A chain-link fence's side gate remained open less than a foot, but enough for them to both squeeze through toward a set of Quonset huts at the rear of the cleared compound.

Heavy lifters, ground steel, dump trucks, and plows were lined with flat gravel precision among every conceivable piece of earth-moving equipment. Charlie slipped into a cracked open sliding door with George close behind. Both men hesitated in the darkness.

"At least there aren't any dogs. Good to get out of that wind." Charlie scanned the interior with his pocket flashlight for any sign of movement. They felt a path toward stacks of drums and spooled cable almost reaching to the ceiling. "Safe as anywhere, I guess." George offered no further suggestions,

removing his blanket and stretching it across oil-spotted concrete.
Charlie's snoring rose from behind him.

CHAPTER

12

A muffled question escaped between scarf layers wrapped around George's mouth. "You see anything yet?" Charlie shook his head, still scanning around the corner. The thin slot of sky beyond overhead rooftops remained unending gray. George huddled forward with arms wrapped around his sides while he hunched on his bag.

An occasional car door slammed, struggling engines rumbled to life, and various hums and rattles sounded above wind-tossed paper scraps down the alley. "I gotta tell you, the bunk on that ship might have not been too much to brag about, but it sure beats oil sludge cement anytime."

"You should have tried a night in my closet," Charlie stretched. He released a low huff after muscles loosened. "You starting to get concerned too? Sunday morning. A place like that even going to be open for business?"

"That's where Sully said we need to go." George nodded at the battered split sign suspended over the porch and two dirt-fogged, double-glass doors. Hazed glass advertised nickel beer nights on Wednesday with All You Can Eat blackened halibut and crab legs. Ragged tugs and draggers bobbed on the water with a matching pair of trawlers resting in slips on each side of the stilt-supported structure. "So now what?"

"Good question. Too much risk heading back to Sully's." The moment Charlie turned for another glance around the corner, the gunshot explosion of a backfiring truck echoed down the narrow building passage. Charlie jumped to his feet. Eyes rolled in their sockets, and he almost swallowed his tongue. He turned as George also rose, and his heaving chest shuddered in the same contractions.

"Oh man, my nerves can't take anything more like that." Charlie laughed off the tension.

"Hey, thought I saw someone go in through the front door. Wait here." Charlie turned again for a glancing peek, braving further neck extension.

"Well?"

Charlie shouldered his duffel, elevating it to block his profile and leapt forward, shuffling his feet in double time until reaching wide stairs leading up the building's front porch. A few overhead gulls screeched and circled. Bells clanked upon his entrance. He cringed while turning to notice George studying his route.

The Point of No Return was a single open warehouse with surrounding windows. The bay-facing window spanned from floor to ceiling. Booths also lined each wall, and a massive rectangular counter sprawled in the center. Rattling pans greeted his entrance and settled back to silence. Several potted plastic birch saplings obscured the front entrance, and Charlie ducked, peering through the spindle limbs.

Grumbling men's voices hacked and coughed, permeating brine-soaked air with a distinctive stew of coffee, eggs, and tobacco smoke. Coughs, stifled laughs, and a general murmuring rolled in early morning light like atonal waves against the dust-tinted glass panes. Through rear revealing windows, men hauled equipment and supplies down the wooden boardwalk stretching the building's length.

Although half a dozen men sat with their backs toward the entrance, Charlie examined each form along with a potential recognizable face. He took second and third verifications for any possible connection to the Triton. Gentle fingers pushed against one of the front doors, easing it open far enough not to dislodge the bells but enough to motion George.

Across Bering, George dragged his bag behind him and shuffled until crouching behind a row of newspaper vending machines, rising over the red and yellow cages to scan for motion. "Come on, toss it over there next to mine. We don't need any more attention." George heeded Charlie's instruction and dropped his bag behind a corner bench. Charlie pointed at the brass bell above their heads and slipped through the opening.

"Where'd all these folks come from?" George hesitated with Charlie behind the plastic leaf camouflage. "Sure it's safe?"

"No sign of Fatso, Chicken Neck, or even Paco. You smell that?" George's own stomach rumbled from the fried eggs and sizzling meat overpowering the collective odors of working men. The blanketing hypnotism pulled them from cover to identify the source. Charlie pulled out a stool at the far end of the counter, ensuring visual surveillance on the front lobby while George kept full view of the single door leading out to the boardwalk. "Let's get on with what we came here for, and breakfast is on me."

"Eighteen!" a barking snap shot through the air after two double doors swung open and slammed against pine siding covered in aging photographs, mounted fish, netting, and corkboards wallpapered with clipboards and business cards.

The squat man's apron and t-shirt were threadbare and splattered with random blotches. He held one tray in each hand above his head while negotiating around chairs and tables without taking his eyes from a back-corner booth. His forearms, tattoos struggling to emerge from layered gray curled hair mats, bulged from the crowded circular dented trays. He swung around and landed each on chipped block tabletops with an aluminum scrape. Steam overpowered the swirling smoke, enveloping the faces of men slurping from tall white coffee mugs. Charlie detected a rustle from behind him.

"You boys need some help?" a voice rose. A younger and less world-wearied version of the first man leaned around the corner. His arms were also covered in an accidental comic book yet almost hairless and ink coloring still pronounced. A broken smile stretched across his tooth-filled, acne-scarred face. The entire right eye from halfway down his forehead to his ears and neck was covered in a deep crimson purple port wine stain.

One hand pushed two somewhat white mugs on the counter without thought while using the other grip to shove back unwashed stringed frantic hair from his eyes. Black coffee spilled from a pocked, stainless-steel coffee pot and splashed dark flecks across the bar surface sheen.

"As a matter of fact, a good friend of ours recommended your place. Thought we might try finding a way up to Skagway." George grabbed a mug. He pushed the hard ceramic to his lips and snatched it back. A thumb brushed across the sear of his lower lip. He winced in silence and scanned the booths.

"Guess this place is as good as any. Hey, Pop!" the boy's cracking voice called. Charlie's shoulders slunked, and his eyes dropped to concentrate on his coffee. Hairy arms turned, a just-lit cigarette bouncing in the corner of his lips. He yanked a once-white hat from his head revealing a crown of twisted black-and-gray hair surrounding his scalp like a frightened halo. After a final exchange of undeterminable table discussion, he dangled both unencumbered trays at his sides and knocked the counter trap open with one knee.

"What is it, boy? Hurry it up. Got three more orders, and Jimmy's in a mood this morning. Better be important or I'm shovin' that spatula in your hands. Maybe then you'll know what it's like to pour sweat over that grill." He turned as if just noticing Charlie and George's presence.

"These fellas are trying to get to Skagway." The boy shrank back, raising a stained mug, and proceeded wiping it with an even darker stained towel slung over his shoulder.

"Skagway? Can't ya just drive like everybody else? Bus runs outta here at twelve and four," he commented and brushed dripping sweat from bulging forehead veins.

"We'd like to but our friends are a little lacking at the moment," Charlie feigned. The man paused with a hesitant exchange between them.

"Hope you got enough for that Joe," he gruffed. George nodded in reassurance, now sipping and flexing his fingers with the returning warmth. A random yell rose behind them. "Yeah, Barnes, keep yer shirt on. Boy, go find out what's takin' Jimmy so long." His son wasn't asked twice, tossing his towel in the corner and sprinting toward the double kitchen doors.

Bells rattled, sending Charlie and George into a hunch. Their heads spun toward the entrance. Eyes turned to meet the tattooed man's furrowed glare. The fuzzed anchor across his right arm now elongated and tightened across his chest, cigarette rolling between his lips. "You boys ain't in any kinda trouble, I hope?" he asked with his cigarette taking a full right to left shift between his lips.

"No, nothing like that," George jumped in to defend.

"I gotta great-uncle lives up around there, and we got word a few weeks back that his health is starting to ail a bit. Thought we might go up awhile, see how he's doing, and if we can do anything for him." Charlie didn't wait for words and sipped. Forearm hair rustled as his arms unfolded and scratched his slick scalp, glistening in the now morning air sunshine pulsing a few shafts through the dense smoke. His head tilted to one side, attempting an expression decipher.

"Well, you fellas don't look too dangerous to me. Hey, Wilson!" he yelled along the back-booth row. A cropped blonde head turned at the call. The stranger rose and approached them.

"What's up, Hank?" a gap-toothed reply rose over murmurs and chortles. "My eggs are getting' cold."

"Ain't you and that brother of yours going back up to the yards?"

"Yeah, this afternoon. Twenty tons o' timber better be there by sunrise. Whatcha wanna know that fer?" the man paused and released an audible belch, rubbing his belly through a faded concert t-shirt.

"These two gentlemen are looking for wheels," Hank shot back a mocking reply. His focus returned to the same monotonous motion minutiae of untold previous mornings.

"That so, eh? Well come on over and have a seat. My food is still gettin' cold," he turned and stumbled back to his booth, the odor of cheap bourbon still exuding from his pores.

"Excuse me." Hank glowered behind them while clinking empty mugs.

"Sorry," George slapped his shirt and pulled a crumpled dollar bill from the pocket. Hank snatched it without further comment.

"So boys, what kinda business you got up around that neck?" Wilson concentrated on the steaming food plate before him with snapping fork cracks. Charlie repeated his earlier line to

Hank. Across the table, a man draped in an almost identical ragged t-shirt and torn jeans hunched over his own plate. "Pretty country up around those parts, but the yards are a good hour north of Skagway. Boys, this is my brother Wade." The other man didn't raise his head or show any sign of acknowledgement other than a brief snort. George extended an open palm but returned to his mug handle and took a deep slurp. "Sorry 'bout that but Wade is a man of few words. Ain't hungry or anything, are you?" Charlie couldn't overcome his unmoving stare at the piled hash browns, toast, and sausages. "Here," Wilson stretched and shoved a plate forward. "Can't eat it this cold." Both hands stretched vertical above his head, and a belch shot forward mixed with eggs and alcohol.

Neither Charlie nor George bothered locating forks and scooped with both fingers, concentrating on reminding themselves to chew. Their frantic food-shoveling caused Wade's robotic movement to hesitate with a sideways glance. "All right then, we're leaving sharp at three o'clock. You know how to get over to the depot? It's off Old Ferry at the end of Northpoint."

Charlie and George exchanged blank stares. "We'll be there."

"Don't worry, ask old Hank over there, and he'll get you pointed in the right direction." Wade dropped his fork on clean enamel with a clank, releasing an identical belch matching his brother's earlier release. A gaping yawn followed. "All right boys, remember, three o'clock sharp or we're leaving without ya," Wilson finished and rose, exiting toward the front double doors with remnants of breakfast scattering a trail behind him. Wade dug several bills from his front pockets and tossed them near the register.

"What do you think?" George asked, still gnawing on toast crust and strawberry jam left on Wade's plate.

"Good as any plan we have right now." Hank's son wiped the booth adjacent to their seats with frantic vigor, stealing a glance in their direction every few moments. "Everything okay?" The boy checked around in each possible direction and shifted to their table.

"Don't know what your real story is and I don't care. Some guy came in earlier and asked Pop if we seen anybody looking like they didn't belong." His restrained voice was interrupted by the crash of a kitchen plate.

Blood rushed away from George's complexion.

"What sort of guy was he?" Charlie matched the boy's tone.

"Look mister, everyone around here looks the same to me."

"What did he say?"

"Never spoke to him myself, but Pop said he was just asking. Think you both better find a place to hole up for a few hours."

CHAPTER

13

The pair of shuddering men huddled, each bent forward at the waist while leaning back and forth. They trembled on top of their bags, hands clenched and shoved as low in their coat pockets as possible.

The horizon mocked with a barren, slick, black strip and far glistening pinpoints breaking smooth lines. Charlie blinked through tearing lids. He struggled for certain identification of his watch's large hand over the three and looked beyond, blinding himself from the sun still struggling through the trees. "Su—gigk hope shhhsk—Wilk—rememers," George chattered between a slit formed from the loosening of his stretched wool scarf. Only his eyes remained visible after a tilt of his head.

"What? Either your vocal cords or my eardrums have frozen over," Charlie laughed although reaction was abrupt, wasted warmth spilling from his lungs. George nudged his scarf wider with hesitation.

"I said, I hope Wilson remembers we're out here," he spurted in a single extracted word, retightening the wrap back around his neck. Right at the conclusion of his statement, an ice-shattering horn boomed across the open field, and black-soot smoke billowed from a semi cab's top exhaust pipe clearing the hill.

"There's your answer." The truck snarled forward as if no driver steered behind the wheel. Its tires slammed across the slick cleared road, and both men jumped in just enough time to grab their bags and leap from the impending collision. Hydraulic squealing sprayed loose puddles of slush, flying mud, and shook birds from low-hanging branches. Wilson tossed a glowing red cigarette butt through his cracked window while the vehicle released a tremendous air brake belch.

The driver side door opened with an abrasive grate, and Wilson clanged down chrome steps. His brother was no more than an outline through the darkened front windshield, but the glowing tip of his own cigarette poked out beneath his red-and-black checkered cap. Wilson clutched a Styrofoam coffee cup in one hand and smiled a two-toothed grin in the meager light.

"Come on boys, times a wastin'. Boss man needs us at first light to get those tractors outta there and drop this load of pine," he said with a leather-gloved slap against a long cut trunk, ice crystals crunching and spraying. Charlie and George shouldered their bags and followed him single file back to the idling semi. "You can toss 'em right up there," Wilson motioned over his shoulder.

"Amazing how small these things are from the outside and can actually fit so many people," George marveled and grasped the door handle with his own glove. "You want us to get in on this side?" he asked and waited for Wade's exit.

"What side are you taking 'bout?" Wilson's voice cracked. "Said we'd get you up to Skagway, never said nothin' 'bout where you was riding."

"Back there?" Charlie asked with his gaze fixated on the looming lumber stack stretched behind the cab. The raw wood jumble was no more than a cut-log-pyramid heap on oil-saturated two-by-eights. Random thick chain links draped the trunks. Charlie attempted ignoring the rust-attached eyebolts linking them together and glanced back in the hope that Wilson would reveal the joke. He spun George around so their backs faced Wilson.

"Look, it shouldn't take longer than nine or so hours, and I think we can make it if we stay huddled against the back of the cab."

"If the cold doesn't get us, getting crushed underneath one of those trunks might be a rude awakening," George turned and scanned down the lengths of bark.

"We'll be there at sunup." Charlie turned, surveying the barrenness surrounding them and a few smoke wisps indicating Juneau's outskirts.

"Boys, no more time. You coming or what?"

"Come on," Charlie grunted and scaled behind the side bars, grasping a chain with both hands and hoisting himself onto the flat. He stretched a hand down to George. The entire vehicle's frame bolted forward with a choking dark-soot cough. The splintered planking beneath them rumbled and swayed as they propped their backs against a metal sheet panel protecting hydraulic and electrical interconnect cables below their legs. Through the narrow back window, saliva poured across Charlie's cracked lips when he recognized steam rising from Wade's coffee. The dozen logs were all between two and three feet in looming diameter and scraped against one another at every passing bump and pothole in the road.

Both men's vision fixated on the raw timber's weight swaying against each other while Charlie and George pushed themselves farther backwards against the rear of the cab. Wade caught their wide focus from a glance behind him after opening the cab's rear sliding window. Their heads turned to the warmth washing and wrapping around the backs of their hoods.

"How you boys doin'?" Wade yelled, raising his cup to camouflage the uncontrollable rise in the corners of his mouth.

"Just fine, almost tropical, got any suntan lotion up there?" Charlie asked. Wade's curving lips were replaced with a slow, gear-grinding expression and wrinkled forehead. His head vanished below the back of the seat and returned with arms full of wool Army blankets. He pushed them out one at a time through the window slit.

"These might help ya a bit. Least they'll keep down some of that gentle breeze," he yelled through a cupped hand to elevate his voice above clanging and grinding metal. The window slammed shut. Charlie saw both of the men's heads swaying and leaning forward, Wade slapping the dashboard. Neither he nor George hesitated to wrap themselves in the abrasive wool reeking of oil, sap, and alcohol. No words escaped their bundles while they watched open fields disappear.

Gradual tightening boreal forest engulfed both sides of the parting log windows opening between jolts. Charlie's head bobbed forward between adjustments to his center of gravity. At the moment an abandoning blanket wrapped around his perceptions, a knock tossed him to one side, and the smash above his eyes shot nerve impulses spinning around to the back of his head.

Once the shock cleared and he pulled the blanket from his face, George's muffled yells rose above the random collisions returning to his ears. He peeked through an opening in the wool. George was flat on his back careening back and forth between the bottom stack of logs. His hands flailed and grasped, scratching at loose bark once within arm's reach while the wood heaved and wrenched above and around them.

Their bodies jostled without control—airborne among the tons of dancing pine. Charlie scrambled on hands and knees retaining as much contact as possible, adjusting his sway to the carnival ride effect. He grasped one corner of George's blanket wrap, now clinging around his waist, and pulled him from beneath the juggling timber.

A thousand rusting chain links squealed in their strain to contain them.

"Here," Charlie instructed and laid a free loose chain across George's lap. He took the remaining slack and wrapped a length around his own waist, never releasing his arm from encircling George. What began as a road became no more than a cleared swath snaking through old-growth shrub and birch-dotted pines.

Trenched pits and mud-covered stones littered the clearing and formed low berms on each side of their crawling path. Previous twilight turned darker. The biting links filtered through their gloves and denim jeans. They doubled blanket layers around their heads. George squinted to identify Charlie's moving lips escape between the layers. "Still glad you came on this little adventure?" Charlie called out.

"Wouldn't have it any other way!"

When Charlie awoke, everything was silent, but he remained locked into the tension of a bird sleeping on a wire, vigilant against the next collision. The stillness remained short-lived. A buzzing chainsaw tooth shrill interrupted his returning awareness.

Pulling apart tightened blankets, a firelight blaze on the trail's side blared against surrounding darkness and the resting logs once dancing above his head. Two figures huddled around the flames, but their backs were turned. The sawing shape was indistinguishable, but the unnatural mechanical engine whirred through the dark.

After swinging his legs to the ground, Charlie groped his way back against the flatbed's side with each wobbling step. Images of black-and-blue bruised mottling across his legs flashed through his thoughts. George turned at the approaching crunch of Charlie's feet into iced snow.

"Decide to get up?"

"Are we there?" Charlie rasped.

"Does this look why we're there?" George returned. Wade stifled a laugh and raised a square brown bottle to his lips. George extended a cup in his direction while steam rose and billowed away into the night. Although he knew the coffee would blister his mouth, Charlie no longer cared from a tingling sensation returning to his fingertips. A moment's indecision swept across his intention to drink it or pour it over his head.

"Trees down aways up the hill. Surprised we ain't seen more," Wade grumbled and continued with another tip of his bottle. "Have a sit, shouldn't be much longer."

"Thanks. Think I'll stand awhile," Charlie answered but crowded next to the fire's edge, crouching close enough for the outer embers to begin singeing the rubber of his boots. Intense blood pumping back through his arms increased in proportion to the thawing of his flesh. Wade gnawed on a chicken leg and tossed spent bones into the ruby, ash-crusted coals.

"Hungry?" Wade's mouth quivered and pushed a cooler toward them. George buried his face into a wing. The three men were abandoned in their gnawing and flipping bones into the fire.

"What are we going to do when we get to the border? Won't they wanna see our papers?" George asked.

"Answerin' your first question, we already passed outta the States an hour ago. As for the second, these parts don't get too many mounted patrols," Wade slobbered with clinging chicken skin on his chin.

None of them exchanged another word even if possible above the rise and fall of the chainsaw blade ripping through frozen wood. George looked up when the rattling saw fell to silence and Wilson emerged from wavering shadows.

"All right, boys, let's get a move on. Daylight's coming in a couple o' hours, and we gotta rendezvous with Mr. Shales in Breakbone. Come on, Wade," he said, motivating his brother in the back with a gleaming chainsaw blade tip nudge. Charlie assisted George to his feet, both men sharing stiff grimaces. Wade kicked surrounding snow clods into embers steaming with violence while Wilson revved the diesel engine back to gasping life. The semi's headlights knifed across a jumbled faint landscape where Charlie identified torn spruce limbs and fallen timber splinters sliced by steel teeth and rolled to the roadside.

"Who's Mr. Shales?" Charlie yelled through the open back cab window.

"Our boss," came the reply. George hoisted himself to his previous position beside Charlie, slinking the cumbersome links back across their legs after rewrapping themselves in their blankets. The window snapped shut and the truck lurched forward. Charlie turned to examine George's profile. His face was a vibrating contortion of clicking teeth between open lips.

"C.S., I want you to know something," he managed to gasp.

"And what is that?"

"If we actually find Absalom's gold and get it home, I don't ever want to set foot in this place again," he asserted with amplified accentuation on his declaration's final word.

"What happened to not having it any other way?" Charlie returned a sagging smile attempt. Any sleep he may have enjoyed vanished, and nothing more remained but resuming his anchoring grasp and witnessing the arrival of dawn cresting the dark.

Sunlight appeared and illuminated the landscape with high-snapped clearings of snowfield slopes reflecting the mirror shine. "Hey, look," George's voice rose with an elbow in Charlie's ribs. A consistent descent of the range turned toward a barren clearing. Trunk spacing tightened again, but the thin snow blanket vanished, revealing browns and grays still clinging to autumn. Both men were slow to exert any motion from clenched abdomens and unresponsive leg muscles.

The chill still clawed across every exposed surface of their bodies although bitter night-wind knives vanished. Charlie batted an eye in the direction of George's shaking pointed finger, and a distinct smoke column rose from around the bend. "What's the matter? You don't seem to be moving very quick."

"You're talking? You almost looked like rigor mortis was setting in no more than an hour ago," George responded. Rubbing his eyes, the moment of mirage passed against the still-snow-covered peaks behind it. Through the rear window, Charlie watched Wilson retrieve a handset above his head, and the motion of his jaws tensed between his straining cigarette.

They arched around a final descending bend, branches parting to reveal a wide-open, flattened expanse with more than a few dozen flatbeds, containers, cargo holds, and sheds arranged in ordered patterns. Several smaller trucks were lined in rows at the central complex's entrance.

Smoke billowed from an aluminum chimney while dots of men milled around on the asphalt, pointing, shaking their heads, and all turning up to observe their arrival. With a final air brake gasp, the semi settled to silence. "Guess we're here," George chattered, unraveling blankets and kicking their bags off the side. Charlie envied their blushed cheeks and fresh warm faces.

"Wilson, can't thank you enough for this. Truly appreciate the lift."

"Don't mention it. Wade was takin' odds on whether or not you two would still be breathin' by the time we got here." He offered a slight chuckle while his brother emerged from the cabin and began uncoupling main hoses with violent hydraulic swooshes.

A round man in a blue jumpsuit and olive drab parka broke through the front door and sprinted toward them, his side-to-side waddle shaking with energetic spasms and breath puffing in the air. By the time he reached them, the man in the parka bent forward with both hands on his knees and an aluminum clipboard trembling against one thigh. Morning sunshine peeked over the horizon and lit the mountain tops in orange-red fire.

"Wilson! Where in the Sam Hill have you been? You were supposed to be here hours ago." Wilson tried replying but was cut short. "Boss is gonna have your hides."

"Shut up, you little tick," Wade scowled down from his straddle between the cab and bed. The little man squinted up with narrowed lids and tapped his grease-covered, gloved finger at the clipboard. Wilson laughed.

"Called Shales hours ago that we might run a bit late. Now won't you be a good little boy and go get us some fresh coffee?" Wilson turned with outstretched arms as if poised to strike. With the clipboard shielding the top of his hood, he turned and sprinted back toward the wide-stretching front steps of the prefab structure.

A red maple leaf flag suspended from a steel pole in front of the building hung lifeless in the morning sun. "Come on, fellas, I want you to meet somebody." Wilson motioned and turned in the same direction as the angered clipboard. Wade remained with the haul, continuing to unhitch the bed while

Charlie and George tripped after his brother through the double doors.

Waves of warmth wrapped across Charlie's face. He staggered at the returning sensation across his ear tips, forcing him to grasp the back of chair. The interior was a vast single room with half-glassed, walled offices surrounding the perimeter. A wide wood-burning stove occupied the center with overstuffed couches, chairs, and short, ragged magazine-littered tables.

The little man earlier greeting them peeked over his office window. He slunk back down to his paper-strewn desk after recognizing eye contact. "Don't mind him, that cockroach is more of a pain than he first appears," Wilson said while unzipping the front of his parka and clanking three empty mugs on the counter. Rich black coffee poured from the spigot. "Cream and sugar's over there if ya need it." George stared in all directions and flexed both hands, focusing on his fingertips in blank preoccupation. "Come on." Wilson led Charlie and George down a narrow corridor jutting off from the main section.

At the end of the hallway, a radio blared twanging guitars and an overwhelming bass thump above intermittent analog static. A woman turned up to smile. Her broad shoulders hunched over, and her eyes were submerged beneath plump cheeks. A single hair braid draped over one shoulder. "That's Rosie—our angel in the night."

"Casanova." She placed one hand across her mouth after rolling her eyes. Wilson stopped at the end of the hallway and knocked before opening the door. Charlie followed. A desk stood at the far end with loose paper stacks scattered across the surface. More clipboards than he could estimate hung suspended from the wall behind him. Tin walls blared with the notes of Johnny Cash vibrating in diminished echoes.

A hunched-over man in a black Stetson turned up at their entrance. He swung around in his chair, rotating the stereo's volume without taking his eyes from them. The hat slunk down on his forehead as he rose from the desk. Snakeskin boot heels clicked across unfinished plywood flooring.

"Wilson, that was a close one. You know that Creevay was about to cancel on us. So who's this? Find some wanderers in the wilderness?" he asked. Charlie judged the man past fifty in his red-and-white checkered shirt and faded blue jeans clinging to pencil-thin thighs. His sunken gray eyes darted in deep sockets and contrasted high cheekbones.

"Mr. Shales, this is Charlie and George." The cobbled man leaned forward and extended his hand.

"It's a pleasure," Charlie offered and winced from the exchanged grip, uncertain if the sensation was his natural force or the result of thawing nerves. George nodded in acknowledgement.

"Have a seat," he motioned toward vacant chairs.

"If you all don't mind, gonna head out and see how Wade's unloading with the Cat." Mr. Shales tipped his hat.

"Now then, Charles is it? You boys sound like Americans. Working this line for another outfit?" he sat back in the creaking swivel chair and crossed one leg, resting interlocked fingers across a sunken stomach.

"No sir, I mean yes sir, we're from the Seattle area, but we came up to visit a friend near Blackhole," Charlie asserted with returning vocal cord sensation and slurped from what remained in his mug.

"Don't know what kinda friends a man has up around those parts but wolves and bears, but if you say so." He slid open a top drawer and pulled out peanut butter crackers, slipping them between thin lips and allowing stray crumbs to snag in his pepper gray moustache. George retained no control over his almost slobbering reaction to the crackling plastic wrapper crinkle. "Wouldn't be hungry, would you? Can't offer much but there should be some leftovers from last night. Hope you like mushroom soup. Listen, I gotta surveyor headin' up that way, and you can catch a ride with him if ya hurry. He's leaving," he paused and yanked the sleeve from over his watch, "in just over an hour."

"Right now, we'd be happy just to lick the pan," Charlie answered with George's head shaking in anxious agreement.

"Head on back down the hallway, and tell Rosie I sent y'all. She'll take care of ya and get you in touch with Sebastian. I'll give him a holler and let him know you're on the way." Mr. Shales crinkled his eyebrows tight enough for his wire-rimmed glasses to bounce off the tip of his nose. He swirled, raising Johnny Cash back to previous vibrating levels. George closed the door to the pulsating notes behind them.

"So you're doing what out here?" came a boy's high voice while his eyes darted across the road ahead of them, and too many sticks of gum smacked between his distorted lips. Charlie belched from the remaining soup in his throat. The entire night's intermittent sleep and rattled muscular ache pushed him deeper into the seat cushions. George's head fell back into unconsciousness.

"Meeting a couple of old college friends for some hunting," Charlie replied.

"Better sit back and get comfortable. It's another good three hours if the road holds up. You sure you wanna drop off there? Those roads haven't seen a grader in years." The truck sped forward fast enough for Charlie to grip the front headrest. The boy held the steering wheel with the fingers of one hand while the other dialed the knob of shortwave radio, diving wide arcs to each side of the gravel-pocked road. They passed collapsed sections so narrow that he didn't believe the tire spread was wide enough to maintain the ten percent grades. "Where are your guns?"

129

"They're bringing them for us," Charlie's own voice almost convinced him.

"Sure wouldn't catch me out here alone. Been doing this surveying gig for almost a year now. Between semesters ya know. Pays good enough for books." Charlie measured a comment but found himself joining George's muted snores.

CHAPTER

14

Sunlight shafts crested lower maples, strangling wild grape and myrtle dotting the elevating wooded floor. Charlie's head rose. Intertwining limbs gave stiff resistance to a rising breeze blowing hair across his forehead.

Suffocating mistletoe clumps attacked older trunks beneath rippling leaves. His feet rose and dropped forward in unconscious mechanical repetition, focused vision locked into discernment of the ancient limb mesh snaking across a canopied sky—centuries-old hemlocks forming cathedral walls while feathered choristers trilled hymns from above.

Each holy leaf crackled beneath their hardened rubber soles. Songs and stories, loud and quiet, joined old growth united in the faint, greenish-glow glimmer between a single leaf's veins. Hovering above a velvet moss beard draped around glowing, cracked gray slate, water splashed, guided, and controlled their descent. Charlie dropped to his knees, a history of decay cushioning the fall. He plunged both hands into a shimmering pool of ice clear water. It splashed across his face and hair. Baptismal shudderings cleared his mind while George puffed up from behind his crouch. Sunken freshwater algae's slithering elongated hairs rippled beneath the surface, anchored to worn stones.

Uncle Tyler's place, Charlie's thoughts continued repeating, was just over the next ridge. But another came and passed. Brush-covered deer paths camouflaged the landscape. George kept his words to a minimum between the huffing of his straining breaths driving the quickened pace.

Immature sapling copses and thin branches whipping across their cheeks stung with increased repetition until tripping back to the tracked whitetail trail. A still moist dung ball pile squished beneath the sole of Charlie's boot. Fleeting sun remained visible through random parting trunks. Nocturnal creatures waited for the vanishing of light, stirring with initial scavenges through hollowed decaying logs.

Dead leaves still clung to dried limbs. They roared like crashing waves when driving gusts blew through the spires. Fading sunlight forced George to avert his eyes from the now chilling wind. Night birds twittered in the low branches with an occasional territory violation protest, their heads cocking from side to side at the erect furless animals below them, upright and without grace.

Charlie sensed George's apprehension with each head turn, but they trudged forward in silence. Charlie's pace increased in relationship to George's struggle. Like a remembered, sacred childhood vision fading from too much experience with this world, a wider stream reappeared through the thicket.

George sprinted after Charlie's path around the mud-crusted bank and granite curve. Focus directed their feet, continuing forward movement regardless of protesting calves. Gurgling water flowed with the expectation of widening into the expanse of Charlie's memory, but varied no more than a few extended leaps across.

A light, fire, smoke, any reassuring sign would manifest at any moment. Nothing came. A vision of himself and George hugging their knees and shuddering around a meager open forest campfire wouldn't shake from his projections.

Catching his breath, Charlie dropped and sat on a log jutting from a collapsed mud wall, roots dangling and poking into his thighs. Water flowed in rapid determination—a combination of spring-fed runoff and the morning's violent thunderstorm. Visions of succulent browned turkey, mashed potatoes and gravy, and buttered corn on the cob infected his thoughts. More cold water splashed across his cheeks, drowning the images. Abdomens twisted with the last fulfillment of mushroom soup fading. Charlie removed his right boot and fished out a pebble that had been torturing his foot for the previous mile.

"Oh, man, that's good. I don't think I got the aches out from riding beneath those jumping logs," George exhaled, splashing and watching his own reflection's water droplets scattering the image while using his duffel as a seat.

"Tell you what, it's gotta be around here someplace," Charlie replied and savored the frigid wetness trickling down the sides of his temples. He turned, calculating trunk shadow lengths in reference to what light remained through swaying branches.

"Don't know about you, but the wind seems to have picked up a might, don't ya think?" Charlie didn't answer, rising and shoving his boots back over once-white socks. Scarce remaining daylight settled a blue haze across every leaf and trunk. Colors faded beneath the decreasing glow. Reds, golds, and oranges trembled back to varying shades of gray like flickering exposures of a silent movie. He rose with an initial forward eye focus and negotiated a deceptive elm root patch, the last desire a turned ankle in their isolation.

A hand shot to George's shoulder, yanking him down before Charlie's voice met George's ears. "Quiet!" Through a downward drifting branch separating from the distant mesh of arching leaf cover, a pair of grayed moss-tinted antlers lifted with almost imperceptible highlights allowing definition from the darkening sky. They counted the passage of time in breaths, waiting for the attached moose rack to charge. "Wait, this isn't right."

Trunks and trails converged into uncomfortable similar patterns. Charlie scratched one eye for a sudden survey of fractured horizontal lines peeking through interwoven limbs. The calculated intersections revealed a noticeable tilt to the right while an image snapped back through his memory.

"Finally," George gasped over his shoulder in the recognition that the antlers were mounted and unmoving. "Some sign of civilization. Wonder who owns that beat-up old shack?" They still calculated their approach, trading head turns but not long enough to lose focus on the structure ahead.

"We've arrived." Eyes adjusting, sunken angles and warped lines remained. Charlie's nostalgia gushed into the moment from the grand log structure cherished in recollections of abandoned ease. A pair of barrels, grayed with the passing years and their iron staves rusted orange, guarded sentry on each corner of the structure.

The suspending broad antler arches hung high but cast no shadow. A split-log fence meandered around a wide flattened stretch of surrounding old growth, distinctive level ground with a distant ascending slope. The depressed fire ash pit was encircled with ankle-high boulders located between the cabin's side and stream. They stumbled forward and caught a steadied pace once reaching level ground, scanning for any evidence of movement.

"Anybody home?" Charlie called to no return above the rippling water murmur or hushing leaves. He turned and saw George's head dropped low in his collar, blowing on his fingers and holding knuckles to his cheeks. A rough-hewn window gaped to one side of the cracked front door opening, nothing more than a few stitched rabbit hides providing a weather barrier across the center window.

No sign of smoke rose from the chimney stack—worn head-sized stones pulled from the stream bed, fitted together by hand, and cemented with dried sedge and rich limestone-silted mud. George trailed behind while Charlie scaled warped plank stairs leading to the porch. Like the chimney, the porch was an endless back-and-forth routine of rounded quartz, granite, and mud daubing until a calculated platform resulted, retaining the integrity of rebar reinforced concrete. Dense, hand-hewn, dried pine planks supported his boots. Years of exposure stretched once-perfect symmetrical alignment.

"Hello? Anyone?" George called through his cupped hands.

"Not yet." Charlie's open palm brushed across the stacked logs, less geometric precision from previous stacked positions and their ends still reflecting original axe-chopped pockets. Moss and fungus scaled a patchwork calico across their rounded faces almost the circumference of his waist.

"He built this himself?" George continued and now joined him on the porch. Charlie inhaled the raw basic pureness into his lungs. He absorbed fossilized sap and long-dead insect carcasses in their vacant, black tunnels—a thousand unseen ghosts forever haunting the grain. "Awful quiet around here," Charlie whispered.

"Almost believe I heard Grampy's stories more than you, and you described this place better than your grandfather. Can't

believe he got these trunks eight feet in the air all by himself."
George's fingers also glided across the sharp-angled cuts.

George descended the steps and turned for the handle of a double-bladed axe head buried deep in a stump of countless crisscrossed cuts. A glinting surface revealed untold seasons of snow and sun. Pushing open the door, Charlie slipped his head into the dim illumination, keeping the rest of his body contracted for extraction.

Shoulders tensed and his legs braced for immediate withdrawal. Earlier leaf flutters now transformed into a bitter, harsh wind. A sudden gale force swirled down through upper pine branches, shoving the door open behind him and slamming split planks against the wall. Enough light entered to reveal the sparse interior. Leaned against one wall, a lashed-branch bed frame stood tossed at an angle.

The massive stream-rock fireplace stretched almost the length of the opposite wall with narrow shelves on each side. The bowed planks displayed carved wooden statues—an elk, bear, squirrel, figures in various poses, and a random scattered chisel set, some still on the shelf and others rolled across the floor among woodchip mounds. Pine sap lingered, saturating the air.

George wasted no time scavenging for food. A pair of lashed pole tables and cabinet discolored with the passage of decades propped against a side wall. Dried fish strips he believed were salmon and other unidentifiable salt-cured meat was wrapped in oiled deer hides. Torn scraps remained but both he and Charlie swallowed with suggested tooth grinds and a hint of taste registering on their tongues.

Charlie swung a disapproving head at George's motion toward the outside stilted cache. "Still hungry too but we don't know if he even still lives here." George agreed and picked the meat between his teeth. "Besides, I don't think either of us is in any mood to catch a lead slug in the back." Charlie pushed aside several half-carved fish, retrieving matches and a tin patched red lantern. The kerosene glow illuminated a stitched deer hide mattress stuffed with dead pine needles and moss. Hardback books of every size and shape covered any shelf space not already occupied with a carving.

A Winchester bolt action 30-06 was propped along the side of a leather chair before the fireplace. George collapsed on a stretched matching leather couch. Charlie returned to the front porch, scanning through the dense surrounding growth for any evidence of unnatural light. Sunlight disappeared. Nothing more than a meager blue dimness descending through vertical cottonwoods blanketed recognition.

Charlie pulled several logs from a stack next to the porch and gripped the axe handle with a firm two-handed grasp, wrestling it from the stump. The suspended lantern from a fence rail provided wavering light. He took broad arching strokes with full arm extensions, allowing the steel head to perform all of the work.

Drifting flurries spotted in swirling cascades, blowing hair into his eyes. Distant hollow cracks and snaps echoed. Differing volumes broke through the forest and his log splitting while wind snapped dead, dry limbs. Underbrush whooshed beneath the collapse. He clutched his hamstrings, cramped from the afternoon's trek of limb-dodging, ankle-twisting negotiations, and unpredictable lichen-carpeted granite. The axe head pace decreased with each successive swing. Even his grip loosened with rising blisters and jerking muscle shots through fingers, arms, and shoulders.

All natural light vanished. Although the silhouettes of the treetops remained discernible if his neck craned high enough, the surrounding wood was complete darkness. Clouds boiled above with his lantern providing the only beacon shining against the black. Previous flurry swirls transformed into broad, fat crystals blowing down from the sky. They clumped one upon another and landscaped the dark forest floor into blue-hazed ice.

Split wood was stacked so high in his arms that Charlie turned sideways and backed up the steps, unable to verify his footing. Wind blasted against the front door, forcing it shut with a slam after he reentered the cabin's shelter and his cramping forearms scattered the wood with a thud at his feet. George rose and shuddered, constructing a precise fire—shredded birch bark tinder, a handful of spindle dry twigs, finger-sized fatwood chunks, and a final crisscross of medium seasoned split pine. The fatwood splinters took spitting flame with a wispy black smoke trail dancing in the stiff draft.

With bare feet and hands, they huddled in front of the flames after pulling a pair of deer pelts from the bed. They wrapped themselves so tight that no more than their heads poked out from the openings. Firelight licked the blackened stone hearth, soot discolored from ten thousand previous fires. The moment allowed Charlie a greater detailed study of the high-arched ceiling, rustic joinery, and basic simple lines he attempted retrieving from memories of his youth.

Walls were narrower and more compact by the passage of time than when he once huddled beneath the same ceiling. The walls were covered in animal skins—some recognized and others mysterious. A rifle carriage hung vacant above the fireplace mantel.

Once warmth returned sensation to both fingers and toes, George stretched and yawned. After rising and breaking the fire's mesmerizing trance, Charlie collapsed back onto the buckskin couch facing the flames. George leaned against the wall in a snoring doze, his legs still crossed.

Yawns muted dry log crackles. Crystal-burning pine sap filtered across the worn hides with elegant perfume. Charlie couldn't recall where consciousness ended and the sweet blanket of dreams began.

A branch snapped. Leaves swirled in mad sandpaper stroking. Charlie's eyes cracked open and struggled to identify dying coal shapes.

Indistinct distant animal grunting broke into a howl.

The room returned to invisible shades with the lamp's kerosene nothing more than a slight whisper and logs glowing crimson-orange embers. George remained an inert, hide-covered lump across the floor. Four distinct porch-planking thuds removed any lingering haze. His stare froze and he crouched behind the backrest, allowing one eye to peer around the side. Charlie's glance darted back above the mantel at the empty gun supports and the rifle a few yards away.

Seconds passed as minutes, sinking to his hands and knees and retrieving an iron poker. He scrambled back to cover. The porch steps were interrupted with more precise lighter taps and eager whining.

"Slow—quick enough—hurry?" Charlie managed recognizing over the wind. The door flew open. Rather than charging out of the swirling violence, an animal leaned forward on front paws and released a lingering, drawn-out, guttural snarl from the most primal throat depths.

A dull gun metal barrel poked through the cracked opening. "You, too?" he heard the whisper more distinct but still muffled. While scented warnings froze the dog in a single, solid contraction, the defined metallic click of a drawn hammer sprouted prickle sweat across Charlie's brow.

"Don't shoo—shoo—shoot!" Charlie stuttered his words as if rising from another voice, hovering above, watching the confrontation. Deciding not to reveal the poker, his full profile appeared around the couch's corner. Nothing more than the man's rough edge of fur, boots, gloves, and scarf were visible.

The dog strained forward, jumping ahead with wild uncontrolled yelping and strained fits from the rope lashed around his neck. Swelling chest muscles bulged beneath twitching gray-and-white contractions. The furred tower's breath shot out in billowing, white-crystal snorts above the animal straining at his side.

"Uncle Tyler?"

"Ya better get out from behind there," he commanded. The rifle barrel lowered in Charlie's direction. His poker clanged against the floor with an echo, but he followed the command, raising both hands above his head and interlocking his fingers. The shadow tilted his head in recognition of no immediate threat. The voice was a massive vague outline with diminishing cloud streams less intense than previous huffing billows of a still-stretching dog at his side. A lantern rose. "Who are ya and what are ya doin' in my place? Give me one good reason why I shouldn't just turn your head into a canoe and feed ya to Frisco," the voice cued through a now visible wool scarf wrapped several layers around his head and eyes poking through a gap.

White ice clods clumped to eyebrows while he kept the wavering barrel pointed toward the floor and the dog from breaking his collared grip. White teeth flashed blue in the kerosene lamp while a charcoal-spotted pink tongue darted and flung splattering saliva in every direction, lungs wheezing from the strain.

"I'm unarmed. It was cold. I'm trying to find Mr. Tyler Sutcliffe."

"What do want with old Tyler?" Charlie stared at the spastic frenzied fur. "You don't want to mess with him. Heard he was one tough, mean son of a buck. A single cold stare stops a beating heart."

"It's been a long time, but I was sure this was his place. I know he'd clear up all of this." Between the now-widened scarf, Charlie recognized broadening eyes glinting in the lamp. The hulking man took one mittened hand and pulled away his remaining scarf, revealing broad, rose-chapped cheeks and a wind-bitten grin.

"So ya think I could clear all this up? You ain't? No, can't be," he gruffed and took a step forward, striking a match across the door frame and leaned at the waist. "Charlie!" he roared. Uncle Tyler's enthusiasm almost removed Charlie's hesitation from the animal snapping at his side. Tyler returned to the front porch and tied the dog off to a rail. He retrieved a jug from beneath the table, refilled the lamp, and snapped another rattling match to life. The wide smile across his lips never diminished.

Uncle Tyler barreled forward, wrapping both arms around Charlie, and lifted him from his feet. The fur of his cap rubbed against Charlie's cheek, and contracting biceps rolled and expanded beneath Uncle Tyler's coat. The embrace released with a final roar, and he fell to the floor. "Whoooeee, son, I was about to mount you up there on the wall with the rest of them," he nodded in the direction of several whitetail and elk glass-eyed stares. Charlie released a shaking chortle, wiped sweat beads from his forehead, and collapsed back into the couch's stiff leather cushion. George's head cracked from beneath his covering, a single eye witnessing their exchange.

"Sorry about surprising you like this."

"Don't worry yourself none," Uncle Tyler snapped an instant reply while stamping snow and ice clinging to his boots. He unwrapped multiple clothing layers. "Whew-hee, listen to that blow." Uncle Tyler whistled a melody with surprising clear notes and tonal depth although Charlie sensed further clarity with thawed cheeks. Numb fingers continued fumbling with what remained of his scarf, revealing discolored rows of incomplete teeth. Two desperate red hair clumps clung to the sides of his head after removing his anonymous furred cap pulled low over his eyes. He massaged the sting from his vision. "That's a relief," he squinted, "blindness ain't too bad."

Leather strappings securing boots to his ankles remained laced. Suspenders popped from his shoulders and fell dangling at his sides. Uncle Tyler dropped in front of the charred fireplace ashes on one knee. He pushed and prodded embers with fresh seasoned pine until his entire profile was bathed in a red, yellow, and orange glow.

"Thanks for not shooting." Uncle Tyler stifled a laugh.

"And him?"

"Uncle Tyler, this is my good friend George." George nodded in his direction, buckskin still drawn around him.

"Sorry there ain't too much room but can't say as that I get a whole lot of company round here." He blew on his fingers, clapping and rubbing his hands together in front of the flames after remounting his rifle above the mantel. A howl cut the wind. "That stupid mutt." Tyler cracked the door, and a gust blew it from his hands.

In the discordant orchestra beyond, Charlie witnessed black spruce peaks swaying in swirls. After unhitching an almost now frozen dog, Frisco slinked in between Tyler's legs, performed several circles around the elk-skin rug, and collapsed in a fire-warming whimper.

"If I didn't know better, almost thought you might have been a bear yourself covered in all of those furs," Charlie joked.

"Bear? Bears got too scared of me. Here, this'll get ya inside warmer than your outside." Tyler motioned well-worn tin cups into Charlie and George's hands. Distilled fumes shot into his nasal passages after taking an initial probing sip. The few drops transformed to fire across the roof of his mouth, coated his tongue, and scorched a pathway down his throat lining.

"What, whew, is this?" words struggled squeezing out, the drink still sucking most of the breath from his lungs and shaking head.

"Like it? Made it early spring. Take some corn, a couple a potatoes, a pinch or two of yeast, lotsa sugar, time, boiling, and then a little special magic. That's whatcha get—pure magic," Uncle Tyler beamed an irregular toothed smile. A looser grin curved across George's lips after finishing his cup and motioning for a refill. Frisco whined and flipped a gray ear, eyes glistening in the firelight—one blue and one green while listening to the men's surrounding voices. "Come on, let me take a long look," he shifted back to stare at Charlie. "How many years now? Son, you and your daddy musta spent near every summer up here. Back then you barely came up past my waist." Charlie crouched in silence to turn and stare into the fire. "You all hungry?" Neither Charlie nor George admitted their earlier rummage.

"Yeah, a little I guess," George responded and Charlie nodded in agreement.

"Don't expect nothin' fancy, but let's see what I got. Plannin' a little trip to the ridge in the morning if this blow finishes off." Frisco cracked an eye open at Tyler's exit. He returned within minutes, both hands full of meat chunks and a bone stuck under one arm.

Once again leaning near the fire, he skewered the meat on long narrow shaved limbs and propped them just above the glowing embers. Crackling fat dripped and sizzled into the ashes. Frisco's head shot erect, tilted to one side, and slobber drooled from slick, black gums. Tyler flung the bone, not even approaching the floor when Frisco's jaws flashed open and snatched it from the air.

All three men sat without speech, listening to the flame crackle and meat-roasting voices. Outside, violence increased above the sporadic gnash of teeth at their feet. Frisco continued his meditative gnaw, sucking marrow and stripping remaining meat scraps.

"Hadn't planned on staying too long. Just a few questions and we'll be heading on our way."

"Sorry to break the news, but I don't think you'll be getting anywhere without a chopper. Take a look," Tyler instructed with a nod towards the window. Charlie rose and stumbled into the table, pushing open the latch. Previous leaves of brown and yellow, rock, shrubs, and every other exposed surface were coated beneath a contouring white blanket. Light escaping the cabin reflected radiating microscopic crystals glinting in fleeting diamond radiance. Although the winds lulled, dense flakes continued descending from the black sky.

"That sure came out of nowhere."

"Better get comfortable." Uncle Tyler bent back over the open hearth by the time Charlie returned to release a slow breath and sank into the cushions. The contents of his now almost-empty cup blurred thoughts and bent straight lines into curves. He rubbed his thighs and grimaced. A skewer of sizzling dark venison waved in Tyler's hand. One quick finger probed the meat, and his hand jerked backwards. "Here." What minimal amount of fat bubbled in the lean flesh glistened and spat in the flames. Hunger forced a larger bite into the block-sized chunk. His teeth tore into it, ripping as the sear peeled back the haze of his focus.

A minute passed and he continued chewing. Tyler threw an amused glance along with a dull pocketknife. "Cut it up and try not swallowing all at once." The bite at last squeezed and dropped to his stomach. Frisco rose from the previous devoured bone and took turns snatching scraps in the air from all three men. "Not sure what you want to do about bedding down, but you're free to use the couch, pull up a space on the floor, or the smokehouse ain't too bad."

CHAPTER

15

Their voices responded as one. "Smokehouse?"

"Yeah, come on." Tyler rose and whistled. Frisco twitched fur on the floor, abandoned in his dog dreams. Charlie's eyeballs teared and fluttered when reemerging into the night. Winds forced his gaze downward at the sinking snow footfalls rising to their ankles. George's huffing behind them struggled against the howl.

The axe and stump vanished, leaving a worn ash handle tip protruding from the white glinting smooth surface. They stomped a trail toward a clearing at the rear of the cabin. A leaning hut sat several feet back. It appeared no more than a hundred-square-foot log-over-log construction with the same cabin foundation and a tin chimney jutting through the center of the upward sloping roof. A snowdrift rose up one side and almost reached the eave.

Uncle Tyler kicked snow from the door's path to crack it open just wide enough to squeeze through the narrow gap. His lantern swung in the darkness, reflecting snow sprays descending from the roof. A massive fire pit excavated the barren dirt floor's center with racks of thin, bark-stripped horizontal lashed poles on each side wall. A table with a cast iron meat grinder stood opposite of the door.

"Not much but with the fire going, you should stay plenty warm," Uncle Tyler said and nodded at the corner split woodpile stack. "Keep those ventilation hatches open so you don't get yourselves smoked out. Uncle Tyler reached a series of ropes and yanked down plank shields where the walls met the ceiling. An instant frigid blast swirled into the room. Uncle Tyler bent down to light the fire pit. Flames rose in the confined space smelling of salt, old fat, and dried fish. "Be right back," he returned to his feet and hung the lantern on a door frame peg. Charlie brushed aside pebbles and debris, clearing a space adequate for fire warmth but far enough not to singe himself from a flare. "Here we go," Tyler returned moments later with an armful of buckskins, mold-discolored wool blankets, and an almost unrecognizable rifle, lines differing from the Winchester hung over the fireplace.

"What's that for?"

"On a night like this, you don't want any unwelcome guests with the wind tossing scents up and down every side of these woods."

"What sort of guests?" George blurted. George realized the question never should have been asked. Releasing an uncontrollable yawn that bounced his glasses across the bridge of his nose, Uncle Tyler stretched in every possible simultaneous motion. "See ya'll in the morning. Coffee'll be hot!"

"Uncle Tyler?"

"Need something else?"

"Good seeing you again."

"You too, boy, you too," he finished, opening and slamming the door behind him with as much possible speed. Scant light filtered through the high, thin slots. Walls shined slick. Years of natural oils and melted fat penetrated into wood grain from the flesh of smoking meat. Removing his shirt, Charlie reclined on worn caribou leather.

The fire's heat glowed across his exposed skin. Both he and George shuddered from the outside contrasting bitter wind howls. Numb fingers and toes faded. They propped their boots to dry by the flames, and steam soon billowed from the seams. Charlie pulled a wool blanket over his shoulders and lay on his back staring at swaying movements through the ventilation slits.

"Still awake?"

"Yeah, can't say how much longer."

"You are the luckiest man I've ever known," George murmured with his gaze captured by the same reflecting ceiling.

"How in the world can you make a statement like that?" Charlie attempted a vain control of his response.

"You still have someone to miss." George's last word was accentuated with the snap of an exploding sap pocket. They listened to winds lulling from earlier gusts but still lingering and pushing through the narrow open gaps.

Stretched mournful moans rose and fell in the pitches of winter phantoms. Charlie pulled his blanket tighter until the wool scratched his cheeks. The specter chorus decreased and intermingled with hazed visions of the earlier day's high-leafed loft cathedrals.

Charlie shivered himself back to consciousness, eyes cracking open to no more than the weak embers of a single red eye staring back through the haze. The initial stir shook his half dream, half hope of Karen still snuggled in his embrace.

A cracked, splitting explosion shuddered the log walls. He distinguished his own breath exhaling in white clouds against morning light through the high vents. Charlie struggled up from his hunch to discover he had no feet; at least none offering immediate control. Through the openings, four distinct blue sky patches contrasted blackened wood. He glanced at the rifle still propped against the wall where Tyler had left it the previous evening.

A scant glow burned through gray ash with curling smoke wisps clouding George's still inert form beneath a blanket. Another report shuddered the smokehouse. Muted shockwaves flooded the forest. Slipping on his boots, Charlie pushed on the door and found no movement. A kick shifted the planks less than an inch.

Charlie lowered his shoulder, leaned forward, and took three full running steps, hitting with full force. The door released a cracking split from ice-shattering frozen wood separation. Still, the door only swung open wide enough for Charlie to slip through if he inhaled and turned to one side.

Snow, compact and crunching, almost rose to his knees. He swung around to the front of Tyler's cabin and noticed two sets of prints trailing down the steps—one canine, the other human. They twisted down to the stream at its most narrow and shallow stretch, disappearing and resuming across the opposite bank. Dotted impressions receded, rose, and vanished over a brief embankment.

One of the buckskins remained wrapped around his shoulders. Jean cuffs tucked deep into his boots, Charlie negotiated ankle high drifts with intermittent success while maintaining a constant resistance to the chill returning across his exposed skin. Another report rang out through the clear air followed by Frisco's howling attention.

The dog and Uncle Tyler sat on the edge of a wide flat clearing, no more than a rolling field. A distant towering hemlock fence bordered the expanse, and mountains continued another ascent beyond. Tyler crouched on one knee, scratching Frisco behind an ear.

"Morning, son," Tyler rose and dropped the barrel of his 30–06 over one shoulder, the strap dangling loose while blowing on his exposed fingers. Cut glove tips revealed naked rose-colored plump fingetips matching the tint of his cheeks and forehead. Charlie brushed flurry crystals from the face of his fogged watch crystal, but both hands remained hidden. Without even the slightest cloud hint, the sky spread pure glowing blue with the sun casting initial long, stretched shadows across the white flatness.

"What time is it anyway?" he stretched and yawned. Frisco trotted circles around his knees, whimpering and begging for another scratch.

"Time to get moving. Early enough to get some real work done. Here," he shoved the rifle in Charlie's free hand. The gleaming worn wooden stock may as well have been an icicle, stealing dear warmth just beginning a return to his knuckles. "See out yonder there?" Tyler turned and nodded across the clearing. Charlie stretched a palm across his brow, shading the sun and focusing intense study across the opposite open field.

"What am I supposed to be looking at?"

"Right there next to that big old poplar on the left, 'bout ten feet up," he pointed and shoved a pair of binoculars into Charlie's chest. He rubbed the ancient Army-issue lenses on his shirttail. After a moment of bouncing and focus, he settled on a long-abandoned beehive dangling from one of the lower thicker branches with distinctive holes scattering its paper-fluttering surface. "As I recall, you were a pretty good shot for somebody so young."

"Yeah, maybe so, but I don't remember any of us who could find it like Benny. I haven't even seen a gun in years let alone squeeze off a round." He stepped toward Uncle Tyler, grabbing the Winchester's frozen black barrel and hefted it in both hands. The stock rose to feather brush across his cheek. The weapon's cloud weight shifted from so many earlier remembered years.

Slamming back the bolt and ensuring he was chambered, Charlie sank to one knee, adjusted a squinting eye through the scope, and rotated metal crosshair knobs as intersecting fine black lines bounced against a background of blurred grays and greens.

"On sight?" Tyler murmured the question in the slow breath of a cracking staccato.

"Near as I can tell." Frisco whined behind still-flowering currants. Charlie steadied his left arm support, breathing pattern shifting to a slower rhythmic flow keeping in time with a mental metronome. The hive, in every clean, sharp detail, steadied to stillness, his contained breath held, and his finger compressed against the trigger's resistance.

Previous cracks motivating his awakening haze didn't compare to the echoing roar washing through his eardrums, down his spine, and ricocheting back up to settle waving tingles across his molars.

Tyler raised the binoculars and released a long, protracted whistle. "Wouldn't be stretching the truth with me a bit?" Charlie didn't reply and settled his scope back on the hive. Now, four distinct holes appeared. The shot could not have been more centered than if performed with mathematical calculation.

"Pure luck. Let's try another," Charlie breathed.

"Nope, that's all I needed to know. Besides, morning's getting along and Creektoe's expecting me at the Falls. Let's get on back and strap on some stompers." Charlie tried returning the

Winchester. "That one's yours. Got my own Lenore back under the bed."

"Creektoe?"

"He's the nearest neighbor. Time for a hunt. Rut's going full on, and we need some meat if I'm making it through the next couple o' months." Uncle Tyler turned, retracing their steps and snapping a finger. Frisco bounded back over the hill crest.

"Hunt sounds fine and all, but George and I need to get on our way pretty soon." Uncle Tyler continued in silence. They stomped snow from their boots after reaching the front porch. Tyler placed dried salmon strips and potatoes across the table by the time Charlie entered. Charlie's eyes widened and saliva drooled without control, pooling in his mouth. "Go on, help yourself but go extra on the spuds. You're gonna need the fat those were drowned in," he pointed with a knife. Charlie's teeth gnashed the first bite while Uncle Tyler spoke his instruction's final word.

"Hello?" George's voice called through the door. A half sleep-drowsed expression peeled away with the steaming plates of greeting food. "Enough to go around?" Uncle Tyler rose to clank another dented aluminum plate across the table. Potatoes and fish flew into piles. Tyler smiled and reclined, sipping his mug after wiping the blade across leather pants and releasing a thunder-rumbled belch. "So how do you do this?" George managed asking and chewing at the same time.

"Do what, young man?" Uncle Tyler's words reacted in utter, earnest wonder.

"This, here. You're miles from the nearest road, no electricity, no running water." His previous whisker tremor widened to a broad smile sweeping across his mouth and eyes glinted in the firelight.

"One day, just got tired of it all. Seems the easier things got, faster time seemed to pass me by. All these modern-age advances may be wonderful, but even with everything they gave, they also took something away," he concluded, tapping an almost black root pipe on the split pine table and bent down to retrieve a burning twig from the fire. He leaned forward and crossed his eyes on the pipe bowl, concentrating while his still-reddened, wind-burned cheeks sucked and exhaled like trilling a trumpet.

"Still don't get it."

"Look, all of these inventions that you and everybody else seem to need as if you can't live without are supposed to make life easier, advance the quality, and give us more time to spend doing the things that make life worth living. Right?"

"Guess you could look at it like that," Charlie tilted his head with a long, jaw-stretching yawn. His vision flopped back to stare up at the still-barked joints crossing the ceiling and random-chopped axe-blade impressions.

"I didn't find that promised time. In fact, found less. Just a lot more things I couldn't do in the same amount of time. I was one of the top brokers on the West coast—near the fastest pace occupation a man can find, but all my gadgets brought nothing. None of it did. Even lost my marriage getting so caught up it blinded me to the most important things a man can hope to find in this life." He paused, choking on pipe smoke rolling around his remaining hair. Charlie closed his eyes. Charlotte's face flashed against the black of his shut eyelids.

"So what makes you happy?" George now slowed his devouring pace. Uncle Tyler released a deafening laughter roar, slapping one knee. Frisco's ears stood on end, and he whined at his slumber's interruption until weighed eyelids clamped shut and snores resumed.

"Happy? Look around. Can't say I don't get lonesome from time to time but look around. This, all of this makes me happy—that first morning smell of fresh pine sap oozing from the bark, wildflowers out in the meadow sparkling your eyes better than any Fourth of July fireworks, fresh venison right off the fire, black coffee boiled over an open flame. Don't get me started. Could go on like this for the whole frozen morning. There's something that can't be described without the experience of it. Here, in this place, a man rediscovers how to be a man." Tyler bent forward and tapped his spent ashes. "Why is it that I gotta feeling you two didn't come all the way up here to stop by and check in on an old hermit?" He stopped with a vague jaw-tightening and glancing jagged-fingernail review. Charlie couldn't decide if either the exhaustion or full stomach caused his words to spill out faster than his mind could register their expression.

"Yes, you're right. We're here to find the gold." Charlie heard the specific words spoken for the first time from his voice and his own listening of those words. Uncle Tyler bent forward, resting his elbows on his knees, and ran an open-fingered hand through short fuzz on the side of his head.

"What about that?"

"What?" Charlie asked.

"That wedding band. You left a wife to look for money? I can tell you right now, the best treasure you're ever gonna find is the gold you already got on your finger. Believe an old man."

"There's something more, my little girl is sick, we need the money."

"You're telling me I got a grand niece I never met?" Tyler's face loosened and his head turned.

"She's an angel dropped down from Heaven, Uncle Tyler."

"Sorry to disappoint you both after traveling all this way, but my brother always had a talent for storytelling." Charlie removed the journal from his coat pocket, and Tyler caught a glint off the worn leather cover. "Let me take a look at that." He pulled the volume from Charlie's grasp, scanning the first pages and leafing through a few in between them. "Yeah, that's

Absalom's hand. Looks like he learned how to write with his feet, don't it? I think he had the same gift as your grandfather."

"Is there anything, any information you can give us?"

"Somewhere in this sweat-washed, wrinkled paper pile should be a mention of the old Stanton place."

"Stanton! That's the name. How did you know?"

"That old fairy tale has been passed around these mountains for more years than either of us has been alive. Never put much stock in it. I put it right up there with the ghosts of unrequited miners, phantom wolves, or the Headless Indian. Sure hope you boys didn't try coming all this way just because of this book." Charlie rose, wandered to the window, and stared at the blanket of white masquerading strained, bent branches. "Now come on, wastin' too much time, let's see if that eye is still as good at shootin' something that moves."

Uncle Tyler rose and stumbled back toward his bed, dropping with a grating squeal of rusted springs protesting his weight. He pulled a pair of rustic snowshoes from beneath it along with a rifle barrel glint. He measured each foot into the center and interlaced straps around his boots and ankles in systematic ceremony. "Lucky I made it back last night without these," he strained without raising his head. "None of us would be getting' too far without 'em," he said as he bent over and rummaged through a trunk.

Two more pairs emerged, one set falling at Charlie's feet with a hollow clunk and the other laid across George's lap. Hide leather was stiff and cumbersome in Charlie's thawed finger joints, but both he and George managed completing their mounting after tugs and strains. Tyler sat at the irregular-sectioned table, cleaning and polishing rounds. He blew and measured each shell. Brass casings gleamed in the bright light, and he loaded them into dull, black-metal clips.

"How far is it?" George rose and slapped his shellacked wooden frames.

"Far enough. We all set?" Tyler rose and stomped both snowshoes around his own feet on the worn floor and shifted toward the open door with high knee steps. A crude bag swung over the opposite side of his weapon. Rope dangled from his belt, its multiple cords slapping leather leggings. Frisco paced frantic paw-stepping in front of the smoldering coals, yelping and snipping at their feet. Charlie slung his own rifle, and they kept pace in their awkward forward motion.

Initial uncoordinated leaning eased into a huffing rhythm, arms pumping at their sides. Frisco managed easing his strides to stay with them at least part of the time until diving through the drifts, chasing unsuspecting birds, or snapping at squirrels twitching down at them from above. The unbroken snow surface reflected iceberg blue in the quiet shadows of silent trunks. Loose powder clouds puffed and broke the line; a contrasting pink tongue dangled in the center of wide jaws. "Dog!" Uncle Tyler yelled at his side followed with sporadic whistles. The animal froze with command recognition—all spastic motion halting, powder dusting back across his fur in white-speck crystals. All four legs settled low to the ground while he whimpered and crawled back in the men's direction. "Ignorant mutt'll scare every bit of game for miles around. You boys still all right?" he asked, hesitating to wipe his glass lenses with a shirttail managing to poke out from beneath his coat.

"Good," Charlie allowed passing seconds for breath control and answered. He stood upright and casual the moment Uncle Tyler turned to survey them. Charlie rotated in the opposite direction. George's lungs heaved and breath poured in dense breath nostril shots like a locomotive smokestack.

Not a single cloud appeared during the morning sky, yet the abundance of sunshine hadn't brought the first warmth to his face. Frisco reached them. His head still hung low, and he offered a sulking whine while muzzling Tyler's knee.

"Toe's probably already there by now. Don't worry, just over that ridge. Gonna start to freeze if we don't keep moving." Charlie slung his Winchester again and followed the broad crunching tracks mapped ahead. Terrain shifted to a sharper slope climb with thinning trunk concentrations.

Charlie's thighs clenched and seared. He and Tyler exchanged few words while George gasped behind them, all men concentrating on each successive step and realizing the economic restraint of their expendable energy. Even when he wanted to speak, numbing wind distorted mouth contractions that should have formed without thought. He didn't need to vocalize that whatever they took required hauling the entire distance back to the cabin.

"There." Tyler stopped short and pointed with his barrel. Charlie blinked from the glare and shaded his brow with one hand.

High limbs parted and revealed a towering, almost vertical cliff face of clinging scraggle brush. Split granite walls stretched high into morning sky. A man's shape jumped up and down waving both hands above his head. Frisco froze, unmoving and lifting no more than his nose in the air. He bolted from Tyler's side, shoulders rippling, toward the base of the cliff. Another dog appeared racing down a jagged-cut trail on a powder spray. Both animals tore toward their impending collision. Progress collided with Frisco leaping high and turning his head to snap back over his shoulder while paws flew past beneath him. The other dog possessed identical gray-and-white fur mottled with black patches. A pink tongue curled up and away from snapping, snarling yellow, sunlit teeth. Brief fur glimpses appeared at any given moment during the melee.

The rolling energy mass appeared as a single roaring animal with five legs, then three, and at times, seven—a demonic-possessed, guttural-growling fury. Kicked snow and yelps subsided once Frisco fell on his back, wriggling and squirming while the other dog licked his face.

The cliff figure descended, lumbering down the same winding path in chugging rhythmic breath gusts and his rifle gripped to one side. It appeared no larger than a BB gun in a child's clutch. His entire face, with the exception of two eye slits, was covered in a darker wrapping than the rest of his body. Other than his fingertips, not a single square inch of skin was revealed. Rather than laced boots, scarves, and buttoned coats, the stranger wore only skins with still-clinging fur clumps and random rags tied around his legs and ankles.

"You old coot!" the man roared in a resonant unidentifiable dialect.

The animal skin-covered man blotted out the sun while slapping Uncle Tyler, who braced himself to keep from falling forward, across the shoulder. "Looking healthy, Toe. Been eating well I see," Uncle Tyler shot back while his friend began unwrapping the rag layers. His skin revealed dark and red as if just crossing a desert, scanning across Charlie and George with a permanent squint.

With straight, gray-stranded hair pulled back in a pony tail, unblemished white teeth spilled out between cracked lips. His nose and cheeks were carved in solid angles, contrasting even more to the uncountable horizontal wrinkle creases across the contours of his profile and Uncle Tyler's age-framed eyes.

"Can't complain—Moomau!" he commanded. The dog froze, glaring back toward the men. Frisco continued taunting nips at the animal whose head now sank between his shoulder blades and exchanged sullen glances between Frisco and his master. "Thought we were running alone today?" he nodded in

Charlie and George's direction without breaking his concentration on Uncle Tyler. Charlie's great-uncle turned and spoke beyond their hearing range.

"Charles, come on over here. Charles, George, this is Creektoe. Creektoe, Charlie and George." Charlie extended his gloved hand in the man's direction but only received a slight head tilt. George didn't engage an effort. "Saw tracks everywhere this morning and they're all heading down toward the Pass." Charlie exchanged glances with his great-uncle, receiving a "we'll talk about it later" look in return. Uncle Tyler rubbed the reddish stubble across his chin. "What are we doin' out here freezing our goods off?" Creektoe uttered a bastardized noise like a phlegm clearing and whistle mutation. Moo trotted to his side. By the time Charlie turned his head, both men and animals crested the hill and began descending. He grimaced from the returning leg burn and hunched forward.

After trudging through ankle-high drifts even in snowshoes, they paused at a brush parting. Moo fell to one knee and pushed his snout into loose powder, coating his nose and whiskers. Where their clumped tracks ceased, a thinner trailing-line depression sank into the snow. Lighter but still pronounced shallow depressions faded ahead where overhead boughs shaded the flakes.

"Ty, up there," Creektoe pointed down the sunken line.

"Now boy, Toe and me are gonna head over that hill, and I want you and your friend to swing opposite up the left. You'll hit a granite stretch you can't miss. Crawl up until you get to the top and by then, you'll see Toe and Moo. Remember," he finished with a vertical exposed forefinger tip across cracked whitened lips. "Something the matter?" Uncle Tyler asked with a scratch across his chin. George gripped his rifle.

"I'm not sure if I can do this."

"Do what?" Creektoe asked, now turning and watching their exchange.

"I don't want to kill anything. How can you end another life with such ease?" George tilted his head and retreated on one heel while Creektoe's sight sank to his toes.

"Listen, hunting isn't taking life. It's giving life. Wouldn't expect you to understand. There is an understood honor of sharing respect. Those eating and being eaten," Uncle Tyler responded. George said nothing further. Tyler unstrapped his snowshoes, lacing them back over his shoulder and cushioning them to avoid the clapping knock.

Shifting birds chattered above, sending brief ice crystal showers across their heads. Towering conifers standing barren no more than a day ago now hung sullen and quiet beneath the blanket. Forest sounds both real and imagined flooded Charlie's senses. No car horns, flashing lights, ringing phones, or anything manufactured by the hand of man distracted him from his focus. Cold, fresh air sucked in and out of his lungs.

CHAPTER

16

Charlie wasn't certain what minute flinch first focused recognition, whether a chestnut fur shuddering against white or a moment's snow disturbance. Through the sight-glass circle, a short hair-covered neck craned high against stark white pine trunks, its coal-speckled tongue curling and licking across bark. Trembling fine down rippled above underlying contractions.

Wide, dark, round eyes glistened in simultaneous scanning as it nibbled, pointed erect ears arching for any random threatening sound. Vertical and horizontal black thin lines bounced until Charlie took a deep breath and held, dropping the crosshair intersection to rest just above the right haunch where blinding, unblemished white transitioned into reddish brown. The massive antler rack trembled, turning and freezing into place, total calm with the exception of mist cloud crystals snorting from its nostrils and a single ear flicker. He squeezed the trigger.

Charlie lumbered forward with gunpowder traces still in his throat. George overtook him. Tyler and Creektoe were already bent over on their knees, hovering above clumped white mounds stained pink with deepening magenta. George and Charlie raised their hands to their hips, leaning forward while sucking forceful chilled-air breaths. Body heat rolled from beneath Charlie's open collar and swirled into exhaling fog.

"That's your shot, Creek," Uncle Tyler nodded. "Boys, how 'bout grabbing us a pole out among those young pines," his head lifted and he tossed George the hatchet dangling from his waist. Frisco and Moo continued wild dances around the carcass, bellowing primal salivating growls. Their paws kicked snow into clouds, and they settled down with bellies close to the ground, ears folded back across their necks, and tails low and straight. Each dog exchanged mutual teeth-baring, prepared to pounce if the deer sprang back to life.

"Settle down," Creektoe commanded while Charlie and George focused on the straightest available sapling. George scaled several feet off the ground, and the slender trunk arched to one side.

"Hold it there," Charlie instructed and threw the initial blow, splintering halfway through the tensed wood. Within minutes, the spruce was down and most of the young, thinner limbs hacked away revealing a straight pole. "This good enough?" Charlie shouted.

"Fine, son, fine. Guess you'll put a smile on Margie's face tonight, Creek," Uncle Tyler nodded.

"Don't thank me, look," he motioned to a deformed lead slug in front of his face, eyeing the smashed ridges and blood-clot-shining sheen. "That's a 30–06 round. Mine's a 223 and you didn't even fire." With his final word, Creektoe turned and dropped the single bullet into Charlie's gloved hand. The deer's eyes glazed over, and the puncture wound an inch below the shoulder continued a slow oozing of sporadic blood spurts. Steam poured from the hole while the darkening pool advanced beyond its wide antler rack spread.

"Enough of this chatter, odds are every grizzly around here ain't holed up yet. Not such a good idea dressing him down out here," Uncle Tyler interrupted and unlashed a rope coil from around his waist, tossing it to Creektoe. Creektoe's spanning wrinkles tightened in recognition of Tyler's comment. He stretched the stripped pole along the buck's body with its onset of rigor mortis. Both forward and rear hooves crossed the cream-white wood, and he lashed them tight, ending with slip knots. "So what do you think? Should we try making it back over to my place, or you think that wife of yours would mind seeing me again so soon?" Creektoe gazed above their heads and examined the clear, late-afternoon sky, scanning shadow angles across rolling unbroken snow.

"Hour and a half, maybe two hours of light left, Ty."

"Yeah, looks like your place it is. Hut!" he commanded Frisco. With a single syllable, Frisco rose from his battle-ready stance, perked his ears erect, and trotted to Tyler's side with his bouncing tongue dangling from the corner of his mouth.

"Uncle Tyler, what about our gear back at your place?" Charlie asked.

"Don't worry yourself none about that. Creek'll have one of his kin run over and fetch it tomorrow if need be. You know something, Toe, it's awful fortunate we have such strong young men along with us," he winked at Charlie and George. Their rifles shouldered, they bent forward and grasped opposing ends of the pole. The other two men didn't wait for them to position the carcass with any degree of comfort.

Snowdrift depth decreased once entering a willow thicket stretching beyond their sight. Charlie turned and watched the red droplet trail vanishing over the hill behind them.

"Just like old times, huh, Toe?" Charlie isolated their chat above crunching snowshoes.

"Yeah, but I'm usually the one bringing home the meat," he said with a laugh. "Remember that eleven pointer with the left droop a couple years back?" Tyler asked, stroking his whiskers and probing the snow with his rifle butt. Frisco and Moomau continued their frolicking dance.

"That was one fine animal," Creektoe stared with sight concentrating on his footing. "Awful slim this year. Been out here for more than a week, and I haven't seen the first tracks before this day," he continued. Creektoe and Uncle Tyler paced several yards ahead. "And this young buck comes outta nowhere and takes down a two hundred pounder." Creektoe's tongue clucked and his head shook. "As far as I can tell, that's the first in almost five weeks." Charlie believed his assessment of the deer's size was a significant exaggeration but offered no objection.

"You hear that, boy?" Uncle Tyler yelled over his shoulder. "Always knew you'd never forget how to fire that thing." Charlie and George leaned forward, the buck's weight now digging into their shoulders and remaining bark splinters scraping against their necks.

"What did he say?"

"Something about weak, couldn't make it out," Charlie gasped.

"You boys okay? Wanna break?" Creektoe hesitated. They concentrated on breathing rather than words with George in the rear. His burden dropped with a hollow thump. Charlie followed, rifle falling to one side, and massaged compressed cramping stiffness. George removed one glove and scooped fingers so full of snow that the whiteness remained between his lips while trying to work his jaws closed. "When I was your age, young men, I could have carried that critter up and down this mountain all by myself. That's the problem with you kids these days—weak and soft."

"Toe, when you were his age," he stopped and rubbed an ear. "Well, we won't go into that now," Uncle Tyler chuckled.

Barren hemlocks melted into black shadows against a sun-vanished, darkening sky. The first noticeable star emerged. All feeling ceased in Charlie's shoulder with the exception of a jolt jerking him forward from George's slip across a camouflaged branch.

All words halted and Charlie no longer discerned the passage of time other than George's constant huffing and heaving. Even Frisco and Moomau ghost-stepped at the side of Creektoe and Uncle Tyler ahead of them. A wolf howl in the blind distance startled Frisco, releasing a growl into the evening onset.

At first, Charlie couldn't determine if he was hallucinating. Sounds, not those of the woods and forest, but more familiar noises rose above quiet, shifting limbs. Focused listening to eliminate all other sensations reassured his comprehension.

"You hear something?" George gasped. Creektoe's pace quickened, even leaving Uncle Tyler to lag in the drifts. Through the parting bark ahead, unnatural light grew more intense with the shrill cries of laughing and singing children. Charlie turned and focused an ear on the noise ahead. "Me too, come on," George urged him forward. As they crested a wide embankment, several doublewide trailers appeared in a clearing with a larger Quonset hut almost identical to the structure where they had slept in Juneau.

Random scattered poles with mounted arc lamps lit the flattened area, and towering pines protected on three sides. Creektoe's pace transformed into a slow jog, allowing his momentum to carry him the remaining descent where terrain leveled. The first trailer's door flew open with a metallic bang, and a child rising no higher than their knees burst into chilled air. "Poppa!" she squealed, wailing forth in a rapid foreign language of nimble tongue and esophagus maneuvers.

"This must be the place," George interrupted the scene after arriving at the front wooden porch. Four steel barrels leaned in the center of an open courtyard between the trailers, fires blazing cast shadows of everyone long and far into surrounding stark forest shadows. Charlie and George once again dropped the carcass with an ice-crunching thud. Both men collapsed at the same time, cross-legged on the snow bank. Slick sweat coated Charlie's temples, and he trembled from initial hypothermia. Shivering without control even through his gloves and hat, he pulled flaps over his ears until the tips brushed his neck.

George's uncontrolled chattering teeth distracted Charlie's focus. "Sort of like being on the back of that truck again," George mumbled. George turned his head to notice the curtain's parting at the end of the far trailer. Several glowing candles illuminated a face.

George's eyes refused looking away from stretching, black, draped hair glinting down both sides of her shoulders. Shivering, numbness, and aching vanished. Her head tilted forward, catching his gaze.

A widening smile advanced across her face, ivory-white teeth reflecting the firelight. Long lashes curled above shattered cinnamon eyes returned his locked gaze while he absorbed her high, thin cheekbone curvature. George no longer chose to blink from the freeze. After rubbing his eyes, curtains closed and the vision disappeared.

The first child was followed by another, then another, and yet a fourth. They could not have varied by more than a few years in age, and they danced around Creektoe, pulling on his coat and stretching up to poke his ribs. Four more figures emerged, slower and more calculated.

"Just leave that over there. Boys, come on." Charlie struggled to shift his calves but almost launched upright without the massive carcass weight. He leaned over and extended an open palm toward George. An older girl whom Charlie judged to be in her initial teens flashed bashful glances and vanished back inside. The other three were older, around the age of Charlie and George, along with two teenagers. "Charlie, George, this is Creektoe's family," Uncle Tyler spoke.

"Yep, the whole rowdy bunch," Creektoe smiled, rubbing the hair of one boy and lifting the smallest girl to his chest. Wild, unkempt hair drifted down past her shoulders and whipped across Creektoe's cheeks, not removing the permanent smile chiseled across his chapped lips. Frisco and Moo skulked away behind a shed, spooked from incessant giggles and laughs.

"Now who is this little angel?" George reached out to the girl in Creektoe's arms. She tore her gaze from her father's face for a moment and lost all expression, chin diving back into Creektoe's chest. "Sorry about that."

"Don't be. She hasn't seen a whole lot of your people," he answered in reassurance.

"My people?"

"Yeah, you know," he repeated and spread his arms to point across the other children, their eyes darting between themselves. George didn't elaborate but shook his head in recognition. "Now I'm not expecting you to remember everyone, but this here is Gracie, that's Annabelle, James, Mark, Jess, Anne who jumped back inside, and Bill. Oldest boy must have got called back into work with this snow, but he should be along soon." Creektoe attempted continuing the introductions, but more yelling reemerged from the doorway.

"Old man, you told me you'd be back by sundown! You have any idea how worried I was? Do you know how much I have to do to get ready for tomorrow?" came a woman's string of words. Charlie judged her to rise no more than five feet tall. She stopped short at recognizing the others and released forehead contractions. Her cheeks and jaws slackened. An instant relaxation flowed across her features. She coughed and brushed imagined wrinkles from her small parka. "Tyler," she nodded in their direction. Uncle Tyler lifted his chin long enough to establish eye contact but gave no more than a grin. "How do ya do?" she asked and stepped down the porch, extending an ungloved hand toward Charlie. He removed a glove and tightened his grip on her palm's coarse warmth.

"Gentlemen, this is my one and only reason for living in this world," Creektoe beamed. Even with her dark complexion and little light emitting from the flames, Charlie still detected a profound blush across her round cheeks while giving her husband a light swat across his forearm. The little girl named Gracie giggled and stretched arms out toward her mother.

"Charles, ma'am, Charlie Sutcliffe. This is George," he nodded to his side. George slipped off his hat and shook her outstretched hand with grasping, downward-curled fingers. Several other figures now emerged from various trailers and surrounded the group. Their faces were older with even more children emerging from behind them.

"Margie."

"I understand formal introductions are good manners, but if everyone doesn't mind, we're gonna freeze out here," Uncle Tyler interrupted.

"Right as always, Ty, come on rascals, inside for bed." A wailing protest chorus returned his prodding, but each filed into a single line back up the porch.

"Oh my," Creektoe's wife gasped after witnessing the buck in the snow bank. She pulled up the hem of her frock and high-stepped toward the deer. "Guess I can't get too mad at you. This'll feed the brood for weeks," she said and dropped to her knees, allowing her fingers to sift rigid fur.

"As much as I'd like to take credit, the trophy belongs to this young man." She rose at the conclusion of her husband's statement, not looking up at Charlie but keeping her sight to the ground. She shuffled back and sideways until Creektoe was almost obscured from her vision. "Now, let's get him over to the barn for a dressing. Ty?"

"Naw, you all go on ahead. I gotta get some feeling back into these fingers," Tyler said and stamped his feet while scaling the porch steps, Creektoe's wife trailing behind in silence.

"Sorry about that, Creektoe, didn't mean to upset her," Charlie spoke.

"Don't think anything about it." Creektoe grabbed one end of the pole and dragged the deer between barrels toward the Quonset hut. Charlie and George, sensation still not returned to shoulders or hands, followed. The door slide clicked to one side, and Creektoe flipped a light switch. The broad concrete floor spanned with tools of every shape and size. A flat-bed Ford was parked at the far end with three adjacent snowmobiles beneath tarps. He reached next to the door and pulled a tinkling link chain hung suspended from a ceiling cross-tie. A blue tarp stretched across the concrete. He unlashed the buck's legs, and with straining thighs, heaved it over his shoulder. "Mind giving me a hand?" he gasped. Charlie leapt forward and dropped a rusted hook into Creektoe's open palm. He swung the deer sideways and over the hook until the chain dangled it above the tarp. From beneath his jacket, Creektoe pulled a long blade gleaming from outside barrel firelight. "You want the honors? Your kill," he motioned the knife toward Charlie.

"That's okay. It's been a lot of years, and I'm certain you've had more practice." Creektoe shrugged. Starting at the bottom of the abdomen, he inserted the blade and pulled down toward the throat.

Already freezing flesh resisted the dissection, but slices and pulls opened until the still-stained belly spread apart. Minimal blood flowed as intestines and other vital organs flopped to the floor with a wet thwack. George winced but refused turning his head.

"Creektoe?" George asked.

"Yeah?"

"I saw a woman through a window down on the end. Who is she?"

"Oh, you musta seen Meredith. That's Margie's little sister. She sort of keeps to herself most of the time. Shame what happened. Husband got killed a few years back. It was the darndest thing getting caught in an avalanche up at the Pass. Grab that bucket," he commanded Charlie. "Might want to take your gloves off for this." Charlie bent over to scoop the intestines, liver, stomach, and remaining organs. Heat still retained within them brought tingles back to his fingertips. "Oh, take care of that," he nodded at the knife tip. "Ever had venison liver?" Charlie shook his head without taking his eyes off the shining, purple lumps of flesh.

"Can't recall," Charlie replied. Creektoe worked with a surgeon's hands, placing calculated cuts at precise depths, peeling back the hide and trimming clinging sinew while progressing down the back and torso. The entire hide cracked away in a single massive blanket, still stiff from the cold. After stretching it full length across one of the few uncluttered floor patches, he wiped the blade clean on a bench rag and returned it to his sheath.

George jumped at the roar of a chainsaw chortling to life. The high-pitched whine echoed off the tin hut's arched walls.

Charlie tried speaking but was met with Creektoe pointing at his ear and shaking his head. Rotating steel teeth sank into the wine-red flesh, severing tendons and bone. He first dispatched the front legs, then ribs, and dissected the carcass's remainder until the torso dangled from the chain. He pulled swinging remnants from the hook and laid them across a bench.

"And here, my boys, is the best part of all," he beamed and retrieved his knife once again. "Gentlemen, this is called the backstrap, and you'll find no better tasting piece of meat off any animal that crawls, swims, or walks across this earth." He worked the knife along the rear of the slab, just above the spine, until removing a long gleaming strip of copper-red meat dangling with admiration in the light bulb glow. "There, hope you took good notes," Creektoe said, wiping his knife for the final time. "Now that's taken care of, let's go see what my beautiful bride is up to."

By the time they returned, the trailing screams of children vanished with no more remaining sounds other than the continuous wind roll through towering cedars or an occasional exploding crack in one of the barrels. Lights remained on in three of the trailers while they trudged after Creektoe's lead. The men removed their boots on the front porch and entered. The rush of warmth across Charlie's cheeks burned, and he leaned against a miniature totem to maintain balance.

Upon entering, a black iron-belly stove stood against one wall with split firewood stacked as high as Charlie's chin guarding each side. Through a half bar into the kitchen, Margie hummed to herself among discordant pot clangs. With little candlelight and the stove's open door, he stared at the remainder of walls covered in shields, carved masks, skins, mounted animal heads, and sinew strung bows.

Elegant detailed moose, bear, elk, and eagle carvings leaned against pine panel siding. No chairs or tables appeared across the floor. A haphazard arrangement of moose and caribou hides stretched to all four walls.

"Where is everyone?" George asked, pulling the hood from his head.

"All my young ones better be off to bed," Creektoe replied and collapsed on what Charlie perceived as an elongated black furred beanbag. He pushed the wood stove door wider but jerked back his fingers. He shoved them into his mouth and used the other hand to add more wood.

"Those all your children?" George asked with a snicker from Uncle Tyler, also falling into a similar bag with an exaggerated sigh.

"Most of them—eight, three girls and five boys. The others are cousins. You already saw Margie's little sister over next to the stream. My brother Red lives beside the smokehouse with his wife and youngsters. Ever met a Tlinget before?" Creektoe asked and sat up cross-legged. He pulled a pair of pipes from a shelf behind him and motioned one in Uncle Tyler's direction. Both Charlie and George shook their heads when he offered an additional two for them.

"We are one of the oldest North American tribes and stretched from your Washington state all the way past the Aleuts," Creektoe spoke each word with slow care, his face illuminating with a broad smile after sucking inward on his pipe stem and the following cherry-glow brightness highlighting strained cheeks. "There may be many houses, but we are considered Dine, or the inlanders. Tlinget just the same."

"You men just gonna jaw there the rest of the evening, or you forgot about eating?" Margie called over the half bar between the kitchen and main room. Charlie jumped to his feet and turned the corner where each man pulled a chair around a stout table. On the stove, a massive copper pot shuddered from boiling, and steam rose, wetting wild hair falling into her eyes. "Ain't much but I didn't know we would be receiving evening company," she grumbled and shot a cool stare toward Creektoe. She grabbed wooden bowls and ladled each to the brim. George's eyebrows scrunched his tongue, and the first spoonful danced between his cheeks. Creektoe didn't turn upwards toward Margie, slurping and studying his bowl's contents in silent meditation.

A knock sounded at the front door. Creektoe tried rising but Margie braked his chair with a hip. "Sit—eat," she ordered. George's spoon fell from his grip, and it splashed soup across the table. The face of whom he had earlier caught no more than a glimpse entered the cramped dining area. "Merry!" Margie's voice rose in an instant while leaning forward to return her embrace.

"Hope I'm not intruding, but I noticed we had company," the woman said as she unbuttoned her parka and let it fall into a chair. She glanced at George and swept a hand across her forehead. Her almond complexion glowed in the light, and corner cheeked dimples spanned upon meeting George's gaping stare.

"Not one bit. You hungry?" Margie asked.

"Oh, no thanks. Just thought I'd drop in. We don't see too many new faces around here." Charlie rose and extended a hand.

"Nice to meet you, I'm Charlie and this is George." He paused, turning and waiting for George to rise to his feet. George remained frozen, locked into his seat while their eyes vanished everyone else from the room.

"Mmmph, nnnnice to meeeeet, niiiice tooo met yoooo, Mere, Mere, Merideth," he stammered and almost tripped forward across the table. A slight giggle escaped from her throat, and she took his hand in hers, applying slight pressure.

"It's a pleasure meeting you. Please, call me Merry. Now, I don't want to disturb you any longer. I can see that all of you men have some appetites."

"No, no disturbance at all," George responded and shot to his feet, pulling out his chair and motioning for Merry to sit.

"Are you sure? If you insist." George scooted the chair in for her and sat next to the kitchen counter. Margie and Creektoe's heads bent forward, and she nudged him beneath the table to interrupt a forming smirk.

"Wow, fantastic, Mrs. Creek—" Charlie hesitated.

"Margie. Glad you enjoy it. You look way too skinny. You could use a little more fat on those ribs. Getting a little worried that meat was getting toward the end of storage," she stopped and took her own sip, a contouring lip smack in tacit agreement to Charlie's compliment.

"So what was that about feeding everyone for a month?" Creektoe coughed and turned to stare into a dark-window sky after Charlie's question. Uncle Tyler joined the exchange.

"Pickings have been slimmer this year, longer than most of us can remember. Salmon runs aren't what they used to be, and the Northers only got a single trip down the White Ash," Tyler said, clicking his tongue.

"Leaf, that's my oldest, gets into Blackhole around once a month for rice and beans," Creektoe's voice lifted toward the same sky Uncle Tyler scanned. Charlie ceased his spoon-to-mouth mechanical rhythm until the utensil clanked into a vacant bowl.

"Well, Margie, it would be my honor if you would take that venison and make better use of it than me," Charlie leaned forward, sipping from his plastic cup. Creektoe's stare broke. Both he and Tyler turned to direct gazes at Charlie whose eyes darted between the two men. Creektoe's chair scooted with a reverse screech across plywood, and he towered to his feet, looming above Charlie's unflinching features.

"This boy your kindred?" Creektoe's voice lowered to a whisper, and he nodded at his great-uncle. Uncle Tyler returned an assenting gesture. Creektoe raised an arm, and Charlie winced, preparing for the anticipated blow only to discover the man's open palm falling to rest on his shoulder. "Young man, we cannot express the degree of honor you give upon this house and our family," he ended and broke eye contact, sight falling upon his bare toes. Margie kept silent in the kitchen and leaned against a countertop. George watched, waiting for development.

"It's nothing, really," Charlie forced.

"You must understand, the giving of food, especially this amount of food, is a particular honor in our culture. And it couldn't have come at a better time," he continued, his voice almost cracking. "Tomorrow is the pottie!" A broad smile snapped across Tyler's glowing face from Creektoe's sudden exuberance.

"Excuse me?" George asked. Uncle Tyler nudged his arm.

"He's talking about a potlatch. Sort of a big party to folks like you and me. Friends and relatives from the whole area around come to eat, sing, eat, dance, engage in competitions, eat, drink, and eat some more," Tyler said and leaned on one arm, staring at distant invisible points of past images.

"Our eldest daughter is joining Suquoaka for a life bond next week. Her seclusion ends tomorrow," Margie chimed in with wetness still clinging to her tightened upturned cheeks.

"It's getting awful late," Uncle Tyler spoke between a wide gaping yawn. "Gentlemen, it would be a good idea if we got back by midnight. There's a good full moon, but I didn't care for the way that bluster was picking back up—could change anytime," Tyler said, rising and stretching.

"Listen, my friend, the hour is too late and the night too dark. You are all invited to the potlatch for our Anne," Creektoe stated and crossed his arms.

"You absolutely have to come," Merry exclaimed. George's head rose and he smiled at her request.

"Thanks for the offer, but that's a personal thing—that's family." Uncle Tyler turned to sit and started pulling on his first boot. Margie sprinted from the kitchen and squatted next to him on her knees, pushing his hands away and slapping the boot with flashing strength. "I believe that means you won't take no for an answer?" Her stern features melted into batting eyelids.

"Your great nephew's generous gift grants conditional family status as far as we're concerned." Margie rose and leaned against her husband's elbow. His head bent forward, and he kissed the top of her forehead while she slipped an arm around his waist.

"Creek, weren't you bragging last month about a carving you were making of that fine dog of yours?" Tyler glanced up with words muted through his napkin.

"It's a beaut. You boys wanna check it out, too?" Charlie was about to answer when Tyler's sock reached beneath the table, and Charlie sensed a tap across Creektoe's foot.

Merry yawned and held one hand in front of her mouth. George sprang to his feet in anticipation of her chair scooting back from the table. He extended a hand and helped her to her feet. They both walked side by side back to the living room fire, exchanging quiet words beyond the hearing of anyone else before settling along the couch.

"Thanks, but hauling that buck so many miles wore us down to the bone," Charlie said. Creektoe broke Margie's embrace with reluctance while Uncle Tyler also rose and followed him back out to the front porch. Charlie positioned himself near the window. Brief comforting exchanges were recognized while George and Merry rubbed open palms in front of the open fire and brushed shoulders.

Both Frisco and Moo continued frolicking and fighting around the glowing barrels, masking Charlie's ability to discern specific words or sentences. Their voices rose and fell among the brief cadence of exchange. Creektoe's arm shadows flailed in sporadic wild gestures while Tyler stroked his chin.

"You need a hand in there?" Merry called.

"That's okay, you kids keep talking," Margie answered and remained occupied in the kitchen, hand washing the bowls, spoons, and pot. Charlie snapped back and sunk down in his bag at the front door handle's turn.

"Old woman," Creektoe released an enormous wailing yawn even stirring protest whimpers from Frisco and Moo now reclining on the front porch. "Don't know how much longer these old eyes are gonna stay open. You boys make yourselves at home, plenty of wood to stay warm, and if you need anything, give a knock to the last door on the right. Looks like we're all gonna need plenty of sleep for tomorrow."

Margie turned and waddled down the narrow hallway, returning with an armful of high-piled blankets. With calculating method, she unfolded each and draped them over the shoulders of Charlie and Uncle Tyler. Ornate dyed eagles and sea birds covered the dense wool smelling of wood-smoked raw forest.

"I guess it is getting sort of late," Merry broke the continued quiet conversation with George and turned toward her sister.

"Well, what kind of gentleman would I be if I didn't at least offer to walk you home?" George stated and jumped to his feet, taking her hand in his own. He lifted her coat from the chair and assisted her arms back into the sleeves. "C.S., be back in a flash," he beamed an uncontrolled smile.

"Very nice to meet you, Charlie."

All cold earlier chilling down to Charlie's core vanished. Even stinging remnants now faded to a tingling glow. He dropped to rest on a brown bear hide where Creektoe earlier reclined near the stove. Charlie listened to the low flame rumble within the cast iron stove walls licking blackened curves.

One fingertip traced the journal's spine tucked into his coat, and he resisted the desire to scan its yellow pages. Brilliant light pinpoints through the stove's side holes imprisoned his vision from focus. "Boy, you still awake?" Tyler's voice rose above dry pine crackles.

"Yeah, Uncle Tyler, what is it?" Charlie asked, hearing his great-uncle roll over on his back.

"Creek and I talked over your little trip. Seems like you might need help, and he's willing to lend some aid with supplies and a few rations. But, he's also gonna give you the most cherished gift a man could ever give."

"What's that?" Charlie asked and rose on both elbows, looking to Uncle Tyler's prostrate body outline lengthwise on the couch.

"He'll only help out on the condition that his oldest son, Leaf, goes with you. Besides Creek himself, there isn't a soul in a thousand miles around who knows this land better than him. I'd do all I could to stop you myself if you refuse." Charlie offered no immediate answer, his mind reeling with the previous weeks' flashing images.

"If you put it that way, I guess my pair has now become a trio." Charlie lay back down and watched flames dance off the reflecting knotted ceiling. "You and Dad very close growing up?"

"What do you mean by close?" his great-uncle's response rose through the dimness.

"You know, did you ever play ball together, go on campouts, hikes?" Charlie continued, now staring up at the firelight shadows dancing across the ceiling.

"There was some of that if I remember correctly, but keep in mind we didn't spend a whole lot of time together. He always did have a peculiar sort of way about him. Most little boys look up to their elders, but I never could tell what he really thought about us being kin," he stopped and coughed. "I remember one time, he was out shooting birds with a BB gun I bought him for his birthday, and he came across this rabbit. Little, white, furry thing, musta been hit by a car or something but squealed to no end. Like a woman shrieking for dear life. Couldn't stand hearing that misery, and I grabbed a rock to end the suffering. Your daddy grabbed my arm and pushed that rock away. Benjy knelt down, took off his coat, and wrapped it up close to his chest. Your grandma woulda had a fit if he tried bringing in that 'wild thing,' as she would have put it, so he kept it out in the garage. Benjy put a pair of popsicle sticks on each side of the broken leg and used band-aids to hold them together. Your grandma couldn't understand why your daddy was all of the sudden so eager to get more helpings of salad at dinner." Uncle Tyler paused and laughed, as if still seeing the young boy stuffing cucumbers into his overall pockets.

Charlie turned and studied Tyler's outlined profile in the shadows, no more than the continuing blare of pipe embers offering a moment's glimpse at his puffed cheeks and wire white chin hairs. "So what happened? To the rabbit?"

"One Saturday morning, he went out to give it an old tomato, and she was nowhere in sight. Not a sign or pellet to be seen. He went playing in the field by your grandma's house later in the afternoon, and we found a popsicle stick with band-aids still clinging to it. Guess wild things are always meant to stay wild." Charlie focused on the conclusion of Uncle Tyler's final statement, picturing the images and a vision never associated with Benny.

"Did he say anything else after about the rabbit?" Uncle Tyler didn't reply. "Then what happened?" he again asked and turned. Smoke ceased rising from his pipe, and the glowing coal turned dark. Charlie rose with cramped thighs, removed the briar from Tyler's lips, and replaced it on the shelf. Uncle Tyler snored. Charlie pulled his blanket high over his shoulders, legs still reluctant for immediate response while the buck's weight still haunted his shoulders.

Charlie thought he heard the front door opening, closing, and boot thuds across the floor. Imagining Charlotte's fine soft hair against his forehead surpassed all exhaustion. If he concentrated enough, Charlie pulled Karen close, snuggling her into his chest.

CHAPTER

17

Engine roars rattled trailer windows.

Sunlight filtered through speckled almond blinds as clad floorboard plywood vibrated beneath Charlie. He rose from a fur shield and blanket still wrapped around his shoulders, calves cramping his balance while leaning forward on the supporting window sill. Crowds milled around the courtyard between trailers.

People of every shape and size wore multicolored parkas, jeans, and leather. They gathered in groups of three or four while even more children than the previous evening played tag and chased after one another. Frisco and Moo remained inseparable, yapping and skipping in between the random bodies.

"Sleepy heads, sleepy heads, the hour to rise and shine," Margie's voice called down the hallway. Charlie blinked back remaining eye film. After she turned the corner, Margie appeared in full-length buckskin. The hide concealed her wide figure with hair bound up in a bun and bleached white bones supporting her tresses. Intricate beadwork adorned a wide collar and pendant covering the top half of her chest. Her shining moccasins reflected with identical red, blue, green, white, and black beads forming an eagle head. She danced a step with one foot extended and the other to her side until shimmying back into the main room. A rising tune humming in her throat deepened, and her lips allowed the tones to emerge with subtle tremors.

"You look beautiful, Ma," Uncle Tyler's head rose from beneath his blanket's fringed edge. Even through morning noise and disturbance, George's snores continued without any wakened sensation, remaining in distant unconsciousness. Charlie kicked his leg beneath the blanket, and he snorted back to reality, mirroring Charlie's earlier expression.

"Hey, stop," George slurred.

"What's the matter with you?"

"Got back kinda late," George said and fell back to his pillow. Charlie raised both eyebrows. Margie's eyes flashed and she stroked the beads around her neck. After collective stretching, yawning, and struggling into their coats, Charlie reached his great-uncle out among the congested throng. Snow was stomped to ground level from people milling in every direction.

Snowmobiles lined the length of the Quonset hut, some still remaining strapped to trailers. Men and women hauled armloads of baskets, trunks, and carved wooden vessels down a trail beside the courtyard and disappeared into dense cedars. Several snowmobiles continued roaring across the side field, crisscrossing one another's tracks and racing with snow-flying arcs cutting behind their paths. Pink-cheeked children's faces bubbled while they rubbed their exposed hands over burning barrels.

"Guess this party is about to get started," Uncle Tyler elbowed George who joined them. Across the sea of fur-lined heads, Creektoe's towering stature rose, and he raised an arm to motion them in his direction. He too was dressed in beaded buckskin leggings and a similar shirt to others in the council circle. A vest bearing the same eagle design as Margie covered the garment but reflected more significant detail attention. A bone band with three feathers hung from the back of his head keeping hair from his eyes.

None of the men spoke, nodding in their direction. Charlie fought the impulse to extend a hand and returned their gestures. "This is a great day for tradition and celebration," Creektoe concluded while the silver-haired Howewia glanced across snowmobiles tearing through embankments and shook his head. He approached, face next to George's chin, and stared straight up, his eyes cringed cracks behind a vast array of folded dough wrinkles spanning his face. He muttered a phrase and Creektoe nodded. George returned a wavering smile.

"What did he say?" Charlie asked Uncle Tyler.

"My Old Tlinglet isn't what it used to be, but I believe he said they're honored that you're here." Charlie turned a glancing expression at his great-uncle who shrugged.

"Enough of this talk, time for the first feast of the day," Creektoe bellowed and motioned the others to follow. Sunlight cleared the sparse canopy, and morning birds continued their songs. Charlie trailed behind Uncle Tyler while Creektoe and George exchanged quiet words behind them. Snow melted and turned to slush beneath their prints. Mud clung to their soles from the returning forest floor. They passed others in both directions along the trail.

The crisp morning scent of thawing wood succumbed to creeping smoke filtering through the limbs. The trail stopped at a looming planked structure in the clearing. Two magnificent wooden totems guarded each side of an oval doorway. A wing-spread eagle perched atop each tower with unique character carved faces descending downwards at specific intervals. The carvings reflected a mixture of comedy, terror, and sadness in blinding shades of paint. Their colored emblems offered a stark contrast against the leaf and ancient wood backdrop.

The elongated structure stretched into vanishing camouflage with a wide wooden chimney centered in the middle of the slanted roof. As they approached, Charlie identified individual hewn planks leaned against a framework composing the walls. Women gathered in groups outside, tending small fires while meat roasted, unknown vegetables sautéed, and pots stirred with universal aromas.

"What is this place?" George interrupted the observation.

"This is the house of my ancestors," Creektoe spanned an uncontained smile and spread an arm in front of his chest, waving across the milling activity. "No matter how modern this world becomes, we never forget the honor of our ancestors and traditions. One of my sons may be my grandfather just as I may have once been the head of Little Birch," his tone shortened.

"Reincarnation?"

"Something like that. Our complex traditions run many thousands of years. Just because we've adopted a few modern conveniences doesn't mean we have to completely abandon our past. Come," Creektoe ordered and stooped low, entering between the totems. They descended several packed-earth steps to the main floor. Skins were scattered in a circle around a looming stone platform in the center. Wooden benches on two levels rose on all four walls while boys placed stoking logs into the main fire. Ember flames rose high, smoke billowing upwards through the center ceiling opening. Open earth patches between the skins reflected firelight from untold ages of elk moccasin polishing. Broad, hand-smoothed logs from iron blades suspended the roof above their heads as Charlie craned his neck to scan the protecting ceiling. George turned with the same wide eyes, not examining the architectural accomplishment but searching the faces it enclosed.

Four men crouched in one corner, one tapping exchanged rhythms on a hide-stretched drum while another slapped mallets on a hollow log. The third clapped shells together in unison to the beat of the other two while the last man circled and swooned in dance, calculating small decisive steps with concentration across the floor.

"Son, over here," Creektoe's voice boomed down the long corridor. One man hesitated and turned, sprinting towards them. "My friends, this is my eldest son, Leaf" he introduced with one hand on the younger man's shoulder.

"How do you do?" came his curt but formal response. "Oh, you must be the great al'ooni everyone is buzzing about this morning," he tilted back his chin and extended a hand toward George.

"Oh no, not me," he corrected and pointed toward Charlie.

"It was a really lucky shot. I haven't fired a rifle in years."

"Nonetheless, my father and I are indebted to you." Uncle Tyler slipped away to the side, engaging in uninterruptible bragging with a pair of young women. Charlie couldn't hear the boasting but watched the fascinating gleam in their young eyes while he flailed with emotive gesturing to relate whatever tale he released. One glance in George's direction, and Charlie was certain Uncle Tyler was more creative with the deer hunt than actual truth.

During the introductions, a consistent crowd filed through the front archway. As coats, parkas, scarves, and gloves fell to the floor, a vast color array reflected across designs covering damp deer hide. "Come, time for the first feast. I would be honored if you would sit with us. Please," Leaf requested and escorted the three men toward the front of five lines forming around the fire platform's center. At the head of each line was an elder who had been introduced earlier.

Voices echoed through the hall with a low murmur until the first bang of a tightened drum's closed-fist impact silenced all voices. The strike continued pulsating through the air after the last word ceased. All heads turned to the front where Creektoe emerged from behind a curtain.

"Friends and family, Creektoe, leader of the Three Feathers, is honored for your presence at this ceremony. This is a time for celebration honoring the marriage of my eldest daughter Anne and the joining of the Suquoaka." Charlie didn't believe Creektoe could have shown any more teeth if he tried through his tightened withered lips. "Anne," he pointed toward his daughter of whom Charlie caught no more than a glimpse the previous night. She swept fleeting eye contact across the crowd and turned away with a chorus of hooting, clapping, and erupting cheers. "We give thanks to Dikaankaaau, and we ask His blessing upon this gathering." At the pause of Creektoe's final word, he clapped twice and took his seat on a low bench at the head of their group.

Most of the younger women rose, gathering single file in the hall's center, and trailed one another back outside. The group that had been chanting in the corner earlier now played their instruments in solid earth harmonies while the fourth man appeared from behind the drawn curtain. His arms and legs were masked in feather coverings; he spread them wide while dancing in circles around the flaming platform.

A grumbling chant rose from his chest although Charlie saw no movement behind his mask. Firelight shone off the blue-and-red feathers while the other men joined in identical chanting, closing their eyes and swaying to the rhythm.

Charlie turned and the procession of women reentered, forearms straining and backs hunched from carrying wide baskets filled with fish, venison, seal meat on skewers, and an unending array of scorched vegetables. Baskets were placed in the middle of the five groups while anxious eyes already ate. With a final drum-pounding succession, the feathered dancer jumped up to the fire platform edge, released a curdling shriek, and dove off through the open curtain, disappearing from sight.

The complete return to silence was broken in an eruption of screams and claps as hands dove into the food. "Go on, try the beaver, it's my favorite," Leaf nudged Charlie. He grabbed a chunk as big as his fist and sank his teeth into the flesh. George still hadn't tried his first sampling.

"Wow," Charlie managed squeezing out through another muffled bite.

"What's a matter my friend, no appetite?" Leaf indicated where both corners of George's mouth drew tight. "Sorry, no eggs and bacon but you might like this," he said, grabbing a pile of olive green leaves covered in pink meat scraps. George sampled a nibble and then shoved the entire handful into this mouth. "Much more where that came from—kelp and smoked halibut." Charlie and George continued devouring without dialogue. Uncle Tyler remained at the far back of the line, taking turns between the two female friends feeding him. "Your uncle, right, Charlie?" Leaf asked.

"Yeah," Charlie almost breathed between bites, "great-uncle—he's my grandfather's brother."

"He and my father go back a long ways. Guess you could say that if it wasn't for your uncle, I wouldn't be talking to you right now." Charlie stopped chewing while he and George turned their heads. "Never told you how they first met and he saved my father's life?"

"No, that hasn't exactly come up in conversation," Charlie replied.

"Many years ago, before I came into this world, Creektoe was ice fishing near the Wilawatu. He said it was near the end of March, but the ice should have still been thick enough. Well, it wasn't. Said it was like a cannon going off underneath him. After the main splinters, he made it nearly thirty feet from the shore and went under. With all of the hollering and splashing, Tyler heard the struggle and came crashing through the trees. To actually hear your uncle tell the story, it was his dog that first heard all the commotion. That would be Frisco and Moomau's father. Fine dog, he said, half wolf. Anyway, Tyler tied a rope around his waist and plunged into the water, grabbed Creektoe around the neck, and dragged him back to the shore. Got a fire going and shook him back to warmth." All other sights and sounds were nonexistent to Charlie's examination of Leaf's face. "You should hear him recount it someday. They're both much better at it, and the story gets more dramatic with every version."

"Good morning," a voice rose behind them. George spun around and one hand wiped crumbs from his mouth at the moment of recognition. Leaf and Charlie stopped their discussion, watching both sets of eyes lock above mutual purple underlying swollen lids. George dropped the biscuit in his lap and leapt to his feet.

"If you all don't mind?" Charlie and Leaf shook their heads in unison. George extended a hand to point a path through the eating, laughing mass sprawled across the floor. Leaf resumed his meal, but Charlie turned in just enough time to see George reach over and take Merry's hand prior to exiting the lodge.

CHAPTER

18

Throughout the morning, sleds and vehicles filtered away with nodding, faded heads and arm waves in the air. Sunlight burned back the morning chill, and Charlie heard branches dripping with melting ice and snow. Charlie allowed the front screen door to spring shut behind him, and he descended the stairs while Leaf and Creektoe turned at his approach.

"So what's this all about?" Charlie yawned and nodded toward strapped aluminum-frame backpacks. Creektoe, unencumbered, rolled back on the balls of his feet and smiled.

"Yours is over there," he nodded to a red pack leaning against the railing.

"This is too much; you don't have to go to all this trouble."

"Speak for yourself. You've been in the city too long," Leaf glanced up after shoving a foot-long Bowie blade into a sheath suspended from his belt.

"My son is right. Ty made me promise to make sure you boys get back safe, and that's what I intend to do. Now it's getting way past time to get you youngsters down the river." Charlie scanned the immediate area and saw no sign of Frisco or any other motion.

"Where's Uncle Tyler, and what river?"

"He was sorry not to see you off, but he kept muttering something about setting traps and he was gone. As far as the second question, Leaf and I figured the best way toward the valley is by raft. You can take Ten Bears' boat; he's trading over in Blackhole for a few weeks, and he said help yourselves. Don't worry, Leaf'll make sure it gets back in one piece," Creektoe said and dropped a furrowed eyebrow.

"That's right," Leaf replied while his hands shifted around various bags, packs, and tools suspended from his skins.

"Now when you get to Mabel's place," Creektoe hesitated and tossed a glance past Charlie, turning with undecipherable lips and a lowered tone of voice. Both men took one step away after locking arms on each other's shoulders. While Leaf's stature wasn't diminished, his father towered above him. Creektoe's single arm melted into an embrace and allowed his chin to rest on the crest of his son's head. Spanning wrinkles shooting out from both corners of his eyes flexed into clenched furrows with the tightening of his eyelids. His mouth continued moving between syllabic half-speak and hum. Leaf broke the embrace, stepping back to place his own arm on his father's shoulder and lifting the opposite arm to kiss the back of his hand across the wrist. They said nothing further.

"Anyone seen George?" Charlie asked with Creektoe still not offering the slightest response or acknowledgement of farewell. Leaf turned and pointed toward the farthest trailer. George and Merry continued walking in pace with one another, eyes reflecting in the morning sunshine sparkles and shoulders brushing against one another without losing a single moment of contact. "So, thought you decided to join us after all?"

"Good morning everybody," Merry pulled her eyes away from George. He turned with his back toward them. She rose on her toes and wrapped George in an embrace. Their lips moved once again but Charlie was too far away to hear their exchange.

Footing was random with stretched mud ruts where snow vanished and the soft pine needle bedding scattered beneath their steps. Splattering trickle streams appeared on occasional slate outcroppings after passing the ancestral lodge. Charlie still tasted roast seal fat in his throat and the full dulling sensation.

"Doing all right back there, Gup?" Charlie cried behind him through bough-filtering sunlight shafts.

"Let's see, my belly can't hold anymore, I can feel actual sun on my face, got more than five hours of sleep, and this pack feels light as a feather. Yeah, you could say I'm doing okay," George spoke with a tone Charlie had forgotten since Seattle. "Who's this Mabel, anyway?"

"Mabel is what you folks might call a witch doctor."

"A what?" George stopped and Leaf turned, a slight grimace across Leaf's mouth expecting the reaction. Charlie continued along loose pebbles and a consistently turning path of descent.

"Before your imagination runs away from you, she's nothing like the images running through your heads right now. Purely herbal, studying leaves, roots, wild animals—harmless, I guarantee. Give me a degreed medical doctor any day, but many of my people still swear by her." Both men resumed their course toward Charlie who was several paces ahead. "My father said she might be able to help us out on this little journey. She's got several good sturdy mules."

"What do we need a donkey for anyway?"

"Who's gonna carry back all of that gold?" Leaf asked. George turned toward Charlie and dropped his eyes.

"So we're just going to stop in and ask for a mule?"

"Don't worry, she'll know we're coming by the time we get there. And my friends, that is how we are getting there," Leaf stopped after a tight maple stand parted, revealing a river bank. Charlie heard the increasing water rush in the background but confused it with the rising wind. George hopped off the eroded embankment, dropping his pack on a boulder. He leaned into the shimmering water. It splashed across his face and down his neck while releasing a satisfied sigh.

"Hold on, don't want to drink that," Leaf knelt and stopped him with a knee tap on his back. "Odds are you may be okay this time of year. But, there's no telling what sort of tiny bugs might be floating around in there, and I can assure you several days of cramping and misery if they get you. Here," Leaf said, grabbing George's water skin from his pack and unscrewing the cap. Leaf dropped to his knees and drank full-throated gulps from cupped hands.

"But you just said—"

"I'm used to it, you aren't." Both men turned to Charlie's voice shouting over their exchange. He called from the raft. George blinked at the bobbing collection of bowed, paint-chipped curves he judged almost twenty feet long and half as wide. The boat's edges didn't quite reach his knees, and the entire vessel creaked and squeaked in the passing current.

"Guess that's our transportation?" George rose and trailed Leaf.

"That's it. You wanna grab that rope?" Leaf nodded toward a frazzled strand of brown cord looped around a broken stump. He removed his pack and leapt off a lower boulder to join Charlie. George shuttled the packs over his head toward Charlie, placing one leg over the low wall, and used his opposing foot to push out into the current.

Water lapped smooth and clear. Leaf grabbed a paddle and dropped to a low bench in the aft. "Gentlemen, if you will both grab a pole, let me do the steering and we'll be miles down the river before you realize we've left. You both need to spot for me. One final request—how about someone tying down that gear?"

"Just how far are we going?" George asked from his side, gripping a bark-stripped hickory pole with both hands and pushing away from impending boulder peaks jutting just above the water surface.

"Considering how late of a start we got, figure about five hours and there's a decent spot to set up camp. We'll get a good night's rest, and it should be no more than a few hours until we reach Mabel's."

Charlie watched the shoreline weave and twist on both sides. He remembered the Triton's acrobatic balancing struggle. Stretches turned dense with hemlock and spruce walls, masking further vision to less than a few yards into the canopy. More turns revealed wide, barren scree stretches.

Other than eroded cliff walls obstructing his view every few turns, high-reaching altitudes towered as backdrops, filtered through clouds. Distinct poplar and tamarack fenced a contrast between elevated blackish green and blinding white. Mountain crests reflected vast mirrors across the landscape.

Occasional caribou wandered from herds and lifted massive antler racks from willows, detecting their passing scent and dashing off into dense brush after lapping from shallow shores. George stood on the raft opposite from Charlie, and their long poles plunged so deep that they skipped along the bottom.

"Good enough," came Leaf's voice rising above rippling water behind them. Charlie over-handed his pole into the raft and wiped ice water running down his wrists. He bent down with his back to the hull.

"Anything I can do?" George asked.

"Sit back and enjoy the ride," Leaf nodded and turned. Charlie's head leaned back, and he savored mid-afternoon sunshine across his face. Continuing cramps faded and he retrieved Absalom's journal from his coat pocket. His eyes scanned pages and columns of numbers, interpreting further deciphers of faded and running scribbles. Spread among multiple pages, analysis of meaningful direction was sprinkled with random bored doodling. He rotated the book at differing perspectives to see if unique angles altered interpretation. Charlie stared and evaluated every letter and word's curve, each choice, and the possible impact of the context of their interrelationship. Many random sentences dealt with hunger, missing his wife, and the struggle for warmth: experiences Charlie had already tasted and realized many more remained.

As with each time he returned to Absalom's writing and struggled to learn new information to assist their search, his fingers skipped through the wrinkled parchment pages and landed on rough stems clinging to the spine where the final keys once flipped. His father's smiling face flashed into dark thoughts. Not realizing the shift, he slipped further down until stretched on his back with his head propped on flour and corn burlap bags. At first, his eyes closed to blot out direct sunshine but soon struggled to open at all.

Charlie couldn't determine the time of afternoon when the first wooden knock thumped beneath his spine. He shot up, startled, and swung his head in every direction. The quiet murmur of passing water was no longer a passive massage in his ears. A rush now churned and boiled just beyond the thin wood shell. To

193

his side, George was down on both knees. He lifted his pole and jammed it forward. The wood shaft jolted in reverse and darted behind his head. Charlie rolled aside and collided into him.

"Hey, think we need some help here," Leaf gritted out between clenched teeth, his own hands rattling in epileptic seizures trying to maintain a tightened grip on the keel with a white fist. Using his pole, Charlie swatted at the massive boulders cracking each side of the raft. Water transformed from a gentle flowing current to a white splashing boil spraying across his face with every pitch and roll. Both he and George grasped the raft's edge while pushing off from immediate appearing rock.

"What happened?" Charlie cried out over the roar, trying to hear the sound of his own question.

"Sorry about this, but I didn't think it would come this early," Leaf shouted a return. George's knees continued slipping out from beneath him, and he took several quick reacting dodges to keep his pole from jumping back up and striking him across the face.

"What? What would come this early?" Charlie panted while thrusting his pole into the boil, arms jerking without control.

"This late in the year, there's still enough heat to melt first snowfalls up in the higher elevations, and it has to go somewhere," Leaf replied. Charlie turned and watched Leaf rise into the air, knees thrown above his shoulders but one hand still locked on the keel handle. He landed with a thump shaking the entire raft, and a contracted wince shot across his usually calm features. He stuck leather boot toes beneath two rope straps just below his bench. "You better do the same unless you feel like a little swim," he nodded at the same rope tack arrangement beneath the other two men.

"This must be sort of like riding a bronco," George shouted and jammed his own boots into his harness.

"Or the Titanic." Charlie quit counting the violent collisions of stone against wood, his eyes continuing a trade between the anticipation of jolts from their immediate course and the possible seepage of water creeping in through cracking planks. The shore was a disorienting rise and fall without bearing. Rather than the previous edging wood copses, canyon walls rose and fell to each side with shattered granite suspensions.

"All right, poles up," came the aft voice. "George, you're on the right and Charlie left. Can't be sure how much more of this we can take. We need some good spotting from both of you. Remember, call out if you see something coming, and if you go in, float on your butt or you might get stuck and sucked under a hydraulic." They followed as instructed, not daring to look one another in the face for a returned glance neither wanted to recognize. Charlie blinked a discern of immense black objects both beneath the water and ragged tips undisguised above sprayed foam. Vision soon adjusted for eddying swirls as possible collision indications.

"Right side, right side, right side," George yelled. Leaf and Charlie shifted as much weight as possible to the left while boxes of glass jars and assorted vegetables collided with the impact. Leaf's keel shuddered beneath his still-whitened grip. Charlie couldn't determine if he steered them away from the boulders or the water controlled their course. The bobbing tip of a slate jagged edge appeared several yards ahead of Charlie. Time allowed for no warning. Again, the three men shifted their weight in the opposite direction with unintentional acrobatics. Charlie exchanged wide dinner-plate eyes with George while wooden crates tossed and glass clinked across the cramped deck. Leaf's cringed stare and refusal to meet either of their eyes responded to whatever questions they could ask.

Charlie focused on the bow of the raft, watching their packs bounce as they flew through the air and crashed back against soaked wood. On the third glance, George leapt from his crouched position and reached out a futile arm. The red packs flew once more, the raft shifted, and they disappeared into boiling foam.

By now, sunlight vanished from their sight. Surrounding hard definitions blurred with hidden, darkened crags while white spray turned blue-gray in the twilight. All three men soaked and squished in the struggle. Charlie caught brief glimpses of George but shuddered from mirrored identification. George's eyes twisted into tight circles of anger. He tasted blood in his mouth, not realizing a bite down on the inside of his cheek.

The shoreline no longer provided an accurate judgment of time passage while he counted the seconds between random thumps and collisions jarring his brace. The second count between thumps diminished. Their hands clutching raft edges eased in deliberation, and the gravel-strewn shore transformed into even, sparse limbs. A sand-stretching line hugged the edge of lapping water.

Charlie turned to Leaf who sat slumped forward with his forearms resting on his knees. Long black hair escaped from his rubber band restraint and hung down over his forehead and across his nose, dripping to the slick jumbled deck. He flexed his hands to return circulation. Charlie looked at his own pale skin and the blisters forming across his palms. George's heaving breaths continued even as the river now no more than trickled and tapped against the hull. Leaf's head rose and he rebanded his soaked braids after wringing out the water.

"Boy, that was some kinda ride. They're gone," George exhaled between forced drawn breaths.

"Didn't I ask someone to tie everything down?" Leaf asked, slinging his ponytail over one shoulder but not expecting a response. "Well, sorry about that. There was a chance that might have happened, and I shoulda known it. We might have done this a little different."

"Let's forget it. We're all still breathing. Much farther you think?" Charlie asked, still balling his hands at the returning tingle while forcing his question through chattering teeth.

"I think we've all had enough excitement for this day," Leaf returned and scanned along the shore length. There," he pointed to an arced cove almost invisible in the rapidly approaching dusk. Charlie grabbed a pole with what wavering strength remained in his biceps. George leaned forward and dropped his head into his arms that were crossed over his knees, avoiding further possible comment. Leaf joined Charlie, and all three men bumped forward as the raft made initial contact with the black sand-covered bottom, lurching to a halt.

Leaf jumped ashore, towing a rope behind him and lashing it to a clawing ash root. Charlie rose and wobbled, using one hand to steady himself against the mast post. George, head still down, remained unmoved. Charlie turned and surveyed the random strewn cargo. Most containers remained intact, but several broken jars were scattered across the deck among torn sacks.

"Not much more light, gentlemen, better act fast. George, how about getting us a little fuel for the fire?" Leaf asked, shoving the axe into his hands. "Charlie, my friend, hadn't planned it this way, but it looks like tonight we're having a dinner of blueberry preserves, boiled corn, and dried fish," Leaf said, looking down and nudging the loose piles with a squishing boot toe.

"Believe it or not, that doesn't sound half bad." Charlie and Leaf took turns flipping the canisters upright and arranging everything back in some sense of order.

"Go on, I'll take care of it. Keep your senses sharp," Leaf requested. Charlie understood. Sloshing in his clothes, he dug the fire pit. A flare of light rose up from behind him.

Charlie turned and identified Leaf's features glowing in a rising lantern hiss. Needing to dry their clothing in the still-falling temperature, George crested back over the hill in silence. The ax handle bobbed in his belt. Both arms were loaded with enough wood that his footing struggled back to the beach.

Leaf and Charlie relieved as much of his burden as they could carry. Charlie was the first to strip away clinging clothes and crouch low to the unlit fire. Leaf huddled over the collection of wood, snapping twigs and hacking splinters off into a pile. He pulled a thin black stone from his shirt pocket and removed his massive Bowie knife, sending sparks shooting into the bundle.

An initial crackle sparked an ensuing flame no larger than a match head. His hands scrambled to snatch more and larger wood pieces until a blaze rose high enough to illuminate the immediate surrounding brush and trunks. It sent a spiral light twist across the smooth-flowing water now widened enough to once more become a river. George and Leaf huddled naked around the fire while Charlie constructed a rough tripod. He filled a pot with water from the river and suspended the handle above licking flames. George gathered broken food containers and sorted their contents.

"Would you both excuse me for a few moments?" Leaf uttered, rising and disappearing over the hill with the drawn knife in his right hand. Charlie glanced across the firelight to watch the reflected whiteness of George's chattering teeth.

"Aw, man, what a failure. Never should have come along, never should have burdened you like this."

"No, no more, I don't want to hear another single word. Gup, he told both of us to lash everything down. This isn't your fault. It was just as much my responsibility as yours. Anyway, we're alive, we're safe, and we have a meal." George allowed the slightest twitch across his still-shaking jaw.

"She was pregnant." George's head dropped into his crossed forearms.

"Who was pregnant?"

"Deb. I never told you. I never told anyone." Charlie listened to the wavers of his cracking voice.

"Aw, Gup." George's back arched and sank in repeated motions.

"The most important woman I've ever known in my life was lost that day along with my son or daughter. Maybe, just maybe, if we can find what we came to look for, you won't have to repeat what I've already lived." Charlie rose and circled the fire, crouching next to George. He leaned over and squeezed George's right hand. George's own head rose with firelight reflecting across his glistening cheeks.

"Don't know about you, but I'm getting a might hungry and we're eating good tonight. Might just eat it raw," he bellowed.

Charlie released a long, low, satisfying belch and motioned the last remnants of his fish in George's direction. "No, not another bite," George signaled a hand at Charlie. Leaf rose, gathered the remaining scraps, tossed them into flowing water, and rubbed sand across the bottom of the pan. All three men reclined around the fire, listening to the sizzle of steam boiling out of their clothing. The rough black sand was dry and cold against Charlie's exposed skin. "So Leaf, your Aunt Meredith, you close with her?"

"Guess as close as any of us. Why do you ask?"

"Just curious."

"You got a little thing for her, don't you?"

"What makes you say that?"

"Because you've been talking about her every other moment since we left," Charlie added. George said nothing more, turning and smiling.

"Anybody else tired as me?" Leaf commented without allowing his eyes to wander from the fire's hypnotism. Neither man chose words to react as George yawned a gaping hole followed by a repeat from Charlie. A brisk wind channeled down the valley with a clear, star-filled sky above. Charlie inched even closer to the flames, drawing a fine line between warmth and discomfort. He approached to absorb maximum heat but not allow the flames to char the hair off his forearms. "If we've timed this right, should only be another three hours or so until Mabel's. Make it there early enough, and we can set out right after lunch. Who wants first watch?" he asked, now sitting up and cross-legged. George offered no immediate reply, and Charlie's head tilted to one side. "Guess that answers my question," he rose and shouldered Charlie's Winchester. Charlie rose with a long stretch and both arms extended. "Remember, there are still a lot of provisions in that boat."

"Come on, Gup," Charlie bent over and extended an open hand. George grabbed it in reluctance and released his own version of Charlie's reaction. They stumbled toward branches spread across the sand.

Charlie's eyelids no longer resisted the weight pulling them together until he saw something. The indecision of whether it was a random shadow cast by the dwindling fire or the haze descending across his vision pushed them into full scanning mode.

A low branch bent with a slow curve, delicate willow fingers pulling it down until snapping back upright. He knew he saw the hand; he knew he saw both the wrist and forearm further rising toward a shoulder. Curling auburn hair bounced over a white knit sweater and succumbed to the swirling shadows absorbing a dimpled cheek. Charlie's head rose and he blinked away the cold. Refocusing, his limbs stretched without movement, and the ground rose to meet nothing more than highlighted stillness. Charlie shook his head, rolled towards the fire, and drifted off to the sound of the crackle.

CHAPTER

19

Charlie awoke to morning sparrow trills. He turned and saw George's vacant bough pile. He yawned, turning over with palms digging into morning-wet, darkened pebbles. George hunched over the fire, pouring coffee as black as used engine oil. His bloodshot eyes strained to see above puffing suspended baggage. Leaf leaned over the raft wall, running his finger along seams between the planks.

After Charlie adjusted his vision, he noticed numerous dents and discolorations from the previous afternoon's constant collisions. "So what do you think? She gonna get us there?" Charlie cried out after George shoved a full tin cup into his hands. Leaf swayed on his heels with crossed arms while his sight remained locked on the dents and paint chips. He scratched his forehead and turned.

"Looks bad but I don't see any separation. At least nothing I can feel, and there doesn't seem to be any sign of water inside. Guess there's only one way we're going to find out."

Charlie detached himself from yesterday's carnival ride by maintaining concentration on Charlotte. Still, his eyes couldn't resist wandering in an examination of the hull plank seams every few moments. Within minutes, he caught George in the same exercise.

Brush trembled at their passing movement. An occasional pair of antlers emerged from black-green branches interspersed with still-clinging gold and yellow. Birds took to flight but calm silence returned. "Don't worry, I'm keeping an eye on it," Leaf tried reassuring them from his aft post.

"Sure was quite a bit of damage," Charlie remarked and scanned across the broken crates and soaked bags.

"Can't argue that but there should still be enough for the exchange, though. She scares a lot of folks, but I always sort of liked her." Charlie's sustained cough punctuated the conclusion of Leaf's sentence. "You all right? That sounded deep."

"It's nothing." Charlie stated, trying to convince himself. He hadn't admitted the cold sweats running down his neck and back since they woke. Even in the chilled morning air, the lump in his throat turned dry and scratching, swelling from a slight itch to where it seemed as if he had swallowed an apple whole.

"Man, you don't look too good. Honestly, your face is white," George commented with a contraction devoid of encouragement. "My own fault anyway. Probably wouldn't have frozen if I had tied everything down." Charlie glanced down at his hands in the sudden realization that they became a pair of swollen hams beyond his wrists, one rising to wipe sweat rolling from his temples.

"Gup, I don't want to hear any more of that."

"Why don't you take a little break—current's strong enough to carry us the rest of the way," Leaf finished and raised his paddle from the water, tossing a water bag in Charlie's direction. He offered no protest and swallowed, wincing at the passage of liquid down his swollen esophagus.

"What sort of exchange are you talking about?" George asked.

"Exchange for the mule to help carry the rest of this stuff and hopefully whatever we find back with us."

"Makes sense."

"There, look," Leaf pointed ahead and to their right.

"I don't see anything but a big log sticking out over the water," George stared with a hand shading his brow. Leaf dropped a paddle back in the water and rowed instead of steered. The raft trudged along rippling water until just nudging the fallen red cedar. George jumped and tied off the rope. Charlie rose to his feet with too much speed, and his knees buckled until he gripped the side wall.

"Easy does it," Leaf approached him and steadied one arm. "Follow me," he instructed after all three men scaled a narrow gap in the hillside and a path appeared. It wound into dense growth spreading apart and forming a tunnel. Little sunlight penetrated through the clogged, intertwining branches. Leaf began chanting again, a rolling hum of his father's language. Through faint bird calls and overhead anonymous screeches, a voice echoed the repeating three-word chant. The duet grew louder until they passed an entrance and all light sources vanished. The pebble-strewn trail beneath their feet turned level, and Charlie strained to identify the two outlines ahead of him. Leaf's voice became an echo, reverberating off stone walls until a glowing light increased in luminescence ahead. As it approached, surrounding walls lit up, and a hunched-over black figure appeared at the far end of the corridor.

The shadow swung a shaking lantern. Charlie and George both stopped while Leaf sped ahead and wrapped an arm around the hunched back.

"Charlie, George, I want you to meet Mabel." They approached with hesitant steps while she raised the lantern in front of her, masking any features. Charlie extended a hand. She moved the raised lantern to one side of her face and took two steps forward. She was wrapped in a bright green, red, and yellow blanket. Her face and a few wisps of stringy white hair escaped from the edges. Her crooked nose taper leapt out from between a pair of sunken eyeballs.

If not from the wrinkles spanning in every direction from where her ears should have hung, Charlie thought her profile would have been no more than the thinnest of skin stretched across a bare skull. Her gray eyes twitched, and her shrinking pupils darted around their sockets. Her head bent even further towards him. She gave a few brief sniffs and released a howling screech causing George to almost loose his footing and fall into a fissure. Her blanket jumped and furled while her feet kicked sand in every direction. The lantern danced and swayed as if she had caught fire while nonsensical wailing echoed from her lips.

"Whoa!" George cried out. Even Leaf leaned back and brought both hands in front of him.

"Charlie, sorry about that. She smells the auineckti."

"The what?"

"She senses you have great sickness."

"Already told you I'm not feeling great, but it's not like the Black Plague or anything," Charlie defended himself with a cough and sniffle. Mabel calmed down enough to again raise her lantern.

However, her other arm shifted beneath the blanket, and the distinctive shine of polished steel rose through the separated edges until Charlie stared down an over-under shotgun's straight barrels. All three men froze while she spit out a two-syllable word.

"So she'll already know we're coming?" George couldn't resist.

"Mabel, Mabel, Mabel, don't get so excited, we need your help," Leaf's voice cracked with one hand lifting the barrels toward the damp passageway ceiling. "The auineckti is supposed to be a sign that you have an evil spirit in you and you're unbalanced with the Earth."

"Hey, this isn't a choice I made to get sick," Charlie exasperated with a nasal-intoned protest. Charlie twinged from the instant waves of regret and his poor word choice. He didn't turn to see George's reaction. Leaf twisted with his back toward them and leaned down to whisper in her ear.

"Come on, Mabel said she'll help you out." The shrinking blanket-wrapped frame tottered to the rear of the passageway, expanding into a high cavern. Oil lamps spanned the room with smaller cubicles dug out around the wall's edges. A blazing fire burned in the center where rolling smoke plumes rose and exited through a hole above their heads. Charlie noticed natural light filtering through the opening. Various proportioned roots penetrated through the jagged ceiling, some dangling low enough to almost brush their hair. Various bottles and carved wooden bowls covered several tables.

George reached out toward one of the multiple dried-leaf platters when a snapping bark rose in Mabel's throat. His hand jerked back in recognition. Leaf said nothing but shook his head with a stern glance reflecting across his eyes.

Mabel dropped her blanket, revealing a thinner frame than Charlie had imagined. Beaded shells were draped around her neck along with the teeth of various animals, dried pods, and wooden trinkets. She clattered while hobbling from side to side like a human wind chime. A few mumbled words in Leaf's direction and she disappeared around a corner.

"Come, sit," Leaf commanded and all three men took to the ground on dust-penetrated caribou hides. Charlie collapsed in a shaking ball while a dizzying array caused his eyes to protrude from their sockets. Mabel returned with two cups, and steam rolled across their tops.

"Nothing for me?" Charlie joked. She vanished and returned with a third cup as she motioned it toward Charlie. He sampled a few sips, and his face contorted in uncontrollable directions he never thought possible. "Hope this isn't what you guys are drinking." Mabel snorted a slight crackling laugh.

"Don't worry, she said it's just what you need to restore your balance and drive out the auineckti." Charlie drank half the cup as liquid heat soothed his swollen neck. Staring down at the cup's rim, he soon counted multiple cups.

Flames phased in and out of definition while he sensed his back folding and his head rolling against the well-worn fur of the hide. Although not abandoned to complete unconsciousness, he no longer sensed the passage of time. Various voices murmured around him while the ceiling and walls melted into one.

"What time is it?" Charlie heard George's distinct voice.

"Late. You know as well as I do that every second we wait, the sooner that snow is coming down to stay."

"I know, I know, but look at him," Leaf whispered a return. Both men returned to silence with Mabel's faint chattering echoing somewhere on his perception's edge. A rank smell entered Charlie's nose so foul he could no longer return to sleep.

"Think we should go back?" George's voice broke the chant. Leaf didn't reply as he stared at Charlie's shaking frame beneath his woolen blanket. Sweat across his forehead and temples trembled while he gripped the blanket's edges, trying to maintain some control over the seizures. One hand slipped from the blanket to grope the journal's hard edge within his coat pocket. Charlotte spun on her merry-go-round, the sound punctuated by calliope notes.

"I don't know how much choice we have. There's no way someone in his condition is going to make it through that kind of terrain. This is my land. I've grown up around these mountains and valleys my entire life, and I know what this territory will do to a man if it doesn't get the proper respect."

"Then I guess it's settled," George said, releasing a reluctant sigh.

"No—no—not going—back," Charlie's voice broke and trembled. His hand darted back beneath the blanket, and his teeth clenched together. He exhaled and rolled to one side, glaring at the two men opposite the fire.

"You're up," George turned and called as if unaware of the words from his previous utterance. Leaf stepped around the flames to crouch down at Charlie's side.

"We, we are not going back. I'm going if I have to do it alone," Charlie snarled with his assertion increasing deliberate punctual assurance.

"Shhhhh, keep quiet, we'll talk about it later." Charlie's head fell back into the fur, releasing any remaining energy he might have collected. Time passed in blurred mental images of immediate and distant memories along with smells and the sounds of cavern echoes. At moments, he saw Leaf and George's faces hovering above him.

Charlotte knelt beside him, swabbing his forehead with a cool wet cloth while he couldn't help but to turn and bathe in her smile. Drops of water trickled into his ears while she brushed his hair back from his forehead. Mabel's chanting notes resonated near his ears.

Rather than a wood-burning crackle, the first sound entering Charlie's senses was the far-away whistle of a morning songbird answered by a more distant, less melodic response. The primal odor of cured hide filled his nostrils, and he shifted with a soft spring lightness against his back. Nausea and delirium faded into intermittent memory with tension returning to his abdomen. He took the first few hesitant gulps of wetness on his lips, and although some thickness remained, he swallowed with less tight, throat-forced resistance.

A repetitive mechanical thrusting scrape became an undertone in the singing bird tempo. His eyes remained closed. Each easier, peaceful, savored breath was interrupted in an instant.

A warm, slick mass curled across Charlie's cheek. It was followed with the breath of rotten decay washing over and swirling through his nose. He inhaled and snapped upright onto his elbows, shaking away any last fleeting cobwebs into the still morning air.

An enormous brown eyeball stared into his own. Thick black eyelashes brushed against his skin while broad yellow teeth reflected dull light. Charlie reverse crawled and a tree trunk halted his backward progress.

"Hey there," George sounded from above him. Charlie saw nothing more than his boot bottom ridges while he roosted in a low-hanging branch and dropped to the pine needle-covered ground. He stooped to one knee, pulling back on the reins of the animal stirring Charlie from his sleep. The mule whinnied and shook its dust-clouding mane, clomping one front hoof and turning to nibble on salmon berries.

"My head," Charlie winced and rubbed his temples.

"Don't worry, Mabel said it'll pass by noon," Leaf joined them. Charlie rubbed the haze from his eyes and scanned the immediate surroundings. They sat on the edge of a wide field with painted aspens poking along the edge of rolling wild grass.

"Where are we?" Charlie coughed.

"Mabel said the last part of your balancing required a reconnection with the land. So here we are, out on the land." Leaf stopped sharpening his knife and wiped the glistening blade on his pants leg. He cut a piece of dried meat and tossed a sliver toward Charlie. His cheeks contracted with the saltiness in his mouth and the return of flavor while George shoved a water bag into his other hand.

"And Miss Maggie has already introduced herself," Leaf followed and rubbed his hand down the mule's back, teeth baring an appreciative whinny. The animal paid no attention to her load of bags and supplies while continuing to forage around the immediate ground. Charlie sat up cross-legged and stared at the hide covering his legs.

"I meant what I said." Neither of the two men answered his assertion. Leaf turned an eye toward George and wandered back to the thinning mix of dogwood and asters whisking around his knees.

"Charlie, gotta admit, you had us awful worried the night before last," George now sat also cross-legged beside him.

"The night before last?"

"You've been out for almost two days." George picked up a pair of brown pine needles, rolled them between his fingers, and stuck them into the corner of his mouth.

"Gup, we've come too far to go back now. Every time I go to sleep, I can only see her face staring up at me in the darkness of that bed," he concluded with the remnant of a cough and took an extended gulp from the water skin.

"You oughta know by now I'd do anything for you, but if you get too sick you won't be doing her or anyone else any good." George pulled the pine needles from his mouth. Charlie laughed. "What?"

"Something Karen said to me. Charlotte and Karen. Sometimes you've just got to believe." The final word of Charlie's statement was accentuated by the previous singing bird exchange.

"Is that what you really want to do?" George recognized the answer without need for a response. "I've known you long enough that when your mind is made up, no more questions are needed. Leaf said the old lady is going to help us out."

"Help us out, how?"

"Take a look," George said and pointed to a pile of gear and backpacks leaned against a boulder. George rose to his feet. "If you're still too ill to walk, I'll carry you over my shoulders. Made you a promise and it's one I intend to keep." George extended his hand downwards where Charlie grabbed his forearm with an exhalation, steadying himself back against the trunk.

"Is the trail cold?" Leaf's voice reappeared.

"Just getting warmed up," Charlie asserted.

CHAPTER

20

$\mathbf{A}$head in varying degrees of perception, a black outline stumbled with increasing repetition as footing approaches shifted over uneven scree and lupine scattered along their game trail. George's body weight shifted above dotting emerald leaves, legs rising stiff with each forward lunge. The path grew more unidentifiable and transformed from intermittent low patched reedgrass and broken shale stretches to a smoother rising terrain, increasing and shortening his forced breaths.

Earlier carefree strides with arms swinging at his sides and mechanical deliberate footing now devolved into short hesitant steps, and by his most recent estimation, four near head-first tumbles to the ground. Each time, he leaned just enough to one side and avoided collapsing.

Leaf was far ahead. Whatever he lacked in speed, he now more than compensated for in distance. George reached Charlie during yet another low ninety-degree bend at the waist, grabbing both knees. George's face faded to slick pale beneath gasps like those of a drowning man just resurfacing the water for a final breath. Charlie knew not to needle George about the earlier harassment of Leaf's pace.

"Hey," Charlie called over to no more than desperate thin wheezing. Charlie hesitated for a moment and reclined on an angled stone slope, first checking for any small animals occupying the stress fractures along its face. He released his own exaggerated sigh and shuddered in hope that understood mutual agony might ease some of George's low-eyed discomfort. Hands dropped and rubbed his hamstrings, over accentuating his own need for a break. "Ain't this one of the toughest?" he called ahead. George squinted behind him, still bent over but his gasps easing once focusing on Charlie. A glint rose at the shared strain recognition. Neither required identifying the scrapes and reddened patches across cheeks and foreheads from pushing through stinging brush. "Thought the mosquitoes were all supposed to be gone by this time of year. Can't tell if my eyes are swollen from bites or sweat."

"Can't keep up with me, huh?"

"Gup," Charlie forced, "Ain't slowing down yet. Almost makes me want to be on the back of that truck again wondering if any of those three-ton logs would roll over on our heads." Once walking side by side, neither spoke again, their matching cadence swooshing through hollow, tall wild rye. Each man surveyed his own piece of territory in remaining twilight.

"Been kinda quiet. Wanna share anything?" George stopped, hesitating long enough to turn and twist his lower back in contortions.

"Just wondering what they're doing right now. What if we've come all this way and discover it was either a hoax or a terrible exaggeration?" Charlie swallowed.

"Look at it this way: Even if we return with no more than the few dollars we had when we left, will Karen love you any less? Or Charlotte for that matter?" Charlie couldn't help glancing from his boots to his ring and turning it a full rotation before forming a smirk. Brushing the gold, a laugh broke from his throat. "What's so funny?"

"Can you believe that no more than a few weeks before Grampy's funeral, I came this close to pawning this ring?" Charlie asked, holding his thumb and forefinger in a narrow gap.

"She would have killed you," George returned.

"Yeah, maybe, but it was our anniversary. I wanted to take her away from everything. Even if for no more than a few hours, take her to a fine meal at an expensive restaurant, maybe a little dancing. You remember how much she loves to dance?" George nodded. "Then, just a quiet, silent evening listening to our old scratched albums."

"Deb and I shared a lot of those times together. She and Karen were a lot alike, but you don't wanna know what would have happened if she saw this ring missing from my finger," he grinned and spun his band. "You think it's strange that I still wear this?" he asked and held up a clenched fist.

"Any stranger than two grown men searching for buried treasure?"

"See Leaf yet?" George asked and peered into the vanishing vegetation ahead with one hand across his eyebrows. Charlie dropped the backpack straps from his shoulders and leaned forward with an audible breath release. Charlie hesitated but rejoined the visual scan, squinting to pick out shapes and forms. "There," he pointed, "that's him."

"Better keep moving." Both breathing rates resumed normal, but their pack remount was in slow motion with deliberate intent. A low crescent moon's faint glimmer guided their forward path. Night sounds scurried around them, snapping twigs and brushing leaves not known from the result of air movement or unseen spectators.

Flashing pinpoints of reflecting eyes peered from long-shadowed bottom and top-reaching branches, and there was chattering over the two-legged wanderers passing below them. From the dusk blend of blue-and-black horizon beyond, Charlie first identified a distant flickering pinpoint of light.

"Am I just tired or do you see what I see?" he stopped, balling up both fists and rubbing his eyes. George's earlier missteps became premeditated and forceful. They arrived with Leaf down on one knee, his cheeks fierce balloons and one ear almost to the ground while breathing life into a struggling flame. His braid fell over to one side, and he whipped it back over a shoulder to prevent catching any of the scurrying embers.

Leaf's fire-illuminated profile turned. Charlie couldn't discern any of his features but sensed a faint relaxing contentment within the silhouette of his face welcoming the arriving stragglers.

"Tonight, we stop here. Don't think I can take another step!" he declared with emphasis and shot to his feet without hesitation. George wiggled his arms from his straps and dropped his load, oblivious to sarcasm, and scooted next to the fire. Leaf resumed his tending of the young embers, now adding thicker, dry, snapped branches. "This fire isn't going to feed itself," Leaf instructed and nodded toward Charlie.

Charlie dropped his own burden. He thought of prodding George's assistance, but his eyes were already flame locked in a hypnotic glow. Maggie's breath was regular and wheezing, mane twitching as her head sank.

"If you think you've got enough to last the night, triple it," Leaf muttered in a partial lecture between his own full lung exhalations and crackling wood, eyes narrowed for heat protection.

"Hope it doesn't get too cramped in that thing tonight," Charlie observed while George stretched on his knees, unrolling the sewn caribou hides across the most open, flattest area beneath a high, branched pine.

"Don't worry, I need stars over my head," Leaf asserted through the twilight and lashed Maggie to a fallen birch. Charlie retrieved a hatchet from his pack, wandering into an ancient spruce cluster with limbs shattered like a giant's random scattered bone fragments. The firelight glow at his back faded into the dusk with no more than the moon's glow illuminating his footing.

Thigh ache pulsed with each swing, but Charlotte's face, scratched forearms, and sunken eye sockets under white linen distilled adrenalin into his bloodstream. With each clear vision, the hatchet head fell in more pronounced chopping strokes. Following Leaf's instructions, a stacked, low firewood wall encircled the fire's edge. By his fifth return, George lashed the ropes and erected the hide structure in a lean-to from arching branches.

Leaf didn't bother looking up, humming a discordant string of notes beneath his breath. Closed eyes and a backward tilted head, he subtly swayed before the fire. Charlie knew Leaf sensed the presence of his return along with every other surrounding sight and sound. He stood waiting for the end of Leaf's prayer, not wanting to break the reverence.

"Thought I might need to go looking for you," Leaf called out with still-closed eyes. "By the way, we voted, you're taking second watch." Charlie poked at the embers with a long shaved stick. "Hope those rifles Tyler gave you won't have to be used for anything more than hunting rabbit. Keep on your senses—Maggie has earned a much longer life." Charlie acknowledged with a nod and slight trigger brush. "You'll take over from Mr. Gupford at one o'clock, and I'll see the early light.

Remember, do not let this fire go out, or we'll all be getting awfully chilled come morning."

Charlie pushed his watch knob and the circular face illuminated. He yawned, recognizing that even near midnight, a thin pink shell's lining haze fringed above the jagged hill contour. His eyes returned to the fire glow without glancing up in agreement. Leaf vanished with nothing but bent twigs into the thicket. George took over, stirring embers and shifting logs.

"Guess it's just us again," Charlie muttered and released another uncontrollable yawn. George remained a thousand miles away, knees folded up to his chin and a slight sway to the few pinpoint embers swirling into purple-black above their heads. "You can't be that tired. We couldn't have done more than fifteen miles today." George's head snapped up and he rubbed his earlobes. "Look, sorry if I got you out here—"

"Stop, don't say anymore," George cut him short and resumed swirling in the ashes.

"Whatever you say, Gup," Charlie stretched and slapped his friend across the shoulder.

"I'm here because I want to be here. It's my own decision to help you." George stared at the fire with reflections glowing across his corneas. "What more can I do after almost getting you killed?"

"You still going on about those backpacks?" George retained his quiet. "Do me a favor?" George flicked an eye across the flames. "No more. We're alive and warm." George turned up to meet Charlie's stare, detecting the faintest glimmer of stained teeth between the stubble of George's jaw. "Hey, at least this is more comfortable than sleeping in that rusty Quonset hut beneath the snowplows. You're gonna be all right," Charlie called out for a final time. He vanished into the lean-to and dropped the flap.

"If I hear a roar, I'll holler out," George replied with a far-away voice, brushing the barrel across one cheek. Charlie took a final cautious glance into the dark brush and rising black mountain outlines. Flames flickered and danced through sewn-hide fissures while he yanked and pulled off his boots. Air rushed across his tender soles.

CHAPTER

21

Charlie returned from chopped, intermittent dream images and cracked one eye. Beyond the gilded prospect of dawn's sunlight shafts spraying shattered diamond-diffused reflections, he noticed leaves trembling in fresh arctic gasps. Auburn curls flashed and skipped into a dogwood copse.

Leaf vanished while George snorted and buried himself deeper into his sleeping bag within the shelter. Charlie sat up, rubbing his eyes and yawning. Once his sight focused, another noticeable shrub distortion concentrated his attention. He slipped on his boots and jumped to his feet, trailing the last obscured branch bend. This time, he knew what he saw.

A narrow stream's gurgle splashed and slapped between splintered granite, disappearing into an open chasm. Emerald green moss defined the mineral contours as the ground swallowed with heaving gulps. A wren sang to her mate and jumped flutter steps between overhead branches. He crouched low beside the stream with dew soaking into his knees, cupping hands into the flowing liquid ice and splashing it across his face. No sooner had he lifted a shirttail to dry his eyes than a screech echoed and shot Charlie backwards onto the reed grass. Less than a few yards away, brown-speckled feathers cloaked the new morning sun's rays. Fine white down feathers molded slick around the contours of a bald eagle's skull. Its head and shoulders dropped low while crystal-yellow eyes locked onto Charlie's own stare of disbelief.

They studied one another. The raptor cocked his head to one side, a perfect black round pupil widening and tightening within a golden-dusted circle. Pulling feathers close against his body, his tail shook and a nubby tongue jumped from between his inward curved beak.

Charlie froze.

Rather than anticipating an imminent attack and placing both hands on the ground, a slow ease rolled across his brow. Their locked stare continued even during the mutual head-tilting study. Charlie examined the lay of his feathers and his strutting balance while the eagle inspected the man's clumsy gestures. After a time passage neither could determine, the eagle released another piercing, glass-shattering screech and leapt into the air. Buffeting air shocks rolled across Charlie's cheeks as the bird ascended and vanished over the treetops.

Charlie sat in silence before another brush movement behind him. "Hey there, C.S., we were getting worried," George called through the clearing. Charlie rose and followed him back to camp. Several far-off gunshots sounded through the air. He knew he would never tell either Leaf, George, or anyone else about the morning encounter. In fact, Charlie knew that one day, there was only one woman whom he would ever be able to tell.

Maggie chortled into the morning's first awareness. She clomped the sponge-springing tundra, nuzzled across thin birch trunks, and peeled away sheets in translucent, speckled-gray paper nibbles. After each nuzzle, her ribcage rose and fell with mucous bursts. Charlie returned to closed-eye solitude and managed drifting back into dreams. He no longer resisted the physical need for urination while buzzing mosquitoes slapped against his exposed nose and eyelids.

Crawling from the shelter, Charlie removed both sweaters required for sleep while the eagle's memory still clutched his thoughts, uncertain if the encounter was real or no more than a dream. The smells of coffee and frying meat pulled his attention toward Leaf and George, huddled around the fire and talking between themselves. George turned at the opening flap.

"Good morning, sunshine," George blurted with annoying chirpiness and a long slurp from his aluminum cup. "Should have met the morning a bit earlier, coffee's all gone." Charlie blinked away the haze. Over George's shoulder, Leaf erected a green stick grid above the flames, and a black soot-covered kettle boiled and shuddered.

Coals were pushed to one side within the stone ring, and five crude whittled skewers stabbed miniature red-brown carcasses. Juices ran down their shining skin and sizzled into red embers. Charlie shot a direct glare at George and disappeared into the brush.

"Yeah, I can tell you two are the best of friends," Leaf commented, retrieving another identical soot-covered cup, splashing black coffee to the rim, and moving it toward Charlie after he reemerged. Smoke billowed from the fire. Leaf tossed short, green spruce twigs into the ring. Setting his own cup aside, he fanned smoke across his face and shoulders with open palms. "Come on, both of you, smoke bath is the best thing in the morning. Keeps the stink away along with these mosquitoes," Leaf motioned. Charlie and George followed his suggestion.

All three men shrouded themselves in billowing rising clouds. In addition to the sizzling skewers, several round pancakes steamed on a flat stone next to Leaf. "Just about done, my friends. This morning is a breakfast of coffee, squirrel, and corn cakes. Eat the bones too if you can, good calcium," Leaf concluded with both arms crossing his chest. Charlie grabbed a skewer. He traded between pulling at the meat and shoving fingers back into his mouth to cool. Each struggling grind extracted minutes between concentrated teeth for the lean scraps.

"Little butter and red wine would make this go down a whole lot easier," George added. No discussion continued as Leaf turned and raised an eyebrow every few moments from Maggie's anxious braying.

"The missus seems a bit antsy this morning, don't ya think?" Charlie interrupted his lip smacking. Even the finches ceased their songs and flutter hopping between the branches.

"Noticed it started yesterday around noon. A mule can sense a lot more than they usually get credit for." Leaf's words remained, scanning brush camouflage to the depth his vision allowed. Sunlight crested the hill with full sparkling reflection off their rifle barrels, shining morning dew in hue and color arrays. He rose, drifting past Charlie and George.

"See something?" George asked and turned, trying to focus on the object of Leaf's examination.

"No, guess it's nothing." He reclined back on the sphagnum with an arm behind his head and released a passionate belch.

"We got a long haul ahead of us, and if you don't mind, I'm heading down to the creek with the old lady here and top off our water," George said as he rose and unhitched the rope. Maggie gave a short-pitched snort, stretching her neck high with sedges poking out between dough-puffed lips. Charlie drank the final sips from his can while George disappeared through the thicket and descended the slope.

"Leaf, that was one fine breakfast considering we're out in the middle of nowhere," Charlie remarked and threw remaining bones into the fire. "How'd you learn to cook like that?" Charlie reclined on the opposite side of the fire with feet resting on the flat stone. He stared between parting overhead branches and through the depth of blue. Charlotte's face mirrored back at him.

"I've been handy at cooking every kind of animal that can walk, crawl, or swim. Mom's always been an excellent cook, but Dad is even better." Leaf now sat up, swirling coals with his skewer. "One of my earliest memories was Mom and Dad in the kitchen or Dad and I out on a hunt. No matter what time of year, snow or sun, he always had some kind of breakfast ready for me and my brothers and sisters."

"Can't imagine Creektoe over a frying pan," Charlie laughed and picked charred meat from between his teeth.

"Oh, believe it. And what he could do with salmon, deer, seal, you name it. Yeah—" Leaf's voice mumbled away with a remembering smirk as he stared into the fire. "How about your folks?"

"Oh, not much. Mom worked a lot and passed early when I was young." Charlie caught himself in the same morning flame rapture while dangling his own twig and watching the flames lick green inner fibers.

"And your dad?" Leaf pressed.

"Rather not talk about him," Charlie's voice snapped from the fire. George and Maggie emerged from the alders, and he released her reins. "Now, my Grampy—Creektoe reminds me a good deal of him." Charlie's words didn't have enough time to register.

A fierce wail sent Maggie up on both hind legs with hooves punching in the air. The birch branch securing her rope snapped tight and splintered from the pressure. Her initial echoing lung gasp was followed by another until a series of terrified screams rose above all other surrounding natural sounds. Leaf and Charlie jumped to their feet in unison. Leaf draped an arm across Maggie's heaving ribs, trying to restore the animal's calm.

"What on earth is that?" Charlie called over the snorting and stomping. George shrugged and shook his head, checking the chamber of his Browning.

"That way," Leaf pointed with his own rifle now gripped tight to one side. He led the other two men down the game trail. Leaf's knees reached higher until breaking into a full run, branches whipping across his face and slapping back across the followers. The yelling grew louder as Charlie plunged downwards, breath struggling to push in and out of his lungs. His legs were slow to respond, and George's flashing shape grew more obscure in the distance.

Fifty yards ahead down the trail, the brush cleared and Leaf sank low behind a massive fallen trunk. Leaf grabbed George by his shirttail, anticipating further questions, and yanked him down to the velvet, green, moss-covered ground. Charlie's pace dropped to a creeping, chest-heaving advance until joining them. He poked above the bark-decaying trunk and saw the figure of man clinging to the highest branches of a young hemlock.

The height attained by the man reached a point where the trunk leaned to one side beneath his weight's pressure. No intelligible words other than an endless yelling of "Go, git, go, get outta here" flew in repeated random successions above their heads.

"What is that smell?" George asked with a contorted expression. Leaf turned as if to place a clamped hand across George's mouth. Instead, he rose and steadied the butt of his rifle against his shoulder. Through a splash of green, splattering ripples and darker defining contrasts, Charlie glimpsed the briefest flash of shaggy chocolate fur tinted with silver tips and washed honey. He turned toward and recognized nothing more than Leaf's profile.

Leaf's breathing stopped; he aimed and squeezed the trigger. The round's crack exploding through the barrel echoed off surrounding hills and tore through a strained sapling's bark. Defiant roars returned in protest, and the grizzly switching back and forth in paces around the tree now rose on both hind legs, broad front claws pawing the air in their direction. Her shadow blotted out the sun while their eyes widened to focus on yellow curved teeth snapping between her jaws, flecks of spittle flinging through the air.

"That's a momma," Leaf observed under his breath. The bear turned its head to one side and released a roar from the depth of her hair-bristling chest. Leaf steadied his rifle one more time, and the shot ricocheted off a granite boulder no more than a foot from her right rear leg.

The impact transmitted more intention than actually penetrating flesh. It backed away, turning and trotting farther down the hill in short snorting gallops. George hurdled over the log after the last brushing twigs ceased their movements behind her.

"Gup! Hold on, make sure that thing ain't coming back," Charlie called out still behind his fallen timber wall.

"You can come down now," George called up at the base of the bent hemlock. Leaf joined him, reloading and flicking his safety back into position.

"If I were you, I wouldn't be hanging around up there any longer than I had to. That was a she grizzly, and I guarantee her little ones are wandering somewhere around here." After Leaf finished, the figure high above their heads turned down to the two men staring up at him. He hyperventilated and shimmied with broken exclamations during his snapping-twig descent. The man's back remained toward Charlie by the time his feet reached the ground and he bent over, rubbing his biceps. His white hair was disheveled, and the yellow smock raincoat he wore was torn in multiple random patches. He straightened gold-rimmed round glasses, squinted, and rubbed bleeding scrapes from bark across exposed skin.

Charlie and the stranger locked eyes.

Neither man spoke, just staring at one another. Leaf and George exchanged glances, turning back to them. Charlie's eye sank to the wetness coating his boot toes. He slung his rifle again and headed up the game trail back toward Maggie.

"Gentlemen, I am forever in your debt," the man said as he retrieved a handkerchief from his pocket and wiped his lenses clean.

"That was close, too close. Lucky you're not in that bear's stomach right now," Leaf commented with steadier words.

"You literally snatched me from the jaws of death, young man," he asserted and extended an open palm toward Leaf. Once George focused on the figure, his jaw moved and swung back in confirmation of the original perception. With one hand on his hip, he could do no more than run his other fingers through his hair. "Ben," George nodded with the final pronunciation of a complete word.

"You two know each other?" Leaf asked with rising eyebrows while leaning forward on the barrel of his rifle.

"You could say that," George replied while the stranger ascended toward Charlie's previous direction.

"Charlie seems to be reacting a little odd, don't ya think? So where do you know him from? Charlie know him, too?" Leaf continued.

"Oh, he knows him all right." George stopped and turned, the corner of his mouth in an upward twitch. "That's his father."

By the time the other three returned to camp, Charlie extinguished the fire, rolled up the tarp, packed his gear, and strapped down the final buckles across Maggie's back. Benjamin hobbled behind Leaf and George.

"Sorry we can't offer you much to eat. Already had breakfast, but you're more than welcome to help yourself to a little jerky," Leaf tossed a few scraps to Benjamin who chewed with frantic vigor and choked, almost swallowing the smoked venison whole. George packed his own gear in silence. Charlie had yet to glance again at Benjamin, still keeping his back toward him. "So, what brings you to these parts, Ben?" Leaf asked, still uncertain in the continuing silence.

"Just a little sightseeing."

"Liar," Charlie muttered in a release low and deliberate, the rush of blood filling the whites of his eyes. He gripped the reins in both hands and held them tight against his chest. "You've been following us for a while, haven't you?"

"Just because a man wants to get in the great outdoors and do some hunting doesn't mean he has some sort of ulterior motive, does it?" Benjamin asked. His voice retained a collective meter.

"Right, Benny, among the millions of square acres in the Canadian wilderness, anyone would just expect to run into their father," Charlie spit.

CHAPTER

22

No longer able to tell the sky's color, Charlie failed to negotiate a blind root jutting from shale projections. Acid, accumulated in his thighs, short-circuited any defensive coordination, and he flew face forward, both palms outward to break the brunt of the fall. Neither George nor Leaf heard or even noticed the impact or collapse. Charlie stretched flat on the pillow-cushioning tundra with one cheek pressed against caressing sphagnum, still moist and cold. Feet throbbed but not enough to exert the energy from his prone position and rub any degree of sensation.

"Here," he heard a voice behind him. Charlie prepared for the offhand lazy or clumsy comment, but nothing returned except a single hawk circling in some far-away sky. He turned over to meet Benjamin's outstretched hand. His face was smooth and relaxed beneath the reddish pepper stubble of his jaw. "Gotta admit, haven't put in this sort of exercise since I was younger than you." Benjamin remained with his open palm extended, but Charlie rose by his own effort, beating the dirt from his jeans, and jogged ahead with a pronounced limp. Benjamin's head dropped in silence, and there were no other ears to hear his breath's quiet release.

"Leaf, hold up a chance will you?" Charlie called out to Leaf's liquid motion across the rolling tundra field. Charlie watched each footfall, and the sponge-springing mass beneath Leaf's soles didn't even appear to depress from his weight. "Think we should be veering a little more to the right, don't ya think?" Charlie arrived beside him and unfolded his map, now stained, wrinkled, and almost torn in half.

"I don't need any directions. You keep forgetting this is my back yard. Creektoe brought us up here. This is like you going to your local shopping mall or taking a tour around your own neighborhood. There," he paused and pointed down the slope toward indistinguishable spruce groupings. Charlie strained toward the direction Leaf pointed until recognizing a jagged, snaking, black line cutting from one valley bend and disappearing into dense forest growth. "That's where we're staying for the night."

"Why so soon? There's gotta be a good four hours of light left," Charlie paused to catch his breath and glance back toward Benjamin.

"Food is just about gone, and we have three more days. Don't know about you, but I'm not particularly fond of lichen and berries. We have to put some protein inside of us, and with the calories we're burning, we'd never make it. Come on." Charlie couldn't argue the logic. Both George and his father caught up with them. Extracted lung huffs traded between them while they leaned backwards to prevent tripping over their own feet. They descended the sharp decline. Leaf reminded them of immediate necessities. Benjamin stopped, wiping his glasses and scanning past Leaf.

"Guess I'll take a spot over there," Benjamin inhaled a recuperative breath and shuffled past them, wading through low myrtles and dropping his pack against a birch. Leaf turned to Charlie, expecting words that were never spoken.

"This is home for the night," Leaf declared, not taking his eyes from Benjamin who sank to his knees and unstrapped his pack, surveying various contents across the ground. "George, how about firewood duty again and try clearing some of this space? Charlie, you're with me."

The meager remaining energy Charlie found was forced steps after Leaf's pace. From the farthest reach of his ears, Charlie heard a distinct water murmur flowing across the top of shallow rock. Reaching the bottom of the decline, Leaf retrieved the hatchet from his belt and stripped limbs from a fat willow. He jumped, grasping to the length of his reach until it bent almost parallel to surrounding skunk cabbage. He hacked into base bark revealing cream-white wood. After four rapid strokes, the strained trunk crunched and cracked into separation. Charlie lagged again until both men reached the stream. Running water was narrow, and underlying tossed stones remained visible shadows in the clear, iced ripples. "You unhappy with me?"

"What?"

"You seem kinda quiet. I figure if your dad was up here hunting it wouldn't hurt to have him join us. As far as he's concerned, we're up here hunting, too. I don't know what history you have between each other, and it's none of my business. Creektoe asked me to get you up and back alive, and that's what I intend to do. Besides, it's not safe a man his age wandering around here by himself."

"No, we need him," Charlie muttered beneath his breath loud enough for no more than his ears, not answering Leaf's concern but his own. They advanced parallel to the water for minutes. It widened and formed a shallow pool jutting to one side. A distant sublime flow disappeared into the lower valley.

"Here's what I need you to do. See this?" he asked and bent down, retrieving a rounded oblong orange stone half the size of his head. "We need these, lots of these," he calculated and hefted the weight, pointing upstream where more stones were visible. Charlie removed his boots and socks, the corners of his mouth tightening with unprotected skin entering the liquid ice.

"And you're going to drag me out when my ankles snap from the cold?" Charlie joked in personal comfort. Even though the water numbed his soles into dense clay, what little sensation remained was soothed with the slick smoothness against deeper muscles and tendons. Leaf contributed to the gathering until they built a stack rising to their waists.

"Toss me those when I ask," Leaf instructed. He braced both legs and laid the stones end to end until a rough arc formed and another layer followed. The wall rose until water pooled and reached high enough to obscure the stream bottom. Chills flushed across Charlie's forehead while the water now severed his feet, forcing a belief that he stood on nothing more than his ankles.

"Now what?"

"Now we wait."

"Can I get out now?" Charlie pleaded. Leaf nodded. Charlie shot onto dry land and collapsed into the high grass, folding his feet beneath him after drying his skin and pulling on his socks. No sooner had he replaced one boot when Leaf leapt into the pooled stream and swung the stripped branch over his head with both hands.

The impact produced a violent thwack and sent splashing spray through the air. The first was followed by a faster, more instinctive motion. His tension eased and he leapt forward, scooping with both hands into the deepening pool. Charlie saw dark, wriggling shapes fly through the air with each successive stroke and water spray. He grabbed a fist-sized rock, gripping still-flexing fish by their tails, and bashed them unconscious. "What are they?"

"Grayling. And by their size, our protein concerns should be over," Leaf managed gasping out between maneuvers. After more than a dozen, Charlie quit counting and strung a boot string through their mouth and gills. "That should do it," Leaf's face remained solid and sure glancing down at the gleaming fish pile. He pulled his Bowie from its oil-soaked sheath and removed their heads just behind the front pectoral fin. Then, a slice down the stomach center and the abdomen contents were removed with a single continuous thumb-flick action. Paco's automated exercise flashed through Charlie's memory. "I'll get a fire going if you want to go back and get the others." Leaf already piled the gutted grays on a bed of lichen and gathered twigs and larger branches.

"Why can't we just take these back up the hill?"

"You're serious? You have been in the city for a while. Remember us eating near the water the other night?" Sparks flew from the back of Leaf's knife as it struck a jagged flint clutched in his opposite hand.

"Thought I heard some howls earlier—wolves? "Wolves, bear, every hungry critter north of Skagway probably already knows we're here. Don't know about you, but I'm beat and we need a full night's sleep. Come on, go get your friend and father." Charlie staggered back up the hill. George had a steady flame dancing up into the twilight by the time they returned.

"Come on down to the stream. George, we got a feast!" Benjamin stuck his head around the corner of a dead fir with his eyeglass lenses reflecting the orange-and-yellow flames in perfect flickering circles.

"Ben?" George called. Charlie's father didn't require a second invitation.

After arriving at the stream fire, Leaf stuck a pole between two Y-crotched saplings and cut the rope into shorter lengths, suspending each fish a few feet from the coals and tying the opposite end around the pole. He used one boot to kick away a stretched area beneath the grayling and laid a fresh bed of dry wood taking almost immediate flame when ignited from the main fire.

"I have no idea what those are, but I can tell they're gonna be good," George said, gleaming from the fallen log where he sat cross-legged.

"If anyone has stayed up on night watch yet, this evening will be the most important so far. Everyone is responsible to stoke our main fire and keep sharp eyes for any reflections, snorts, growls, or shakes in the bush." He paused, taking a step toward Charlie and motioning his head in a jerk over his shoulder. Charlie nodded his assent. "You too, Mr. Sutcliffe. Better pull up close over here next to the light."

Leaf's eyelids tightened and his eyeballs darted around the illumination. Benjamin followed his scan. Initial flowing juice sizzled from pink-rose flesh suspended above the flames.

After returning to their main camp, random unconscious belches rose from the men while they reclined their heads against logs. All daylight now vanished. Leaf continued evaluating each direction with his rifle cradled in his lap and one finger remaining on the trigger. "Charlie, how about first watch?"

"Yeah."

"Ben, you didn't hike all the way from Skagway, did you?" Leaf asked. Benjamin held one hand to his stomach and struggled forward to a sitting position.

"Heavens no, caught a lift with a buddy of mine, Hodges. He runs a Cessna out of Chilkoot." Benjamin's hands frisked his front pockets for his pipe. A snapping match flared the curve of his short, bearded jaw. He extinguished the flame with a loose shake while smoke snaked through both nostrils.

"And you know an Alaskan bush pilot?" Charlie couldn't resist.

"You'd be surprised at how many people I know. Hodges is a good man but a bit misunderstood by some folks." He paused. "Real misunderstood by others. Got himself into a little trouble while I was on a state shoot quite a few years ago. Let's just say he owed me a favor." His head turned up to blow smoke toward the stars. Charlie shot to his knees, stomped away from the fire, and stroked Maggie's mane. Benjamin also rose, tapping his pipe bowl on a flat stone. He staggered toward the edge of the fire's light. "Thank you again for allowing my company. Anyone is welcome to share the tent," Benjamin's invitation rose.

Charlie wouldn't turn in his direction. The zipper closed. Leaf rose, his rifle lanyard dangling at this side, and he pushed aside a clear area next to the fire after resurrecting the flames back to waist height. George crawled inside the hide covering, and no more than moments passed until wood crackling was the only remaining sound.

Charlotte smiled and laughed in Charlie's phasing degrees of consciousness. Stars above spanned the purple-black where he couldn't decide if his eyes were open or closed. Perception of time was impossible until he felt a nudge across his boot.

"Hey, Charlie, hey," George's yawn reflected in dim light. "My turn," he said, collapsing with a blanket still wrapped around his shoulders. Charlie snapped upright, convincing himself of his own remaining alertness.

"No excitement yet."

"So what do you think about this?" Charlie didn't need George to explain the question, allowing his eyes to refocus on the flames.

"I need to tell you something."

"What?"

"Actually, I need to show you something." Charlie pulled the journal from his coat and dropped the warped book into George's lap. He bent forward and rubbed his hands above the heat.

"So? I've already seen this a dozen times."

"Look in the back." George opened the front cover and shifted to the rear of the spine where his forefinger ran the tip across jagged edges. He said nothing, lifting his head to notice Charlie's reflecting eyes.

"Seems to be a few pages missing." Charlie now collapsed backwards against a log, words flowing from his lips faster than he believed George would understand. After his final statement, George imitated Charlie's earlier release. "After all of this, how are we going to find it?" Charlie said nothing, now hunched on his knees and praying for the fire to tell him what to say next.

"Benny has them. It's late and we'll talk more in the morning." Charlie found no further energy, crawling on hands and knees toward the tarp. George clutched his rifle and arranged the coals. Every twig snap and wind brush brought a quick head jerk. One finger traced the length of his trigger. Above the most recent wood-crackle rush far below the stream, George convinced himself of a low-snorting sniff. Squinting and peering through the brush, his mind decided certitude of a flashing glare contrasting the black. Faces appeared in the contrasting light and dark shadows of twisting branches with gaping sorrowful eyes and spiked teeth. His rifle rose in the glint's direction.

The flowing-water effect was just audible in the valley a few hundred yards away where George hunched over and pulled a dense cloak across his eyes. Increasing weight pushed down on his lids. In the middle of his struggle, he leaned forward and his head snapped back to clear the fog. Although the fire burned with clear, high flames, he tossed an additional log for nothing more than physical activity.

The earlier flash now faded beneath the strain of muscle and tendon numbing. George couldn't identify the first sound stirring him back to the cool Canadian night, nor was he aware of the length he had succumbed to sleep's irresistible pull. But the sound was loud enough for his thoughts to register and react.

In the branch above George's head, an owl hooted and spread flapping wings. George jerked forward with his finger still on the trigger, his hand shifting and sending an explosion roaring from the end of the barrel. Leaf, sleeping with his back to the fire, shot to his feet in a single eye blink, knife drawn and held up swaying in front of his hunched-over frame, steel reflecting the light. Benjamin's grumbling voice mumbled.

"What? Did you see something? Where is it?" Leaf stammered and spun his gaze in a complete circle around the limits of the fire's illumination. By now, Charlie emerged waving his own rifle. George sat back down on his stump.

"Sorry about that, guess I got a little jumpy." George shouldered his rifle and kicked at random twigs beneath his boots. Benjamin returned to his snores while Charlie latched the safety on his gun and shoved it back through the flap. Leaf remained in battle-ready stance, continuing his survey through close-spanned trunks.

"Don't worry yourself. I'd rather have a shot fired at nothing than not firing a shot at something really there." Leaf sought comfort as he inserted his long, glinting blade back into the sheath at his waist.

"Besides, if anything is getting close, it'll think twice about a visit now," Charlie added and slapped a reassuring hand across George's forearm. "Why don't you call it a night?"

"My turn," Leaf glanced at the other two men.

CHAPTER

23

Late afternoon sunshine managed curving over strewn boulders and clumping brush high above their heads. Actual rare warmth across Charlie's scruff and forehead lasted a flashing moment before chilled wind peeled it from his skin. Charlie squinted at random reflections off the churning water. Broken alder fences lined the canyon rim edge. Hushed water whispers pushed past them.

An occasional loose stone skipped down near vertical walls while a circling eagle's echo reverberated off millennia of erosion. Through the wide parting walls on each side, Charlie shuddered at the visible snow-covered peaks and knew little time remained until frozen crystals settled into lower valleys and remained. Their brilliant mirror shine intensified the cold although no more than subjects in a landscape photograph.

At the wide section of the water's flow, a carved pool formed with high reeds and cattail lining the shore. Clear water rolled with the exception of slight shimmers blurring perception as George gazed into the depths of sunken boulders. Although his eyes stared above at the few wisp-strewn clouds and allowed sunlight to rob his immediate sensations, Charlie kept alert for any loose debris or jagged shards leaping from overhead splinters. He admired struggling shrubs and stick spindle bushes growing from the cracked stone and dangling roots.

A click across Charlie's chest snapped his abandonment. "Are you insane?" he asked, rising on his elbows. George stood at the shelf's edge with both arms folded across his paste-colored chest. Stripped down to his boxer shorts, he dipped one foot in the water while trying to maintain balance with the other. His toes flinched back as fast as they entered.

"Thought I might wash off a bit. I'm telling you, brother, you might want to try and scrub a little of your own odor away," he smirked.

"Washing is one thing, hypothermia is another." Charlie sat up, wincing at the swirling flow while imagining air sucked from his lungs and the burn of water only a few degrees from freezing wash across his skin. George approached the edge slowly, taking a seat on the cragged black-and-white-speckled granite. He allowed both feet to enter up to his ankles. He bent forward and splashed water across his shoulder blades, tensioning and releasing with each droplet. "What's your wait? Just jump in."

George turned and raised his eyebrows. "On second thought, maybe just a splash will do," he responded. Charlie rose and squatted next to his friend, dipping his own fingers and soaking his face. Sunlight flashed above the canyon edge, and he shuddered back to his previous reclining. Hawks continued their distant circling caws above them, two black pinpoints against increasing darkened blue.

"Daddy?" Charlie heard and shot upright.

"Gup, you hear something?" George turned and shook his head. Charlie rubbed his eyes and returned to shut out as much stimulation as possible. A cheek tap caused Charlie to brush his face. Seconds later, a subsequent harder tap followed. He cracked one eye and saw George with his back toward him and legs still suspended in the water. Closing his eyes once more and releasing a sigh, a third poke into his eyelid stung, and he leapt to his feet.

"Ow! That hurt—what are you trying to do? Cut it out!" Charlie's irritation sputtered.

"What are you talking about?" George called backward, his gaze remaining fixated on the swirling black liquid. At that moment, a hushed audible giggle bounced against the sheer overhanging face ahead of them. An immediate "Shhh" followed. Both men exchanged glances and turned upwards toward the cliff edge.

Charlie raised a finger across his lips in motioning silence and rose to backtrack up the loose pebbled path winding to the top. He calculated each measured footfall to eliminate all possible sound. Fissured granite shelves to each side bore the brunt of his weight. Charlie dropped to his knees and parted thin golden stalks. Two figures lurched over the cliff's edge and peered through the brush for a better view below.

"Who might you be, my friends?" Charlie rose and blurted. The boy, whom he judged not old enough to shave, turned and stared at him with an open mouth and wide white eyes. The girl released a shriek, jumped to her sneakers, and fell backwards over a jutting root rising to catch her heel.

The boy lunged for her legs but was not quick enough to grasp one of her jean cuffs. She vanished over the side, and the straight stalks whipped back upright. Silent seconds seem to have lasted hours before an echoing splash unlocked their paralytic stare. A howling, soprano, bloodcurdling scream followed the impact. Charlie grabbed the boy by a belt loop preventing him from following her same fate.

The boy remained almost suspended in the air as the path cleared. The girl thrashed in frenetic splashes while George struggled to drag the uncontrollable energetic explosion back from the reeds. Arms, legs, and every other possible appendage flailed in resistance. George ducked and weaved to prevent a fist across his jaw. He yanked her by the back of her collar and pulled with a single forced contraction, bracing both legs across the granite. She still kicked and punched in the air, collapsing on her stomach and coughing water down her chin and neck. The boy huffed up behind them as her animation subsided, and Charlie tracked close in his steps, half walking and sliding.

"Janie!" the boy squeaked out and knelt at her side.

"Get your hands offa me, squirt," she coughed and shot a dead glare into his still-wide eyes. "What?" she both asked and yelled at once. "I mighta drowned," she protested in Charlie's direction and rubbed matted hair from her eyes.

"Well, you didn't, young lady, did ya?" George lectured back with his hands on his hips in his best scolding parental voice, gasping to regain his own breath. "If you and this young man hadn't decided to throw rocks at us, none of this would have happened." She shivered in silence, scowling with her knees raised and pushed against her chest. She wore nothing more than a thin jacket over a blue t-shirt. She shook and water pooled around her jeans.

George removed his own coat and draped it around her shoulders. She neither spoke nor flinched, grabbing both sides and pulling it tight against her soaked skin while continuing her stare and listening to the clacking of her own chattering teeth.

"What's the big idea?" Charlie added.

"Henry, you don't have to tell them anythin'," she trembled. The boy's orange flame hair appeared blonde as he squinted against the last sunlight shaft moments creeping behind Charlie's hovering outline. In the exact breath of her final word, a distinct gunfire crack compressed down the carved water channel.

"Come on," Charlie called after cinching his final lace. "Better get her somewhere warmer before she catches something." The boy named Henry knelt to assist her upright, but she shoved him away. George followed everyone, hopping on one foot while trying to force his other into a boot. A second report echoed the first. "Shotgun?" Charlie hesitated and turned. George nodded in agreement. "We don't have any shotguns." The statement wasn't required, quickening their pace. Once clear and returned to the top of the ridge, both men spotted a figure lying prone across a fallen trunk in the gradual sloped clearing below. The man turned, eyes squinting while trying to identify the other two figures approaching him. Once close enough, the man jumped to his feet and charged towards them, stumbling and shifting before catching his boots on a sprawling fireweed patch. Charlie and George vanished as the man stooped to one knee and extended a hand to the girl, his shotgun broken in half and slung over the opposite shoulder.

"What happened to you? You're soaked," he exclaimed while she stomped past him.

"They did it, it was them two, made her fall in the water," the red-haired boy spit out every syllable. Sparse sun lingered with tendrils of light breaking the valleys between crests. The girl, still bent forward, remained a shadowed figure against the darkening lavender brush canopy. The man raised his head with a stone glare and squeezed the shotgun butt hard enough to whiten his knuckles.

"Get yourself back to the house, and get some warm clothes on before you get sick," he barked behind him. His words carried down the slope and echoed against surrounding granite.

"Now hold on just a second there," Charlie protested. "This young man isn't quite telling the entire truth. We weren't doing anything but relaxing by the river when these two decided they wanted to start using us as target practice," he defended and put his hands on his hips. The man exchanged a glance down at the boy who had no more than a cluster of red hair sticking out from behind the man's pants leg.

"Henry Scott, any truth to that?"

"Like you care anyway? I hate this place. I hate it. I hate it!" came his mantra's final repetition, and he tore away in the same general direction as the disappeared girl. The man's gun grip loosened, and he removed his bush hat revealing a pale, thinning scalp. Long breath blew through pursed lips.

"This isn't the way I typically like to meet folks, but the name is Bill," he said as he stepped forward and nodded, face drawn with a waxed sheen. Charlie couldn't resist noticing his belt, notches drawn through holes tighter than a previous worn lighter hole further along the length.

"Charlie," he hesitated, "and this is my good friend George Gupford. Honestly, we had no ill intentions whatsoever."

"We didn't even know anyone else was there until the rocks started coming down," George added.

"I believe you," Bill released each word in a single extended breath. "Take them to the woods I told myself. Get them out of there and you'll see a change. You're doing it for their own good." The man's voice faded while gazing toward some invisible point past George.

"We're sort of surprised seeing anyone out this far. Haven't seen or heard anybody in more than a few days."

"Well, light's almost gone and I gotta get these back for dinner," Bill patted the tan speckled guinea hens dangling from his belt loop and tied with a shoelace. Evie's gonna wonder if I got eaten by a bear or stomped by a moose," he laughed, framing his words with spirit-affirming reassurance. "Boys look like you could use some meals yourselves," he nodded at George who hadn't yet finished buttoning his shirt.

"Bill, the offer is appreciated, but we have two more with us and better be getting back ourselves," Charlie said and brushed a gnat from his eye.

"Nonsense, got enough here to feed you and every animal within twenty miles. And like you said, we don't get much company up here. See that point down there next to that old spruce stand?" he asked and turned toward the lake with an extended finger. "Head on back to wherever you left your friends and meet down at our place quick as you can. Evie's gonna be thrilled to see some new faces." George shrugged his shoulders and Charlie nodded. "Then it's settled. See ya in a bit." Bill turned and glided down the path, his shotgun still over one shoulder and whistling a tune fading in the distance.

"Where did he say their place was?" Benjamin called from a few yards away, curved thorns tangling his trouser legs.

"Over that ridge near the spruce grove by the water." No sooner had George stated that they noticed illuminating light flares. They shimmered on the lake surface and shot out like beams across still black water.

"Anybody seen Leaf?" Charlie asked and turned.

"Don't worry, he's around." The night above still hadn't turned black beneath the sky. Across almost indefinable hills, swirls of red, purple, and green danced like waterfall delicate crinoline. Various caws, shrieks, and night chatters stirred. Pairs of close-set eyes reflected in lantern light. The brief shines flashed above a shrub clump or fungus-covered slate pile shatter.

243

Charlotte's face carrying Charlie's steps was interrupted by an additional sound overtaking those of water and wood. Specific notes rose and fell with wind pushing through branches. Faint at first, they grew stronger with each successive step. "Anyone else hear that, or have we been out here too long?"

"Yeah, music. Down there," Benjamin pointed his stick down to the lake's edge. "Not every day you hear eighteenth-century Italian opera in the North woods." Violins and cellos roared into dusk as a structure of weather mutations grew from prehistoric ferns and bulrush near the shore. Tiki lamps, set several yards apart, now guided them along a widening path until reaching a pebbled stretch and warped wooden steps. A dilapidated porch stretched along the face, prepared for collapse with the first intentional gust of wind. George noticed Maggie's twitching ear silhouette against a faint glow from within, her reins lashed around a broken post.

"Guess that answers the question of Leaf." Frayed nylon fishing nets, hung out to dry, stretched the porch's length while white-and-red, chipped cork floats dangled and issued hollow knocks, dancing in the night currents. Decaying fish odor filled the nostrils of all three men while they ascended the stairs. Piles of more netting, fishing gear, and canoes in varied degrees of seaworthiness were scattered haphazardly and spilled across the gravel.

Floorboards contributed unique vocals with each successive step, and Charlie snatched a handrail for support. He knocked above crescendo notes. Now, louder closed-fist bangs rattled torn screen-door hinges. The distinctive scrape of a needle across vinyl amplified in their ears and was followed by echoing boot clomps across the inner floor.

"Glad to see you could make it. The wife was wondering if I was starting to tell tall tales. Come on in," Bill beamed, holding the strained door open with one arm and guiding each man inside. "I know it's not much to look at, but consider it a work in process. Can't expect miracles in a couple of months," Bill said and crossed his arms. A lantern and random half-consumed candles provided the cramped space's only light. A long narrow hallway ran the building's length with three rooms jutting off at the far end. The barren wooden floor supported a scattering of stick barren furniture—a couch, an over-stuffed faded chair with padding spilling from its seams, and a round table with four chairs. Towering cases occupied one entire wall filled with books. George glanced across the titles and raised his lantern—the complete Foxfire series, edible plants of the Canadian Wilderness, wild game-dressing manuals, gun care and maintenance, frontier first aid, and stacks of magazines. "You a reader too, young man?" Bill asked, noticing George's interest.

"Yes, sir, but mostly Classics," he replied.

"Me too, can't read enough of them. Have been all my life, but what would anyone else expect from a lawyer?" George and Benjamin traded glances from his last statement. Benjamin wandered past Bill to a magazine stack spilled across a side table and pulled corner-tattered pages into the dim light. His eyes opened full as he looked beneath the bottom rims of his glasses, his gaze shifting beyond them.

"Find something interesting?" Bill noticed.

"Amazing how ten years can pass in the blink of an eye. Africa can be an unforgiving land." Benjamin realized all eyes focused on him, and he tossed the magazine back on the sliding stack. George glanced down after turning toward the hallway. He read the name "Benjamin Sutcliffe" credited at the bottom of the photo. Two tribal-dressed women crouched over a stone mortar and pestle.

"You all gonna chatter away the night in there, or is anyone gonna help me get some dinner going?" a voice called out through the back door.

"Come on, boys, meet the wife, Eva." Bill rose and turned, releasing no sound from the lurching chair, but the wrenching frame betrayed excessive armrest use. They passed through the door where his shotgun hung over the frame and exited another screen door louder than the entrance. They stepped across a broad deck with a single continuous bench encircling the wooden platform.

Screens once protecting the inhabitants from weather and insects succumbed to neglect, scattered random shreds clinging to their posts. In the center of the expansive platform, flames licked and danced beneath a turning spit. Charlie was certain the shining, naked birds were the same ones seen earlier dangling from Bill's waist. Even in occasional night gusts, the aroma of sizzling fowl permeated the air. Juices and fat bubbled within the crisp skin, and their golden brown reflected the firelight, causing audible grumbles in George's stomach he knew everyone heard. After all four men creaked onto the deck, Leaf looked behind him, still sitting cross-legged facing the fire with a tin cup raised to his lips.

"What took you so long?" he called and returned his gaze to the light.

"Where are my manners?" a woman said and rose upright, wiping her hands on a crimson-stained apron struggling to cling across her gaunt hips. Bill dwarfed her frame. She leaned forward and shook Benjamin's hand. "Eva." Her handshake was almost as strong as summer breeze through lace curtains while her lips curled and breath focused upwards at a tress of dangling hair. White down remnants still clung above her ears. Her mouth never moved while crow's feet spanned the corners of her eyes and disappeared behind her temples. She wore a simple summer dress beneath an Army-issue olive-drab coat and fur-lined hood extending past her knees.

A constant suspended stare loomed in the depth of her eyes. The backs of her hands were harsh and defined in almost mechanical contrast. The spoon in her opposite hand was in a gripped clench while she poured liquid across the spit.

"Smells good, woman. Never thought we'd have company for dinner when I woke up this morning," Bill sniffed and bent down, removing the lid from a blackened cast-iron Dutch oven. Melted brown sugar and beans bubbled within and joined the smell of the roasting fowl. He dipped a finger and stuck it between his lips to both taste and cool. "Beans are done."

"Bill, I gotta tell you, we've been tracking for days, and the last expectation we ever thought we'd see is you and your family out in the middle of this nowhere," Charlie remarked.

"I can see how this might be a surprise. Life in Vancouver was getting too much. Kids were getting too soft, and I thought it would be good getting them back to a little self-reliance. This old fish camp and shack has been in the Stanton family for generations."

"Stanton?"

"Yeah, Bill Stanton, told you that earlier." Although their heads didn't indicate the slightest twitch, Charlie and Benjamin's eyes locked in an instant.

"But if you're in the legal profession, Vancouver is a long way from here," Charlie continued.

"Look, I have my reasons and we don't know one another well enough to go into any further details," he said, the ease melting from his features.

"Come on, these are guests," she chided. "May I offer you all something to drink?" she asked in a voice so quiet, Charlie questioned if it was even a request.

"Anything would be fine, ma'am," Charlie said. Benjamin collapsed next to Leaf and rubbed his hand near the flames.

"Janie, be a help and get some cups," she called into the shadows. The sulking black outline on the far bench didn't stir but released a defiant gasp. Eva shook her head and pulled the pot of water suspended by a rusted metal ring. "Can't do everything myself."

"Henry! Get me some cups out here," Bill called through the door. The red-haired boy Charlie and George met earlier bounded through the exit with a smash against the frame. His springing step wilted.

"What are they doing here?" Eva said nothing, again shaking fine white feathers from her unkempt hair while turning the spit and mixing the beans with her other hand.

"That's not your concern, boy. Do as you're told," Bill's words grew sharper with each utterance. No reply returned except bangs and wood slamming against wood.

CHAPTER

24

Water flicks across Charlie's exposed face roused him awake. Random spasms trembled beneath the green nylon sleeping bag wrapped around George and signaled a sputtering return to life. Thunder cracked and echoed across mountains towering on the lake's opposite shore, and the peal rumbled over open water. No visible sunlight appeared while Charlie unzipped his bag, rising and stretching tightness while thin smoke wisps rose and dashed in increasing gusts beyond the encircling barrier wall.

"Rise and shine," Leaf called with no more than his head appearing above the deck edge. He swung over the railing with scattering rain droplets across his features. Benjamin appeared in the rear doorway with a lit pipe between his teeth, puffing and staring up at the overcast sky still spitting rain. Another lightning flash and immediate thunder crash shot George upright.

A slow sputtering transformed into full droplets slapping the oxidized tin roof. Open patches splattered wetness down onto vast stretches of the deck forcing Charlie to scramble back beneath his bag's cover. Charlie and Benjamin's eyes glanced across one another in their head turn, but his father disappeared back inside.

"So how did we sleep last night?" Bill's voice reached them as he turned up the stairs, a fishing pole in one hand and a pair of lake trout in the other.

"Like babies," Charlie replied. Bill darted through the open door and returned without the fishing gear. Through the raised kitchen window, Evie scooted from counter to counter with the sound of her cleaver whacking and breaking the rain pelting above their heads. "Bill, we can't thank you enough for the hospitality, but we really have to be on our way." George tightened his boot laces and shouldered his bag.

Leaf stood next to Maggie under a broad overhanging eave, shifting a short-haired brush across her coat to gentle neighs. Raindrops pounded an incessant, constant beat across the metal and grew so intense Charlie shouted to be heard.

Henry appeared.

"They're still here?" the boy blurted out with strained nostrils flaring translucent pink against his freckles. Bill turned and shook his head at his son.

"Quit being so rude," he scolded.

"Rude? Why don't you shut your face? You wanna see rude? I'll show you rude!"

"Henry Scott!" the group heard a yell through the open window. At the sound of his mother's voice, Henry threw down the dangling fish and stomped up the stairs before stopping in the doorway, each connection reverberating across long-settled timbers. Lips drew into a thin pout, and his eyes never left the ground.

"I still hate you. You never listen to anything I have to say. I don't even exist." Charlie wasn't certain what had started the argument or what were the events prior to their arrival. Benjamin reappeared, hearing Henry's final statement, and tossed a fleeting look toward Charlie.

"Son, that's no way to talk to your dad," Leaf interjected. "If I ever took that tone with my father, I wouldn't be able to sit for a week. I have no idea what started this between you two, and I don't even want to, but there's no possible excuse for that kind of attitude."

"What do *you* know? Some ignorant backwoods Indian," the boy stopped and folded his arms across his chest.

"I know enough that if he doesn't do what should be done, I could." Henry unfolded his arms, tilted his head to the side, and stepped back with one leg in the kitchen.

"You're just like him. Like everyone else. I wanna go home." Henry turned back to his father. "Sounds like everyone has a dad who cares about him except me," he yelled and sped inside before any further words reacted. George caught Charlie's gaze across the open water but kept silent. Bill removed his hat and ran his fingers through dwindled strands, releasing a breath.

"Sorry you had to see that. You all think it's wise to head out in this kind of weather? I mean, do what you want, but you wouldn't catch me out in that." As if to emphasize the point, another lightning flash and thunder clap followed his statement. "Besides, we can't eat all of this," he stepped to one side. His wife exited onto the deck carrying a wide platter covered in pancakes and dark syrup. She clanked the plate on the table.

"All you hungry men aren't doing anything until you get something into those stomachs. Come on, don't be shy." George leapt towards the table, forgetting to unleash his pack and grabbed a pancake in each hand. "Now that's what I like to see— a man who knows how to eat. Like a little homemade blueberry jam on those?" George glanced up and nodded. Through the open door, Charlie noticed the two kids' shadows inside shifting and clinking forks against plates. Charlie joined Leaf who chewed in silence beneath the constant rain-slapping roof.

"You know, he's right," Benjamin reappeared and joined them, blueberry jam specks and pancake crumbs clinging to the edges of his short chin hairs.

"Look, why doesn't everyone just settle down for a while until this rain lets up a bit, and then you can get on your way," Bill said, slurping coffee. Leaf and Charlie recognized mutual nodding agreement. Charlie stood and wandered to the railing, scanning the usual calm lake surface churn beneath the downpour. Leaf joined him.

"Time is a critical commodity, Leaf. You know just as well as I do that the first sticking snow could be here anytime, and it's going to take at least an extra day to make it around this lake." Charlie kept his voice to minimum volume, but Bill felt his head spasm at the conclusion of his statement.

"If that's your big worry, why don't I take you across?"

"On what?" George decided inquiring between pancakes and coffee gulps.

"Our raft, of course, right over there," Bill turned and pointed. Charlie leaned over the railing and saw the partial section of a mast floating above a cleared cove. "Can't take you all at once but two trips oughta do it if you can get your animal up over the side. An hour of rafting sure beats a day of walking." They couldn't argue.

George spent the morning's remainder and start of the afternoon dozing in and out of rest while Henry and Janie disappeared. Charlie paced in a constant back-and-forth motion across creaking deck planks while rain showed no sign of easing, falling in solid gray sheets across the sky. Even the range tips across the water were no more than fog-obscured haze allowing random portions of black-green to appear at any given moment. Although thunder decreased and intervals drifted from their ears, the lake surface indicated no hint of cessation.

"Might as well sit down and conserve some energy," Leaf interrupted Charlie's concentration. He jumped at the sudden startle of Leaf's instruction, breaking study from the ragged paper scrap once defining a clear map. He hunched over in automation as if concealing it. "Didn't mean to startle you."

"Sorry, just a surprise, that's all. Come, take a look at this."

"We should still be moving in the right general direction."

"Close as I can tell. If Bill can get us across this lake, we have to make it over this mountain and through here where the ground levels. Looks like a tundra field near as I can tell, but I don't know about this river," Charlie said.

"Only went to that area once when I was a kid. There's a narrow section where we should be able to get across with relative ease this time of year—even Maggie. If it was break-up season, forget it, the entire area is one big floodplain." Leaf sat next to him with their backs against a wall, slipping his Bowie knife from its sheath. Steel glinted even in the dim light. He spit on a rounded whetstone and began making methodic blade strokes. "Fifty times, both sides, every day. Dad never stopped saying a sharp knife will always be your best friend. Whether you use it or not, keep an edge and you'll never lose yours," he said and stared into foliage without a first glance at the whetstone caresses.

"If this weather sticks, no telling how long we're gonna take."

"Sure we'll hit some snow up there. Couple of degrees colder and this would all be turning white and staying even this far down." Leaf pointed over to where Maggie hung her head, half dozing. "That old girl is tough, but I can't guarantee how she'll do in the drifts."

"We should make it in—two more days?" Leaf took a sideways glance at the unfolded paper and dotted his knife tip across the surface.

"Three full days and at least most of a fourth. Stop thinking like a flatlander. See, after this field, we got a whole additional range. We'll be lucky, I mean really pushing it, if we get anywhere from eight to ten miles a day. Seen your dad since breakfast?"

"Last time I saw Benny he was still reading in the chair inside," Charlie's atonal words fell.

"I'll see if the missus in there can help with any restocking before we head out. You two really don't like each other, do you? Won't ask but if you finally decide to, I'm sure you'll tell me in your own good time." Charlie turned his head.

"What if Creektoe dropped out of your life for seventeen years?" Charlie asked. Leaf's blade thwack hesitated, and he stared across the open water. "I'm going to try and get some more rest." He folded the beaten piece of paper back into a tight square and stuffed it between the journal pages now sealed inside of a plastic bag. He scaled back up to the deck and positioned his bag next to the fire.

Trout sizzles dripped into the embers. George remained in his tightened cocoon. Charlie's head lay back with the constant thumping drumbeat of rain against metal. He attempted concentrating on Karen and Charlotte, but the closer they became, the further he drifted. His heartbeats accelerated after rolling between sides. The incessant rain drops forced Charlie upright, and his boots collided with the steps. He swung the back door wide.

"Still hungry?" Eva asked with a frying pan in one hand and a motioning spatula. Full light brought a previously unnoticed feature. Even through caked mascara and base, distinct purple-and-green shadowing underscored her left eye. Her smile slipped to her feet after full eye contact with Charlie, head turned down with a collision of the pan into the side of a soapsuds-brimming bucket. The fractured posture accentuated swelling down the side of her cheek.

"No ma'am, thanks anyway," he replied. "Are you feeling all right?"

"Just a few sniffles," she returned and raised one hand to block the side of her face as if scratching her temple. He entered the main room with Benjamin reclined in the chair, pipe in hand, and tilting his head to one side. His chin rose. He scanned through a magazine suspended in dimmed light shafts entering the window. Smoke swirled in clouds around his head, drifting to the chinked ceiling.

Charlie stopped and pulled away the passing of years. He constructed a fuller, lower hairline, graying removed and wrinkles vanished, the circumference around his father's waist eliminated. Occasional eyebrow flickers moved and hums sounded while Benjamin flipped the pages.

"Gonna just stand there or read a little with me?" Benjamin murmured, pipe still clenched in his teeth and not looking up to acknowledge Charlie's presence. Charlie cleared his throat. He advanced toward the shelves and read the titles to himself in silence. He removed a volume and scanned pretext illustrations. Pages flipped between his fingers before he slammed a cover shut and spun around toward Benjamin.

"Where've you been?" he both asked and yelled. Benjamin continued puffing, not offering the slightest flinch. Charlie leaned forward and raised a wavering foot but allowed it to return to the floor. Through the still-open rear door, the silhouette of Leaf's head peeked around the corner and nodded.

"Come on, have a seat." Benjamin still wouldn't lift his chin to look at Charlie but released a low giggle with a rising and falling throat extension. He reached the magazine's back cover. He knocked his pipe on the chair's side table, eyes not examining the task. "It was a hundred and twelve degrees. Never felt a sun like that."

"Excuse me?"

"Tanzania. Dodoma. Not really Dodoma, about thirty miles outside. Little village near a river. These two women, a daughter and her mother-in-law, spent a literal week gathering up this wild wheat growing in the valley. Then, they'd drive a pair of oxen in a homemade grist wheel, separating the chaff, and beat the husk from morning 'til night." Charlie sank to floor with his knees against his chest.

"So you're telling me that you've spent the last seventeen years living and taking pictures in Africa?"

"No, not all the time. Took assignments in Portugal, Great Barrier Reef, Brazilian tribes who hadn't seen a white man in decades, Serbia, had a little commercial venture outside of Dublin, the list goes on and on. Now the Hutus, those are real men." Another crash in the kitchen jarred Charlie from studying the worn, almost flattened soles of Benjamin's boots.

"Yeah, you would know what a real man is supposed to be."

"I took whatever assignment the office directed. Kept moving, kept traveling. Kept putting as much distance between that town and myself as possible. Every time the angel's face appeared in my mind or her voice sang inside my head, I knew it was time to move on." Charlie's vision moved from his father's almost worn heels to his own clearly defined sole ridges.

"So you're such a famous photographer, why aren't you retired in a big mansion somewhere?" Several inhalations from Benjamin's stem passed before the first chortle emerged. Charlie thought he choked when the first was followed by another and then rapid increases until wheezing laughter almost dropped Benjamin's glasses from his face.

"Son, I hardly have a cent to my name. If I was so loaded, you think I'd be staying in that roach-infested dive of a motel?" Charlie's face loosened and he twisted the strings of his coat.

"That's it. That's why you want the gold. Know what? You're not gonna see the first dime," Charlie shouted and jumped to his feet. Benjamin's head rose to study Charlie flashing down the hallway past Eva, slamming the screen door behind him.

"You okay?" Leaf called from his recline against the steps.

"Let's just say I see things a little clearer." Charlie's head dropped against his bag. His eyes closed. Charlotte stared back across her pink tea table with inanimate stuffed animals slumped over in opposing seats.

"Come on, you gonna sleep all day?" George called. Charlie rose on his elbows and blinked, scanning in all directions. The mist-obscured water remained, but the rain roar against the roof ceased with a few spattering thuds dripping from branches in random thwacks. Charlie glanced at his watch and noticed the late afternoon hour. He sprang to his feet, stretching and yawning during the ascent. George laced his boots and shouldered his pack, calling from the shore below. "Go on, get your stuff together. We voted. Bill is taking Leaf, Maggie, and me across first with the gear, and then he'll come back for you and your dad." George turned and headed down the beach toward the raft, avoiding any protests.

Charlie jumped and sprinted after George without bothering to tie his laces. Benjamin sat on a log pile with outstretched legs, waving as the raft departed. Maggie released several indignant neighs and clomped the raft hull. Bill and Leaf pushed forward from the sand.

"Hey there, might as well sit awhile. Right now we have nothing but time," Benjamin called to the back of Charlie while they watched the raft drift into deeper water. Oars replaced poles.

"We have nothing to say to one another." Acid rose up Charlie's throat and into the back of his mouth. His fingers clenched and uncut nails bit into his palms, skin separating beneath the incisions.

"Come on, son, I am still your father," he commented while whittling on a stick of seasoned pine. Charlie whirled around, raising both fists at his side.

"A father would never sentence his own granddaughter to death!" The words shot from Charlie's lips in a tense machinegun sputter while his entire frame shook without control. "Why'd you do it, huh? Why? Are you just the greedy parasite I've always thought you were? It was you. You tore out the pages didn't you?" Charlie's chest heaved and he clutched both hands together to control his seizures.

"Look son, I—" Benjamin's knife stopped.

"No, I don't want to hear any kind of explanation. There are no words you're gonna find to explain it or where you've been for almost two decades." Charlie spun around again and sprinted back up the deck stairs, rubbing his fingers to concentrate on reducing the blood-rushing torrent through his arteries. Charlotte's face wouldn't shake from his mind although he managed easing his swollen chest by folding both arms across it.

A muted sigh released in his throat after breathing returned to normal and mist scattered across his eyebrows. "Even though she's never met you, she still asks about you. We can't lie to her. Karen just keeps telling her that you're on a long trip and someday you will come and see her. What do you think of that?" Charlie's head rose in anticipation. No sound met his ears but the chirps of songbirds reemerging from secure warm holes. Dusk now approached with longer shadows creeping across the setting sun. "I said what do you think of that?" his voice now rising. "Nothing to say?" he asked again with eager venom in his tone and turned. Benjamin no longer perched on the logs. Instead, he was waist deep in water pulling an aluminum canoe behind him. "Hey, where do you think you're going?"

Benjamin grasped the gunnel with both hands, flexing his arms straight at the elbows and hooked a leg over the side, jerking himself up and landing with a thump, the canoe rolling to each side. "I'm not sitting here on this beach all evening waiting for them to get back. We have something to find, and I can't sit any longer."

"Are you insane?" Charlie half cried while taking no more than a single leap down the steps and racing across packed sand. He stopped at the water's edge. Benjamin hadn't yet put an oar in the water. He turned and grinned. "How do you know that thing even floats?"

Charlie danced, trading between feet, with his hands on his hips. He turned back to the camp and then to the canoe, finding himself sprinting through the shallow water. Stinging ice bit his ankles, and cold clenched his calves.

"Decide to come along?" Benjamin now back paddled a few strokes in his direction. Just as the water reached his hips, Charlie's trembling ashen knuckles gripped the canoe's edge, and he pulled himself over in a single thrust. Benjamin shifted to the boat's opposite side and counterbalanced the weight. Charlie bent forward and shuddered from a whispered wind working across the lake, leg hairs standing on end. "Here, grab a paddle."

Charlie had no further words nor could he trust what would emerge if he spoke. He turned and witnessed deck lights fading behind them until they reduced to no more than pinpoints against the darkened spruce dotting the shoreline and what remained of the red-lined, pink horizon beyond them. Both men took long, plunging strides into now still water. Charlie rubbed one eye at a light flickering ahead of them. At first it flashed on and off multiple times until remaining a constant light stream shining a bleached sliver across the water.

"Uh oh," Charlie murmured. He turned, glancing beneath the cross-strut where he sat. By now, drenching pants legs and boots should have dripped drier from previous sloshing, but water still soaked to his skin. With each stroke, a shallow water pocket moved from aft to bow. He squinted with just enough light remaining to identify several missing rivets once joining two aluminum panels and an unbroken water stream spurting beneath their feet. "We have a problem," he observed and dropped his paddle, feeling around for anything to bale.

"What are you talking about?" No sooner had Benjamin turned to ask the question when he recognized the concern. He pushed his hat high up on his forehead and released a low whistle. Both men said nothing further, gripping their paddles and leaning both shoulders to the length they could reach, massive strokes pushing as much water behind them as possible. Bared, white teeth and mutual grunts were exchanged in the approaching night. Although light grew brighter and steadier ahead, water now surfaced past the tops of their boots.

"Don't know if we're gonna make it," Charlie forced out between his clenched jaw.

"Shut up, boy, row!" Water flecks from his father's paddle sprayed across Charlie's face, flung back through the air. Random familiar yells rose along the opposite shoreline. Charlie's eyes rose just high enough to identify a pair of figures dancing and hopping on the beach, their bodies no more than black silhouettes against the firelight. Their spasms ceased and they jumped aboard the raft. Charlie spotted Leaf's outline lunging forward and pushing with a long pole.

"Benjamin! Charlie!" Bill's shrill voice called out to the frenzied paddle splash. They recognized how low the canoe sat in the water. Charlie no longer felt his shoulders. Forearms burned with a diminishing knowledge that they were somehow joined to his body further up his frame.

Ink-black water now swirled almost to their knees. Their forward progress crawled. Charlie watched water lap over the dim aluminum hull. The raft's outline was visible and no more than twenty yards from their splashing paddles. With a final forward stroke, the fire in his shoulders was extinguished by water soaking through his sleeves. Charlie watched his father rise and jump from the bow, putting as much distance between himself and the now submerged canoe. Charlie sloshed in his general direction.

White water kicking up beneath his legs was the only navigational point of reference. Vision and hearing both blurred from the chill while he struggled to keep his eyelids separated.

Legs and arms turned more unresponsive with each contraction. He no longer sensed forward movement. With what hearing remained, frantic cries and shouts continued but in intermittent chopping shakes. Charlie rose and fell beneath the surface, forcing one final eye opening to see shimmering shapes hovering above the water.

The last image identified through Charlie's perception was Leaf's outline looming from the raft's edge and the sensation of a hand grasping the back of his collar. Clear evening air washed across the droplets pouring down his face.

An eagle's screech echoed. Charlie stirred, shaking his head at heat baking his cheeks and forehead while the remainder of his body shook beneath a blanket. He turned and winced at the throbbing pangs throughout his entire core. He heard muted whispers beyond the fire and knew he was still alive, each heartbeat slamming blood through the ache in his ears. After three momentum turns, Charlie rolled to one side and raised himself onto an elbow, squinting to focus on the shapes of Leaf and George sitting with their backs against a stump.

"Look, see, I told you he'd make it after all," Leaf commented with a curling grin at the corner of his mouth. "Here, take some of this," he asked, crouch stepping over Charlie and shoving a tin cup in his open hand. Charlie sipped and grimaced.

"What is this?"

"Hemlock and wintergreen tea. It'll take the chill out of your bones and the ache out of those muscles." Leaf returned to his seat next to George. "Bill was sorry he couldn't say goodbye but said he had to get back before his kids burnt down the shack." Leaf and George sipped from their own cups.

"C.S., I thought you were a goner for sure," George hushed and dribbled tea down his chin. "You shoulda seen your face, your lips were purple as dawn." Charlie shuddered with the sudden memory snapping back into his thoughts through slow-motion scenes.

"Leaf, your family may have been grateful for the venison but that's no comparison. I can't find the words to thank you enough for saving me from freezing to death out there," Charlie said, nodding over his shoulder and wrapping the blanket tighter around his neck.

"As much as I'd like to take the credit, don't thank me, thank him." Leaf motioned his cup behind Charlie. Charlie turned and saw his father's outline standing on the shore, pipe in one hand and his weight propped against his willow eye walking stick. Gold-rimmed spectacles were a pair of glowing orange circles glinting firelight on a black silhouette. Charlie refused to meet his glance, and Benjamin's chin lifted to examine unfolding stars. "Well?" Charlie said nothing.

George turned toward Leaf as he interrupted. "Looks like night has arrived and Maggie is done for the evening after that little trip. Think it's best we all get a fresh start in the morning.

George volunteered for first watch, and I'll take the second. Charlie, you need some more sleep to recover. Benjamin's going to relieve me, and you get to watch the sunrise."

George yawned. Maggie chortled and muzzled an ancient birch. Charlie stood and turned, unlaced leather straps securing the hide flaps, and entered in silence, collapsing on the soft, napped-leather flooring and allowing the hot tea to continue washing through his body. Just prior to a drift into waning consciousness, he reached into his pack for reassurance of the journal's spine beneath his fingertips. He pulled out the plastic bag-covered book and stuck it beneath his head.

Sleep came with the imagination of Charlotte cradled in his arms while he brushed her hair and clean fresh breaths rose and fell against his chest. When he heard the sound of another voice, Charlie jumped and released a snort. The sudden wrenching sent spasms through his back, legs, and neck. Charlie couldn't determine the passage of time.

CHAPTER

25

Piercing stabs diminished. Charlie discovered maintaining balance no longer required leaning forward. Briars and thorns decreased to a level stretch of immature pencil maples dotting beneath their parents and grandparents. His steps were crunching sponge bounces across the layered dead-leaf carpet. Sunlight had not crested encircling mountain walls guarding each valley side. What sky appeared visible swirled in royal purple and green.

Charlie swatted a mosquito, and his vision rose high enough to recognize George's head and shoulders through the brush. "C.S., get on over here." Charlie stabbed a foot forward to scratch a blistering itch. Devils club and chokecherry brush slashing parted like walking onto a beach. To his left and right, a distinct snaking path stretched beyond the reach of his sight.

"This doesn't look like any sort of game trail I've ever seen."

"You are correct, my friend, almost forgot this was here," Leaf turned from his kneeling position. His knife point twisted into one of Maggie's hooves while her knee shuddered and he dug away an obstruction.

"Any more time in that and we would have bled to death from a thousand cuts," Benjamin wheezed and hunched forward with both hands overlapping the top of his willow stick. "Young man, where and what is this road?"

"Old miner's trail. I thought by now all these years would have grown over it, but I'm obviously incorrect. This is good. It may add a few hours to the trip, but I think we can all use some relief."

"If we don't have any blood left in our bodies, it's not gonna matter whether it's a few more hours or weeks," George's voice rose above the others. He lay stretched prostrate on his back across the now earth-gravel ruts, one arm draped across his face. Both Charlie and Benjamin bobbed in concurring nods.

"Mr. Sutcliffe, would you mind keeping Maggie company for a moment?" Leaf asked. "Just to be sure, I want to scout down a ways and make sure this isn't just an oasis." Charlie collapsed next to George and watched Leaf's form grow smaller as he jogged down the winding double path.

"I'm getting even more tired just watching him run."

"Know what I'm thinking about right now?" George asked.

"My thoughts are reeling."

"A nice, huge, sesame-seeded bun, a half-pound burger dripping so much grease that the bread can barely stay together; loaded with onions, tomatoes, mayo, ketchup, the whole works." Charlie's eyes glazed over from his description. "Oh yeah. And then, I want a whole 'nother plate to hold the fries, not just any fries. I want the ones not too thin but not too thick," he continued now rising on one elbow and ensuring Charlie understood his description by two fingers articulating the exact measurement. "Ones turned to just the perfect caramel glaze with a hint of transparency crunching between your teeth, oil still hot on your tongue."

"George?"

"Yeah?"

"Shut up."

Maggie's lip-flapping lung snorts disrupted their route's relative rise and fall. Spanning mountain crests appeared in random stretches on each side of their advancement. Charlotte was no more than a breath away from every muddied boot print. While his pack straps dug lower with each step, he saw her ahead of him. She crouched down to pick up a leaf and spin the dry, flat geometry in front of her wide eyes. She marveled at dew-jeweled spider webs suspended and dripping in the constant wetness. Loose curls bounced over her shoulders while she skipped. Eyes caught every dark crevice and uncertain twist, but each time, they turned to identify the glance of her father's guiding reassurance.

Charlie stopped to release a tightness in his right boot, collapsing on a moss-carpeted stump. From the corner of his eye, his little girl continued dancing through a maze of low fern. Cool air rushed across his sock during the ankle rub. A honey sunlight glow filtered through the branches, catching her tresses and tossing them across her eyes. Far off, the crack of a falling branch snapped him back to the forest depth on each side of the road.

"Hey, Gup, you still thinking of that burger?" Charlie continued massaging in response anticipation, but his words were met with no more than a blend of colliding insect hums. "Gup?" Charlie called out with Charlotte vanishing and leaping more indistinguishable into the woods. Even Maggie's struggling breath failed to reach his ears.

Lacing his boot, Charlie rose and turned a complete circle to find himself in total isolation. He turned back to their just-traveled route and scanned ahead. Blisters and soreness vanished as he approached a rising hill. His pack rose and fell across his shoulders in unbalancing jerks. Just as he crested the rise, Benjamin's thinning, white scalp bounced through a maple clearing with Maggie's swatting tail flicking her wrinkled buttocks. "Hey!" Charlie called before Leaf turned.

"Looks like we are at the end of the road, gentlemen. Thought you were taking a little nap back there," Leaf gestured. Benjamin scanned the surrounding foothills while George sucked from his waterskin. "Charlie, can we talk for a minute?" Charlie nodded and made his best attempt at breath control. "You still got that map?" Charlie nodded while he and Leaf dropped behind the others, shielding themselves with a wide hemlock. Charlie removed the crumpled paper and held it up to what light remained.

"What do you think?"

"See this, here? Road's run out. Need to get through this stretch, and I don't see any other option but going up here. How are you? Still got enough breath in your lungs?" Leaf asked.

"Just fine as anybody else," Charlie straightened his back and forced a smile across his lips. Leaf reemerged around the trunk to meet Benjamin's lower, slow-moving whistles and George staring up at the rising terrain ahead of them.

"Gentlemen, we need to go that way," Leaf gripped Maggie's reins and pointed toward a consistent rising path reaching to a height they couldn't recognize beyond a hundred yards.

"Up there?" George pleaded. Leaf grabbed Maggie's reins in both hands and advanced, not bothering to answer his question. Benjamin's whistling returned to its previous volume. While Charlie followed the others into the hazed soup above, he caught Charlotte's auburn dancing hair flash from behind a thin splatter of pine needles trembling in the breeze.

Men and animals no longer lifted their eyes to gauge their advancement. They concentrated on their feet, counting one successive step after the other. None of them could recognize the outline of the other. Wind brushed up the mountain cliffs. "Leaf," Charlie called. His immediate surrounding was enveloped in milk-white fog, visible no more than a few yards in any direction. Charlie heard Maggie's hoof falls, but her low-belly frame was a vague darkened blur drifting in and out of focus.

"Up here." Charlie stopped when Leaf materialized out of the clouds. "Mr. Sutcliffe, George?" The other two men appeared, mutual gasps trading between them. Each man drew their collars up closer around their necks. "Look, over there," Leaf pointed.

Charlie struggled through the haze but identified his direction. A black stretching mass both rising and falling enveloped another distant peak. He recognized its movement toward them.

"That's going to be here before we can get down out of this altitude. I wanted to get off of this mountain so we can reach it by morning, but I don't think we have a choice. Down there," Leaf stopped and again pointed, this time to a closer point. Charlie shuddered and drew a line from his fingertips. Further down the clearing, granite shelves suspended above the black. "Years have passed since my last stay, but Creektoe and a cousin holed up there a short while ago. Ben?" Leaf asked and motioned the reins toward Benjamin.

Leaf darted ahead of the others, checking for any threats and the path integrity. Ozone electricity lined the passages of Charlie's nostrils, the hairs of his arms stood on end, and pebbles clung to the soles of his boots. The cloaking fog lifted in a rub and blink of his eyes. Leaf's pace increased until he was no more than an outline in the trail stretch descending without distinct identification. The first raindrops were wind-shot stings across his face.

George nudged Maggie from behind in conjunction with Benjamin's stick prodding. The cliff's edge descended into black-hazed pinpoints of anonymous forms. Charlie jogged past the others and gripped the fractured stones until reaching a granite platform where Leaf crouched and rubbed loose sand over the solid floor. Upon entering, the buffeting chill tossing Charlie's hair diminished. Leaf retreated to the rear of the overhang when the outline of Maggie's head first cleared the side ledge. "Everything safe back there?" Benjamin called out with a match-head flare. From the flicker's rise and fall, Charlie believed he saw vague intersecting lines spanning the smoothed walls to each side of them and minute, glistening quartz flashes catching the light. All fell to silence with the exception of distant indistinct rain-slapping echoes against stone and a wind rush up the mountainside. It tossed what remained of each man's hair back over his head. Leaf's soles scrunched across the grit-dusted stone floor where he untied bundles of earlier gathered kindling and dry branches.

With twilight shimmers contrasting the surrounding darkness after the match extinguished, Leaf was a crouched black shape almost indiscernible as human with the sound of snapping twigs and crunching tinder. Brief flashes like miniature flashbulbs broke out until both flame and smoke remained. It grew wide enough to illuminate a loose boulder ring encircling stacked branches.

The wall and roof spanned in hand-drawn characters scattered among images. Maggie stepped back with one eye widening at the growing fire until her regression was halted by the tightening of Benjamin's rein grip.

"You sure this place is safe?" George continued scanning. Charlie's boots slipped from his feet, and he released an audible sigh, head dropping back on his pack to watch the flames dance shadows and images across the low ceiling.

"Safe as anywhere else around here," Leaf returned and rummaged through one of the packs across Maggie's back. Benjamin's walking stick dragged beside him as he removed his glasses and squinted through them. He studied stick-figure representations of men hunting what appeared to be caribou, more groups in boats harpooning seal, and a settlement with huts and kneeling women. "From what I can tell, it looks as if it's only been a few months since someone was last here." He nudged George and pointed at a firewood stack lining one of the walls.

"Amazing, saw something like these out in the French countryside caves years ago," Benjamin continued in his rapture.

"Mr. Sutcliffe, I don't believe they're that old, but some of the ones further that way go back more than a few thousand I'm sure." George required one more scan before catching sight of Charlie and dropping his own pack. He rotated both arms at his sides and yawned. "Creektoe and I even stayed here once in a while when we were up this way on a hunting trip with my grandfather."

He stood beside Benjamin and raised a hand to brush the lines and shapes. Leaf closed his eyes, tilted his head back, and inhaled to the point of his chest straining his vest buttons.

"Don't know about the rest of you but I'm starving. Any more of that seal fat left over?" George rose on one elbow.

Various belches emerged from the men, their sleeping pads encircling the fire. "Don't think we're going to have to worry about visitors tonight, but I think I'll keep my place toward the front. I'm sure Maggie here will let us know if there's going to be any excitement." Charlie lay on one side opposite of Leaf while George picked crumbs off his blanket. Benjamin continued staring above, rotating his head on occasion during the interpretation. "Even though we only stayed here overnight a couple of times, this place really brings back some good memories," Leaf said and joined Benjamin's overhead stare.

"I must say something, young man, the way you talk about your father, I absolutely have to meet the man one day," Benjamin whispered.

"I hope you do, sir, he is the best man I've ever known or ever will know."

"I can tell. Your voice changes when you say his name, and I recognize the thousand memories swirling in your eyes when you talk about him." Benjamin released pent-up breath-full lungs.

"You okay?" Leaf asked.

"Sure, must be the altitude." Benjamin rolled forward and crouched toward the stack of split wood. He grasped a log in each hand and tossed them into the dwindling coals. The impact sent spiraling embers rising and splattering across the black soot circle fading toward the hand-painted drawings.

"I'm as sore to the bone as any of you, but there's an energy here. Almost feels like the arms of my people wrapping around us tonight." Leaf stuck both hands behind his head. Charlie's eyes closed and he pretended not to hear their conversation. "You wouldn't believe how many of my cousins, aunts, uncles, a lot of them, have forgotten how things used to be. I guess it's why I still dress this way, acting like my forefathers in many ways, to honor my dad. Mr. Sutcliffe, I can't think of anything more I'd like to do than introduce you two. Mom might take a little offense with all of the stories you'd be trading all night."

"That's it for me. Young man, mind if I take a few?" Benjamin asked, camera in hand and adjusting the aperture.

"Sure," Leaf yawned and rolled to face the fire. Charlie's eyes snapped shut in anticipation of the movement. George's snoring cut through flaring wind stoking the fire.

Within moments of the final shutter click, everyone snored except Charlie. He sat up and poked at a falling chunk of ash while hugging his knees. He watched Benjamin's chest rise and fall.

CHAPTER

26

Each time Charlie turned his shoulder, Benjamin paused, leaning against trail-projecting boulders or bent over at the knees. He grasped his thighs with both hands. As their ascent continued winding upwards, rest break intervals lengthened. Alders thinned as more fireweed replaced the devil's claw thickets biting exposed skin.

Thistle and scrub, still waist high, scraped across opening and closing gaps around their ankles. George's coat zipped until reaching the limit around his head so only his nose and cheeks poked through the drawn cord.

The air was not cool enough yet to see their own breath, but brown and gray ground stretches started coverage again between shallow, clinging snow mounds. Maggie matched Leaf's consistent pace while clopping ahead of him. An occasional swat across the hindquarters with a broken willow branch corrected her direction when straying too close to the drop-off masked in unfathomable fog. She whinnied, shook her head so both ears flopped on the sides of her head, and redirected her hooves back toward the cliff face inner wall. George stopped several yards behind Charlie when Leaf paused.

"What, what are you slowing down for?" Charlie drew a sucked breath and asked the question in a single exhalation.

"Old girl is favoring that other leg." He bent down and lifted the mule's front right hoof, examining the texture and cracks for any lodged stones. Charlie didn't drop his pack. He allowed the weight to pull him backwards so the sheer granite provided support. Still, quiivers spasmed his shaking knees. He forced himself back up to disguise the strain. One straight leg followed the other. He peered over the cliff edge and their traveled path. Billowing, blind mist haze continued cloaking them after rising above cloud level.

"Let's take a few minutes. Benjamin isn't looking so good. Air's starting to really thin out this high. I want to know if anybody starts getting the first sign of a headache," Leaf muttered, still examining Maggie's hooves and brushing the bottom of each with a flat palm. George stared straight at the ground in front of him, examining the destination of every stride placement.

When Charlie returned to a somewhat normal breathing pattern, his previous rasping was replaced by George's fresh croaks and suffocating air gasps. He didn't bother resting against the crumbling face. His pack leapt from his back, shoulder straps snapping from his upper arms in conjunction with both legs buckling beneath him. His pack contacted scattered asters, absorbing his body jolt. Both boot tips stuck straight out. His arms flopped to his sides, and he leaned back with closed eyes. Only his mouth remained open, drawing in vast lung-fills of the altitude's diminished air.

"Am I gonna have to carry you the rest of the way, Gup?" Charlie asked in his direction, not quite finding the right amount of breath to complete his statement with the intended passion. George scrambled at his hip for a canteen. Benjamin's outline formed through the mist.

"Mr. Sutcliffe, how are you coming along?" Leaf noticed his approach.

"Look at all of you young men. Here I am hardly in my fifties, and I bet I could outrun every one of you," he exclaimed, lifting his chin and lecturing beneath the rims of his glasses. He turned in the opposite direction, removing a handkerchief and wiping moisture from his lenses. Charlie perceived noticeable chest heaving and a stifled cough.

"Just the same, Benjamin, would you mind walking along with me? I think these heights are spooking Maggie, and you seem to have a calming effect on her." Leaf straightened and placed the animal's leather reins in Benjamin's outstretched hand. He stood next to her and ran an open palm across her ribs. She released a reassuring chortle and stomped a hoof, wandering to the embankment for a short gnaw. "Charlie, come here," Leaf directed. Brief breaks in the coverage allowed him to catch glimpses into the valley. "See, there." Charlie focused in the direction of Leaf's pointing finger. Clouds parted, revealing distant painted tundra below. "That's our direction?"

"Yes. Come on. It's getting late and we'll barely make it off this mountain. We're gonna need to get a fire going." Leaf turned to where Benjamin and George advanced well ahead of them. The trail arched around the side of vertical granite. The path was no more than a few yards wide at stretches where two men elbowed walking abreast and Maggie clopped in the rear.

"How much longer do you think?" George asked above the sudden wind increase. Dry-stalked brush whispered beneath his yelled question.

"Shouldn't be—" Charlie began.

"I reckon about—" Benjamin added at the exact same moment the first word fell from Charlie's lips. Charlie shot a side glance at his father who released a brief whistle, removed his glasses, and wiped the lenses clear. "As I was going to say, I reckon about the time Charlie and Leaf say we're there, we'll be there." He replaced the glasses on his nose, adjusted his straps, and whistled an off-key tune while swirling his walking stick like a baton. George continued, outpacing the others with longer strides as the descent angle increased.

"This little leg of the trip wouldn't be so bad if it were all downhill," George laughed at his own joke. Maggie froze in her tracks, the rhythmic clop of hooves against stones silent and wind sounding in their ears. She released a high-pitched whinny, clopped with her front legs, and rose on her haunches. Her load shifted backwards, and hooves punched the air. Flashing eyelids spread wide and revealed hairline capillaries in the white surrounding her chocolate brown eyeballs, bulging from their sockets.

"Whoa, whoa, whoa there girl," Leaf cried out, snatching the reins from Benjamin. He leaned back at the waist to avoid catching a random hoof across the jaw. Maggie continued her shrill neighing and sniffing once all four hooves returned to the ground, but she still shook in spasmodic fits, kicking ragged mane dust. "Shhh, shhh, there, there." Leaf took extended rubs down the side of her ribs until bucking settled to concentrated lung gasps and a short sneeze.

"Was it something I said?" George stopped and turned to glance back up the path.

"Leaf, she okay?" Charlie added and also took soothing strokes along the side of her neck. Maggie turned her head and nuzzled against his chest.

"Can't really tell. She seems okay but her heart's beating a mile a minute." A sound rose above the wind but ceased in an instant. It was a low rumble of tremendous weight spilling into the open valley. Charlie glanced down to his boots and noticed gray, sharp-edged pebbles dancing around his soles. Before his mind grasped awareness, the vision of Leaf, Maggie, and George vibrated before his eyes. He leaned to one side and placed an open palm against exposed basalt, feeling tremors beneath his touch at the same time the tearing of earth echoed in his ear drums.

"What—what—what is this?" Charlie yelled above the constant thrum of stone grinding against stone, vegetation and roots tearing from the ground.

"Come on, let's move! Earthquake!" Leaf yelled. Benjamin shot past them with his stick clicking across shattered quartz. Maggie leapt down the path, almost dragging Leaf who struggled to maintain his own footing. No sooner had George appeared around the bend when Charlie looked up in just enough time to hear a fading yell vanish over the cliff's side, George swinging futile arm circles at his sides.

Charlie's brain could not register what his eyes conveyed. Every image of the trip flashed through his thoughts in cascading, scattered photographs. Talus and shards skipped down the side of the mountain face while Charlie held an arm over his head to cushion the glancing stings. Charlie threw his pack from his shoulders and dropped. He crawled forward.

With each advancing foot toward George's last spot, the moment's realization solidified, and nausea forced out the contents of his stomach. He couldn't determine if the dizziness resulted from shifting ground or an acid burn lingering in his throat.

As quick as it began, the ground rested still. Even though earth no longer moved beneath their feet, random cracks and bangs continued ringing out through the valley along with the creaking of timber until nothing more than wind hushes returned. "Everyone okay? Ben?" Leaf called and coughed the dust from his lungs. Maggie shook her head and bent down to nibble on a clover patch.

"Gup! Gup!" were the only words Charlie found in his throat. He jumped to both feet and sprinted down the hill toward the cliff edge, allowing his own momentum to almost drag him over the side. Charlie flushed all thoughts from his mind, preparing for whatever his eyes were about to witness. The image of George's broken, mangled body flashed without control. He inhaled to full lung capacity, sticking his head over and through the tall weeds.

"C.S., you gonna make me wait down here all evening?"

"Gup! You made it!" Charlie cried, now joined by Leaf and Benjamin.

"You must have an angel on your shoulder, my friend," Leaf called down. "You hurt?"

"Nope, just a scratch or two," George said, returning back up the ten yards above him. He remained flat on his back in a dense sage patch, pressing on legs and arms to validate absence of injury. "See? Right as rain," he grinned and glanced down to notice a red wetness coating his fingertips. "Well, maybe more than just a scratch," he replied and wiped the blood from a gash across his chin.

"All right, you guys hold me, I'm getting down there," Charlie exclaimed, jumping to his feet and turning to prepare for the descent.

"Hold on there, you're in no condition, none of us are in any condition to try scaling down that overhang. Anyway, there still might be loose rock, and you'll bang him up good. Ben, grab that rope."

Benjamin handed him a rope coil, and Leaf knotted one end around the mule's harness. She glanced up at the commotion and protested with resistance but still pulled forward. "Charlie, take this end and pass it over those roots."

"Gup, grab a hold and tie it around your waist," Charlie called over the side. He nodded back toward Leaf who slapped Maggie across the hind quarters. She reversed back up the narrow trail. The rope tightened, and loosened roots strained under a grown man's full weight. Leaf continued making sharp clicking snaps with his tongue and teeth while Maggie pulled and whinnied.

George's head cleared the weeds, and he held a shirt against his chin while dangling. Leaf and Charlie each grabbed an arm and pulled him the remaining few feet back to even ground. All three men reclined in silence for a moment, staring up at the now cleared sky and an initial star scattering gaining hold in the expanse.

"Gup, don't ever do that again," Charlie cried in mock condescending tones.

"Wasn't my idea to go sightseeing." Leaf pulled back his shirt to examine the injury. George winced when the cloth pulled away, and Leaf splashed canteen water into the cut.

"At least it's not too deep, and I think I got most of the debris out. Enough of this. We now have two reasons to get off this mountain."

"Earthquake?"

"This part of Canada and Alaska lay across one of the largest fault lines on the planet," Benjamin added, shouldering his pack again and wiping his glasses.

"Yeah, but that was nothing more than a tremor. And when there's one, there's likely to be more," Leaf finished and extended a hand, helping George to his feet. "My friends, let's go. Remember, fast pace but steady and sure."

CHAPTER

27

George stopped and adjusted his straps. "What's that?" he asked and leaned forward against an eroded crumbling shelf, blocking any further advancement without a crouch. He pointed down into an unfolding valley. Charlie also paused and dropped into a squat to stretch his calves, regulate breathing, and retie a loose boot string. They both squinted at an elongated rectangular yellow dot with masking brush obstructing a clear view.

"Looks like we're going to find out," Leaf responded after scanning the sun's height-to-horizon relationship. "That takes us right along our route." He guided Maggie down the uneven descent where each man passed no more than single file to maintain balance with the vertical mountainside's assisted support.

Maggie started and stopped, shaking her head and yanking on her reins. Charlie traded glances between the route of his feet and the approaching object's increasing clarification. Benjamin's whistling rose and fell in random, jabbing notes. Spinning around with a glare, Benjamin's melody ceased in recognition of Charlie's downturned eyebrows. Mosquitoes bounced off foreheads while swatting their ears with autonomic repetition. Maggie also flicked what tail she possessed to slap the buzzing.

"I don't believe it. How on earth did someone manage getting a school bus out in the middle of this nowhere?" George asked. Flat, rotten tires grew visible with spanning rust patches splotching the vehicle's metal surfaces. Curves and lines retained artifact pale yellow but still suggested the representation of a vanished age.

"Never know what you're gonna find out here. This whole landscape is littered with vehicles of every size and shape: beaten-down old shacks, plane wreckage, you name it. Most are fixed up for hunting camps, were abandoned when the pipeline went in, or leftovers from the Army. My cousin Damien told me last year that he found a phone booth washed up on the shore of Little Catooga," Leaf responded. George asked nothing further, shaking and scratching his head. "Hey, anyone home?" Leaf shouted.

"Take some care," Benjamin stopped and leaned on his willow-eye walking stick.

"Don't worry. I know you should always announce yourself coming up on something like this." With no response, Leaf circled the entire bus. Not the slightest interior movement indication appeared through several spider web-shattered windows. "Looks abandoned, gentlemen." Packs fell to the ground in almost simultaneous thumps. "Don't know about you, my friends, but I say we take a little breather." George explored both the hard pack and tundra to the front and rear of the vehicle.

"Doesn't even seem to be a road here," he commented and wiped sweat from his forehead with a handkerchief, beating away the same bouncing insects Charlie continued battling.

"Ben, why aren't these things biting you?" Leaf asked.

"Skin's way too tough for these little flying needles."

"They probably know they'd be poisoned if they drank his blood." Charlie's comment drifted just quiet enough for no one to hear but Leaf. Leaf's head shook and he turned up a corner of his mouth. Leaf pulled a corroded tin bucket from the weeds, holding it to the sky and checking for holes. He tipped his waterskin and poured.

Maggie's ears twitched. Her head sank and she lapped sloshing water. Lips smacked and she clopped several appreciative hoof stomps. George dropped and rested on an even patch of tundra, unlacing his boots. His face contorted while twisting and turning each boot. A loose expression washed across his stained face after both freed his feet. Charlie imitated the exercise and released a long breath. "Got any blisters yet?"

"My blisters have blisters. My entire right foot is one big blister. Better get some fresh socks. So what do you think about her?"

"About who?"

"C.S., you know exactly who."

"Oh, Merry. She seems nice. Guess we can't really consider it a rebound attraction after the amount of time that's passed." He pulled a stalk of grass and stuck it between his teeth, chlorophyll biting his tongue while the end rolled between his fingertips.

"When Deborah died, I swore I'd never, ever allow myself to become that way again. Didn't see it was worth it. Don't get me wrong, I'm not saying the memories were bad or anything. But, but it was just too much. Musta lived on Oreos and root beer for a year."

"Yeah, I remember." Leaf allowed Maggie to roam the immediate area and nibble across lupine while Benjamin vanished around the opposite side of the bus.

"Oregon plates, guess his registration is overdue," they heard Benjamin's voice call and the rapid clicks of his camera's alien mechanical shutter.

"Never in a million years would I have thought I'd meet someone like her out here. We must have talked half the night. We are so much alike. Her husband, Rick, was a mechanic in Blackhole. She was born there and always had a dream of moving back near her mom and dad's home but they sold their property and moved to Fairbanks. Her voice, her eyes, her everything, man, I felt like a babbling idiot when we were introduced. I was so tunneled into her face I couldn't speak a single word anyone could understand," George continued with hands no longer rubbing his toes but flying in wide circles at his sides.

"Can't tell you how happy I am that you met her."

"But, man, this is tougher than Basic."

"You were a younger man then, also," Charlie sipped from his waterskin, droplets dribbling down his chin's whisker stubble and cutting paths through the grime.

"But even when I catch myself thinking that I'm half dead," he paused to concentrate on wriggling pink toes, "I don't know if I've ever actually been this alive." Charlie's head dropped and he rubbed grit from his wrists.

"You should see your face right now," Charlie smiled and smacked the side of his head.

"I know. Long overdue for a bath, but I can't look any worse than you."

"Not that. It could be darker than the middle of the night now, and I think the glow on your face could light our way. That's better," Charlie sighed and curled his toes inside new cushioning socks. "I'd give anything not to put those boots back on."

"Gentlemen, you may want to come take a look at this," Leaf called from inside, the shock springs creaking with his footfalls. His head appeared through the open side front door with a hand covering his nose and mouth. Charlie ascended the steps and turned to look down the interior length.

"Man, what is that?" Charlie furled his nose and stuck the inside of his elbow across his face. More mosquitoes buzzed and slapped the glass. All seating was removed except a pair in the front. Squat shelves with assorted dusted cans and bags lined one side. At the rear, a table jutted against the back window covered in plywood with a low stool. He took exploring steps forward to a rotten cot occupying the opposite side where Leaf stood with his head bent down and nodded. Escaping from beneath the edge of a red-and-black checkered blanket, a single boned hand descended, naked skeleton fingertips pointing to the floor. A gold band dimmed with dust around gray mummified skin.

"How long?" Charlie's muffled voice rose through the cloth of his sleeve.

"No telling for certain, but I'd have to say not more than a year. Kinda shocked he's actually still here. Bears or wolves should have torn into him within a week." Leaf lifted the blanket's edge where dried tendon and flaking skin still anchored the upper arm to a shoulder. "I don't see any obvious trauma."

"What should we do?"

"If he's been here this long, let's let him keep resting. I'll get in touch with the authorities when we get back. He might have some family still missing him. Besides, we need to keep moving if we're going to reach the mine by tomorrow. As I've said before, this land not only requires respect, it demands it." Charlie nodded in silent agreement. "No need to mention this."

"Almost thought you two went to sleep in there. Anything we can use?"

"Nope," Charlie replied with a lifting chin. Exiting the bus, his pack crawled back over his shoulders. He extended a hand toward George and lifted him to his feet.

Charlie scanned the rolling hills while keeping distance behind Leaf and Maggie. He selected a marker—a unique tree, rock, or discoloration convincing himself that he only had to make it to that one point. After arrival, he found and concentrated on another until accomplishing the goal of reaching it. Markers came and passed, each one an image of Charlotte getting closer. Air remained silent and still across the landscape. Their path opened to a wide tundra field scattered with dotting, short wildflowers, no more than purple-and-yellow specks stretching across frozen waves to the distant mountain range melting against the skyline. "Anybody hear something?" George's question broke the repetition.

Leaf stopped, turned his head to one side, and brushed a hand across Maggie's back. A single wind gust blew a loose strand of hair across his eyebrows. Kneeling to the ground, his hands shifted and rubbed the moss tips.

Beneath the soles of his feet, Charlie sensed a confused, random, vibrating thrum. Distant lowing intensified from a vague whisper to a rising rush in his ears. On the horizon, black specks bobbed and leapt like a vast ant army. At first, the shadows formed no more than an amorphous thin line. Then, the line thickened where he identified specific galloping pinpoints growing and advancing.

"Anybody else feel that?" George noticed the focus of Charlie's stare.

"Uh, young man," Benjamin stammered towards Leaf. "I think I've seen something like this before." Leaf's cringing eyes opened, now wide blinking flashes.

"Me too. Run!"

"Run where?" George's voice rose in recognition of the advancing herd and increased hoof-beat volume like water rising in a flash-flooding river.

"There," Leaf pointed to a crevice where a thin slit opened in the field of vision and scattered lichen-covered boulders descended a rim.

"Think we can make it in time?"

"Guess we're gonna find out," Leaf cried from behind, dragging Maggie's straightened reins and pulling her as fast as she allowed. George high-stepped across the sponge-springing ground, pack bobbing across his back. Benjamin huffed with an open mouth and thwacked Maggie across her rear with his walking stick. Leaf noticed George's head turn. "Don't look back, keep going!"

Charlie couldn't resist.

He turned and now saw specific arching antler points bobbing and shaking above wide, glistening, brown-eye reflections. Rumbling beneath his feet shook his vision.

The crevice grew closer.

The bolting, antler-headed sea advanced as a single massive shadow across the land, galloping and bumping against one another. Those in front attempted adjusting in recognition of the human obstructions but were pushed forward by the advancing hoofed ocean, unable to perceive a need for direction change.

Tundra vanished and loose-graveled ground appeared beneath them. One side of the crevice opened where Leaf pulled Maggie down below ground level. With a final head-turn to watch tundra clumps and debris raining upwards and through the air from ten thousand hooves beating the ground, Charlie lost balance and tripped over an untied lace. He landed on his side with the herd's vibration resonating through the length of his body.

"Charlie, what do you think you're doing? Get down here," George called from the narrow fissure, his voice almost inaudible from the braying and antler-clicking collisions. The animals advanced close enough for Charlie to examine neck and shoulder muscles rippling beneath their short, tan fur and white necks. Mustard-chipped teeth bared and nipped at one another. His eyes clamped shut, and he braced for the initial impact.

A force grabbed his backpack and lifted him to his feet. No time remained when Benjamin wrapped his arms around Charlie's neck and both men fell backwards over the crevice's side, landing several feet below into dense ferns.

Charlie lay with his eyes staring upwards, backpack shifted to one side. The sky melted to a crimson yellow through the opening above his head. Shapes of flying furred bellies blotted out the light in intermittent flashing obstructions, leaping across the crevice and continuing a rain of descending splattered mud and moss clumps. He wriggled from his pack and rolled to one side where Leaf attempted calming Maggie beneath a slight overhang.

Pebbles and shards separated from the wall and dusted their hair. Rock continued vibrating and shuddering. "You sure it's safe here?" George yelled.

"Safer than up there," Leaf returned, flashing an upwards thumb.

"Son, you just about got yourself stomped to death," Benjamin called, stooped on both knees. Charlie rubbed dust and grime from his palms and said nothing to his father. The constant rumble ebbed to random, occasional thumps in unison to a decreased and final absence of the blotting shadowed bodies leaping above their heads.

"They're gone? What was that?" George yelled even though volume was no longer required. Leaf crept up the incline and glanced over the edge. One hand motioned the others to follow.

"They're gone. Caribou. Lucky again. Herds run these parts in the thousands, and once they get spooked, best thing to do is anything you can to get out of their way." All three men emerged from the crevice and stood behind Leaf, surveying what was, a few moments before, a green, even field. The ground stretched in a mud-caked stew of torn vegetation and random puddled water. "Gentlemen, the hour is getting late, and it's time we holed up for the evening. Let's head for those poplars and get some shelter."

"Boy, get up, your turn," Charlie heard a gruff through the shelter flap and Benjamin's stick jabbing his toes. Charlie pulled his rifle from the side bag, checking for safety latch engagement, and crawled into the night.

Above the fire crackles, George's snoring rose through the thin nylon walls of Benjamin's tent. Charlie's cough produced no reaction from his father who sat cross-legged on a goldenrod mound, his knife whittling away at an anonymous stick. He released quiet, soft whistles in an obscure tune. The black outline of Leaf's body was camouflaged beneath deer skin layers with his back toward them. Charlie checked the pot for any remaining tea.

"Looking for this?" Benjamin ceased his whistling and motioned a cup. Charlie snatched it and downed the final remaining sips swirling at the bottom. His neck arched while examining the vast star field array. "That son of Bill's—Henry? He was something else, wasn't he?" Benjamin commented to himself. Charlie huddled with his knees drawn up to his chest and his rifle propped to one side. Flames dwindled. Charlie tossed additional split wood into the embers, blowing until flames resurfaced.

"You can go to sleep now, Benny. Sun's gonna be up in a few hours," Charlie uttered, still bent over and blowing across the coals.

"I'm aware of that."

"Pulling me up from getting stomped to death and dragging me back. You know you didn't have to do that," Charlie said, tapping his rifle stock.

"Yes, son, yes I did." Both men paused.

"Just tell me one thing—why did you leave for so long? Huh? Why did you do it?" Words spilled forward with the cadence of a university professor.

Moments passed with no more than burning wood and the muted hush of night air blowing in from across the open field. Whistling stopped. "Because I'm weak." His blade also ceased skipping across the wood's surface, studying the metal's shining reflection. "Everyone handles pain in different ways, son. When I sat in that office and the doctor told us about your mom, it almost seemed like I was on the outside looking in on someone else's life."

"I've learned a little about pain. And the one thing I do know is that it's not something to run away from like you did," Charlie's voice rose.

"Oh?" he scanned the melting terrain and gave a sideways glance through the edges of his gold rims, now teetering on the end of his nose.

"Don't try confusing this with what you did. I'm doing this for my little girl, and if I didn't at least try, both she and I would never know a more significant regret. At least whatever life she has left."

"Look, okay, this is it. When your mom died, I died too. Well, at least the most important part that I've ever been or will be. I did everything I could to shield you from those long agonizing hours of moaning and suffering. I would have given my very soul to enjoy even a single peaceful moment before passing on. But I couldn't do it. I couldn't take any more pain. So, I buried myself in work, traveled, and tried putting as much distance and time between myself and that memory." Benjamin's knife resumed and increased with each shaving flying faster than the previous one.

"But you did lose again, Benny, you lost me and your granddaughter. Oh, I see, that's why you haven't seen Charlotte yet." Charlie sat back, blowing on his fingers. His father's whittling now flew at a frenetic pace, brief white slivers shooting from his hands.

"If I can help find this gold, if I can give something back of what I should have been giving to you and her for all these years, maybe it'll compensate for even the slightest of my weakness." Benjamin released an extended exhalation, and his blade ceased any further cuts, dropping to his side. "You may be right. I've obviously lost my only son, but I can't lose my granddaughter too."

"It's never been about the money. Look at Karen and me, we can't even pay the electricity bill to keep the lights on half the time. But you know what? We're family. I can't begin comprehending running away from them no matter how bad things ever got." Charlie now leaned forward to stare at his father, both of their faces framed in the fire glow.

"And do you know why?" Charlie shook his head. "Because you've become a better man than I could have ever hoped to be." Benjamin removed his glasses and rubbed the lenses with his red checkered flannel. Both men crouched in silence with no more than a dry crunch in the distance rising above the voices of burning wood.

Both of their heads lifted to watch the faraway dense star concentration spanning the sky. "Remember looking at those same stars by the campfire in Yosemite? When you look out at them you, we, are looking back in time—a lot longer than the last time we looked at them together." Benjamin's hand rose and opened a shirt-button flap, removing folded pages. "Here," he muttered and leaned over, dropping them into Charlie's lap. Charlie unfolded them and recognized Absalom's handwriting in an instant, turning the images toward the light. His lips moved without sound as he scanned down the entries.

"This is it. Everything makes sense except for this—what does it mean? Look to the Cross?"

"That's the only part I haven't quite figured out. After hours at the library, I figured he must have hid it somewhere near the old Stanton outfit," Benjamin found his own voice rise and fall in the same tenor as his son. "Seems we came to the same conclusion."

"That could mean anything."

"No matter what, at least he put the latitude and longitude of the general area. He may have not known how to read or write very well, but at least he was good with numbers." Charlie folded the pages back and motioned them toward Benjamin. "No, put them back where they belong." Charlie crawled inside but returned, both men resuming their universe examination.

"You remember going to Uncle Tyler's when I was a kid?"

"Some of the best days of my life, son. No matter where I was or what I was doing, I will never forget that happy pureness in your eyes even during my last breath." Benjamin's gaze returned to the flames, wrinkles spanning at the corners of his eyes and the tips of his moustache rising to touch tightened cheeks.

"George and I stopped by to see him on the way up. Can you believe he still lives in that old cabin?"

"Sure miss him too, sometimes. Who do you think taught me how to shoot? Well, I guess you could say he taught the both us since I taught you. What do you know? This started out as a flute but now I don't think it'll be good for anything more than a toothpick." Benjamin rolled the white spindle between his thumb and forefinger. Charlie allowed his eyes to drift down and lock vision onto this father.

He had no control over the corners of his own mouth, rising to mimic his father's expression. Both men proceeded to identical yawns. "Think I'll take you up on that offer and rest my eyes awhile. Benjamin rose with a protest and stretched, rubbing his hands for a final time over the flames. "That lake water was sure cold, wasn't it?" he turned and headed toward his tent. "Good night, son." Charlie hunched forward and loomed over the embers.

"Dad?"

"What is it, son?"

"Thanks." His father moved slowly but deliberately while Charlie crouched in his coat and lost sight of his father. Charlie no longer identified between the star swirl above and the sparkle of Charlotte's eyes.

CHAPTER

28

Charlie scanned ahead while knee and ankle wrenching faded with a rapid pulse rise. "This supposed to be it?" Down the now even slope of their descent, parting spruce revealed glimpses of rust orange iron and crumbled tin sheets. Distant mountain range peaks across the valley were cloaked in colorless obscuring mist.

Benjamin stayed behind with Leaf and Maggie. George huffed, keeping pace with Charlie. They reached the slope's bottom. He stood surveying the scattered landscape of half-collapsed structures with hands on his hips, breath still bolting from his lungs. A stark orange set of disjointed tracks wound through the center of the open, gravel-floored field with multiple I-bars turned to one side and massive iron spikes squeezed from the split trestles. Bits of weed and sedges poked up beneath them like unshaven stubble.

Charlie wandered to the largest building's gaping collapsed wall. A century of snow falling, settling, and melting across metal and wooden surfaces reduced the once solid shelters to shambled skeletons: bowed planks and gaped joints, cracked splits with the hue of bleached bones offering uncertain support to the corrugated tin and weak iron. Several side and storage sheds remained almost intact.

The vast array of iron and steel wheels, shafts, gears, and multiple more unrecognizable shapes were strewn in random piles while others remained stacked with precision. The oxidizing assortments appeared as if some giant hand had rolled and scattered them around in every conceivable direction and angle. Charlie beat the burnt orange dust coating from his palms when the sound of Maggie's clomping hooves crunched in his ears. "Doesn't look like much, does it?"

"Can't say that it does, but this is definitely Stanton. I think there were two brothers." Leaf's expression shifted into an easing of normal tightening around his eyes, staring back to the past. "It's been almost twenty years since Dad and I were here last. Doesn't look a bit different than it did then." Leaf tied off Maggie to a splintered wall protruding timber.

Ragged tin corners bent just within reach for the animal to rub against and offer multiple satisfied chortles. A tremendous wind gust descended into the valley and swirled uncovered scalps in white crystal flurries twisting through the air.

"If this is supposed to be a mining operation, where is the mine?"

"Come on," Leaf motioned and both men exited from beneath the open roof. Leaf straddled the crusting dilapidated iron rails and pointed. Charlie followed the line of sight from Leaf's extended finger, and a black, almost visible rough rectangle appeared from the brush. Scrub shrouded beaten squared oak timbers. "That's the main entrance from what I can recall. There should be a couple of others scattered at different points around the base and one way up at the top. All depends on how much has collapsed since then."

Leaf's words resurfaced ignored objective reasoning. Truths squeezed through that had managed suppression since the Majestic left Seattle. Leaf's scan continued, unaware of Charlie leaving the tracks and half jogging to where Maggie still nibbled.

"So this is Absalom's hiding place? Thought he might have done a little better. Not quite what I pictured, to be honest," Benjamin's pipe appeared from his shirt pocket after he rubbed sweat and dust from his glasses. George entered the main structure, his shape no more than a black outline against the Swiss cheese holes spanning the rear wall and several wide light shafts descending through the collapsed roof. Benjamin followed, coughing from kicked-up specks and the weighted odor of kerosene-soaked burlap. Charlie didn't notice their presence.

George released a slow whistle and ran an open palm across the adz head-hacked beams once supporting a massive water wheel. The axle had long since been displaced from its shaft and tilted at a slant against a stacked granite wall just below ground level. Trickling water gurgled through a narrow slot, open on one end of the cavernous room and struggling to force its way through to the opposite side.

A teetering open sluice scaled along the entire back wall, but several sections collapsed, seeping dew and condensation from higher elevations. George nudged a pile of scrap iron with his boot but retracted it, turning upwards at the sound of scurrying feet scratching against thin metal sheeting.

"Looks like we aren't the only ones here," George muttered and bent down to examine a scattered roll of dung pellets. "Rabbit or raccoon?"

"Sounds more like rats. What do you think you're doing there, son?" Benjamin asked and looked up after serious concentration on his pipe bowl's cherry-red glow. Wind-swirled smoke spun around his head the moment it drifted from beneath his moustache.

Charlie almost tripped over a pipe and broke his concentration while heaving a shovel in one hand, a bobbing lantern in the other, and a rope coil looped over one shoulder. Leaf appeared around the corner at the first footfall of Charlie's exit from the wheelhouse.

"Whoa, hang on there just one minute. It's going dark in an hour or two. There's no use trying to get in there tonight. None of us are thinking very clear right now."

"Leaf, I appreciate everything you've done for us, and there's no way we would have ever made it this far without you, but I have to see, I have to find out." Charlie leaned to one side as if to pass Leaf. A hand came to rest on his shoulder.

"He's right. If Absalom's haul has been holed up in there all these years, I can't see that twelve hours is gonna make a whole lot of difference," his father advised, pipe clenched back between his teeth. "Besides, I'm starving." Charlie examined the shovel in his hands, released a complicit breath, and rested the handle against a pump.

Maggie neighed with the rope slung back over her side. Charlie bent down, striking a match and hissing the lantern to life. The entire room glowed in a slick yellow dullness, filling their nostrils with age's decay.

"I'm on firewood detail," George called out and headed back toward the earlier descended slope with the axe bouncing on his shoulder.

"Hold up, I'll give you a hand," Charlie called and pursued.

George released his accustomed belch even startling Maggie. A wide vocal yawn howled above the calm. Wind quieted a return back to occasional air rushes but still enough to send ghost voices through the myriad of holes in ancient metalwork. A breeze played loose, flapping tin sheets with pinging thwacks against decayed wood.

Leaf tossed another log into the rapid ember descent, kicking up sparks to whisk away in the night sky. He returned to the incessant click of his knife angled against a sharpening stone. "Listen to that, you'd think we landed in the middle of hell itself with all of that howling and carrying on," Benjamin commented through peaceful stem puffing.

"Tell you something, we got here without a minute to spare. I can smell it on the air. If we're gonna have any shot at making it back, there can be no delay past tomorrow, or we'll need three dogsled teams to get back over those mountains," Leaf uttered beneath his breath as if struggling with each successive word. Charlie stretched and yawned, the last taste of dried salmon still in his throat.

"Who's up first?" Charlie asked with no immediate replies.

"Shouldn't be a danger anymore. Food is just about gone. I figure two us can stay in here, and the shack across those tracks is in good enough shape to keep out any wanderers," Leaf reassured after rolling his padding over the pebble-covered ground around the fire ring. Diminished light contrast remained through the holes and open, torn wheelhouse wall. Heaving clouds brought premature dimness, and the appearance of night returned. Leaf rose and swung the lantern through the opening. "Snow hasn't stuck yet, but I guarantee it will any time now. That's a nasty front coming through. George, why don't you and Charlie bed down for the night? We'll all get a good rest and fresh start first thing in the morning. George—George?" Leaf's words were met with a muted snore managing to rise above the growing howls and shrieks.

"Forget it, he's out," Benjamin rose in slow motion and draped a blanket across the length of George's reclined body where he used a pile of rotten sacks as a pillow. "Can't believe a man could fall asleep that fast with all of this racket."

"Well, that settles it. Charlie, Ben, I'll come get you at first light. Okay with you?" Leaf asked, casting a glance between Charlie and his father.

"Yeah," Charlie struggled a response. He threw his pack over his shoulders and trailed behind Benjamin, already across the tracks and pushing in the creaking shack door hanging by a single hinge, grinding above the wind. Benjamin raised the lantern above his head for a quick survey, and he suspended the handle on a rail spike pounded into the door frame. More debris, litter, and animal dung were scattered across the splintered floor with wide gaps dividing planks. Billowing dust clouds rose and resulted in several exchanged sneezes.

"Hey, take a look over here," Benjamin called and fell to one knee. He opened the front door of a potbellied stove in the cramped room's back corner. Fingers explored up the pipe's rise leading to the ceiling, and he nodded to his son in confidence. "Seems okay, let's try it." Benjamin gathered strewn splinters and sticks, kicking them into a loose pile at the base of the stove. A low flame emerged. Charlie rolled out his pad and took the first few waterskin sips. "That's nice, don't see any smoke filling up the place," Benjamin scanned the ceiling while stroking his whiskers, the firelight dancing reflections off his lenses. "Think we might need a bit more fuel, though. You still have that axe handy?"

"Sure, over by the door," Charlie pointed, rubbing his hands to thaw over the crackling flames and heat funneling through the wide opening. Benjamin hadn't opened the door more than a crack before a rush of wind pushed it wide and pulled him forward into the night.

"Would you listen to that? It musta dropped another twenty degrees since the sun went down."

"Here," Charlie rose, removing his coat and draping it around his father's quivering torso. He stumbled but caught the fall. He hunched against an ancient desk collapsed against the low window with several missing panes.

"Thank you." His father grabbed the axe and disappeared into the darkness with the lantern swinging in his one free hand. Charlie huddled cross-legged in front of the fire with a blanket wrapped tight around his shoulders. Creaks, pops, wails, grinds, and a symphony of other sounds cascaded with random notes in no particular sequence. Although he was surrounded by four walls, the entire structure leaned to one back corner, and Charlie forced himself to ignore wide black gaps for possible eyes returning his glance. He groped the floor for his rifle behind him and pressed the chilled metal barrel against his cheek.

The front door bang creaking back to life startled Charlie from a doze with his eyes clamped and his head leaning against the wall. "Sorry to wake you," Benjamin's words emerged between chattering teeth while dragging splintered dry pine through the doorway. Stove flames roared with rejuvenation from the cross-ventilation.

"Let me help." Charlie dragged in three more armfuls. "We're only going to be here for the night. How much did you get?" Charlie's own words stumbled with the effect of blowing wind, sensing the fire's previous escaping warmth.

"Never have enough." Benjamin slammed the door shut behind him. "Ain't gotta pee or anything?" Charlie shook his head. With the understanding, Benjamin slid what remained of the desk in front of the door with jamming hip motions. "Now, let's get this fire really roaring."

"Dad, you remember much that summer after the eighth grade when we went to Yosemite?" Charlie managed keeping his question coherent after rewrapping himself in the blanket and allowing the fire's heat to warm his throat.

"As I recall, I promised you a camping trip if your team won your division. And boy, did you ever. You guys clobbered 'em. You had what? Seven runs all by yourself?"

"Five."

"Yeah, well, it might have been ten as far as I was concerned." Benjamin took a tentative seat in a creaking Windsor spindle chair and tested its strength. His entire weight strained the grain. One hand fumbled through his flannel pocket for crumpled Borkum Riff. "Your mom had to tie me to the bleachers to keep me from floating away." Although faint light filtered through the stove's open door, enough emitted for Charlie to recognize distinct twitching whiskers.

"When we were at that old settler's town camp near Silver Falls, I remember sitting around the fire, you telling mom and me ghost stories, and then the next morning we went and swam at the lake all day."

"The water was almost as cold as our unexpected dunking. A little early good practice for the both of us, you think?" his question diminished as if not expecting an answer.

"I remember you taking mom's picture."

"Oh yes. We were driving down this little winding back road deep in the woods, branches making a tunnel above us. A stream ran down right along the side of it. Your momma carried on and on about how beautiful she thought it looked with the sunlight filtering through the leaves and the way the white water splashed against the slate and boulders. It was an opportunity not allowed to go to waste." Charlie watched his father's words, hands moving in contortions, and his pipe bowl glow swirling through the air. "Mom put on her black coat and light stepped across the smaller rocks to reach one particular boulder almost in the middle of the stream. Oh, I tell you, your mother was one beautiful woman. I decided to leave her alone, enjoy the moment, and went back to check on you. When I looked back through the tree clearing and saw her perched on the rock tossing back that fine corn silk hair, I could have sworn Heaven opened up and an angel fell right out of the sky." Charlie bent forward to get a clearer look at his father's face.

"Then what?"

"Well, I grabbed my camera 'cause I couldn't let that moment get away. Snuck down behind a stump, leaned over the lens, and froze time. I've been around this world ten times over, visited more places than my memory can begin to recollect. My eyes have seen wondrous things but much more than a million miles later and almost as many photographs, that was the closest to perfect a man could ever take. You remember how much your momma hated having her picture taken?" Charlie nodded.

"You know something, Dad, there's more that I can't remember than I can by now. Her face is almost starting to fade from memory." Charlie choked on his last words. He grabbed a splintered rail from the floor and stabbed the logs, flipping one over to a raw side.

"What do you remember?"

"She always smelled like honeysuckle. Whatever happened to that photograph?" Charlie sensed Benjamin rustling in the shadows and his stomps sounding across the floor, nails creaking beneath his weight. One arm reached into his back pocket and removed a wallet, two fingers pushing around until pulling out a creased square. It dropped into Charlie's lap. He opened the worn folds, and his mother's profile stared back from a warm, late summer day, in the middle of a rushing California stream. Charlie turned to look at his father but remained silent not by deliberate decision.

"Yeah, does that to me too." Benjamin returned to his chair and continued silent puffing behind the cracks and hisses of burning pine resin. "Go on, take a good hard look. Don't you ever forget the face of that angel." Charlie reclined on his padding, no longer finding the strength to remain upright. He settled a position, allowing firelight to illuminate the photo while his eyes studied every curve, angle of light, and dimensional perspective. His eyes closed a final time with the image still dancing across his retinas.

CHAPTER

29

Charlie swatted specks pelting his nose and cheeks, stirring him back from scene-twisting dreams of Charlotte's eyes and Karen's voice. The night's howling wind vanished, and silence replaced it with distant-morning bird chirping. Chattering claws on wood stirred apart his eyelids.

The previous evening's vague recollection struggled back into his thoughts, still trying to disseminate the dreams. High in the rafters, whiskers twitched over shadowed beam edges followed by another claw scamper. Charlie scanned the dusty, debris-covered floor and pushed back his blanket.

Charlie probed just below his chest for the journal. He collapsed back beneath the blanket's lingering warmth but snapped upright recognizing an absence of the cover's familiar touch. He shoved and scattered every surrounding object. His pulse quickened while crawling around the cramped room on his hands and knees.

Benjamin was gone, his pad rolled up in a bundle and pushed beneath the chair. He remembered wrapping his coat around his father's shoulders. The memory returned at the same time he noticed the desk pulled back and away from the door.

Charlie leapt through the creaking, one-hinged door, looped his laces, and sprinted toward Maggie. She turned and heaved a muted whine at his arrival. Leaf disappeared but George's still sleeping body lump continued snoring in the new day's air.

Charlie grabbed the coil of rope again, throwing it over his shoulder. His shovel and lantern bounced beneath a clear blue morning. His thighs pumped down the scattered tracks until taking a hesitant glance at the looming black opening. Timbers framing the mine entrance appeared more splintered and lopsided than observed from yesterday's distance. There was no indication of any interior light as he struck a match and the lantern burped to life. He inhaled a concentrated breath, pushed any sensation of collapsing, crushing walls from his thoughts, and replaced them with Charlotte's frail pale face. Ducking into the entrance, he raised the lantern as high as the low-cut ceiling allowed.

Narrow walls glistened with dampness. Like the wheelhouse and shack, the floor was covered in rusted metal carcasses and mysterious mechanical skeletons. Tracks remained clear enough to judge direction, jumping and dodging a path farther down the tunnel. The passageway descended while Charlie noticed pick-axe iron grooves in the quartz-splotched walls. He paused, catching his breath, and witnessed the mine entrance no more than a pinprick of light behind him.

With each footfall, Charlie imagined more of the mass above his head, but Charlotte's tightened eyebrows pushed aside sweating palms and the blood rush beating through his eardrums.

"Hello!" he shouted down the corridor to no response but his own returned echoing inquisition. He approached an intersection where the tunnel opened wider into a high-vaulted ceiling room. Pick-axes, shovels more rust than metal, and other manual digging implements were scattered among loose chipped quartz. Ash handles had been long since eaten away by insects as he kicked them with a boot. Several side tunnels split off in four different directions from the oval domed chamber. He swung the lantern in each direction, searching for footprints, but the floor was too covered in strewn gravel to leave any identifiable trail. Scanning into the first tunnel, a complete rubble collapse blocked any degree of forward movement. He approached the second-to-last opening and strained his vision. Above the opening, Charlie made out the shape of a cross. Distinctive white quartz edges were rough, but there was no mistaking an extended milk-white line intersected by a shorter line perpendicular to the first further down its length. His father's words from the missing pages surfaced. He gulped a heaving swallow, ducked his head, and entered.

If Charlie believed the previous corridor was narrow, clearance was almost spacious compared to this current diminishing passage, wide enough for no more than one man to pass without having to turn to one side. At least the ceiling was higher and the lantern rose above his head. The winding path curved and gave a slight rise above the previous descent. Charlie lowered the lantern and stopped.

A faint glow appeared at the end of the passage. At the moment of recognition, a slight thumping shuddered through his boots. The blows like popping flash bulbs were followed by drizzled dust and splinters into his scalp. Somewhere far away through the density of granite, Charlie strained and heard the sounds of grating stone as if crews paved new road above his head.

Sweating, tingling pricks across his slick skin now clawed up from within, intestines squirming and tightening acid regurgitations in his throat. He shook the images aside and rubbed the dust from his eyes. His pace increased toward the glow until he rounded a corner and saw another lantern. It lit up a wide, cleared-out section. Although less spacious as the initial cavern, the excavation allowed for comfortable movement. On the room's far side, the floor disappeared into blackness along one entire edge. A single rope was tied off to a crossbeam buried in the wall, and the opposite end disappeared over the contrasted rim. "Anybody here?"

"Charlie, boy, that you?" Benjamin's voice rose from below. Charlie first studied the anger he would hurl down while approaching the drop-off and swung his lantern over the side. His father turned up to glance toward the additional light. "It's here, Charlie! It's really here—look!" Benjamin stepped aside and allowed the full lantern to reflect across a faded rectangular red trunk obscured under fallen rock.

Charlie stared.

His mind attempted separating the rage of betrayal and witnessing the actual manifestation. Another floor shudder beneath his feet jolted him from achievement. More chips cracked and splintered from the walls, sputtering across loose gravel.

"Come on, Charles, pull it up. There's not much time. This whole place is gonna—" Benjamin couldn't finish his command when the most violent shake yet knocked Charlie from his feet. The lantern fell from his hands but remained lit, the glass shroud searing a burn across his wrist. Throbbing peaked with each heartbeat. Fine particle clouds kicked through the air as he choked and held his collar over his mouth.

"Dad, you okay?" Charlie coughed and stumbled, swaying to his feet. Nothing but a low whimper met his question. He again leaned the light over the ledge. Benjamin lay on his back squinting toward the blinding flame. He hugged the chest with one arm while the other pushed boulders from his waist. Charlie noticed an immediate crimson spreading across his father's leg. Fine haze powdered his glasses, shoved high on his forehead at an unnatural angle while his beard twitched and grimaced. "Hold on, I'm coming down to get you."

"No—no more time, the next one is gonna bring tons down on both of us." Charlie lashed one end of his rope around the same post, securing the other rope, and tossed the free end over the side.

"Tie this around your waist and legs, and I'll get you and the chest up," Charlie commanded with adrenaline forcing each motion in subtle choreography and direction while the opposite length of sisal landed across his father's chest. "Yeah, that's it, now push through there."

"I know, I know, who do you think taught you this knot?" Benjamin coughed and winced. Another jolt rumbled the cavern walls, smacking Benjamin with colliding debris and more rolling further past him, vanishing without impact echoes. "What do you think you're doing?" came a protest as Benjamin's rope became taut. "Don't worry about me, I'll be fine. Get the gold first. That's why we came here in the first place, remember?"

For an instant, Benjamin's line slackened and Charlie stretched for the first rope.

Several shards raining from the ceiling glanced across the crown of his exposed head. Grit and powder filled his lungs. He rose to both feet and ran Benjamin's rope around his waist, dug in at his heels, and staggered in reverse. On the twisted cord's opposite end, guttural gasps echoed over closer rumbling shakes. Charlie's eyes strained through the clouding dust until a hand appeared over the edge and then another.

When he believed enough of his father cleared the edge, Charlie lunged forward while retaining tension, grabbing Benjamin by the collar and pulling him the remaining distance to the floor. His father rolled to one side, releasing an excruciating yell almost as loud as the surrounding chaos. His right leg followed the rest of his body, but the other foot didn't respond and failed to realign, still horizontal against the even ground.

Benjamin pulled his glasses from his forehead and blinked into Charlie's eyes. "Yeah, it's broke all right," he strained between teeth. His face slipped to slick white beneath the grime. He didn't have enough time for another word when the floor swayed beneath both men and a deafening thunder-crack peel crashed through their ears.

The remaining rope snapped tight.

Charlie rose from his father's side and swung the lantern over the edge. Benjamin exhaled and rolled to also glance down. A snapping pop exploded while they watched the shelf where he had just lay split into multiple fissures and collapse into the dark chasm.

The red chest tumbled into blackness.

Charlie registered a split second of the splintering strained wood and ducked the trailing rope and post flying at him from behind.

Rather than the rumble returning to calm, rolling vibrations continued as echoes of the falling ceiling reverberated down narrow passages. "Come on, can't think about it anymore, we've got to get out of here!" Benjamin shouted and propped himself up before recognizing Charlie's search for splint material. Charlie knelt down, strapping broken shovel handles to each side of Benjamin's leg and used his t-shirt as a securing tourniquet. He threw his father's arm around his shoulders. Both men's jaws clenched as Benjamin's weight pressed against him. Charlie stumbled and strained back down the passage, using his own body to cushion the wall impacts until they reached the first cavern.

"Charlie, is that you?" a voice rose into the corners of his awareness. Two silhouetted figures appeared in the open archway.

"Come on, give me a hand," Charlie choked and gasped. Leaf and George each took an arm. As they progressed back up and toward the hole of light growing larger ahead, supporting wall beams squealed and fractured from tons of pressurized granite squeezing in from every side. Behind them, the ruptured crashing echoed in their eardrums.

Violence vibrated through their skeletons. Charlie sensed the initial stages of lost consciousness. The last image in his vision was an ever-widening hole of light at the tunnel's end where chills melted into warmth.

Charlie awoke to the icy wetness of a handkerchief across his forehead. He coughed a violent tremor from the deepest passages of his lungs. The ground no longer shook, and he heard a braying mule. His eyes remained caked over, and he rubbed his lashes, removing the blur. "He okay?" Charlie managed a gasp from tightened neck muscles.

"Just fine, don't worry. Put your head back down and take this," Leaf instructed, raising a hot cup of tea to Charlie's lips. The liquid heat soothed throat-lining scratches, still raw from inhaled particles.

"That you, son?" Charlie raised his head once again and saw Benjamin stretching opposite of him. Benjamin's reddish-gray beard was mottled and clumped. Gashes and cuts of crusted, dry blood pitted his wrinkled forehead. "Boy, you should see yourself."

"You're talking. You don't look a whole lot better," Charlie tried smiling and coughed. He turned back to stare up at the blue expanse poking through surrounding aspen bending in the breeze. "It's gone, isn't it?"

"Yes, son, it is."

"Charlie, you need more rest. I don't see any significant injuries inside or out, but Benjamin needs some attention. I set him up with a better splint and stopped most of the bleeding, but some of those ribs aren't much better than the ankle. Not much more I can do up here. At least he appears over the shock," Leaf towered above them. George knelt next to Benjamin, tilting his head to drink from a cup. "Should be able to make an improvised gurney with the stuff laying around here, and Maggie can do most of the work taking him back. If we can at least get to Mabel's, he should be okay. She can keep him stable until we can get word back to Creektoe." Both Leaf and Charlie turned to a gurgle growing in Benjamin's throat. The slight chuckle transformed into a belly laugh, but the shooting trauma forced him to stop.

"Imagine that. We brought that mule all the way up here to haul back a treasure of gold, and it winds up what we really needed him for was to haul back a broken old man," he allowed his words to trail off, followed with a few additional snickers.

"Rest, Dad, rest," Charlie whispered. Benjamin's eyes closed once more, and George continued swabbing the dirt from his face.

"That goes for both of you," George commanded.

"I think we all need to lay low for a while. I'll get everyone something to eat, and we'll head down in a couple of hours," Leaf finished.

CHAPTER

30

Keeping eyes focused toward the tips of his boots negotiating bone-snapping granite, Charlie hacked beneath his breath. "How much farther, you think?" Naked thin weeds struggled up between the crevices.

"Depends, not sure about that sky. Luck's been with us so far," Leaf concluded and leaned against moist rock. The monochrome gray sky betrayed any sense of the afternoon's late hour. Most of the previous day's altitude descent remained silent with the exception of required communication.

Charlie and George tended to Benjamin, taking turns mopping the sweat from his forehead gashes and cushioning the lashed gurney Maggie guided down the trails. A stifled moan from the rear of the mule caused Leaf to turn once their procession heeded his rest. He shot a glance at Charlie but was too slow to masquerade it once recognized.

"Me too," Charlie acknowledged. "The fever doesn't seem to be easing, and his color's getting worse." George remained busy bending over Benjamin, pouring from his waterskin, and swabbing a soaked handkerchief across his face. Even in the late afternoon chill, sweat continued forming across his forehead.

"We have to get moving. Feel that wind?" Leaf turned as he spoke, eyes scanning a horizon shifting to darker gray tones swirling into invisible hazes. "Better make camp soon."

"No estimate on my first question?" Charlie prodded with a lowered volume.

"I'll be honest with you. Took a look at that leg and I think it's already starting to go a little septic. I assure you there's no way we're gonna make it all the way back to Dad's. But, with the rate we can travel and his condition, we can at least reach Mabel. I know the fish camp is closer, but you saw those people. They can't even help themselves." Charlie offered no protest to his logic. He also caught the unmistakable odor of Benjamin's main injury.

"Yeah, but Mabel? You think she can?" he now stood, voice still diminished, and returned to Leaf's blinking eyes.

"Hey, look what she did for you. She may not have university training, and I'm making no promises that your father will be dancing any jigs in a few days, but at least she can stabilize the wound, and infection I'm afraid, until we can get him some modern medicine."

"Guys, he's starting with the crazy talk again," Charlie turned to see George rounding the corner. His drawn face was caked with grime, detailing the cringes beneath his eyelids and a reddened creep around the corners of his mouth. "I—I—" his voice diminished.

"I know," Charlie replied.

"This is the plan," Leaf whispered. "We're setting up accommodations for tonight. The fish camp is no good, so we're gonna have to go around the lake. It'll probably add a good seven hours of footwork, but there's no other choice. Stay concentrated, keep focused, and waste no movement. There's no reason why we shouldn't make it by tomorrow night unless there are other events we can't control."

"Like what?" George asked as a wind gust blew hair across their scalps and answered a simultaneous response.

"Like that. See where the horizon gets fuzzy just over that ridge?" Leaf directed with his knife tip now unsheathed and pointing back over his shoulder. "That's one big blow, and only time will tell if it's coming this way." He turned and rose, scanning the immediate area.

"Here, give me a hand," Leaf jumped and disappeared into a low branch wall. He paused. "George, how about getting us the first load of fuel? We have to keep him extra warm tonight." Charlie followed, negotiating the waist-high juniper islands in his path. Leaf dropped to his knees and cleared dead brush and limbs from the ground. A single massive Sitka spruce rose like a spire above the younger saplings, and he evaluated the slope.

"Need some help?"

"We need shelter and we need it fast. The tent's no good. Cut off a few of these old limbs," he nodded at a twenty-foot log. Charlie snatched the axe handle from his shoulder blade, and the weight pulled at his stretched forearms. Chill permeated through his gloved fingers, and the handle was a slight sensation in his grip as it swung away, stripping branches. Leaf pulled his Bowie and hacked smaller limbs after tying off Maggie. Random gibberish continued dripping from Benjamin's lips with short jerks and spasms all concluding in sharp, breath-shortened gasps.

Both Leaf and Charlie concentrated on their tasks. "Take it easy—no sweating." Charlie nodded.

"Think that should about do it." Charlie accomplished a final dead-wood thwack.

"Good, come on," Leaf grabbed one end of the trunk while Charlie heaved the other side. With a breath whoosh, Leaf jerked the load over his head and jammed it into a crook where a thick limb met the trunk. "There. With that, get more branches and we'll throw the tarp over the top. At least most of the wind should stay blocked. I'll finish it off if you want to start on the fire pit. I'd say we've got about an hour of daylight left, and the temperature is gonna drop more than any of us would like."

"Already has," Charlie stood up from his cleared circle and shuddered at the two-dimensional sky. Far black peaks were Halloween-masked in gray mist, and although sleet diminished, fine flurry flakes danced and scattered, twirling and melting by the time they approached ground.

George returned for the axe. He tucked in Benjamin's hides and blankets again before disappearing once more. "Leaf, you think it's that bad?" Charlie spoke the words they both had so far avoided.

"Yes, yes it is. You got a whiff when I changed that dressing a little while ago. He needs more help than we can give him out here, and he needs it soon." Leaf completed anchoring the tarp. He pulled a tinderbox from one of Maggie's side bags after pushing together a leaf-and-twig pile. Crouching down in the fire pit, sparks flew from his flint until a glimmer of flame appeared. A breath released with the return of darkness.

"Let me help," Charlie said as he crouched down and blocked the gales with his body. The fire relit while both men fed twigs into the meager flame. Charlie watched the same filth and sweat coating across Leaf's features. He knew he appeared no different.

"You might want to clean some of that off yourself," Leaf commented between puffed air cheeks. Charlie wiped the back of a hand across his forehead and studied the dirt and black remnants of dried blood where his scalp split apart. George reappeared.

"I don't want to cause any unneeded alarm, but something shook the bushes down the hill. It was too dark to see, but it was big and moving." He dropped his armload of wood and bent forward over the flames, hands rubbing together in rapid succession.

"One thing you can always be certain of out here—you are never alone." Above the crackle of flame, a howl rose and whipped the overhead branches. George jumped while Leaf turned his head to one side, staring at the ground and pushing loose hair from his ears.

"Wolf?" Charlie asked while all three men swung their heads around even though they knew the practical hopelessness of identifying the wail's origin.

"Sounds like it. Don't worry, we're all staying close tonight." Leaf offered his most reassuring tone while fingers traced across his rifle's safety. He pulled a pack from Maggie, laying the ground blankets over cut boughs lining the shelter floor. "Even so, we stick to sentry rotation. Bears may not be a concern anymore, but that injury is sending signals in every direction high on this evening wind. With Ben out, it's gonna make our shifts a little longer. Stay close to the flap and holler out at anything suspicious."

"I shouldn't have any problem," George laughed.

"I mean it, shoot first. I'd rather lose a little sleep than anything else." George winced after unstrapping the poles tied to the mule's saddle and Benjamin's full weight bore down on his lower neck and shoulder. Charlie grabbed one side while pulling him back toward the shelter, positioning his father horizontal to now stretching flames and heat pouring from the pit. Cheek hairs twitched but Benjamin's eyes remained closed, flinching his hands in a lucid dream.

Charlie poured water from his canteen into a handkerchief and wiped his father's forehead. Droplets beaded into his eyebrows and reflected the firelight. Benjamin released a cough after Charlie wet his lips and forced a few drops down his throat.

"Here," Leaf motioned a few shreds of dried salmon in his direction.

"No thanks, appetite is off right now," Charlie replied without looking and continued stroking the wet cloth across his father's face.

"I'm not taking no for an answer," he now insisted and dropped the scraps into his lap. "We already have one down, and there's a long serious hike tomorrow. You're gonna need every calorie you can put down. That better be gone by the time I get back." Charlie still wouldn't turn from his task. "Hey, we're all worried but he'd say the same thing to you right now if he could." No longer resisting, Charlie chewed the salt-tinged stringy flesh with meditation. Leaf disappeared into a starless night with flurries still falling and sparkling against the burning wood.

"C.S., it's like he said, everything is going to be all right."

"Thanks, Gup." The wolf ghost again called out far across the valley above the whoosh of wind through branches and their flapping tarp. George decided continuing in silence. Leaf reappeared within minutes but wasn't quiet enough to keep Charlie from grabbing his rifle and laying a light finger across the trigger.

"Easy, here," he said and tossed leafed twigs into Charlie's lap. Leaf pulled a cup from his pack and filled it from his canteen. "Strip off some leaves, mash them in your fingers, and boil." Leaf suspended the cup from a stick propped in a granite fissure until boiling-steam pockets rolled across the surface. Pouring more water from his canteen to cool the mixture, he knelt next to Benjamin whose most recent spasms had subsided.

"What is that?" George rose on his elbows.

"Willow. Won't heal a broken ankle, but it should help a bit." Benjamin cringed and tightened as he struggled to drink, drooling from both corners of his mouth and liquid pooling down into a brown gray depression at the base of his neck. "Here, see if you can get him to drink as much as he can," Leaf motioned the cup toward Charlie and folded back the blankets covering Benjamin's legs. Charlie turned. In the firelight, Leaf unwrapped more flannel layers to reveal the swollen, yellow-purple section of leg and blackened, blood-sharp edges.

"You were right," Charlie could no longer resist turning his head.

"Hold his shoulders," Leaf continued and George scooted to the rear of Benjamin's head. Even though Leaf applied the lightest possible touch, a diaphragm-generated groan bellowed from Benjamin. He lifted the trembling leg to remove and replace the rotten bandage with a new flannel rag.

Further whimpering continued while he splashed cold water across the wound and allowed the chilled wind to blow it dry. "I'd give anything for some alcohol right now." Leaf rewrapped the bandage. Benjamin's strained neck slackened white-rope tendons stretching through his pale skin, and he drifted back into sleep.

"This actually isn't bad," George remarked after sipping the rest of the cup.

"All right, that's it for now. George, you take over for me. And Charlie, you want to bring up the sun?"

"Right on it." George crawled into a rear corner of the shelter, pulling several blankets over him, stifling wind that managed knifing beneath the tarp edges. Charlie flipped charred logs until flames rose to eye level.

The eventual return stirred practice of what he would tell Karen when they again met face to face. Words catalogued and reeled through his thoughts about the explanation, recount, and every minute detail's expression of the previous weeks. His free hand went on instinct to the inner pocket of his coat. The fleeting panic almost sweeping across him vanished in the remembrance of leaving it with Maggie and no longer requiring previous vigilance.

Even though appearing asleep, he noticed the shake of his father's blankets in trembling seizures. Charlie pushed his pack to the rear of Benjamin's head, pulled down his blankets, and lay with his chest against his father's back. Charlie stretched the blankets back over both of them. Benjamin's shuddering settled to slower spasms with transferred body heat.

Charlie listened to each drawn breath and exhalation through his father's lungs, concentrating to the point of holding his own breath to detect even the slightest rhythm variation or fluid gasp. He raised a hand, examining the finger silhouette bending and opening against firelight cast across billowing walls. Periods of eyelid opening and closing grew in length until exhaustion no longer allowed regrets of the foolish.

All four men reached the lake before noon even with the night's flurries settling a sticking snow blanket several inches on level ground. Most of it melted to a mud-stained slurry. Leaf kept the blankets layered across Maggie's back, allowing her to nibble and graze where blueberries still managed poking up beneath the white coating.

No conversation of significance was exchanged since breaking camp. Neither Charlie nor George questioned the confidence of Leaf's return route. He paused long enough for water refills at passing streams or hoof examinations. "As I've said, my friends, it would be shorter getting across this lake back to the White Ash, but that's not gonna happen." Charlie's father remained unconscious for much of the morning, still drifting in and out of delirium.

"Sure wish there was some way to get a signal over there," George paused to recline on a wide stump surfacing from the bank. Charlie took every break for a return to Benjamin's side and placed a palm across his forehead.

"Leaf, check this out," his hurried words commanded. Leaf stood over Benjamin and placed his own hand across the wrinkled skin above his brow.

"Good, good, looks like the fever's starting to break a bit. We have two choices: we can sit back and rest our feet awhile or we can eat on the go."

"Someone pass me a fish," George exclaimed, straining upright as he pushed on the stump and mounted his pack.

"Yeah, me too. Sooner we get back, the sooner he gets help."

"Very well, let's move out."

All three men wrapped their faces in scarves, warding off pure white-reflecting sunlight. Charlie kept the opposite end of his scarf wrapped around the handle of his rifle to prevent skin sticking to metal.

"Char—Charlie, boy," a voice broke the monotonous forced men's gasps as they struggled through the drifts. Charlie stopped and spun, trucking through swallowing snow pockets.

"Dad?" Charlie knelt down beside the stretcher after Leaf tightened Maggie to a halt. "Hold on there, take it easy," Charlie whispered while Benjamin propped up on both elbows. The smooth expression across his face scrunched in an instant with tight eye corners, and he fell back with a whimper. "That ankle is still broken, and Leaf thinks you might have fractured a couple of ribs, too."

"What's a man got to do to get some water around here?" he offered a frail smile. Charlie shot a glance at Leaf who nodded in consent. He lifted the waterskin to his father's cracked lips. "Ahhh, better than the finest wine I've ever tasted."

"Guess we don't have to ask you how you're feeling?" George reappeared, drinking his own water. Charlie poured more into Benjamin's eager mouth.

"Feel like I got hit by a ton of rocks." He laughed at his own joke, but a sudden coughing fit terminated any further stretching. "What is this?" he asked, turning first to his feet and then behind him where Maggie's tail continued whisking across the top of his balding head.

"Pretty ingenious, huh? Leaf came up with the concept."

"Still cracks me up. You brought this old mule to haul away old Absalom's treasure, and what did she end up hauling? A broken old man with the patience of a teenager." Charlie said nothing, bending over him and brushing back fine white hairs.

"Enough of that talk now. Leaf says only a few more hours and we should be back to Mabel's. She'll fix you up just fine."

"That wrinkled old witchdoctor?" he protested.

"Here," Charlie pressed on his father's chest to keep him down and reached into his coat pocket. He retrieved a folded snapshot and dropped it onto Benjamin's chest. His father grasped the photo and stared at sunlight shining across its gloss surface.

"Your mother was one beautiful woman, wasn't she?" he asked with a permanent smile pasted across his lips.

"Yes, she was, now lay back and enjoy the ride," Charlie commanded and pushed both of his shoulders back until he again reclined.

"As I recall, she could get a little stubborn at times too. Did I mention that? Because you sure didn't get it from me."

Benjamin obeyed his son's instruction, folding his fingers across his chest with the photograph nestled secure between them.

The afternoon continued clear and cold while negotiating rolling hills, shallow streams, and intermittent stretches of open field and strangling forest. Although they had traversed the identical path days earlier, unbroken snow blankets with the exception of random animal tracks obscured certain identification.

George started taking silent but questioning glances at Charlie in periodic intervals but, like Charlie, kept his head down. He reserved remaining energy to concentrate on picking up one knee after the other. "There, hear it?" Leaf stopped, held up a hand, and pulled back on Maggie's reins.

"What?" Both Charlie and George stood without motion, straining to hear anything more than a surf-crashing whir of wind through clinging spruce or an occasional songbird breaking the silence.

"Come on, let's pick up the pace," Leaf huffed. Neither man questioned him. The sun was now below the lining mountain crest, and the chill numbed their cheeks from burn exposure.

They located a game trail and entered a tangled grove of old-growth birch. The paper-peeling trunks turned their immediate vision into shadowed blue while Charlie struggled through slit eyelids. George tended Maggie with Benjamin in the rear. The mule whinnied and complained with the rapid energy expenditure.

After Charlie crested a snow embankment, trunks opened and revealed a narrow stream, Mabel's stream. A thin white smoke column rose from several hundred yards down the bank. Through the quick-approaching evening haze, the obscured outline of a hunched-over, red shawl-draped woman contrasted against the background. Leaf threw his pack to the ground and sprinted along the bank. Charlie found no power to keep pace. Their words remained imperceptible, but he approached close enough to witness Leaf's wild gesticulating arm movements. He grasped one of Mabel's elbows and pulled the woman across the ground, keeping her balance and almost falling several times from her walking stick while it poked holes in wet sand. George also dropped his pack and collapsed on a barren crag where snow hadn't managed to stick. Eyes closing, his head dropped into his hands.

The ancient woman shuffled past Charlie as if he wasn't there. She grabbed one of Leaf's hands for balance, shifting the rest of her weight on her stick and knelt over Benjamin's body. He remained fast asleep. Mabel's single bone-stretched hand reached down to unwrap the flannel bandage from his leg in a single swift motion.

Benjamin snapped forward with his knuckles gripped tight around the gurney edges. "What do you think you're doing, old woman?" he howled. She said nothing through what remained of her darkened ivory teeth, bending further down and inhaling extended sniffs of his wound. The same skeletal hand reached beneath his parted coat and pressed, sending further tremors rippling through his body to the point where he couldn't even gather enough breath to cry out a second time. Mabel muttered three words to Leaf.

"Come on," Leaf instructed after unlashing the poles from Maggie's back. Charlie grabbed the front two handles while Leaf lifted the back end. They negotiated over the uneven rocks and damp sand until entering Mabel's cave.

CHAPTER

31

At first, Charlie couldn't determine if he remained locked in a disjointed hallucination of faces and falling. Above faint, distant bird trilling, a combustion engine's roar throttle churned and revved through the air. He ignored sensations, burying his nose deeper into the massaging caribou fur caressing his cheeks.

Immediate past events filtered back into his thoughts— hot soup, the fire's warmth, chanting, and unfamiliar scents in his nose while Benjamin shook and howled. "Hey buddy, come on, time to get up, they're here." Charlie rolled over and saw George across the glowing coals near his head.

"Gup, what is that?"

"Our return to the civilized world." Charlie threw aside the hides and grabbed his pack.

"Forget it, you won't be needing that anymore," George coached. Charlie chased close behind while shifting through the tunnel. They emerged to a profound blue morning sky even though more snow had fallen, transforming the terrain into an alien world. Lined along the bank, four snowmobiles huddled in single file. The fourth rider cranked a throttle, poked a screwdriver to make adjustments under the hood, and once again fuel injected.

Birds shook from their branches. The figure beneath the hood rose and leaned into Leaf, almost knocking him from balance. Mutual laughs rose between them following the head butt. He turned to notice Charlie and George's emergence.

"Charlie, you're up. Damien, this is Charlie Sutcliffe."

"So you're the famous American I've heard so much about," the man smiled an adolescent smooth-cheeked grin and extended a thin, uncalloused hand from beneath his red parka sleeve.

"Charlie, Damien here is one of my cousins, those are his two brothers, and I don't know where Matthew's run off to."

"Probably getting more of that magic coffee," Damien coughed and blew on moisture-wrinkled fingers.

"Let's get whatever gear you want and saddle up," Leaf turned back toward the cave. Charlie struggled behind through the snow with dragging laces.

"Not sure I'm following this," Charlie puffed crystal billows.

"Guess Creektoe got a little anxious. Damien told me he sent him and the other boys to check up on us. I realize you were looking forward to another few days of hard slogging through the countryside, but we're going back in style," Leaf said and slapped his cousin's snowmobile seat. Charlie chased Leaf back through the tunnel until returning to the central chamber. Benjamin remained propped in one corner, a steaming bowl balanced across his stomach and bare feet dangling next to the coals. His splintered ankle remained dressed in tight, white wrapping.

"Well, Dad, this is it. Come on and I'll give you a hand. Think we can make a crutch out of something around here," Charlie's voice sang with a rolling cadence.

"Uh, Charlie," Leaf interrupted.

"No, he has to come back with us. You said it yourself. I'm not leaving my father, my dad, out in these woods a second longer. What about your pilot friend Hodges? Isn't he supposed to rendezvous with you after a week?" Charlie heard his own questions rise and shorten.

"Son, he's right," Benjamin joined the exchange, cracking his eyes.

"Charlie, after what we've been through together, you know I wouldn't risk anyone's safety. He must have a few more days. I guarantee the moment he's safe for travel, we will get him out of here. Mabel's the best care for him right now."

"Besides, I think she's getting a little sweet on me," Benjamin guffawed. Mabel, whose back was turned during their entire exchange, rapped a brief walking stick tap on the stone next to Benjamin's head. "Old Hodges will get along after he sees I'm not there. I'll get in touch with him after we get back and let him know I've still got some breath."

"I thought she didn't know English?" Charlie asked. Leaf shrugged. One thin finger rose to her narrow clay lips and blew a hush.

"Here, take this," his father extended the photograph towards Charlie.

"No, Dad," Charlie bent down to grab his vacant hand. "Give that back when we all get home." Charlie rose toward George, kicking up dust from his pacing at the cavern's entrance. Charlie absorbed a final scan of the chamber. After reaching the arching entrance, he paused and turned. "Dad?"

"Yes, son?"

"I love you."

"I love you, too. See you on the outside."

Although the snowmobile pace slowed enough at moments for Charlie to inhale suffocating, smoked engine oil and hot-grease breaths, most time elapsed in vision blurring whites, grays, and intense greens. Every slightest rise and fall sent pangs shooting through individual joints and tendons. Skin blistered and once fallen from his feet began healing but remained raw while rubbing against the interior of his boots.

All four changed lead positions through open fields and single-file progress. After clearing a quick, direction-altering stretch through a valley rising on both sides of them, the group reared back on their throttles and rested.

"Whoa boy, I gotta get one of these!" he heard George shout out after dropping his parka hood. Charlie said nothing, dismounting and kneading some degree of sensation back into his face. The sky was once again overcast with the threat of another whiteout. He couldn't determine the length of the trip so far, but his back's stiffness told him it was too long.

Walking toward George, Charlie's knees hesitated seconds after being told to rise and bend by his brain. He swung them in full extension, side to side, and scuffled through low snowdrifts. George removed his waterskin, and no more than a trickle leaked from the black plastic spout.

"Here," Charlie motioned his own water toward George who nodded in acknowledgement.

"We're gonna have some kind of story to tell when we get back." It was too late for George to realize his words after they escaped. Charlie wasn't fazed from a thousand-mile stare at the snowmobile ski impressions behind them ribboning into darkened forest. "Hey." Charlie didn't offer a flinch's hint in his singular concentration. "I said, hey!" he exclaimed louder with a slight hand wave and whistle. No more than Charlie's eyes shifted toward George. "Quit worrying, he's going to be all right."

"You think, Gup?"

"Would Leaf have taken us all this way just to leave your dad with someone who couldn't help him?"

"Yeah, guess you're right." Charlie's sight dropped to the snow with a continuing cross expression as if kicked ice clods manifested reassurance.

"Come on, boys, light's wasting away on us, and I promised Ma we'd be back before sunset," the younger ponytailed cousin called. He straddled his Sno-Cat and throttled back, roaring the shrouded cylinders. Charlie took a sip after retrieving his waterskin and forced his legs back across the padded seat. He wrapped his scarf around his eyes, arms encircling the driver's waist, and he crouched low to block the wind.

The constant jostling and racking of a mending body loosened enough for Charlie to drift into a doze with spiraling images of hiking, Maggie, the mine, and Charlotte in a cascading vision swirl. Complete consciousness returned when forward movement reduced to a crawl and the idling engine hum was interrupted by a dog's incessant yapping. Creektoe's trailer collection appeared after sweeping around a broad hill crest. Moomau's distinctive gray-and-white coat bounded across the flat snow, kicking up spray with each wide paw beneath a pink dusk.

Charlie scanned for Frisco, anticipating Uncle Tyler barreling through a door, but only the single gray dog flailed toward them. They pulled up beside the trailer, and Leaf blew a short whistle. The dog stopped in its tracks and dropped to the snow pack.

After another growling yipe, Moo jumped back to life and sprinted toward Leaf, leaping so high in the air that his front paws landed on both sides of Leaf's shoulders as he caught the animal in mid-flight. "Someone's glad to see us." Leaf couldn't help laughing and twisting his head from the massive pink-and-gray tongue licking across his face. "Come on," Leaf directed toward Charlie and George while the others filtered back to their homes. Leaf opened the front door.

"Hello? Anyone home?" Charlie called out after all three men entered. George collapsed into the same bag from the journey's beginning, releasing a sigh. In the kitchen, a low simmering liquid gurgled above the ticking kitchen clock with the aroma of melting fat and marrow.

"Where is everyone? This place was like a subway station before we left," George muttered and leaned his head down the dark hallway. Leaf held a hand to the stove's iron surface.

"Nobody's been out here for a while." Leaf's observation drawled out an extended yawn. Charlie noticed the puffing beneath his eyelids. His skin stretched taut and paler than the once olive, energetic confidence vibrating through his complexion.

Charlie gathered split logs and tossed them across the few glowing embers remaining in the stove's belly. Leaf tiptoed down the hall. George rolled to his side so the flames brightened his face.

"Gentlemen, I can't believe I'm saying this, but I do believe I am too tired to eat," George spoke without opening his eyes. His quiet, strained words rose above the burning wood whirl as wind gusts blew down the aluminum chimney.

"Quiet!" Leaf's head stretched back around the corner. "They're asleep," he motioned with a single finger to his lips. Charlie also leaned back, stretching his arms over his head and releasing an uncontrollable yawn. His face still twitched in aching distortions. "Charlie, you want something to gnaw?" Leaf whispered through the darkness after removing the pot from the stove. "Charlie?" No sounds returned other than short snores emanating from Charlie's curled-up moose hide.

Crashing boulders and shaking earth shook Charlie. He jerked and realized the boulder tumbling was no more than an exploding pine knot in the fire. His head sank back down to a pillow, and he pulled blanket layers over his shoulders without memory of covering himself.

A faraway humming rose above other random voices. The woman's hum broke brief notes between the hushed tones of other familiar voices. He rolled and turned. Around the kitchen table, Leaf sat with Creektoe, George, and Merry leaning her head on George's shoulder while they bent forward and sipped from chipped mugs. "Rise and shine!" George called, noticing a stir beneath the blankets.

"Gup, how long have I been out?"

"Still dark out there, but I'd say a good twelve hours. Here," he answered, rising to grab another mug from the sink when Margie's quick-draw hand shot out to slap him across the back of his wrist. Her brows furrowed but dissolved back into a wide-toothed grin.

"Look at all of you, you're nothing but skin and bones. My sons are home," she sang out in a continuing light lilt.

"Feels like I've been asleep for a year," Charlie yawned.

"My son has been filling me in on your adventures." Creektoe pulled a chair back from the table and put an arm around Charlie's shoulder. "From what I hear, every one of you is a true hero." Charlie flicked an eye toward Leaf.

"Don't know how you'd arrive at that conclusion," Charlie replied. "No gold, I nearly got my dad, best friend, and your son killed, and wasted weeks' worth of time I could have spent with my daughter." Charlie stopped, pushing his coffee to one side and dropping his head against the table. He pulled back from a sharp, poking edge hitting his forehead. "What's this?"

"Open it. Ty couldn't make it to welcome you back but thought you and your friend here might put these to some use,"

Creektoe winked and nodded at the folded pamphlet. Charlie unfolded the document and rubbed away the last remnants of sleep.

"What is this, really?"

"What's it look like, son?"

George leaned forward with both hands flat on the table. "C.S., that's a one-way ticket to Seattle. Here's mine," he waved an identical slim, folded envelope in the light suspended over the table. Merry turned with a grimace, studying George's profile.

"Grab yourselves another couple of hours—your flight leaves at six fifteen this evening. Skagway to Anchorage. Anchorage to Seattle."

CHAPTER

32

Charlie allowed the sedan door handle to drop from his grasped hand. It creaked shut as usual, but the locking mechanism didn't catch. He turned, banging it closed with a hip. The parking lot was almost vacant. A few wheelchair passengers scooted or were guided along the hospital's front tented walkways, scarves bundled tight around wrinkled, pale throats. Plows pushed towering berms of gray-blotched, salted snow toward pavement edges.

Sneakers sloshed through the slush. The pneumatic whoosh of the front double doors poured heat into the open, still air. He pulled his own scarf back and blew across the fingers of his one free hand with Charlotte's present wrapped in blue-and-pink ponies tucked beneath the other arm.

The purple coat he found for Mr. Snuggles at his favorite thrift store jostled in an over-sized box. His fingers tapped on the wrapping paper while waiting for the elevator, but he turned, feet moving without will. Breath was forced once exiting into the open courtyard.

Most of the snow was shoveled from the walkways. Flowers bent and huddled in an almost complete white blanket. Bronze angels, animals, and koi wore their own iced coats. Charlie sat on his bench, placing Charlotte's gift beside him. He leaned forward with both eyes locked on the ground and hands in his pockets.

Charlie read the memorial dedications carved into the benches like an old familiar book. A curled forefinger traced along the routed grooves, and the image of Charlotte Casey Sutcliffe followed by a pair of dates blurred into his mind's eye. He felt spasms of shivers down his spine while he fought a hot wetness forming at his eyelid corners. "Thought I might find you out here."

Charlie shook. He spun around and Charlotte's box dropped to the concrete. "You gonna sit out here all morning and freeze or go see your little girl who can't wait much longer for her daddy?" George implored. He bent over to retrieve the package and shoved it back into Charlie's hands.

Moments passed during Charlie's straight-focused stare. "Gup, how can I possibly go in there?"

"Charlie, look at me." His eyes turned in reluctance. "We tried, man, we tried. I nearly died falling off a cliff, you were frozen and deathly ill, almost shot, and a cave collapsed on your head. So we didn't get Absalom's gold. Maybe you found something a bit more important. Now come on, I'm tired of this cold." George stamped his feet. Charlie rose after grasping George's open palm and followed him back inside toward the elevator.

"What? What is that?"

"What's what?" George replied also warming his own hands.

"I don't know—something about your face."

"Have no idea what you're talking about other than getting some feeling back into these fingers. Here we are." The simultaneous ding of a parting elevator door broke his comment. The corridor was shadowed and narrower. Charlie glanced toward the nurse's station half island. The dyed-black head of thinning hair didn't look up but was replaced by a gray, hair-helmeted scarecrow with frightened strands escaping a pinned bun.

"Hello there. Rosie off today?" Charlie asked, tempting further delay.

"And you are?" the scarecrow's monotonous tone drawled.

"Mr. Charles Sutcliffe and I want to see my daughter," his voice rose.

"Miss Whitehall is off running charts, and I believe Miss Sutcliffe is at her exercise period. You are more than welcome to visit after completion." The advancing simmer at the back of Charlie's neck grew hot and his molars clenched. He contributed nothing further to the exchange and clomped, echoing determined heel stomps across the linoleum, as he advanced down the corridor.

"Mr. Sutcliffe, please!" she rose with a screeching chair. Her penciled eyebrows furrowed towards George. His head shook and she returned to furious keyboard clicks. Charlie stopped at the hallway's end, peeking through Charlotte's cracked room door while he ran a finger across the wooden letters painted in butterflies and flowers spelling her name.

Mr. Snuggles was gone among her other stuffed animals arranged and laid across the top of her bed. Different-sized paintings wallpapered the gaps between monitors, tubes, and other anonymous white plastic-cased equipment. They were scrawled with basic stick figures in coats and backpacks tossed among towering crayon mountains and deep, blending-green forests.

"Guess Karen has been telling her some stories," George coughed.

"Yeah. What's that?" Charlie noticed a square corner poking from beneath her tightened sheet. In the dim light, he stared at a creased photograph of his mother sitting on a boulder in the middle of a stream. "You wouldn't know anything about this, would you?" George shrugged his shoulders. He chased behind Charlie who shot another glare down at the nurse. "Hey, where is everybody?"

"Does seem kind of quiet," George interrupted, holding one hand across his mouth and dropping his chin to his chest. "Come on, let's head up to the rec room and find that beautiful little daughter of yours." Charlie caressed the remaining stuffed animals. The elevator ding snapped his trance, and he just brushed through the closing doors. Again they encountered a darkened corridor after doors parted. Their soles tapped across the shine-reflecting floor until they reached a doorway at the end of the hall reading PHYSICAL THERAPY—ROOM 501.

The moment Charlie entered, the room exploded with light and color. The space was crammed with faces both small and large—some registering immediate recognition and others foreign, yet all screaming and giggling in abandon. Streamers stretched from opposing corners. Multi-colored balloons bobbed and floated in the air rush from bodies jumping toward them.

"I—I—I don't understand," Charlie stammered with George racing up behind to stop him from staggering back against the wall. "What is all of this?" Karen twisted and waded through the sea of little bodies screaming and dancing around her feet. She pulled the box from her husband's open-mouthed grip and wrapped her arms around him.

"Surprise!" Karen squealed in the same tone as the other children. "Yes, I know this is our daughter's birthday, but she also has a little surprise for you." Charlie craned over Karen's shoulder. Charlotte was tucked beneath white sheets with Mr. Snuggles cuddled into one elbow.

"Daddy!" She leaned forward and Charlie stooped to encircle her. All light, sound, smell, and every other sensation blanked into fog beyond the embrace of her wrapped arms.

"Hey, my little Sweetpea, did you miss me?" Charlie's eyes grew wide, and he released a breath not exhaled in years. Behind him, a familiar voice rose above the laughing. He turned.

"Boy! You made it." Charlie gave a double take. Standing behind George, Uncle Tyler rocked back on his heels with both thumbs in his suspenders, and Benjamin sat in a wheelchair at his side. "Well you don't look too worse for wear," he released a full belly laugh and slapped Charlie across the shoulder.

"Uncle Tyler! How did you get here? And Dad, I don't—"

"Not important, just that we are," Uncle Tyler interrupted. "After that beautiful wife of yours there got worried and told me more about my little grandniece here, it's about the only thing that would have gotten me out of those woods for a spell." Charlie noticed Karen's blush. "Now, before we really get this party started, I believe your daughter has a present for you," he beamed a wide Santa Claus grin. Charlotte reached behind her pillow and removed a wrinkled envelope. Her meticulous petite fingers pulled back the flap, removing and straightening the enclosed single page.

"Dear Kate, cannot say, say, now, how, how much longer I got. Tommy is gitin, gitin, gitin. What's that word, Momma?" she asked, turning to look up into Karen's eyes.

"The word is supposed to be suspicious, but why don't we let Daddy read the rest of it." She lifted the document from Charlotte's hand, dropping it into Charlie's lap. An immediate recognition of penmanship met his vision as he read to himself. His lips curled while rubbing his forehead.

"I'm still not understanding all of this. No date but this is undeniably Absalom's hand. See? He talks about the Stanton Mine down here," he pointed.

"Remember this?" Benjamin leaned forward, waving the journal in front of him with a smile beaming almost as wide as Tyler's tooth-filled flash. Charlie rose to his feet. He cradled the journal in one hand and held the trembling letter beside it. He could not locate anymore words but exchanged a glance between the two men.

Uncle Tyler interrupted his father. "Well boy, let me shed a little light. As you already know from the journal, my great granddaddy was getting a bit nervous about his partner, Thomas Murphy, and he was already starting to feel the effects of typhus. He didn't—"

"How did you know anything about that? You've never read the journal," Charlie interrupted.

"Slow down, slow down. Anyway, Absalom sent a letter, this letter, to his wife at the same time he was finishing up the last entries in this book. Let's cut right to the chase—I found this letter years ago. It's an abbreviated version of old Abe's journal. I already unloaded that trunk years before you were even born. With the help of my good friend Creektoe, of course."

Charlie grasped the railing of Charlotte's rolling bed, both legs quivering in anticipation of a sudden meeting with the floor.

"Then if you have the gold and there was as much as he said there was, what are you still doing living in a cabin out in the middle of nowhere?"

"Already answered that question the first night we were there," George jumped into the exchange.

"But if you knew we were looking for nothing all along, why on earth did you still let us go?"

"I believe I can answer that one. Son, I already stopped by Uncle Tyler's a few days before you and George showed up. Like you, I thought if anyone knew anything more about Absalom's gold, it would be Tyler. He didn't even tell me he'd already gotten it. But, he realized our paths would eventually cross and one of two things would happen: either we'd kill each other or start acting like a father and son again." Benjamin reached out and placed an arm around his son's waist.

"Here, I believe this is yours," Charlie turned and held out the photograph.

"Your mother was one beautiful woman. And yes, she did always smell like honeysuckle."

"Gup, guess you're ready to settle back into your place," Charlie said and turned.

"Well, you're probably not going to believe this but I'm moving," George replied with both hands in his back pockets.

"Come on."

"I'm serious. I'm moving to Alaska." Charlie shook his head.

"From the man who said he never wanted to set foot in that state again?"

"Meredith said I can stay at her cousin's next door until I can find some work around there, get on my feet, and find a place near Fairbanks. And then, who knows what might happen next?" George winked. Charlie's eyes wandered to Charlotte's smiling face peeking at him just over her covers. He rose and turned, wading through the little bodies toward a massive window at the room's far end and overlooking the frozen courtyard of bronze angels. Karen's hand touched the back of his head, and she ran her fingers through his hair.

"Don't think I'm not grateful, but—but, our little girl." She reached up on her toes and kissed an ear lobe.

"There's more, look." she whispered, leaned against his chest, and pushed a stack of legal-sized folded papers into his hands. The University of Utah letterhead stood out in bold black against the paper's lavender hint. He scanned them, flipping one after the other with increasing speed.

"Does this mean what I think?"

"Yes, Charles, yes it does. We're going to spend a little time in Utah." Charlie returned his glance at the papers and then back toward George, Uncle Tyler, and his father. Tyler caught his wordless face and roared once again into howling laughter.

Snohomish County, Washington
Many Years Later

Wisp-thin, barren apple branches whisked and snapped against smooth-painted eaves underscoring what few gale gasps struggled to continue the storm. A young man hunched forward with both knees together, stealing glances at the second and minute hands of his watch when he thought it went unnoticed. Karen rose, wandering past Charlie who sipped his Earl Grey and flexed fingers at the warmth filtering through his joints. All three heads turned in simultaneous reaction to each occasional flickering headlight beam.

Sparkles shot illuminations through ice crystal-coated window panes and splashed specters across faded rose-patterned wallpaper. "Robert, try relaxing a little, looks like the worst of the storm has passed, and I don't believe the authorities would allow anyone to drive if the roads weren't safe enough." Studying her words, he collapsed backwards into the elongated sofa cushions.

"You too," she brushed a hand across the back of Charlie's exposed neck when he coughed and the teacup trembled in his grasp.

"I'm not worried," Charlie's chin rose and an eyelid winked through firelight reflecting initial crow's-feet spanning both corners of his eyes. He still studied and admired the curve of Karen's jaw. "Still think we should have picked her up."

"Thank you, Mrs. Sutcliffe. Do you need any help in the kitchen?"

"Why that would be lovely, thank you. Did I hear that you're considering the medical field after finishing your degree?"

"Yes, ma'am. My father was a surgeon," Robert stammered and stole a decoding glance toward Charlie while rubbing his index finger. Karen started responding but stopped with another pair of headlights winding down the hillside, descending, but fading back to nothing more than a memory of snowdrifts costuming the barn and vacant front steps. She forced a smile with Robert tracing each footstep back into the kitchen.

Charlie's cup rattled in his stiff-fingered grip, making the saucer tremble. He scanned bookshelves reaching almost to the ceiling with vision still sharp enough to identify and return the associations of their titles. Fireplace flames rose and flickered light across their spines while he listened to murmuring conversation just beyond the reach of identification.

"Here we are," Karen and Robert returned. Robert remained standing, scanning and reading the library, his outline silhouetted against the sputtering logs struggling to maintain flame. Karen's eyes flexed to the front windows each time lips met her cup's rim. Charlie couldn't remember the final time his eyes succumbed to the weight pushing down on them other than Karen rising to wrap an afghan around his shoulders. When he snorted himself back awake, Robert appeared in profile with a thin volume open in his palms.

"What ya got there, boy?" Charlie croaked.

"This has to be old," Robert's unchallenged features glowed smooth and loose. Charlie's eyes widened when he rose and snatched the book from his hand. Robert quivered and fell against a shelf. "I—I—so sorry," he jumped back toward the couch. Charlie lifted the book and parted the cover. His head tilted back toward the ceiling, and he caressed the open pages after collapsing back into his chair.

"Charles, behave yourself," Karen whispered and took a hand into her own grasp. "He's not hurting anything." The distraction focused all attention away from the front arching driveway. A car door slam halted their exchange. Both Karen and Robert leapt from their cushions.

"Hey everyone! Sorry I'm so late but everybody got stuck at the airport. Lucky to even make it out after half the flights were canceled," a voice called through the open front door. Robert sprinted to her side and pulled her bags through the doorway. She turned as if expecting more, but both she and Robert glanced in Charlie's direction. "Daddy!" Charlotte spun and dropped to Charlie's side, wrapping both arms around his shoulders. He sneezed with the scratch of her scarf across his cheek, and he released an uncontrollable laugh.

"You go away for one semester and I don't hear from you anymore. What? Two phone calls in three months?"

"Sorry, Daddy, everything is much busier than I expected," she frowned and brushed his thinning scalp.

"That's okay, Pumpkin." His head tilted to catch the full fire glow reflecting across her wide-open eyes. "Guess I'm just being a bit grumpy."

"Robert, I need a little help in the kitchen again," Karen asked.

"Sure." Charlotte and Robert turned, exchanging an extended glance at one another before he exited. Charlotte kept one arm around Charlie's shoulders as she pulled the book from his hands and collapsed into his lap.

"What's this?" he asked and rubbed a narrow silver ring around her finger.

"Robert gave me a little early birthday present. I can't believe you still have this old book." Charlie shifted to one side so his knees didn't support her full weight. "Are you comfortable? I must be crushing you," she jumped to her feet and bent over to scan for any discomfort in his eyes. Charlotte turned and rubbed her hands together in front of the fire. Weight returned to his eyelids.

"Oh no, I'm fine. But you know what?"

"What?"

"You—you will always be my little Sweetpea." Charlotte smiled. She opened the chain-link screen and stirred the logs with a poker, shooting embers high up the flue.

"I'll be your Sweetpea from now until the end of time." She turned and met Charlie's head slumped forward with muted snores rising and falling from his chest. Charlotte pulled the scratched-leather book from his grasp and replaced it on the shelf where pages still smelled of smoke and forgotten wood.

About the Author

Philip P. Thurman lives and writes in Lake Mary, Florida, with his wife, Donna, and three children, Matthew, Elizabeth, and Paul. He has written several books, but *The Gilded Prospect* is his first published novel. His personal and professional life has brought extensive domestic travel, international journeys in Europe and Central America, and childhood in the Alaskan and Canadian forests. He is an avid outdoorsman who enjoys hiking, camping, and fishing with a particular appreciation of North America's remaining wilderness. An English major and graduate of Stetson University, he is employed as a manufacturing quality assurance executive.

Contact Philip Thurman by visiting www.philthurmanfiction.com or emailing philthurmanauthor@hotmail.com.

Follow him on Facebook.